It Happened at Whisper Lake

a novel

D1714013

CEONE FENN

outskirts
press

Prologue

Knees shaking, eyes downcast, Luella gripped her husband's hand as they squeezed through a gauntlet of shouting reporters.

"Coach Laurent, do you plan to take the stand in your defense?"

"Augie, has Jolliet University asked you to resign?"

"Mrs. Laurent, do you still believe your husband didn't rape those boys?"

The gusting wind tossed Luella's hair across her face and into her mouth. Russet leaves swirled over the courthouse lawn. The temperature was cold for late October in northern Wisconsin, although sunlight streamed through seams in the gathering clouds, giving the false impression of warmth.

Climbing the thirteen marble steps to the courthouse door required concentration. She focused on her feet, willing one foot and then the other to clear each riser.

She shouldn't have been in this place. She should have been in her classroom at St. Eligius School teaching rambunctious eighth-graders how to write linear equations instead of attending court in this remote Northwoods town; but that's where the charges against August had been brought, the alleged abuse having taken place at Laurent's Basketball Camp on Whisper Lake. That's how, at nine o'clock on a Tuesday morning, she found herself heading into Ojibwe County Court.

Luella took her seat on the bench behind the defense table, close enough to smell her husband's Brut after-shave and at an angle that allowed her to see his partial profile, as well as the back of defense attorney Thomas Lowery's balding head. Between them, she had a clear view of the judge's platform and, to her right, a slightly obstructed view of prosecutor Adlai Fett.

She quickly scanned the room looking for Beth, hoping that their daughter had changed her mind about coming to court. There was no sign of her.

Franklin slid in beside Luella. "Thank you," she mouthed and squeezed her brother's hand.

August turned and shifted in his chair. He appeared distinguished in his dark gray, tailored suit, looking more like an attorney than a defendant. He'd been blessed with his father's good looks, a Roman nose as straight as a ruler and a full head of wavy, silver hair.

Despite attorney Lowery's thorough briefing, yesterday's jury selection was more of an ordeal than Luella had imagined. Although she wasn't on trial—never received as much as a speeding ticket—she felt the enormity of the situation as surely as if she'd been the one charged with the crime.

The jury, twelve strangers—seven women and five men—entered and sat in two tiers just beyond the prosecutor's table, looking somber and intent. Jury selection had been painstaking. During *voir dire*, the judge and attorneys had sought to expose bias and uncover anything that might disqualify prospects. The prosecution favored churchgoing women with children; the defense, professional, childless men. At the end of the day, Luella left with the sinking feeling that the prosecution held a clear edge; or maybe it was just that since August's arrest she'd stopped trusting in good fortune.

Chapter One

~The Arrest~

Luella's face lit with a satisfied smile. The opening week of summer basketball camp had gone perfectly. She and August made it to June 20, the final day of the first session, without anyone rushed to the emergency room, caught using drugs, or sent home for disciplinary reasons.

In the camp kitchen, while loading plates into the dishwasher, Luella sang "Jeremiah was a bullfrog, was a good friend of mine..." Preoccupied with reviewing everything to be accomplished before the end of the day, the lyrics soon turned into a hummed melody. Beside her, Rosie tunelessly hummed along, scraping remnants of pancakes, eggs, and sausages from the breakfast plates into an over-sized garbage can.

The familiarity of the routine enveloped Luella like a favorite old sweater. The physicality of camp life was a welcome change from the mental rigors of nine months teaching mathematics, and the serenity of the forests and lakes was a welcome respite from the city.

Contentment. That was it in a word.

A breeze infused with pine, its temperature inching into the mid-seventies, sifted through the screens. The sound of basketballs ar-rhythmically bouncing against the paved courts some forty yards away drifted in, punctuated occasionally by a referee's whistle. August's commanding voice carried over the erratic pounding, while Beth's voice was rarely heard above the din.

Beth had shadowed her father since she learned to dribble a basketball at age six. She'd been on the staff through college and during her first years of coaching, but this year, after winning a high school state championship, she'd come with bona fide credentials, ready to hold her own among the cast of prominent coaches. Now her son, Wyatt, had become her shadow and a mascot of sorts among the campers.

Marilyn turned the radio to a local oldies rock station. She wiggled her substantial bottom over to the refrigerator, took out a container of deboned chicken, and sashayed her way back to the stainless-steel prep table. Rosie, taking her cue, bobbed her head, twisted her shoulders, and moved her feet to a different rhythm.

"We're in the groove now." Marilyn threw her head back, laughing.

"We're a team." Rosie gave Marilyn and Luella each a high five, a gesture that had August's influence stamped all over it.

Luella put the fully loaded rack into the dishwasher, closed the lid, and turned it on.

Steam rose from the kettles of potatoes boiling on the stove. Marilyn slid four giant pans of brownies into the ovens.

"I get to lick it," said Rosie, eyeing the large wooden spoon coated with brownie batter.

Marilyn winked at her.

Luella raised her eyebrows, signaling to Marilyn that eating batter containing raw eggs wasn't a good idea. "It hasn't killed her yet," said Marilyn.

Marilyn handed Rosie the spoon. She wrapped her fist around the long handle, opened her mouth wide, and shoved the spoon into her mouth, clamping her lips around it, then extracting it slowly. Her mouth comically rimmed in chocolate, she closed her eyes tight and licked her lips, as though savoring a taste of heaven. Luella envied Rosie's childlike unselfconsciousness, the way she lived in the moment, appreciating the smallest pleasures.

Bringing Rosie to live with them four years ago had not been easy. She missed a mother who had cared for her all her life, but who lived out her days in a nursing home, a victim of Alzheimer's. At age forty-eight Rosie still needed supervision, a task that had fallen mostly to

Luella, given August's busy schedule. When he was home, he doted on her. Despite Luella's efforts to improve Rosie's nutrition, he would often bring home a bag of her favorite strawberry daiquiri-flavored jelly beans. "Aw, Lulu," he'd say, "she has so little pleasure in her life. What's the harm?" Watching Rosie laugh and dance and savor brownie batter, Luella decided August was wrong about the lack of pleasure. Her delight in the smallest things was not a failing; it was an enviable gift.

Luella's thoughts were abruptly interrupted by a breathless camper, who lunged through the kitchen doorway. "There's trouble. Beth, I mean Coach says to come fast."

"Is someone hurt?" Luella pulled her apron over her head and tossed it on the counter.

"No. The police are here."

"Police?"

Luella rushed from the kitchen toward the basketball courts. What happened? Had one of the players gotten in a scrape? Some kids came from pretty rough backgrounds. August had always been able to handle the toughest characters, drawing the best from them. There must be big trouble if *he* couldn't defuse the situation.

An Ojibwe County Sheriff's SUV was parked alongside the chain link fence. August was flanked by two officers. Their daughter, Beth, stood several yards away. The other coaches corralled the campers on the next court, obviously trying to keep the kids, who chattered among themselves and craned to get a better look at the action, from getting too close to the trouble.

When she came up alongside Beth, Luella looked over at August, whose hands were cuffed behind his back, his face crimson, his eyes flashing.

"August, what's going on?"

"This is a big mistake!" August hissed, the cords in his neck bulging. "I don't know who put you guys up to this, whose cockamamie story you've been listening to, but believe me, when I find out, there'll be hell to pay!"

"What's a big mistake?" Luella, looked at August, then whirled around to Beth, her voice rising. "What's going on!"

"Dad's being arrested!"

"Arrested? You can't be serious. August, what's this about?" Luella stepped toward him, but an officer who looked too young to be a deputy blocked her way.

"Step back, ma'am," he commanded, holding up his hand.

"If this is a practical joke, it isn't funny," said Luella.

The coaches were known for trying to outdo each other with escalating pranks. But no one smiled. August sounded like he wanted to kill someone. Luella looked anxiously from one officer to another, then at August, searching for an explanation.

"August?"

He glanced at her. "I told them at the station this is a ridiculous, goddamned mistake!"

The station? What was he talking about?

A swarthy officer, built like a wrestler, forcefully grasped August's upper arm and turned him toward the open rear door of the waiting squad car.

"This is fucking ridiculous!" August seethed.

Bird, the family's one-hundred-twenty pound, black-and-tan Newfoundland-Retriever mix, barked as he ran ahead of Rosie, who'd trailed Luella down the path to the courts. Rosie hollered after her big brother. "Augie! Augie!" Batter smeared around her mouth, her eyes wide with alarm, she thrust both arms toward him, pleading with him to come back. She stumbled and fell.

Luella and Beth rushed to her.

"I want to go with Augie!" Rosie cried, as they knelt to help her.

"He'll be back soon," Beth reassured her. Holding Rosie's arm, she lifted her to her feet and brushed dirt from her hands and knees.

As the older officer placed his hand atop August's head, bending him into the SUV, August yelled to Luella, "Call Franklin! Now!"

She stared at him, stunned.

"I want to go with Augie!" Rosie whimpered as the officers drove away.

Luella took a deep breath, placed her hands on Rosie's shoulders. "Listen to me, honey," she said, bending down to look her in the eye. "It's going to be okay. Augie isn't hurt. He's just mad. He'll be gone for a little while, but he'll be home soon."

Tears ran down Rosie's cheeks; her nose dripped.

Luella pulled a tissue from her jeans pocket and handed it to her. "Augie wants us to be brave, sweetie. Do you want to help him?"

Rosie, sniffling, eyes glistening, nodded.

"Then wipe your eyes and nose. Augie needs you to help Marilyn get ready for lunch." Luella struggled to keep her voice even, knowing that what her sister-in-law lacked in intellectual ability, she made up for in uncanny emotional radar.

"Go tell Marilyn that Luella will be there soon." Rosie sniffed and wiped her eyes. "What will you tell Marilyn?"

"Luella will be there soon."

"Good. And please take Bird with you."

The thought of August cuffed, furious, and humiliated made Luella's stomach turn. She tried not to panic. The arrest made no sense. Who was accusing him, and of what? This *had* to be a mistake. The timing felt like a setup or some kind of retribution. Her fear slid toward anger. When August was released, he would find who was responsible and make them regret it. Whoever they were, they'd miscalculated if they thought August Laurent would let this go. Reputation meant everything to him.

Luella's inclination was to dash to her car and drive to the sheriff's department. First, there was the issue of what to do about the campers milling around on the courts. Should they upend the day's plans? Or should they find a way to continue? It was unlikely that August could get back quickly enough to finish out the day. And what if it took longer to sort out the mistake? This was Saturday. On Sunday afternoon, another group was scheduled to arrive, a cycle that would repeat for the rest of the summer.

How many times had August reminded her of the pact they'd made when they'd purchased the camp? "I'll run the courts, you run the rest." She'd never bargained to shoulder the entire responsibility. But Luella had dealt with trauma involving many of her adolescent students—divorces, deaths, suicides—and had always kept her composure. She could get through this. She had no choice.

The quiet that had descended on the courts began to lift, escalating as though some unseen hand slowly turned up the volume. The shaken campers would need reassurance that Coach would be okay, and that the best thing to do would be to get on with everything as planned. Kent McElroy, one of August's oldest friends and coaching buddies, who'd worked the camp for years, was here. And there was Beth. She could capably step into her father's shoes.

Luella twirled 360 degrees looking for her grandson. Breathless, she turned to Beth. "Where's Wyatt?"

"I asked one of the players to take him down to the beach. I didn't want him to see his grandfather carted off in a squad car."

"Thank heavens." At least that was one positive, Luella thought. "Do you have any idea what this arrest is about?"

"I don't know, Mom. I was two courts away. I ran over when I saw the commotion."

A few basketballs bounced. Luella, vaguely aware of the sound, turned and saw that Kent had begun to reorganize the players. He looked at Luella and nodded. She nodded back and mouthed, "Thank you."

"Mom, I've got this," said Beth. "I'll talk with the coaches. They're all pros. We'll keep the kids busy while we figure out how to handle the rest."

Luella thought she detected a slight quaver in her daughter's voice, a trill that belied her air of confidence. Beth was a born leader who would take control no matter how flustered or frightened she might feel. She was her father's daughter, and that was reassuring.

"This has got to be some royal screwup," said Beth.

"I'm sure of it," said Luella and then hurried up the path toward the house to call her brother Franklin, an attorney.

With each mile Luella's anxiety grew as she made the forty-minute drive along the treelined back roads and two-lane highways to the Ojibwe County Jail, determined to speak with August.

After waiting a half hour in the lobby, she was led by the desk attendant into a room with beige block walls, a spare wooden table, three brown plastic chairs, and harsh light, all, it appeared, purposely designed for discomfort. The place smelled of guilt and desperation, as if over the years an accumulated shame had seeped into every surface.

The muscular officer who'd made the arrest entered the room, this time accompanied not by his baby-faced partner but by a woman with a blunt-cut hairstyle and crow's feet bracketing wide-set, penetrating eyes.

"Mrs. Laurent, I'm Sergeant Fossmeyer," said the stocky male officer, who sat down at the table across from her.

"And I'm Officer Smolinski." The female officer pulled out a chair and sat next to Luella. Her closeness, probably meant to be reassuring, made Luella wary.

"I want to speak with my husband," said Luella, lifting her chin, pulling her shoulders back, and feigning self-assurance.

"Mrs. Laurent, Luella, may I call you Luella?" asked Officer Smolinski.

"I need to speak with my husband."

"I'm sorry." The officer laid her hand on the table reaching toward

Luella's arm, but stopped short of touching her. "Believe me, this is really hard to tell you, and it's going to be even harder for you to hear." She leaned in, head tilted, expression pained, and cleared her throat. "Luella, your husband has been charged with multiple counts of first-degree sexual assault of a child."

Luella gasped. "No! It can't be! This is a mistake!"

"I'm so sorry. It's no mistake," Officer Smolinski said softly, eyes glistening. "He's been charged with engaging in repeated acts of sexual assault, assault by a person who works with children, causing mental harm to a child, exposing his genitals, child enticement, and possession of child pornography —all serious felonies."

Luella heard little after "sexual assault of a child."

"Ma'am, for years your husband has been having sex with under-aged boys." Luella turned toward Sergeant Fossmeyer, who looked her in the eye. "Some of those kids were only eleven years old at the time the abuse began. We believe that the assaults took place at your basket-ball camp."

"I know this is a lot to take in," Officer Smolinski added quickly.

Luella looked from one to the other, eyes blinking rapidly. "This is crazy. I know my husband. He's a good man. He loves children."

A look passed between the officers.

"I'm telling you, this is impossible." Luella's eyes welled.

The sergeant leaned toward her, an edge creeping into his voice. "This is ugly business. The truth is your husband has been molesting kids for a number of years, kids whose voices haven't changed yet and who aren't old enough to shave."

"It's not true!" Luella argued, struggling against mounting hysteria. "You have the wrong person. August has helped more children than you can count."

Officer Smolinski fixed her with those sympathetic eyes. "We have numerous witnesses who have come forward."

Witnesses? How could anyone witness something that never

happened? Luella felt desperate to make them understand that she was married to an honorable, faithful husband who would never damage a child or betray her trust. "You don't know him like I do. If he were doing the horrible things you say he did, I would know."

The officers again made eye contact with one another.

"Ma'am, I know this is hard to process. Just take your time," said Sergeant Fossmeyer.

"How about a glass of water or a cup of coffee?" The woman's offer struck Luella like a mother giving milk and cookies to a child to blunt the hurt of a bruised knee. This was no minor hurt. This was a nightmare.

Luella shook her head.

"We believe he used the Hoops and Hearts Foundation to recruit his victims." Sergeant Fossmeyer leaned in so close she felt his hot coffee breath on her face. She grew more nauseous each time he exhaled.

She fingered her gold necklace, an outline of a heart with a basketball dangling in its center, a cherished gift August had commissioned for her and Beth when they'd launched their foundation. The glare of the overhead light made Luella's eyes burn. Her head ached. There had to be an explanation for this horrendous mistake. She crossed her arms over her chest. "I want to talk to August. He can make you understand this is an ugly lie."

"I know this is shocking news," said Officer Smolinski. "It's hard to believe someone you love could have molested children, but we wouldn't have arrested your husband if we didn't have the evidence."

Luella clenched her fists and jaw. Clearly nothing she said would make them change their minds. The less said, the better.

Sergeant Fossmeyer sucked his teeth, then rubbed his forehead. "So far you haven't been implicated in any wrongdoing."

Luella flinched. Implicated?

"What he means, Luella, is that since you help run the camp and the Hoops and Hearts Foundation, we would appreciate any information you have that would be helpful."

Helpful to whom, Luella thought. She locked her fingers together to keep her hands from shaking. The airless room grew stiflingly hot. If only she could breathe. "Am I in trouble?" she asked. Perspiration beaded on her upper lip.

The door opened. A uniformed officer peered around the doorway. "Mrs. Laurent's brother is here. Says he's her lawyer."

Franklin strode through the door, graying temples, designer glasses, and thick briefcase making him look every bit the intimidating attorney. Relief flooded through Luella. Sergeant Fossmeyer, exhaled loudly, pushed back from the table, and stood. Officer Smolinski pulled her hands into her lap.

"I'm Franklin Martin, representing Mrs. Laurent. I trust there is nothing further you need from my client."

"She's free to go," said Sergeant Fossmeyer.

"Come on, Luella. We're going home." Franklin rested his hand on her shoulder. She stood and teetered on wobbling legs. Franklin took her by the arm and guided her out of the room.

"What about August?" she asked.

"I'm sorry, Lu. That's more complicated."

Chapter Two

~Still Waters~

Two days after returning from the jail, Luella still couldn't sleep. She sat propped in bed, cheaters on, book in hand, the reading light turned down low, unable to concentrate on the paragraph she'd tried and failed to read a half dozen times. Sergeant Fossmeyer's and Officer Smolinski's words played on a continuous loop in her mind. *Sexual assault. Molested children. Implicated.*

August lay next to her, sleeping, his breathing deep and steady. Since he'd returned home after his arraignment few words had passed between them. When she'd inquired how he was doing, his response had been abrupt. "Later. I'm exhausted."

"Can't you at least tell me what's going on?" she'd persisted.

"You were in court. You heard the charges."

"But—"

"They're a damn lie. It's all fabricated bullshit."

"August, I'm really scared."

"You have nothing to worry about."

"I just—"

He turned off the lamp on his side of the bed. "Please, Lulu. I can't. We'll talk once I get some sleep."

She watched him now. Outwardly he appeared to be the same man who had always shared her bed, yet the ordeal had transformed him into an intimate stranger. In the shadowed light she studied his features—closed eyelids, pinched brow flexing and then relaxing, parted lips moving as though he were conversing in his dreams. Throughout their marriage, whenever she'd looked at August, she'd seen goodness, openness, a man who strove to do right in the world. Unimaginable, the terrible accusations against him. She could not believe them, *would not* believe them, no matter how adamantly the police insisted her husband was guilty.

"We're a team, Lulu," August had said countless times. "My life doesn't work without you by my side." He was the sleek sailboat, she the stabilizing keel. Her task was to keep them balanced. She'd embraced her job of holding August the dreamer, the big idea person who eschewed mundane matters, upright. Their pact relied on trust. They'd had their separate roles, but never secrets.

August shifted and muttered something unintelligible. Settled.

Luella turned her book to the front cover. *Go Set a Watchman.* Beth had given her the book as a Mother's Day present. "I know *To Kill a Mockingbird* is your all-time favorite novel and that there's a lot of buzz about Harper Lee publishing a second book," she'd said. "I hope you're not too disappointed. Sometimes things don't live up to expectations."

Losing her thirty-two-year-old husband to a heart attack two years ago, left alone to raise their son when she'd imagined life stretching into a charmed future, had turned Beth from an inveterate optimist to a guarded realist. Luella hoped this would be the summer her daughter regained her bearings. She had been doing well that first week at camp. Then, the arrest.

Setting her book down on the nightstand, Luella eased open the drawer and pulled out her journal and a pen. She ran her fingers over the embossed pine tree stamped onto its leather cover. August had given it to her as a surprise years ago. Recording her thoughts had seemed self-indulgent until she decided that writing could be a conversation with Nell Wooden, her role model, the wife of the most successful and revered college basketball coach in history.

August's admiration of John Wooden bordered on worship. He'd recited Coach Wooden's accomplishments so often Luella knew them by heart—first three-time consensus All-American, ten-time NCAA Division I champion, seven Henry Iba Awards, five-time college coach of the year, Presidential Medal of Freedom.

Most people who knew of John Wooden's storied career never heard of his wife. For twenty-five years, every month on the day of her death, John faithfully wrote a love letter to Nell. On the night August read the dedication Wooden had written to Nell in his book, *They Call Me Coach,* aloud to Luella, she'd been deeply touched. "Her love, faith, and loyalty through all our years together are primarily responsible for what I am."

As they'd made love that night, August whispered in her ear, "You're my Nell." Luella vowed then to shower her husband with the same love, faith, and loyalty. She would be the heart behind August the public man. After that she'd begun writing to Nell as though speaking with a dear, albeit deceased, friend.

She opened the journal to the ribbon marking the page with her most recent entry.

August confided that he thinks this will be our most successful summer ever. I believe he's right. Registrations are full. The courts are resurfaced and look great. Beth is showing glimmers of her old self and stepping up as his assistant. Besides, the Farmer's Almanac predicts a warm, dry summer. You couldn't ask for a more reliable source than that. lol.

Luella frowned. How naïve and trivial those words seemed now. She clicked open the pen and began to write.

Nell, August had his arraignment hearing today. I was worried that the judge might keep him in jail until the trial or require an exorbitant bail. Franklin stepped in and made a compelling argument, saying that August has a spotless reputation and a history of philanthropy, so the judge ordered his release on a signature bond, which means we won't have to take out a second mortgage. As a condition of his release, she ordered home confinement, that he not leave the state, and that he have no contact with minors.

I don't know if he was more disappointed that he will not be running camp this summer or that he will not be able to have contact with his grandson until the trial is over. Beth asked Franklin to take Wyatt to his house tonight until we can figure out the situation. August was upset, but it can't be helped.

Franklin told me he will not be August's attorney through the trial. He said that August needs a first-rate criminal lawyer, not a tax attorney. The word "criminal" hit me hard. He said he'd recommend someone. Small comfort. Maybe it wasn't what he said but the way he said it.

Luella remembered the geyser of panic she'd felt when Franklin broke that news.

"Surely you don't think—"

"It doesn't matter what I think," he'd said, looking her in the eye with an expression as close to revulsion as she'd ever seen. "It will matter what the jury thinks. And from the looks of it, he's going to need a damn good lawyer if he's going to avoid a long prison sentence."

She'd fought back tears, letting the weight of his words sink in.

Luella continued to write.

Beth and I sat together behind August in court. She didn't say a word. Still waters run deep, which is what worries me. It's been two years since Gabe died. Outwardly, she acts strong. But I can see that she's still grieving. It's as if she's emotionally frozen. I feel terribly selfish. I want to help her, but I can barely keep myself together.

August turned on his back, his deep breathing revving to a

full-throttled snore. Luella resisted the urge to nudge him. His jaw slack, hair disheveled, he appeared aged. Luella thought of the viral YouTube video Beth had shown her. It contrasted his triumphant press conference after Jolliet University captured its first NCAA tournament bid in a decade with newsclips of him entering and leaving court. It presented him in the worst light, weary and humbled, his confidence extinguished. The limelight August relished had shape-shifted into a voyeuristic frenzy of media attention.

Overwhelming despondency washed over Luella. She gripped the pen harder and pressed down more forcefully on the page.

I don't know what to do. This is such a nightmare! I want to pinch myself awake. It's so unfair. August is a good man. Nell, you know about living with a moral and honorable man. What would you have done if John had been arrested for sexually abusing children? I can barely write the words. You can't imagine it, can you? Until the police came, neither could I.

My life will forever be divided into "before" and "after." I know what before looked like, but after?

Luella heard footsteps in the hallway and put down her journal, took off her glasses. Bird, lying on the floor next to the bed, perked up his ears.

Quietly, Luella slipped out of bed, put on her robe and slippers. "Stay," she said softly, holding up her hand, and tiptoed to the bedroom door, closing it carefully. First, she peeked into Rosie's room. Rosie lay asleep. That meant Beth was up.

By the time she reached the top of the stairway, Beth was out of sight. Luella went downstairs and into the kitchen, where she assumed that she'd find Beth foraging in the refrigerator or making a cup of tea. The room was empty. The front porch door closed. Luella retraced her footsteps into the living room. She opened the door and walked onto the screened porch that covered the width of the house, thinking that perhaps Beth had decided to sleep out there on the daybed. Still, no sign of her. Out of the corner of her eye, Luella caught movement. She squinted into the darkness. Beth's receding figure moved down the path toward the lake.

Luella drew her robe tighter. Concerned, she followed.

The night air, a pleasing blend of pine and lake, was June-mild. A three-quarter moon hung over the water, its soft light dancing seductively on the surface. From its perch in a nearby tree, an owl hooted.

She slowed and watched Beth, who'd slipped out of her nightgown, walk into the water, never hesitating, until all but her head disappeared into the blackness. Worried, Luella wanted to call out, but resisted. Beth was a strong swimmer. As a child, Luella had taught her to float and dive and swim until she was certain Beth could fall out of a boat a mile from shore and make it to safety.

Still waters run deep. Anxiety niggled at Luella.

Beth swam, gliding otter-like, a gentle wake breaking behind her, the simple elegance of it striking. She passed the raft. With each glide, Luella became more agitated. "Beth! Stop!" she yelled. "Stop!"

She looked around frantically for a means of rescue. A life preserver hung on the bench at the end of the dock. Still, if Beth struggled, she'd never reach her on time. She ran toward a canoe pulled up onto the beach, dragged it to the water's edge, and pushed it until it was no longer hung up on the sand. Then, stepping into the water in her slippered feet, she steadied the canoe by bracing her arms on each side of it, and climbed in. Plunging the paddle into the lake, she pushed against the hard bottom, sending the canoe adrift.

"Beth!" she screamed as she paddled furiously, her biceps burning.

Beth turned, treaded water. Then she swam toward the canoe.

"What are you doing?" Luella demanded, tears brimming.

"I couldn't sleep," Beth said, swimming alongside. "Mom, are you okay?"

"I called out to you."

"I didn't hear you," said Beth, taking in a mouthful of water and spitting it out in an arc.

Luella's shoulders slumped. Fear. Anger. Relief. It was an emotional roller coaster familiar to every parent whose child courted danger and emerged unscathed.

"I'll meet you on the dock," burbled Beth.

Luella said nothing. She paddled toward the beach, her heartbeat slowing with each stroke.

Once on shore, Luella pulled the canoe securely onto the sand. Beth strode out of the water, picked up her nightgown, and wrapped herself in the towel she'd dropped on the beach. They walked out to the end of the dock and sat on the bench.

"Mom, I called Gabe's brother. Anthony invited me to stay at his place. I'm going to leave in the morning, pick up Wyatt, and hang out there for a few days, then head home." Beth wiped her face with the corner of the towel.

"You and Wyatt are supposed to stay here for the summer."

"Mom, camp's over." Beth stared out at the water. "You know once Dad's arrest hit the news everyone cancelled."

"We don't know how this will play out," said Luella.

Beth twisted the ends of the towel. "No one's coming. You know that, right?"

"We can't be sure."

"There isn't a parent in her right mind who'd let her child come to a camp where the head coach is accused of molesting kids."

"But *you* could stay."

"I need time to think."

"You can think here as well as at Anthony's."

"That's just it. I can't." Beth looked down at her hands. "Not with Dad in the house."

Luella's eyes narrowed.

"Multiple counts of sexual assault," said Beth, shaking her head.

Luella's hands trembled.

"Mom, he's accused of having sex with six different boys all under age thirteen."

Luella shot up and stood glaring down at Beth. "He's your father. You can't think that he's capable of doing such a thing."

Beth rose and faced her mother. "I want to believe he's the dad I love and admire, but what if he molested those kids?"

"He's innocent!"

"I hope you're right. But what if he isn't?" Beth countered, her voice rising. "What if he's guilty?"

Luella's open hand whipped across Beth's face.

Beth dropped her towel, the handprint on her cheek visible in the moonlit night. Without a word, she turned and strode from the dock.

Any thought Beth had of waiting until morning to leave camp left with the sting of her mother's hand. Taking the steps two at a time, she raced upstairs to her bedroom to pack.

She dried herself with the damp towel with an urgency that left her breathless. From the top dresser drawer, she selected a pair of panties and a bra. The silky undergarments clung to her moist skin. She tugged on a pair of jeans, grabbed a T-shirt from the bottom dresser drawer, then ran a large-tooth comb through her wet hair, hastily banding it into a ponytail. She slipped on a pair of flip-flops.

Racing around the room, she gathered her basketball shoes, sneakers, and sandals, then emptied each dresser drawer, and jammed everything into a large duffle bag. Pulling the clothes in the closet from their hangers, she stuffed them into a second duffle. From the top of the dresser, she retrieved the pair of aquamarine post earrings Gabe had given her the day Wyatt was born and her cell phone, which she dropped in the zippered side pocket.

After a cursory glance around, she hoisted the duffle bags and raced down the hall to Wyatt's room. Earlier she'd packed most of his things before taking him to Franklin's and Denise's house. Now she flew around the room grabbing the remaining clothes and toys, cramming them into a laundry basket.

Her mother's knee-jerk defense of her father was maddening. How could she be so certain of his innocence? Unquestioning? Naïve? Regardless of what her mother thought, Beth wasn't heartless. She loved her father. She'd give anything if the accusations were untrue, to discover that he was innocent. *But six boys.*

Maybe once she would have jumped to his defense without question, but experience had taught her that pedophiles hide in plain sight. Donald Vincent. She would never forget that name. Donald Vincent had been a teacher at her high school, a faculty darling, popular, charismatic, willing to put in long after-school hours. He chaperoned dances, taught summer school, coached the junior varsity football team. Then he'd been arrested for having sexual relations with a fifteen-year-old boy. Once that single crack appeared, the dam broke; stories of multiple assaults over a number of years surfaced. Shock waves rippled through the faculty. Beth was blindsided. Stunned. Not Gabe. He had never liked the man. "Can't put my finger on why, something just doesn't jibe," he'd told her long before the arrest. At the time, she'd dismissed his dislike as some unconscious professional envy. But Gabe had been right.

Now the stakes were higher. She had Wyatt to protect.

If Gabe were alive, he would do whatever it took to keep their son safe. She imagined his voice urging her to trust her instincts, to leave. *Go, Beth. Go now!*

Bird loped into the room, cocked his head, and looked up at her with penetrating eyes. Beth ran her hand from his head to tail.

"What are you doing?"

Startled, Beth jumped. She turned. Standing in the doorway in his pajamas, circles under his eyes, hair disheveled, her father still cut an imposing figure.

"I'm leaving."

"It's the middle of the night."

A vice tightened around Beth's chest. She stared down at the basket in her arms. She inhaled the little-boy scent of Wyatt's clothes. There could be no question where her loyalty lay.

"I'm disappointed in you. It's not like you to cut and run."

"Disappointed in me?" Beth glared at him. Heat crawled up her neck and into her cheeks. "Are you kidding me?"

"You can't possibly believe these ridiculous accusations." He took a step toward her. She took a step back. "I'm your father for Chrissake. You know me better than that."

"Do I?"

"Be reasonable, Bethy. Think." His tone softened. "You've been helping me for years. Have you ever seen me harm a player? Sure I can be hard on kids sometimes. I want to get the most from them. That's good coaching, not abuse."

"I'm not doing this now."

"I thought I taught you something about loyalty." The sharp edge returned.

"You did." With the basket in her arms, Beth pushed past her father and out the door.

"If you leave now, don't come crawling back!" He shouted.

His words shot through Beth like a poisoned arrow. Gasping for air, she fled down the stairs and out to her car. After loading the laundry basket in the backseat, she started the engine. Her fists gripped the steering wheel until the color drained from her knuckles. The duffle bags. Shit. She considered leaving them. The thought of facing her father again make her quake. Clothes could be replaced. But she'd put the earrings from Gabe and her cell phone in the pocket of one of the bags.

She had to go back.

She closed her eyes, sucked in a deep breath. Now or never. Eyes open, back straightened, she forced herself to walk through the door. Both duffle bags lay upside down at the bottom of the stairs as though they'd been kicked from the top of the landing. Her father was no-where in sight. Beth righted each bag and wrapped her fists around the handles.

Bird ran down the stairs, tail wagging, as if signaling that he was ready for the trip.

"Sorry boy."

Beth hoisted the bags and hurried out of the house. She lifted the car hatch and loaded the bags. As she opened the driver's side door, she heard her mother calling to her as she came around the side of the house.

"Beth! Please don't leave. Stay!"

Hurriedly Beth slid into the driver's seat and closed the door.

"I can't."

Chapter Three

~Fourth of July~

"**M**om! Mom! Watch me!" Wyatt called out as he bobbed up and down in the shallow end of the swimming pool, his dark hair slicked back away from his face, his skin bronzed despite Beth's best efforts to keep him slathered in sunscreen.

Beth, a glass of Sauvignon Blanc in hand, waved from her perch on the chaise.

"Uncle Anthony's going to throw me into the deep end!"

The late afternoon sun shone in a cloudless sky. Heat radiated from the concrete deck, surrounding Beth, bikini-clad, in cocoon-like warmth. Sunglasses hid her weary eyes. She squinted toward the shimmering water, creating a visor with her free hand.

Anthony wrapped his hands around Wyatt's waist, hoisted him, and launched him in a high arc toward the deep end of the pool. As Wyatt landed a glimmering spray fanned into the air.

Anthony's muscled arms and upper body reminded her so much of Gabe that being in his presence was at once comforting and disquieting. His smile was Gabe's smile, his voice Gabe's voice. When she closed her eyes, she could hear her late husband in every bass note. It made her insides ache. Fortunately, Anthony's eyes were chestnut brown instead of intense blue, and he had the gregarious personality of a middle child rather than Gabe's firstborn introversion.

Beth leaned protectively forward until Wyatt's head popped above the surface, his hair as sleek as a baby seal's fur, his eyes blinking rapidly. He inhaled an exaggerated breath, submerged his face, and paddled furiously toward Anthony. As he reached the shallow end of the pool Beth gradually eased against the backrest. Wyatt was a natural in the water. Still, she couldn't erase the anxiety she felt whenever he wasn't by her side.

"He's quite the fish," said Gina, Gabe's and Anthony's younger sister, who lounged in the chaise next to her.

"At camp he swam every day," replied Beth.

"How is Wyatt handling everything?" asked Gina.

Beth sipped her wine before answering. "Pretty well, I think. Of course, he lobbied to stay up north, but he's obviously happy to be here."

Wyatt had put up some resistance when she'd told him that plans had changed, that they needed to leave the morning after her altercation with her parents. "I could stay at Grandma's and Grandpa's and you could go home and come back and get me later," he'd reasoned. She couldn't bring herself to fabricate some fairytale about why they were leaving, nor could she tell a five-year-old the unvarnished truth. In the end, she'd simply said, "I would miss you too much." Wyatt had sighed and resigned himself to leaving. It broke her heart that, at such a tender age, her son had become so accustomed to disappointment.

"And how are *you* handling everything?" inquired Gina.

"I'm fine."

"Funny, you don't look fine." Gina's straightforwardness came as no surprise.

Beth slid the stem of her glass between her fingers, cupped its bowl in her hand, and languidly swirled the wine. Gina was right. She was not fine. Far from it.

She closed her eyes and thought about how perfect life had seemed when she met Gabe. He'd been hired to teach English and coach football at the same high school where she taught mathematics and coached basketball.

"So, you're not just a pretty face," he'd said the first time he spoke to her.

She'd rolled her eyes. "Next you're going to tell me you're a huge Jane Austen fan."

He'd laughed. "Pretty lame pick-up line, huh?"

"Beyond lame." She'd feigned disinterest, pretending that his striking blue eyes and deep dimples hadn't made her heart flutter.

After weeks spent dancing around each other, Gabe had surprised Beth by inviting her to an open-mic poetry reading at a local coffee shop. She remembered how out of place he'd seemed at first—tall, muscled, athletic—in a room filled with bookish types, until an elderly man, hands shaking, voice trembling, read a love poem written to his departed wife, and Gabe's eyes welled. He'd turned to her and said, "He's a lucky man." She knew then that she was falling in love.

"Mom! Mom, watch me!" hollered Wyatt. "I'm going even higher!"

Beth opened her eyes and resisted the urge to warn him to be careful, to stay on the shallow end of the pool. A world in which a young husband could drop dead from a heart attack or a father, whom she worshiped, could be arrested for molesting young boys had become a menacing place. The threat, she realized, was not the deep water but her constant sense of dread.

"I'm watching," she yelled, lifting her sunglasses to the top of her head, pointing to her eyes, then resting her glasses back on the bridge of her nose.

As Wyatt catapulted through the air, her muscles tensed. Protect him, she told herself, but do not make your fear his fear.

"I don't mean to nag," said Gina, "but it might help to talk about it."

"Please drop it."

Beth's response sounded brusquer than she'd intended. She turned toward Gina, whose look of concern was touching. "I'm sorry. It's—it's just that this is the first decent day I've had since the…in a long time. I don't want to spoil it."

"No big deal. Seriously, it's all right."

"When I've had a lot more of these," Beth raised her wine glass, "then, who knows?"

At eleven o'clock in the evening, Beth and Gina sat conversing with Anthony in his living room. Miles Davis played in the background, the volume low enough for their voices to be heard over his soulful trumpet. Lightheaded, Beth curled up on the opposite end of the couch from Anthony and swayed to the rhythm of "My Funny Valentine." She inhaled the peachy aroma of the wine, tilted her head back and let the liquid slip down her throat, welcoming the dulling of her senses, the weightlessness of her thoughts.

The day had gone well. Anthony entertained Wyatt in the swimming pool for hours. At dinnertime, he cooked perfect steaks on the grill, making Wyatt his assistant, while she and Gina worked in the kitchen, creating a leafy salad with warm pears, goat cheese, and toasted pecans. When it was Wyatt's bedtime, Gina read *Today I Will Fly* until he fell into a child-exhausted sleep.

"You guys spoil us," said Beth. "We'll never want to leave."

"If it was up to me, you wouldn't. We love you guys," said Gina, who sat with her legs slung over the side of the armchair across from Beth. Gina placed a hand over her heart, patted it, and glanced over at her brother, as if seeking his agreement. "Wyatt looks just like Gabe when he was that age."

"You weren't even a glimmer in Mom's and Dad's eyes when Gabe was five-years-old," said Anthony.

"But I've seen tons of pictures of him at that age. Tell me he's not the spitting image—"

"Hard to dispute that."

Beth had also seen countless childhood photographs of Gabe in the family albums. There was no denying the resemblance—intense blue eyes, dark curly hair, olive complexion—but to her, Wyatt had inherited his slender frame and full mouth from her side of the family. Still, it heartened her that they wanted Wyatt to be a replica of their brother.

"You're always welcome here," said Anthony, moving closer to Beth and laying his hand on her knee. "You're still family."

She knew that Anthony meant the touch as a brotherly gesture, physical affection being akin to breathing for the Mancuso clan. The first time Gabe had taken her home to meet his family she'd commented on the constant hugging among his relatives. "We're Italian," he'd said, wrapping her in his arms and kissing her on the neck. "Get used to it because, trust me, if you stick with me, you'll never escape it." There was nothing suggestive about Anthony's demeanor. Still, the heat of his hand melted into her flesh, and she had the urge to move his hand up her thigh. It had been two years since she'd felt the warmth of a man's touch. Plus, he reminded her so much of Gabe.

You're drunk. Quit being an idiot.

"I miss Gabe," she confessed. "I miss him every minute of every day."

"He was special," said Gina, raising her glass.

"It's as though he's been gone for ten years or for ten minutes, and I can't figure out which it is," said Beth. "Some days I can barely remember his smile or his voice. Other days, it's as though he just stepped out to go to the store and I expect him to walk through the door at any minute."

"You've been through some pretty tough stuff in the past few weeks." Anthony removed his hand from her knee. "It's got to have thrown you off balance."

"You have no idea." Beth kneaded her forehead, as if forestalling a headache. She took another swallow of wine.

"This whole thing would really piss him off," said Anthony.

"Big time," Gina agreed.

"Gabe took his big brother role seriously. If I'd step out of line, he'd let me have it, but if anyone else tried to mess with me, he'd go after them with a vengeance," said Anthony. "Now that he's gone, Gabe would expect me to look after the family, to man up."

It was so like the Mancuso men to be defenders. Anthony was a year younger than Beth, but that wouldn't keep him from acting as protector. She'd accused Gabe of being paternalistic when they'd first dated, but quickly realized that he respected her independence. He'd simply had her back. Always.

Beth hadn't spoken to anyone about her father's arrest, the arguments she'd had with her mother and father, or the way she'd fled from the camp. It was her nature to keep her thoughts to herself, to carry responsibility alone, or it had been until she'd met Gabe. He'd taught her the comfort of having a partner to help carry the load. Then he was gone. Now, she ached to cry on his shoulder, to have him fold her in his arms.

"I don't want to pry, but it might help if you talked about what's going on," said Anthony, his voice beckoning her to reveal more.

Trumpet music swirled in her head, stirred her emotions. Like morning dew from summer grass, her resolve evaporated.

"I'm…so… angry." Beth balled her hand into a fist. "I'm afraid if I speak, it will make things real. As long as I keep everything in my head, it might just be a fantasy. Maybe I'll wake up and none of it will have actually happened. I don't want to believe my dad did anything to those boys. It's too disgusting to imagine." She spoke emphatically, her words saturated in despair. "Sometimes I think maybe they're all just making things up, that they're out for some kind of revenge."

Gina shot Anthony a look that signaled disbelief.

"Six different boys come forward accusing him of the same thing," said Anthony, shifting his position. "A conspiracy doesn't make sense."

"This is something that happens to other people's families, you know? Not mine. I mean, if I heard this on the news about someone I didn't know, no problem. I'd think, put the sick bastard in jail and throw away the key." Beth wiped her dripping nose with the back of her hand. "But he's my dad."

"I'm sorry." Anthony edged next to her and put his arm around her.

She buried her face in his shoulder and cried quietly.

Gina handed Beth a tissue. Gradually, Beth regained control. She sat up straight, pulled away from Anthony's embrace, blew her nose.

"How could I have thought that he was such a great person all my life when he's a complete skeeze?"

"I guess sometimes people aren't what they appear to be. Maybe people can be both good and bad. Like the light-side and the dark-side," said Gina. "Maybe he's like those people who have multiple personalities."

"What did I miss? Were there clues I simply ignored? I feel so damn guilty."

"Beth." Anthony looked her in the eye. His tone was sharp. "Get that out of your head right now. I mean it. Don't do that to yourself."

Beth nodded, although she didn't know if she believed him. She may have been blinded by a lifetime of hero worship.

"And there's my mom. We had this huge fight. She simply refuses to be realistic about any of this. I wonder if she suspected my dad and turned the other way. I mean, she still sleeps with him. Aren't there things that you would sense? I can't bear the thought of being touched by him. How does she continue to share the same bed? I mean, for fuck's sake!"

"Mommy, I'm thirsty." It was Wyatt, who'd wandered sleepy-eyed into the living room.

Beth prayed that he hadn't heard her. A good reason to keep your mouth shut, she thought. She started to rise but tipped unsteadily.

Gina scrambled up. "I've got this." She smiled at Wyatt. "Hey, baby, Aunt Gina will get you a nice cold glass of water and then tuck you back into bed." She guided him down the hallway to the bathroom.

Beth tried to rise again and then sat down. "And then there's Wyatt." Her voice cracked. "How can I keep him from the grandparents he loves?"

"Try not to get ahead of yourself," said Anthony.

"I can't help it. My head is spinning with all this crazy stuff. I have a meeting with my principal next week. I haven't been able to face anyone at school yet. I can only imagine the gossip floating around that place. 'Did you hear about Beth Laurent? Turns out her famous father is a child molester. Oh, how the mighty have fallen.' And there are my students and players. How do I face them?"

"You'll handle this like you do everything else—with that steel backbone of yours."

"But what if I can't handle this, Anthony? What if this is all just too much? What if this is my breaking point?" She sniffled. "I've always had Mom and Dad as my safety net, and now they're the problem. If Gabe was alive, it would be different. He gave me courage." The more Beth talked, the thicker her tongue became. "I have a confession to make. I'm mad at him for leaving me to face this mess alone. How pathetic is that?"

Anthony's eyes narrowed. "I don't know how many ways to say this. You're *not* alone. You have Gina and you have me."

Beth rose awkwardly. "You know I'm grateful for…everything." As she lurched sideways, Anthony scrambled up to help her. She waved him off. "I'm okay. I just have to get to bed."

She staggered toward the hallway. Then she turned back toward Anthony. "And you want to know something really sick? Despite everything my bastard-of-a-father has done, I still love him."

Luella loved everything about the Fourth of July. The parade in Givens Knoll, a touch of small-town Americana with floats, horses, fire trucks, antique cars, clowns, and the high school marching band. The picnic with hot dogs, hamburgers, potato salad, watermelon, and Marilyn's special flag sheet cake topped with fresh blueberries and strawberries. The boat parade, a Whisper Lake tradition. The fireworks bursting in the night sky. The sing-a-long around a bonfire at the beach. This year everything was ruined by August's arrest. Even Marilyn, who'd cooked at the camp for twenty years, had to be let go.

Sitting on the screened porch with August and Rosie, Luella waited for her brother and sister-in-law to pick up Rosie for the parade. It was mid-morning. The temperature climbed steadily toward the low-eighties. A lazy westerly breeze skimmed across the lake, carrying a blend of music, voices, and boat motors, punctuated by the occasional boom of a firecracker.

She was preoccupied with the conversation she'd had with August about the charges brought against him. "Honestly, I *can't* explain them," he'd said. "I don't know who has it out for me or why they're trying to hurt me. They're bullshit, Lulu. You can't believe any of this fucking nonsense."

When she'd pressed him, asking why he hadn't told her that he'd been questioned at the Sheriff's Department before the arrest, he'd said, "It was so ridiculous, I didn't want to worry you. I thought the police would see that this was bogus and just drop it. I had no idea how stupid and relentless they are."

She understood. Her body stiffened at the mere thought of being in the same room with Sergeant Fossmeyer and Officer Smolinski. She could only imagine what it must have been like for August.

"Lulu," he'd said, facing her, drawing her to him, and looking her in the eye. "After thirty-five years together, you know me."

She did know him. He was her lover, her friend, the father of her child. He was energetic, ambitious, generous to a fault. For his charitable works he'd been named Philanthropist of the Year. He was no saint, but he wasn't the devil. And she was his partner, who'd vowed to love him for better, for worse.

"We're going to trial. I promise my lawyer will get to the bottom of this. I need you by my side. I can't survive this nightmare without you." There was no doubt; she would stand by him. They would fight this together.

Her thoughts were interrupted by Franklin as he strode around the corner of the house and up the porch steps, yelling, "Hey, Rosie, you ready?"

Rosie, dressed in navy blue shorts, red t-shirt, and white headband, dragged the toes of her tennis shoes along the floorboards to slow the porch swing to a stop. "Ready!" She sprang to her feet. As an afterthought she turned to Luella and August. "Are Beth and Wyatt coming?"

"No, honey, they're not coming this year." Even as Luella spoke the words, she held out hope that Beth would show up later and bring Wyatt, if not to the camp, at least to Franklin's. They hadn't spoken since the night of the confrontation when Beth had left in anger.

Rosie stuck out her lower lip.

"It's okay, Rosie Posie. They're with their friends," said August.

"Oh." Rosie smiled, as if that were the most reasonable explanation possible. She let the screen door slam as she hurried down the steps to Franklin's waiting Land Rover.

"I'll be right back," Luella said to August.

As Franklin slid into the driver's seat and closed the door, Luella caught up with him. He rolled down the window.

"Isn't Denise going to the parade?" Luella was disappointed that her sister-in-law wasn't waiting in the car.

"She decided to meet us in town," said Franklin.

"Are you coming back later to watch the boat parade and fireworks?"

Franklin hesitated, stared at his hands gripping the steering wheel. "We're planning to watch them at our place."

"But we always—" Luella resisted the urge to plead with her brother. He loved her, she knew, would stand by her, but he would not countermand his wife's wishes.

She and Denise were close, at least that's what Luella had believed before the arrest, but they hadn't spoken since. Her lack of loyalty stung. Although her sister-in-law was a generous and good-hearted woman, it was evident that she intended to steer clear of the camp. What Luella didn't know is whether Denise's aversion extended to her as well as to August.

"Let's just get through the Fourth." He offered her an apologetic half-smile. "We'll talk later. I promise."

"Um...One more thing." Luella looked down, swirled a patch of loose gravel around with the toe of her shoe, then shifted from one foot to the other. "Have you heard anything about whether I'm going to be charged and arrested, too?"

"Lu, I know you're worried. I spoke with the D.A. It's clear they have no evidence to charge you."

Rosie fidgeted in the passenger's seat. "Rudy's my friend. He's in the parade. He says he's going to throw candy from the floats."

"I'll have her home tonight after the fireworks," said Franklin, his window easing upward.

Luella watched his vehicle disappear around the bend in the long driveway. Maybe she should feel grateful that her brother and sister-in-law were willing to entertain Rosie for the day, but all she felt was debilitating loss.

Laughter echoed across the water, and the aroma of suntan lotion, charcoal, and grilled meat drifted on the breeze, teasing Luella's senses, reminding her that on the 4th of July she should not be spending the afternoon sitting on the porch, alone.

She heard the rumble of boat motors before she saw them. She checked her phone—five o'clock, time for the boat parade, a Whisper Lake tradition extending back to Luella's childhood. Residents decorated their boats—all craft eligible—and cruised around the perimeter of the lake single file as people gathered on their docks to wave and applaud. In years past, Laurent's Basketball Camp would have participated. Throughout the week leading up to the Fourth, the kids would have vied to ride on the pontoon boat by competing in a game August devised to improve their shooting skills. The remaining campers would gather on the beach and boisterously cheer.

Luella called to August, "The parade is starting."

Half expecting him to remain in the house to finish watching *The Patriot*, she was surprised when he appeared on the porch and sat next to her on the over-sized couch.

"It's okay if you go down to the dock," he said. "The view isn't great from up here."

"I'd rather stay here with you."

She allowed August to believe that she stayed for his sake. In truth, she couldn't bear to sit on the dock, exposed, the object of people's pity or derision.

She leaned back against the couch cushions. Their mustiness reminded her of hot, muggy nights spent on the sleeping porch at Aunt Mavis's and Uncle Walter's cottage, her child's body enfolded in the soft mattress resting on a plywood platform fastened to the ceiling by lengths of chain that squeaked whenever she turned. The smell, evocative of comfort and security, made her long for the simplicity of those days.

The first float, a pontoon boat decorated from stem to stern in red, white, and blue, slowly motored past along the shoreline. Through the trees, Luella couldn't make out the lettering on the sign hanging over the side of the boat.

"Can you read that?" she asked, pointing to the float and wishing she had a clearer view.

"Something about Whisper Lake veterans, I think," said August, squinting.

An electric-green ski boat, christened the Tequila Express, followed; its engines rumbled a low guttural growl; its occupants, twenty-somethings in muscle shirts and bikinis, sang "Margaritaville" at the top of their lungs.

"I hope they have a designated driver," mumbled August.

The third craft was a rickety pontoon boat with Chinese lanterns swaying from its dented canopy. Its sign in bold block letters read, "SHI-TANIC."

August laughed.

Luella couldn't remember the last time she'd seen him smile, much less laugh. She reached for his hand. "Let's pray that one makes it back to port."

He squeezed her hand. "Let's hope the passengers are exceptional swimmers."

Next, a bass boat, the prow decorated like the mouth of a shark, its jagged teeth exposed, its engine emitting a low growl, rumbled into view. The driver's malicious voice exploded up from the lake and through the trees. "That's where the pervert lives."

Luella's body went rigid.

"Laurent, you sick bastard!"

The slur jolted her like a taser current. She turned to August, his face red. He stood and, without a word, walked into the house.

In that moment Luella understood; she was not safe anywhere.

Chapter Four

~St. Eligius~

B oredom, unimaginable in previous summers, had set in. Luella used to long for a moment to herself, a moment in which she could escape the demands of running the camp, linger over a second cup of coffee in the morning, sunbathe on the dock in the middle of the afternoon, skinny dip in the moonlight. She did none of those things.

Days were bookended by a sixty-mile round trip to Horizons Sheltered Workshop that Rosie attended now that there was no longer work available in the camp kitchen. At 8:00 a.m. every weekday morning Luella left to deliver Rosie, and at 4:00 p.m. she left to pick her up, always dreading what she might encounter. Between trips, she occupied herself with housekeeping tasks, meal preparation, walks around the camp with Bird, mail retrieval, and her e-reader loaded with enough books to stock a small-town library.

After the first weeks of media frenzy, the cars, trucks, and vans parked at the end of the driveway had mostly disappeared. Then, randomly, some reporter would show up. It happened frequently enough to keep her vigilant. A particularly unflattering photograph of Luella, taken by one of those bloodsuckers, had appeared in a statewide newspaper under the headline, "Did She Know?" The bags under her eyes, gaping mouth, and dazed expression looked like the mug shot of a guilty woman, even to her.

In mid-day, the sun half-hid behind a lofty cumulus cloud. As Luella walked from the house down the winding driveway to collect the mail, gravel crackled beneath her feet. She glanced down and saw a line of pronged tracks in the mud alongside the driveway, a sign that a herd of deer passed through after the thunderstorm the previous night. In mid-July, the forest was a verdant mix of evergreens and deciduous trees, the air a pungent stew of pine and earth. The beauty was marred by a scrim of anxiety that overlaid everything.

As the road came into sight, she slowed her step, hoping that there wouldn't be a reporter or some other curiosity seeker lurking. Cautiously, she stepped onto the road and looked in both directions. The coast was clear. Luella walked toward the mailbox, which stood about forty feet across the road. As she came closer, she saw that the mailbox was misshapen, deeply dented on the top and sides. It appeared as though someone had bashed it with a bat.

Her shoulders slumped. Who would be so cruel?

The door of the mailbox would not open. She pulled and pried until it finally gave way. She rifled through the stack of mail. Sandwiched between the fliers and catalogs was an official looking envelope from St. Eligius School. She hesitated before running her index finger under the flap of the envelope, then began reading:

Dear Ms. Laurent:

This is written to request that you attend a meeting on Thursday, July 30 at 1:00 pm. at the St. Eligius School office to discuss circumstances related to your employment.

Please confirm your attendance by calling my office at 773-555-8600. Sincerely,

Ardan J. Connelly
SECS Board President

Cc: Sr. Marian Lee
Principal

Luella's heart beat double time. Was *she* in trouble because of August's arrest? She'd learned that you could be innocent and still be blamed. Panic crept from the ends of her limbs, up her spine, and into her chest. She needed to speak to Franklin. She pulled her cell phone from her pocket and pressed his number. No answer. She hung up, not bothering to leave a message.

As she staggered back down the long driveway, Luella's stomach churned. Maybe it's nothing, she told herself. She was an exceptional teacher, a faithful employee. Her students loved her. Her colleagues valued her. Maybe Ardan Connelly just wanted to discuss the situation, to manage the fallout. Still, this wasn't a good sign. She feared the worst. She could not lose her job, not on top of everything else.

The forest surrounding her suddenly seemed dark and foreboding, the driveway narrower. Overhead, the large cloud obscured the sun, throwing her path into shadow. She spotted a long, straight stick protruding from a stand of ferns at the edge of the driveway and grabbed it. Flinging the letter to the muddy ground, she stabbed it with the stick. Again. Again. And again.

Rounding the curve toward the house, Luella, heart pounding, clutched the muddied letter in her shaking fist. You're overreacting, she told herself. Connelly mentioned nothing about firing. Still, it was the first time in all her years of teaching that she'd received such a curt letter. Previous summer correspondence always welcomed her back to another school year, not summoned her to the meet with the school board president.

Returning to school had been nagging at her. Since August's trial was scheduled to begin on October 26, she'd hoped to take a leave of absence. She was in no state to teach. With no emotional reserves, in a profession as much about example as knowledge, it was hard to imagine facing her students or colleagues. It was all she could do to get through each day.

She'd promised herself a dozen times to call the principal, Sister Marian, to discuss her options. Too embarrassed to confront the reason she required a leave of absence, she'd procrastinated. Now, the letter had put an end to avoidance.

Whenever August secured a new job as he rose through the coaching ranks, Luella had been forced to start over at a new school. In the early years, her salary helped keep them financially afloat. With August's current salary and lucrative endorsement deals, it was no longer necessary for her to work. But she loved teaching, loved being around children, loved having something that belonged strictly to her. Of all the places she'd taught, St. Eligius School was her favorite. The thought of being fired was crushing.

As she neared the storage shed, she heard a thumping sound. She peered around the corner. August stood with his back to her, his legs braced in a wide stance, his muscles taut, his bare upper body glinting with sweat. He swung a splitting ax high above his head and brought it down forcefully on the log balanced on the chopping block. He bent to retrieve the pieces that toppled to the ground, tossed them into the pile, then picked up another log and set it down. Luella studied him as he repeated the sequence. He wore jeans and a blue baseball cap turned backwards. From behind, he appeared to be a man half his age. "I can't insist my players keep in shape if I look like a pot-bellied couch potato," he'd say. So, at age fifty-seven, he was still in top physical condition. His tanned athlete's body, having thickened slightly, was still sculpted and strong.

Luella had always thought of herself as cerebral, bookish, physically average. Five-feet-four-and-a-half inches tall. One-hundred-forty pounds, twenty more than the day she and August met. Brown eyes. Hair, the color her mother used to refer to as "mouse brown," now dyed a shade darker. A face that others often referred to as "pleasant," neither beautiful nor homely. She wondered what August saw when he looked at her. Whenever she'd complain about her widening hips, he'd say, "You'll aways look beautiful to me." Yet she wondered if August, a man who valued physicality, meant it.

August was a doer accustomed to constant activity. It was a relief to see him outside working instead of inside pacing. Coaching Division I basketball was more job than most men could handle. In addition to recruiting, practices, and game preparation, there was a long season, which meant extensive travel and grueling hours. There were press interviews and endorsements and outside business dealings. Yet all of that had not been enough for August; he ran the summer camp for aspiring players plus sat on the board of the Hoops and Hearts Foundation. Confinement was tantamount to torture. She dreaded to think what prison might do to him.

August turned around. "Jesus, Luella!" he shouted when he found her standing behind him. He grabbed the T-shirt slung over the open shed door, and wiped the sweat from his face.

"I'm sorry. I didn't mean to startle you."

His brow furrowed. She followed his gaze, moving from her face to her fist, wrapped around the crumpled, muddy paper. "What happened?"

"I—I got a letter from Ardan Connelly."

"Oh?"

Luella handed him the letter. Raising an eyebrow, he scanned the dirt-streaked page with holes poked in the paper.

"Do you think they'll fire me?" she asked.

"You've done nothing to warrant firing," he said without looking up.

"But with the pedoph—the scandal still tarnishing the Catholic Church, they might let me go. They might not wait until your name is cleared."

"Outstanding math teachers aren't a dime a dozen. I think they need you more than you need them." He handed the letter back.

She wasn't confident he was right.

"Ken Lauterbach called." August wiped his chest and arms with his T-shirt. "Courtesy call, he said. He just wanted to give me a heads up. The university will name Johnny O'Brien as interim coach. Johnny O'Brien for fuck's sake."

"He called today?"

August hesitated. "A few days ago."

"And you didn't think to tell me?"

"Of course, I did. But I needed time to get used to the idea that I will no longer be the Jolliet University coach."

"Don't say that!" She heard the hysteria in her voice. "You said they appointed Johnny the *interim* coach. That means it's *temporary*. After the trial you'll be reinstated and we can get back to our lives."

August scoffed. "I appreciate your faith, Lulu. Truly, I do. But you're being naïve. Even if…"

"When," she corrected. "We have to stay positive. You're the one who taught me that. You've never thrown in the towel."

"Okay, *when* I'm found not guilty, the university is still likely to cut me loose."

"But you were Conference Coach of the Year! You just signed a five-year contract extension!"

"With a morals clause," August reminded her. "Lauterbach will undoubtedly advise the Board of Regents that the taint of scandal harms the reputation of the university nearly as much as actual guilt. Plus, he'll get to pick his own man. I think he's been itching to do that ever since he came onboard."

"That's not fair."

"It's reality. Appearances matter."

It was all too much—her job, his career. She felt the ground opening beneath her. The weariness in his eyes, the defeat on his face, a face that normally was the picture of confidence, mirrored her weariness and defeat, and it frightened her.

"What are we going to do?"

"Hell if I know." August leaned the ax against the shed. He pulled the sweat-stained T-shirt over his head and pushed his arms through the sleeves. "I'll probably get a job coaching at Podunk High School."

"Where does that leave me?"

"Teaching math at Podunk Middle School."

The hallway of St. Eligius School, lined with student desks and stacks of undersized chairs, smelled of spicy floor wax. By the time the students returned in September every floor in the building would shine with the luster of a Marine's shoes. Now, the place had a ghost town eeriness, with only the sound of a floor polishing machine thrumming in a distant classroom.

Luella made her way toward the main office at the intersection of the primary and intermediate grade wings of the building. She was tempted to bypass the office and head to the security of her classroom, but she realized it would bring little comfort to sit in an empty room. The lights would be off, the bulletin boards bare, and without children, the room would echo lifelessly.

She veered into the faculty restroom, examined her reflection in the mirror. After a six-hour drive, her cerise skirt was wrinkled and a crescent of perspiration shown under each arm of her V-neck cotton blouse with flowers delicately embroidered on the placket. She ran a comb through her hair, applied lip gloss, smoothed the front of her skirt, and dabbed the moisture under her arms with a tissue. She hadn't been this nervous since her first day of teaching.

When she stepped into the principal's outer office, she found the desk usually occupied by Carmela Parolini, the receptionist, vacant. Uncertain what to do, she checked the large round clock hanging behind the desk—12:58, two minutes before her appointment. It was unlike Sister Marian Lee, who prided herself on punctuality, not to be early. She was usually the first one in the building in the morning and the last one to leave at the end of the day.

Luella liked and respected her. Although the nun was self-disciplined and held herself and others to a high standard, she also displayed compassion, laced with a sense of humor. Luella recalled a time at a faculty meeting when several people walked in after the meeting had started and Sister Marian quipped, "You know what Franklin P. Jones said: 'The trouble with being punctual is that nobody's there to appreciate it.'" One of the teachers had asked, "Sister, who is Franklin P. Jones?" "I would love to enlighten you," she'd said, "but unfortunately, we're out of time."

Luella walked around the receptionist's desk and stepped into the doorway of the adjoining office, but no one was there, either. She'd read the letter summoning her to this meeting at least a dozen times. It wasn't possible that she'd gotten the day or time mixed up.

"You're here."

Luella jumped. She turned to face Sister Marian, who looked different somehow. Perhaps her hair was cropped shorter, or maybe those tortoiseshell glasses were new, or maybe she'd lost weight. The change, although positive, was a bit disorienting. Ardan Connelly, with the air of a man who loved being in charge, walked in behind her. His presence was not a good sign.

"I—I didn't mean to pry," stammered Luella. "It's just that when no one was here—."

Sister Marian smiled reassuringly. "I should be the one to apologize. I meant to be here to greet you, but something unavoidable came up."

"Mrs. Laurent," said Connelly, stepping forward and extending his hand. "Thank you for coming."

His hand was clammy and smallish for a man. By reputation he was a bean counter, dedicated but humorless. Sister Marian, large-boned and nearly six-feet tall, towered over him.

"Please," he said, indicating with a nod that she should enter the office. "Have a seat." He gestured toward an empty chair on the public side of the desk. He walked around to the other side and assumed the principal's chair. If Sister Marian noticed, she gave no indication that she objected. Instead, she lowered herself into the chair next to Luella.

"As you're undoubtedly aware, we have a very awkward situation here," said Connelly.

So, there would be no preliminaries, no pretense of sensitivity.

"I know my circumstances have put you in a difficult position," she admitted, forcing herself to look him in the eye. "Because of my husband's trial, I'll need to take a leave of absence for the first semester."

"I'm afraid that's not possible." Connelly, leaning forward, cleared his throat, laced his fingers together, and rested his folded hands on the desktop. "Mrs. Laurent, regrettably, the board has decided to terminate your employment with us."

"But why?" blurted Luella "Surely you can find a math substitute for one semester."

"The charges against your husband are extremely serious," Connelly said.

"But he hasn't had his day in court. What happened to innocent until proven guilty?" Her voice edged from desperation toward anger.

"You have to understand," he said, glancing down at his hands, "the Church is under a public microscope when it comes to—um—sexual misconduct."

"But what have I done to warrant firing?" Luella turned toward Sister Marian, seeking support from the other woman in the room.

Sister Marian touched Luella's arm gently.

"Sister, you know I'm a good teacher. You know how much I love these kids." Luella felt her dignity teetering like a boulder on the edge of a cliff.

"Your competence isn't at issue." Connelly's tone turned hard-edged. "Are you telling me you had no idea what was going on right under your nose?"

Luella flinched. His accusation landed like a sucker punch. There it is, thought Luella, the ugly question that no one had the courage to ask to her face. "My husband couldn't possibly have done the awful things he's been accused of. There was nothing to see! Why must you assume the worst?"

"Experience," said Connelly. "The Church turned a blind eye for too long. We simply can't afford the taint of scandal here at St. Eligius. Parents send their children here because they are seeking a moral education. For us, the suggestion of this sort of—of—impropriety is as detrimental as actual guilt."

So that was the bottom line; it was about enrollment numbers. Fairness be damned. She was to be sacrificed on the altar of expediency. She told herself to accept her fate and go quietly, preserve her dignity, leave the bridge behind her unburned. Instead, she heard herself say, "What happened to 'Let whoever is without sin among you cast the first stone'? What happened to Christian charity and compassion?"

Connelly glowered at her.

Believing he was a lost cause, she turned to Sister Marian.

The nun's face looked like a tragedy mask, her forehead creased, eyes narrowed, mouth downturned. "I'm sorry," she whispered, as though the decision to fire Luella truly pained her. Sympathy was a poor substitute for defense. Luella wanted her to stand up to Connelly and convince him he was making a mistake. The banner over the main entrance of the school read: *Welcome to St. Eligius School—a values-centered community*. Values when expedient, she thought bitterly, not values when courage was required. The hypocrisy infuriated her.

She imagined Connelly and Sister Marian staring at the neon-red flaring above her collar, evidence of her humiliation.

"Luella, is there anything I can do?" asked Sister Marian.

"No," said Luella, rising. "You've done quite enough."

Chapter Five

~Two Teachers~

lthough Beth's after-school coaching duties wouldn't begin for almost two months, like her mother she'd always relished the first day back in the classroom teaching mathematics, delighting in the eager faces, the optimism, the air of possibility.

This year she was filled with apprehension. Trying to muster enthusiasm by rimming her classroom with posters of famous mathematicians past and present, she made certain to include different genders, races, and ethnicities as inspiring examples to her students. As she stood at the lectern waiting for her first-hour class, the eyes of Pythagoras, Emmy Noether, Alan Turning, Maryam Mirzakhani, Elbert Cox, and Katherine Johnson stared at her, as if imploring her to summon courage. She'd prepared fresh lesson plans, pored over class lists; but she was anxious about the students' reaction to her since everyone knew that she was the daughter of August Laurent.

The days of teacher in-service leading up to today had been a strain. Her colleagues weren't cruel, quite the opposite; they were cautious and deferential, their awkwardness reminiscent of the days when, after Gabe's death, still in the depths of grief, she'd finally returned to work. This proved to be worse. No hugs. No I'm-so-sorry-for-your-loss. No glowing testimonials for the object of her bereavement. As she'd sat in the middle of the tiered classroom unable to concentrate on the address given by the Superintendent of Schools, her mind turning in circles, she'd felt her colleagues' collective stare. If there had been a spotlight focused on her, she could not have felt more conspicuous.

Teenagers were not so circumspect. There was the possibility that some hotshot might attempt to score points in front of his peers by trying to embarrass her. Ordinarily, such behavior would not have intimidated her. Humor went a long way in deflecting the occasional showoff. She was a teacher who commanded respect. But this was not ordinarily. The Laurent name had been on the airwaves, in newspapers, and on the internet all summer long. The stench of her father's offense clung to her like dried perspiration.

She doubted that he understood the pain his actions caused, too wrapped up in his own anger to know or care how devastating his behavior had been to those closest to him. She resented his selfishness, the way he acted as if the offense was done *to* him, not caused *by* him. Bitterness would be counterproductive today. Determined not to allow him to sabotage the day, she tried to calm herself by taking a deep breath and counting to ten.

She thought of her mother, whom she hadn't spoken to since leaving camp, wondering how she also was coping with the first day back in the classroom. Since beginning her career, they'd phoned each other at the end of the first day to compare notes. If only she could talk to her now.

A piercing warning bell sounded, alerting Beth class would begin in four minutes. She straightened the papers on the lectern, ran her fingers through her hair, removed a tube of lip gloss from her pocket, swiped the tip across her mouth. She stationed herself outside the classroom doorway, greeting students as they entered the room, calling the ones she had taught previously by name and vowing to memorize the names of those she didn't know as soon as possible.

When the bell sounded again and everyone was seated, Beth began: "Good morning and welcome back." She forced a smile that she hoped would not be read as disingenuous. "I'm Ms. Laurent. This is Advanced Algebra. You're in the right place if you have successfully completed algebra and geometry. If you find you're in the wrong place, no harm, no foul." She gestured toward the door. She paused for a moment, but no one got up to leave. A few students smiled back faintly, most looked at her with unreadable expressions or didn't make eye contact.

She took roll call, struggling more than usual to pronounce the unfamiliar names. The students seemed curiously quiet, as though holding their collective breath, or maybe she was the one who couldn't breathe. When she finished calling out the final name on her list, Beth glanced down at her notes.

She cleared her throat. "Some of you find mathematics easy." Glancing at the class roster, she saw the names of two gifted freshman and several sophomores. "Some of you find the subject intimidating but are here because you know you must pass it to get into a four-year college." Several of the juniors and seniors shifted in their seats. "Undoubtedly, some of you have already decided that this is the last lousy math class you will ever take, and if you never see another equation in your life, it will be too soon."

As she looked around, the students' expressions became slightly more scrutable. A few of them exchanged surreptitious glances.

Beth felt off her rhythm, wearing her discomfort like an ill-fitting suit. She pressed her lips together and wished that she had remembered to put a glass of water on the lectern shelf.

"No matter what your previous experience, in here you'll discover that math is not just for brainiacs." Beth thought of her mother, who'd instilled that attitude in her from early childhood. "It's not a subject that only a few smart people can get. It's a system of logic which is knowable, and it's my job to help you know it." As she looked at their faces, she could see that she was not connecting, not because they were being disrespectful or antsy but because they were being uncharacteristically still.

"My goal is that by the end of the year all of you will have the confidence to move on to trigonometry. I hope that also becomes your goal."

Skepticism was written on their faces and in their body language, but they remained silent.

This was the moment in her pep talk that she'd planned to drive home her point, allaying their fears, reassuring them that she would not let them stumble. But how could she reassure them when she felt so unsteady? It was as though she was on the basketball court and every time she drove the lane to make a layup she took one too many or one too few steps, the ball never reaching the hoop. She paused, hoping to regain her balance. Scanned the faces looking up expectantly at her. Glanced at the clock. There were forty-three minutes remaining before the bell would ring. She resisted the urge to dash out of the room.

Then Gabe spoke to her. *Keep it real, kid. It's now or never.*

"As most of you know, my father's name has been all over the news this summer." There was no turning back. "He was charged with molesting six boys. I am deeply sorry for the young men's pain and deeply ashamed to have my family's name associated with such terrible acts."

She looked around the room. Not a cough or whisper broke the silence. Beth felt tears welling but fought to keep control. She straightened her spine. "If any of you feel as though it would be too difficult to remain in my class, I understand. You can go to the guidance office and request another teacher. I promise you, there will be no hard feelings."

She waited. No one moved.

"Ms. Laurent?"

Beth found the voice attached to the raised hand. She checked her seating chart. The voice belonged to Lila Patel.

"Yes, Lila?"

"My brother said, if I really want to understand math, I should make sure I got in your class."

"Mine, too," came a voice from the back of the room.

Relief poured over Beth like a cleansing rain. Despite her Catholic upbringing, she had never understood the value of confession. Perhaps it was good for the soul after all.

She stepped from behind the lectern and walked toward the bulletin board where the class rules were posted. "Okay then. Rule number one," she said, pointing to the top of the list. "No cell phones are allowed in my class. That's non-negotiable. Leave them in your lockers."

A collective groan filled the classroom.

And Beth smiled.

While Rosie enjoyed a favorite movie on her iPad and August watched sports on television, Luella escaped with Bird to the solitude of the lake.

She'd never been at the camp in September on the opening day of the school year. Ordinarily, she would have been at her home in Lake Bluff just north of Chicago. After a day of teaching, Beth would call, eager to compare notes about their day back in the classroom.

Instead, she'd spent the afternoon with August at Thomas Lowery's office discussing the upcoming trial. Lowery advised against August taking the stand, despite August's reassurance that he could handle the cross examination. There was no upside and too much opportunity to be trapped by problematic questions. However, Lowery insisted that Luella must testify. She'd agreed for August's sake, but the idea made her queasy. Although it was nearly two months away, the attorney fees were adding up. It became likely they would need to take out a second mortgage. They'd been in good financial shape until August was put on unpaid leave, his endorsements dried up, Luella was fired, and the camp closed prematurely. It would take a long time to dig out of this financial hole.

Bird sniffed the ground, caught a scent, and disappeared into the woods.

In the waning light, the water appeared ethereal, as if lit from beneath the surface. A symphony of lapping waves, birdsong, and rustling leaves blowing in a westerly breeze masqueraded as silence. The night was jacket-cool. It surprised Luella how emphatically summer weather changed in northern Wisconsin after Labor Day, as though Mother Nature ignored the Gregorian calendar and summoned fall three weeks early.

She thought nostalgically of St. Eligius School, the air abuzz with conversation and eagerness, students arriving in their new clothes, modeling the latest in junior high fashion. The room, freshly decorated, would smell of floor wax and hair mousse. Luella imagined the students looking up at her as she explained the Pythagorean theorem. How she missed the immense satisfaction of watching their expressions turn from confusion to understanding.

The lights in the windows on the far south shore shown through the trees like a sprinkling of earthbound stars, creating a sense of isolation. She missed her friends, colleagues, and students, all of whom dropped out of her life with the abruptness of an earthquake. She grieved the loss of her close-knit family, the thread connecting them as fragile as spun sugar. She and August maintained the illusion of closeness, going about housebound days together, yet separated by their private thoughts, at night sharing a cold bed.

They'd both tried to protect Rosie by feigning normalcy, yet she seemed to sense the shift in atmosphere the way a person with arthritic joints senses an impending storm, tiptoeing around them as if, somehow, she was to blame for the tension.

Then there was Beth. Over the past two months, Luella had swallowed her pride, called and texted, but Beth ignored all attempts at détente. Luella knew of parents estranged from their children. Until recently, the possibility of that happening seemed unimaginable. Now she wasn't sure of anything. Beth's absence also meant Wyatt's absence. Luella ached to hold her grandson, to ruffle his mop of curls, to read him his favorite bedtime story.

She pulled her jacket tighter, massaged her arms. Looking back at the house, partially visible through the trees, the glow in the windows reminded her of a Thomas Kinkade painting. Despite the dropping temperature, she decided to linger a bit longer. She turned back toward the lake, shifted her weight on the bench, and stretched her aching legs. She rubbed her heart necklace with the basketball charm dangling in its center between her thumb and index finger, as though it were a talisman powerful enough to change her fortunes.

About a quarter mile from shore a boat, its running lights glowing, its motor quietly humming, skimmed across the surface. The soft, one-note hoots of a loon, calling its chicks and mate, punctuated the air.

Tempting as it was, she could not linger on the dock forever. She stood, placed her hands on her hips, and arched her back. Overhead, the sky was freckled with stars.

Her phone chimed. She pulled it from her pocket. Beth. Luella stared at her name with a conflicting wave of hope and apprehension.

"Hello?"

"Mom?"

The phone call began awkwardly, as though Luella and Beth walked through a bog, choosing each step carefully to avoid sinking into the mud.

"So, you made it through another first day of school," said Luella, perching on the bench at the end of the dock.

"I survived."

"Just survived?"

"I suppose it could have been worse."

Beth was not going to make this easy.

"Tell me about the best part of your day," said Luella. It occurred to her that this was the same tactic she'd used when Beth was a sulky teenager, when an inquiry of "how was your day" was met with an eye roll or a monosyllabic "fine" or "lame." She'd learned then never to ask questions that could be answered with a single word.

"When I gave the students the opportunity to opt out of my class because of—um—well—everything that's been in the news, Lila Patel told the class her brother said that if she really wanted to understand math, she should make sure she got in *my* class. And she wasn't the only one."

"That's quite a vote of confidence."

"You have no idea how much I needed it."

Actually, thought Luella, she *did* know. Since August's arrest she felt diminished, avoiding public places, venturing away from the camp only when she saw no alternative. She spared Beth the details of her experience at the sheriff's department, the lingering humiliation and terror. She imagined how difficult it would be to stand in front of her class projecting confidence she no longer felt. "Never let 'em see you sweat," August was fond of saying. This was especially true when facing a classroom of tweens and teens. But what if you no longer had it in you to feign confidence? What if you used all your resources to simply exist? She wanted to explain to Beth that she knew how much the kindness of Lila Patel mattered, but words failed her.

Seconds passed.

"I wasn't expecting you to call tonight," said Luella.

"I wasn't going to," Beth admitted. "But Wyatt changed my mind."

"Oh?"

"When I picked him up after school, he complained that he missed his grandpa and grandma. He insisted we come see you."

A glimmer of hope. Luella imagined her grandson's little-boy arms encircling her neck.

"I told him that with work and school that wasn't possible right now. I promised him we would call instead."

Luella leaned against the back of the bench.

"I'll put Wyatt on the phone."

There was rustling and fumbling as the phone was passed.

"Hi Grandma. I miss you and Grandpa so-o-o much." The sound of Wyatt's voice, cloud-soft and laced with love, made Luella ache. "I want to come and see you really bad, but Mommy said we can just call because she has to work and I have to go to school."

"I miss you, too, sweetie." The temptation to sprint from the dock, jump in her car, and drive the hours it would take to arrive at Beth's was nearly overwhelming. Luella gripped the edge of the bench. "I bet you had fun at school today."

"Uh-huh. I teached Jordan how to shoot a basketball like Grandpa showed me. He's not very good, but I'm going to help him practice."

"I bet Jordan is glad to have you for a friend."

"He's my best friend."

"What else did you do with Jordan?"

"We played on the big slide. It's really high and some kids are scared to go to the top, but we climbed all the way up."

"That sounds like fun. And what did you learn at school today?"

"I made a long number line."

"Number line?"

"Uh-huh. I wrote numbers on a long piece of paper that stretches all the way across our room, and I rolled it up and put it in the special box Ms. Baker gave me so it doesn't get wrecked. I'm going to write bigger numbers on it tomorrow so none of the other kids can ever catch me. Ms. Baker says I'm a math-a-titian."

"You sure are." Luella smiled.

Overhead a pinpoint of light blinked its way across the sky. A plane, Luella thought, not a satellite.

"Can I talk to Grandpa?"

"I'm sorry, not tonight. I'm down at the dock and Grandpa is up at the house. I think he's taking a nap." Luella didn't know whether that was true, although it could have been, but she didn't have the heart to tell her grandson he wasn't allowed to talk with his grandfather. "I'll tell him you're teaching Jordan to shoot baskets. He'll be proud of you." She pictured Wyatt grinning.

Luella heard Beth speak to him, her manner gentle and patient.

"Mommy says I have to say good-bye."

"I'm very happy that you called tonight. I'll talk with you again soon."

"I love you, Grandma."

"I love you, too."

Beth told Wyatt to put on his pajamas, then pick out a book, which she promised to read after she and Grandma were done talking about grown-up things.

A mosquito buzzed by Luella's ear, then landed on her forehead. She fanned the air, brushed it away.

"Mom?"

"I'm here."

"I haven't asked. How was your first day back?"

The image came to Luella of Ardan Connelly stoically sitting behind Sister Marian Lee's desk, his voice devoid of compassion, informing her that she was fired.

"There was no first day. I was fired. I'm still at the camp."

"You can't be serious!"

"I guess the scandal hit too close to home. I offended the hypocritical morality of Ardan Connelly and the board's righteousness," Luella said, bitterly.

"I'm so sorry, Mom. You don't deserve that."

There was a long pause. Luella feared that the call had dropped.

"And, Mom, I—I'm sorry about the way we left things this summer. My quarrel isn't with you." Beth's voice quavered.

"I know."

"This is a nightmare, and I keep waiting to wake up."

"Me too."

"It just feels so unfair."

"It's unfair to all of us. Your dad…"

"Please don't bring *him* into this," Beth interrupted, her voice suddenly edgy.

"But this is especially unfair to him."

"You don't know that."

Again, silence. Luella wanted to argue, to make Beth come to her senses, to make her understand that disloyalty equaled betrayal. But she forced herself to wait, sensing that to travel down that path meant shutting the door, perhaps permanently.

"Beth, are you all right?"

"If you're asking if I'm going to get through tonight, and tomorrow, and the next day, the answer is I have to. I have a son who needs a mother who doesn't fall apart because life is hard. I survived when Gabe died. I'll survive this. What choice do I have? But the truth is, I'm not all right. I'm sad and angry and lonely. Sometimes I feel like I'm going to explode and other times I feel like I want to go to bed, pull the covers over my head, and never wake up. If I had the luxury of disappearing, I would. For Wyatt's sake, I have to get up."

Besides her own overwhelming sorrow, Luella felt Beth's pain, the innate concern a mother carries for her child deep in her marrow. She would not argue with Beth because she intuitively understood that it is a mother's responsibility to nurture the child and not a child's responsibility to nurture the mother. Hadn't it always been so? Hadn't it been that way with her mother and her mother's mother before that? The commitment to nurture did not disappear when a daughter became an adult, or when she married, or when she gave birth to her own child. It didn't go away when she vehemently disagreed.

"Beth, I'm sorry. I'm sorry for all of it. Believe it or not, I do understand."

"I believe you."

Luella heard Wyatt's voice.

"I have to go," said Beth. It's Wyatt's bedtime. I have to read *Today I Will Fly* for the hundredth time."

"I remember." After spending weeks with her grandson at camp, Luella could practically recite all of the Elephant and Piggie books by heart. "Give my favorite little boy a big hug and kiss from Grandma."

"I will. And Mom, I'll call again soon."

After the call ended, Luella's tears flowed. It was as though a relief valve finally released the pressure that had built up since the night Beth fled from camp. She knew that circumstances had not changed; August was still facing trial and the family was still fractured. But she and Beth had taken a step, albeit a small one, to repair the divide between them, and that was, for now, enough. In time, Beth would come to see that she was wrong about her father, wrong to judge so quickly. In time, they would all learn to forgive.

An owl hooted in a nearby tree. It swooped from one perch to another. Luella wiped the tears from her eyes and tried to focus, but by the time her vision cleared, the owl had disappeared into the darkness. She rose from the bench and inhaled the fresh air, cleansing her lungs and clearing her head. Before turning up the path toward the house, she took one final look at the shimmering lake.

Bird appeared, nose and paws muddy. He dashed ahead up the path.

She would not tell August about Beth's phone call. Perhaps, she told herself, it was to protect him from disappointment. Perhaps it was because she resented playing referee. Wasn't it enough that she mended her fences with Beth without taking responsibility for mending August's, too? Perhaps it was simply because she needed this little nugget of normalcy for herself. The phone call on the first day of school had been a tradition between Beth and Luella that had never involved August. It might be selfish not to tell him, but she didn't care. She would hold on to this memory the way a child cradles a small rock in his hands, then hides it in a treasure box.

Chapter Six

~Divided by Zero~

After the arrest Luella stopped attending Mass. She missed the ritual, the security of being a true believer, the comfort of having an anchoring tradition in her life. Now she couldn't bear the thought of people staring at her or refusing to sit near her. Now she wasn't sure she believed in God.

Before church services let out on Sunday morning in mid-September, Luella drove into the parking lot of McBride's Grocery, praying that the aisles would be deserted. Relieved to see only three cars in the lot, she stepped through the store's automatic doors, greeted by a premature display of jack o' lanterns and skeletons. This year on Halloween there would be no costumed ghosts, pirates, or action heroes appearing at her house in Lake Bluff. Instead, this year she would be in Givens Knoll attending August's trial.

She glanced at her grocery list—beef, potatoes, green beans, butter, bread, eggs, bacon, potato chips, oysters, and butter pecan ice cream. This was not the health-conscious food she typically purchased, but she wanted to treat August to an array of his favorite comfort foods.

Luella pushed the cart with its wobbly front wheel through the produce aisle and selected a couple of handfuls of green beans and placed them in a plastic bag. She chose a five-pound bag of russet potatoes and put it in her cart. As an afterthought, she grabbed a bunch of bananas at least a week from ripeness, then turned down the aisle with two small shelves devoted to bread. Her conscience told her to buy the whole wheat loaf, but she knew August preferred white, so she chose white. Her cart limped through the canned goods section, where she picked up a tin of smoked oysters plus a large jar of peaches for Rosie.

An elderly man stood at the end of aisle four looking perplexed. Although she didn't recognize him, she slowed down, accepting his unfamiliarity as a small gift.

"Can't find the damn Wheaties," he grumbled. "Used to be a few reasonable cereals to choose from. Now every kid in America needs his own special brand. More like candy than breakfast for Chrissake."

"Here you go," Luella said, retrieving the Wheaties box from the bottom shelf.

"Thanks," he said, softening. "Damn little courtesy left anymore."

Luella agreed but only managed a faint smile. She was beginning to feel claustrophobic.

On her way to the coolers, from which she selected butter and a brick of extra sharp cheddar, she picked up a large box of potato chips. She turned toward the meat section, eyed the cuts of beef, and then, ignoring her penchant for watching August's cholesterol, selected a marbled chuck roast. She also chose a package of extra thick bacon. From the display rack at the end of the meat cooler she picked out a large leg bone filled with marrow for Bird.

Lastly, she made her way to the freezers in pursuit of butter pecan ice cream. A pint would have been adequate, but she grabbed the half-gallon container, reasoning that if ever there was a time August needed a bit of indulgence in his life, this was it.

Eager to escape, she headed toward the front of the store. As she rounded the corner, Patty Maier, the mother of local former high school basketball star, C.J Maier, stood in the lone available check-out lane, loading her groceries onto the conveyor belt. Luella froze. The woman had the reputation of a pit bull: protective, aggressive, and unable to let go once she sunk her teeth in you. She'd been indignant when, after her son had attended camp for two summers, August informed her that C.J. didn't have the quickness to play Division I basketball. She hadn't been quiet about it.

As the conveyor belt moved, the cashier glanced up and spotted

Luella. "You can start to unload, ma'am," she said. Luella slowly placed each item on the belt without encroaching on Patty's groceries.

Patty turned and looked directly at Luella, eyes narrowing as recognition spread across her pinched features.

The cashier, a chubby teenager with porcelain skin and blue braces, loaded Patty's plastic bags into her cart. "Have a nice day, Mrs. Maier," she chirped.

Patty didn't move but waited for Luella, who had no choice but to approach.

"Hello," Luella said, fixing her gaze on her groceries while she finished unloading the cart.

When she looked up, Patty glared at her as if she had leprosy. Luella's throat closed. The cashier pretended not to notice and continued scanning.

"How could he?" Patty fumed. "How could *you?*" She tapped her foot, as if waiting for an answer.

Luella stood mute.

"You're disgusting. Both of you should be locked up for life," Patty snarled and huffed away.

Luella swallowed hard, desperate not to cry in front of the pubescent cashier. She fumbled around in her purse, retrieved her wallet, and pulled out her debit card. When she swiped the card, the scanner instructed her to try again. Luella bit her lower lip, swiped the card, and punched in her pin number. The message on the screen informed her that the pin number was incorrect. She stood there, confused, staring at the keypad. Her fingers refused to move, as though the four-digit code she'd used a thousand times before had suddenly become unknowable.

Luella heard someone say her name, looked up. Several patrons had entered the store and walked past the checkout station. She needed to leave, get back to the refuge of home.

"Ma'am, would you like to choose credit instead?"

"Y-yes," Luella stammered.

After paying, she wheeled the defective cart, its front wheels shimmying over the pot-holed asphalt of the parking lot, to her vehicle. The hatch of the Lincoln Navigator seemed exceptionally heavy, the morning air unusually thin. She loaded the groceries into the back, shoved the cart into the adjacent parking space, then keeping a hand on the car for balance, stumbled to the driver's side door, opened it, and sunk into the seat. She stepped on the brake. Her hands shook as her finger pressed the ignition button. The engine purred to life.

She brushed away tears clouding her vision.

As Luella backed out of her parking space, a horn honked, startling her. She stepped on the brake, saw that she'd barely avoided hitting the oncoming car, whose driver gave her a withering look. Heart pounding, Luella cautiously turned out of the lot and turned onto the highway, only then realizing that she'd forgotten to buy eggs.

Luella removed towels from the washer, loaded them into the dryer, and pushed the start button. The motor rumbled and then settled into a vibrating tumble. It was just a matter of time before the dryer needed replacing.

She dreaded the thought of shopping at the local appliance store. The scornful salesperson wouldn't confront her directly—unlike Patty Maier, people rarely had the courage to look her in the eye—but she knew what he would be thinking. *There's the child molester's wife. She's got nerve coming in here acting so innocent.* For now, the dryer motor would have to vibrate.

Luella heard a knock at the door. Her impulse was to hide. These days, with the exception of Franklin, no one came to the house uninvited. It might be an emboldened news reporter knocking, although until now, none had been brazen enough to pound on the door. Maybe it was a Jehovah's Witness zealot. In either case, she didn't intend to open the door.

The knocking persisted. Luella peeked through the kitchen window. A white mini-van sat in the driveway. She sidled along the wall toward the mudroom and sneaked a quick glance around the corner. A woman she did not recognize stood at the door. Luella pressed against the wall, backstepped into the kitchen out of sight of the intruder. She slid down the wall, slumping to the floor.

Her thoughts flashed back to the time, as a teenager, she'd crawled on hands and knees under the picture window of her parents' living room and hid behind the sofa to avoid detection by a persistent ex-boyfriend. He'd rung the doorbell again and again. "I know you're here," he'd said, but she'd remained hidden until he'd given up. She'd felt cowardly and foolish then; she felt even more cowardly and foolish now.

She rolled onto her hands and knees.

August entered the kitchen. "What are you doing?"

"I—I…"

"Didn't you hear? Someone's knocking."

She looked up at him. "I was—hiding."

"Oh, Lulu." He offered his hand. She grasped it and let him help her to her feet. He guided her toward the door. The woman held up a bouquet of flowers.

"Can I tell the secret now?" It was Rosie, standing behind them, a broad grin on her face.

"It's time," August reassured her.

"Happy birthday!" Rosie shouted, clapping her hands. "We got you flowers, but I wasn't supposed to tell."

"You did a good job of keeping our secret," said August.

He opened the door, took the bouquet from the woman, and placed a twenty plus a five-dollar bill in her hand.

"You already paid with a credit card."

"I know. It's your tip."

Her eyes widened. "Thank you!" the woman said, then turned to leave. If she recognized them, it wasn't evident in her expression or demeanor.

August handed Luella the crystal vase with two-dozen yellow roses and a card that read "Happy fifty-sixth birthday to the love of my life."

A tear trickled from the corner of Luella's eye. She had never considered herself a crier, but these days tears flowed readily, as though the banks of a reservoir had been breached. Was it because the flowers reminded her of life before, or because she had forgotten it was her birthday, or because of the embarrassment of hiding in her own home?

"Are you sad?" Rosie rested her head on Luella's arm and hugged her awkwardly.

"No, Rosie Posie," said August. "Sometimes people cry when they're happy. Right Lulu?"

Luella nodded.

"You go work on our puzzle, and I'll come and help in a minute," August said to Rosie. "Then we'll all have some birthday ice cream."

After Rosie left the room August took the flowers from Luella and set them on the kitchen counter. He wrapped his arms around her.

"I didn't even remember my own birthday," said Luella. "How pathetic is that? Time no longer means anything."

August lifted her chin and looked into her eyes. "I love you. You don't doubt that, right?"

Luella bit her lower lip.

"Listen to me, Lulu. I can't get through this without you. You're my rock. You have to stay strong. Do you understand? If you collapse, I collapse."

She inhaled a stuttering, rose-scented breath.

"It's you and me against the world." August kissed the top of her head. "Now let's have some ice cream."

Mid-morning, on a Thursday in late September, Luella stood at the kitchen sink washing breakfast dishes, gazing out the window at the forest. Almost overnight, ferns turned brown, poplars bright yellow, maples vibrant orange, and oaks deep rust. Abundant pines rained down a steady shower of golden needles, creating a carpet that obscured the driveway. A beam of sunlight fanned across the counter and spilled onto the wooden floor. Bird, basking at her feet, glanced up, tongue lolling, patiently waiting for their morning walk.

Her cell phone rang. She dried her hands, pulled the phone from her jeans pocket, and eyed it suspiciously. Calls from reporters and foulmouthed strangers received on the camp's landline had been relentless when the news of August's arrest first broke. Once every parent had been informed of the camp's closing, she'd cancelled the line. Then calls began to come on her cell phone even though she'd always been careful to only give her number to family members and close friends, who, of late, had dropped away like leaves from a dying tree. She believed that reporters must have gotten her number from former friends. Betrayal hurt.

She was reminded of Franklin's advice to avoid talking to the press, advice that had been easy for her to heed but not for August. "Remember they are *not* your friends," Franklin had warned. August seemed to believe that past relationships and charm would influence reporters to stand up for him. Untrue. Scandal overrode decency every time.

Luella stared at the screen. The number 502-555-9824 was unfamiliar. She decided to reject the call, then hesitated. *B. Thibodeau.* Her thumb hovered over the decline button. Slowly, recognition dawned. Brett Thibodeau was a guard from Louisville, Kentucky, who had played for August nearly twelve years ago.

She waited for another ring, then pressed accept.

"Hello," said a male voice.

Luella remained silent, deciding whether to respond or hang up.

"Hello? Mrs. Laurent?"

"Yes?"

"This is Brett Thibodeau." The voice was deep and familiar.

In the past she would have been delighted to hear from one of August's former players. Recent experience warned her to proceed cautiously. Few who had been considered friends remained allies.

"Mrs. Laurent, I just wanted to let you know how deeply sorry I am for all that Coach is going through and to let you know I'm in his corner."

Luella's shoulders relaxed. Her grip on the phone loosened.

"It's good to hear from you, Brett." She pictured the lanky, blonde, blue-eyed young man with a healthy dose of the South in his voice.

"Thank you. I owe a lot to Coach."

"He always believed you were an exceptional talent."

"I had raw talent, but Coach made me work hard to harness those skills. I wouldn't have been an All-American if it hadn't been for his pushing me and helping me to believe in myself."

"That means a lot coming from you, Brett."

"It's true. Coach taught me to be a better basketball player, but more important, he taught me to be a better man."

"Kind of you to say." Over the years, Luella had heard many of August's players make such statements, had come to expect such praise. Now, the young man's words brought tears of gratitude.

"It's impossible for me to believe the things I read in the press, the terrible accusations. The person I know could never have done those things. Never. No way."

Luella drank in Brett's words as though they were an elixir.

"I don't know if you remember, but junior year my dad died."

"I couldn't possibly forget that."

"I took it pretty hard. Decided I had to quit school. When I told Coach, he listened. He never pressured me about basketball, never played the you-owe-it-to-the team-to-stay card. He didn't harp on me about throwing away my scholarship. He just listened."

Luella leaned against the counter, smiled to herself.

"When he found out my mom didn't have the money to pay my brother Patrick's tuition to St. Ignatius his senior year, and that I planned to get a job to help out, he made phone calls and worked his magic. The school waived Patrick's tuition. Later that year Coach flew down to Louisville and put on a clinic at St. Ignatius. Of course, I returned to school."

"I remember."

"While he was in town, he stopped at our house, stayed for dinner. My mom thinks he's a savior. My brother still says he's the coolest guy he's ever met." Brett's voice was thick with emotion. "My family owes Coach big time."

Luella wanted to hug him through the phone. "Your call is payment enough, Brett."

"Mrs. Laurent, is Coach available?"

"Certainly. I'll get him for you." As she hurried from the kitchen through the living room and toward the sun porch, with Bird at her heels, she said, "I do have one question."

"Anything."

"How did you get my cell phone number?"

"Beth gave it to me. I hope I didn't overstep my bounds."

"Not at all. It's just that I have guarded my number pretty jealously."

"Don't worry. To put it mildly, she was reluctant to share your number. She's fiercely protective of you, gave me the third degree, but I finally convinced her I wanted to help."

Luella had thought Beth was too angry to care. Deep down she knew better. That steely façade belied her vulnerability. It was frustrating that Beth was so judgmental, so quick to distance herself from her father, so entrenched in her certitude. Yet Beth had to be heartsick over August's arrest. Luella had to admit that, despite their very different perspectives, Beth's pain was no less real than her own.

When she opened the French doors to the sun porch, she found

August staring out at the lake, a book splayed open on his lap. He glanced up at her.

Luella pressed the phone to her side and stage whispered, "Brett Thibodeau wants to speak with you." Luella handed August the phone.

He looked skeptical, palmed the phone as though holding a live grenade.

"Go on," she urged. "It's a call you should take."

August held the phone to his ear. "Hello. This is Coach Laurent."

As he listened, Luella hovered, waiting for his reaction. The crease between his eyes relaxed. He nodded several times. "Thank you, son. I appreciate you saying that. Loyalty is hard to come by these days."

August continued listening. A smile, like the sun inching above a dark horizon, lit his face. "That was some prank you played on Zemsky," he said, chuckling. "If you hadn't been a hotshot three-point shooter I might have benched you for that."

Luella marveled at how quickly August's voice and demeanor changed. The man who retreated into himself of late now sounded like a man without a care. She caught August's eye and gestured, indicating that she was going back into the house.

Bird danced in circles as if sensing a walk was imminent. As she headed toward the kitchen, she heard August's hearty laugh, grateful for Brett Thibodeau's call, but mostly, envious of August's temporary amnesia.

Unable to sleep, Luella, still in her nightgown and carrying her journal, tiptoed downstairs before sunrise and made herself a cup of orange spiced tea. Then she shambled from the kitchen to the porch in her slippers and curled up on the daybed.

Anxiety crept into her thoughts like a thief intent on stealing her wellbeing. August's trial was scheduled to begin in less than a week. She tried not to think about the ordeal ahead or the possibility of conviction. He had a top-notch lawyer, strong character witnesses, and innocence on his side. And yet...

Fog surrounded the house like a gossamer blanket. She set the cup on the side table, turned on the floor lamp, wrapped the afghan hanging over the back of the daybed around her shoulders, and placed a quilt over her lap. She leaned against the cushions, cradled the warm cup, sipped the tea, holding the tangy liquid in her mouth for a few extra seconds before letting it slip down her throat.

Luella tried to concentrate on pleasant memories—Beth's college graduation, her wedding day, Wyatt's birth—but anxiety returned the instant she let down her guard. She peered out into the predawn stillness. A dim halo ribboned with pink shown above the tree line.

Setting down her cup, she opened her journal, pen poised. Write something; write anything, she told herself. She scrolled Nell's name at the top of the page and waited for inspiration. Her hand moved as though guided by an unseen force.

I think nothing, feel everything.

Luella read the words as though they didn't belong to her. She was a math teacher who loved mathematics because it was a system of logic, a method of thought that required order. Now she lived a life that had no recognizable order. A fifty-six-year-old woman, fired from her job, married to a man about to stand trial for molesting children, equaled what? It was as if all her life before the arrest, all her effort, all she had become had been divided by zero. In mathematics that meant her life had become undefined. Her life simply didn't make sense.

I no longer am master of my fate. My mind will not obey me. I am adrift.

Mulling over those sentences she saw how close to the edge she wandered, and it unnerved her.

She thought of one of her phone conversations with Beth. "So, you made it through another first day of school." Beth had replied simply, "I survived." At the time she'd been frustrated with Beth's response, believing her daughter should be less self-indulgent, more positive. Now she understood that survival was not a given. It was something she had to fight for.

Scrawling *SURVIVAL* across the entire width of her journal, she traced the word again and again, the letters growing thicker, bolder, until it screamed from the page.

I've been so angry. With all my heart I wish Beth could see things differently, but I've asked too much. She is incapable of more. I see that now.

I am incapable of more.

An ache in Luella's temples foreshadowed a migraine. She massaged them, then placed the splayed journal on her stomach and rested her head on the throw pillow. Her eyelids grew heavy and slowly closed. It was a though the mist from the lake washed over her, and she drifted off into the fog of sleep.

Someone lurked behind a tree, threatening, as Luella walked down a street lined with stately elms that shouldn't have been there since they'd been cut down when she was a child. The figure was hidden, but she felt it looming. As she walked, she kept glancing over her shoulder. She picked up her pace, at first moving briskly, then breaking into a run. The day was overcast, foreboding, the air viscous, making her struggle for breath. She couldn't remember where she was going. Home? But her childhood home was in the opposite direction, she was almost positive.

Panic rose as she scoured for a fence or a rock to hide behind. The houses on either side of the street—a mix of homes from her childhood neighborhood and from various neighborhoods she and August had lived in—looked abandoned.

A low, growling, disembodied voice coming from behind her threatened, "You better run!" Her heart beat double-time. She turned, saw a shadowy figure dash between the trees.

"Come out you coward!" she yelled, trembling.

Nothing.

Luella's legs grew as heavy as steel posts. She spied a red house with the porch light on. Frantically, she pounded on the door. The light went out. She peered through the sidelight and saw a tall wom-an—Sister Marian Lee?—she couldn't be certain. The woman abrupt-ly turned away and walked toward the interior of the house. "Wait!" Luella begged, but the woman disappeared.

She ran to the yellow house with the green shutters. "Help! Help!" she screamed. The front door opened. Wyatt stood behind the locked storm door. Relief. "Open the door, sweetie!" Wyatt stared at her, con-fused. "Mommy said not to talk to strangers." The door closed in slow motion. "No! Please!" Luella pleaded.

The shadow pressed closer, closer.

She fled, trudging along the street's centerline, her legs so heavy she could barely lift her feet off the spongy pavement. Desperate, she waved for the boys streaming by on their bicycles to stop and help her. Brett Thibodeau cruised by. She called his name, tried to flag him down. He didn't recognize her. Everyone was deaf to her pleas.

A horse-drawn hearse rolled down the street toward her. August peeked out of the window. A veiled figure dressed head-to-toe in black floated behind it. Gloved hands lifted the veil.

Beth!

She felt a hand on her shoulder.

"Luella."

She heard a man's voice far away, then near.

"Lulu"

She squinted and licked her dry lips. August knelt beside her. She tried to figure out what time it was and what she was doing on the porch. It was as though she swam through glue, recognition dawning one labored stroke at a time. Morning light flooded through the porch windows. Fog had lifted from the lake. Her closed journal lay on the porch floor, the pen a couple of feet away.

August sat down at the end of the daybed, removed her slipper, and gently massaged her foot. "I didn't want to wake you, but it's time to drive Rosie to the workshop."

Luella's head felt as heavy as a boulder.

"I think you were dreaming." He brushed the hair from her eyes. "Care to share?"

"I don't remember much. Someone was chasing me."

"Who?"

"I don't know."

"Did you get caught?"

"I don't think so."

"Good. Then you're all right."

The enticing aroma of freshly brewed coffee wafted from Gina's kitchen.

"I didn't mean to sleep this late," said Beth, scuffing into the room, hair uncombed, still wearing her nightgown. "I haven't slept this well since...you know...since everything." She poured a cup of coffee into a large mug sitting on the counter.

"No offense, but you needed the beauty rest. A woman your age shouldn't have bags under her eyes." Gina, hair in a ponytail and wearing a cherry-red apron over a T-shirt and pajama bottoms, stood at the stove. She placed a generous pad of butter in a hot, copper omelet pan, swirled the butter until it foamed and then, from a stone-ware bowl, poured in the egg and cream mixture. She added grated gruyere plus an herb blend of chives, tarragon, and chervil. With the panache of a French chef, she vigorously shook the pan. In less than a half minute the omelet set. Gina slid the folded omelet expertly from the pan onto a plate and sprinkled it with chopped parsley before handing it to Beth.

"This smells and looks amazing."

Gina beamed. "The secret is in the butter, the wrist, and the super-hot pan. The French have a love affair with butter. It would be considered a violation of international law to use cooking spray."

"Yet they're so thin compared to Americans."

"I wouldn't worry about the butter. You could use some fattening up," said Gina. "You're looking a bit anorexic, if you don't mind my saying so. You could be mistaken for a Kenyan marathon runner."

If it had been anyone else making such a brutally honest observation, Beth would have been offended, but Gina had an unusual blend of disarming directness and a big heart. No one else had dared to be that truthful. Colleagues tip-toed around her as if she were a porcelain doll. None had been brave enough to face her. If there was anything Beth needed, it was a compassionate, candid friend. That was Gina.

In the past several months, Beth's appetite had disappeared. Her usually form-fitting clothes hung on her frame, as though she were a child playing dress-up. After Gabe died two years ago grief had stolen her appetite, but it had slowly returned, until she'd begun to look like her athletic self. Then her father was arrested.

"You're a lifesaver," said Beth, changing the subject. "Wyatt was so excited about staying overnight at your parents' house, I couldn't admit to them that I didn't want to be alone. My house feels cavernous with Wyatt gone." She sipped her coffee. "I felt foolish calling you and inviting myself, but I couldn't bear being alone this weekend, and I couldn't face anyone else. You and Anthony were so welcoming on the

Fourth of July, I just thought...well...anyhow, I promise not to make this a regular thing."

"Don't be ridiculous," said Gina. "I didn't have plans, and even if I had, I'd change them."

Of the people in her life, Gina was the most sensitive to Beth's anguish. Others seemed to understand grief over losing a husband, a grief that, for her, lingered like an incurable virus, but not grief over losing someone still alive. It was as though estrangement from a parent for just cause should bring relief, not heartbreak. But it didn't work that way. She wanted her father back. She wanted her husband back. Sometimes the longing became so intense she doubled over, as though she'd been punched in the solar plexus. No matter how many times she silently begged God to hear her plea, He appeared to be deaf.

Gina cocked her head, leaned forward, made eye contact. "You look a million miles away. And you haven't touched that perfect omelet. I'm going to be mighty pissed if I don't get at least one ooh and aah from you."

Beth cut off a bite-sized portion and scooped it into her mouth. "Yum, yum, yummy, yum, yum," she said, hugging herself and swaying as if dancing with a lover.

"Enough already," Gina giggled.

Beth ate several more bites before setting her fork down and pushing her plate aside. She cradled the warm coffee cup, took another sip. "You make a mean cup of java."

"Lots of practice. Seriously, it's the only thing that kept me awake through college."

Beth smiled. When Gabe was alive, Beth had thought of Gina as his fun-loving little sister. Lately, Beth had come to appreciate her as a generous, talented friend, someone with whom she could relax and be herself.

Even the décor in Gina's apartment, eclectic and reminiscent of Great Aunt Mavis's cottage, made her want to curl up on the windowsill and purr. Gina had transformed the rental in the old Victorian into an inviting home. Periwinkle walls set off the crisp, white cupboards. She'd converted two tall shelving units, separated by an attached sheet of wainscoting that served as backing for an upholstered bench, into a substantial piece of furniture, painted white to match the cupboards. Vintage cabbage rose pillows functioned as a backrest. The black, lacquered dining table provided an unexpected contrast.

"You have a real knack for interior design," said Beth.

"I could help with your place, if you like."

"That's a great offer. First, I have to figure out whether or not I'm staying."

"You're thinking of moving?"

"Right now, I don't know what I want. Just keeping my options open. So much feels out of my control."

"Because of your dad."

"His trial starts this week. It can't be over soon enough."

"How's he doing?"

"I tell myself I don't give a fuck. The truth is, I haven't been able to bring myself to talk to him. I'm so angry I'm afraid I'll say things I'll never be able to take back."

"It sounds like you believe he's guilty." There it was, the thing that no one else dared say.

"I don't *want* to believe he is. I *want* to believe he's the moral pillar of the community that he's always portrayed himself to be, but…"

"But what?"

Beth brushed the hair from her eyes. "It—it's something Gabe said. He asked me why my dad insisted on doing bed check at the camp alone. Gabe thought it was strange. I thought he was being ridiculous. My dad had done that for years. I took it for granted, thought he was being thoughtful. He always claimed it was to spare the staff so they could turn in early."

Gina raised an eyebrow.

"I know it sounds naïve. At the time, I got defensive. Gabe said maybe he was just being paranoid because he worked in a public school where, for your protection, you never want to be alone in a room with a student." Beth shifted in her chair, downed the last of her coffee, curled a strand of hair around her finger. "I chalked up my dad's insensitivity to working at the college level where being alone with students is no big deal. They're all adults. I thought he was just oblivious. Now I believe he saw it as—an opportunity."

"Oh, Beth!" said Gina. "It makes sense that you would second guess everything."

"And I've been thinking about Mikey, a friend I had when I was about nine or ten. He would come over to my house a lot to play, and then one day when my dad happened to be home, he acted really strange, made some weird excuse about why he had to leave. After that, if I'd see him when I was with my dad, Mikey would pretend he didn't see us or make a beeline in the other direction. He never came over again, ever. I just can't shake that memory."

Chapter Seven

~One Step at a Time~

The first day of the trial finally arrived.

Before leaving the house, Luella downed the ten milligrams of anti-anxiety medication her doctor prescribed. She wanted to feel nothing, simply to survive the next step. She remembered reading an article about a man who'd walked the length of America and wondered then how such a thing was possible, her bunioned feet aching at the mere thought. "One step at a time," the man said. "That's how you walk 2,800 miles." That's how she planned to get through this day, and the next, and the day after that, until this trial was over.

One foot in front of the other. One step at a time.

The jury filed in and sat in two rows on the right side of the courtroom. Luella avoided looking in their direction. What if they mistook her terror for guilt, misread her stoicism as defiance? There was so much to lose, so much of her future riding on appearances that she could not bear to look them in the eye and see condemnation or pity written on their faces.

Her phone pinged. A text from Beth. A simple heart emoji. Luella turned off her phone and slipped it into her purse.

Beth had decided not to come to court. She had math classes to teach. Her high school basketball season had just begun, and as head coach, she could not easily get away. Plus, she would have to pull Wyatt from kindergarten for the duration of the trial. Luella knew all of that was mere rationalization. The truth was that Beth had already made up her mind about her father's guilt.

An image came to Luella, Beth at five years old—the same age as Wyatt—her stick-figure legs straddling August's neck, riding his shoulders, using his ears to steer, turning his head to the right while August veered left, as he ran into walls, staggered in circles, Beth hiccupping with laughter, shrieking, "Not that way, Daddy, you're supposed to go the other way!" The memory soothed Luella and broke her heart.

"All rise," the clerk said.

Judge Emmeline Richards, a jurist with a by-the-book reputation, her black robe flowing over a petite frame, entered from a side door and proceeded to her place on the platform. The courtroom, smelling of old varnish, was a space locked in another era. Its gray terrazzo floors, deep mahogany woodwork, and tall mullioned windows conspired to make the judge appear all the more diminutive. The only thing keeping the room from echoing was the number of bodies packed into it. Luella felt the capacity audience filled with reporters, relatives, and spectators crowded in behind her. She imagined their eyes on her, judging her, assessing her culpability, condemning her for loving the defendant.

They didn't know August the way she did, hadn't loved him for more than three decades, raised a child with him, built a solid life with him. They knew only what they'd heard and read, knew what the gossip-mongers spread, knew with certainty they would never walk a day in her shoes. Their smugness rankled. Their pity stung. It pained Luella to admit that before this nightmare began, she would have been among them, presuming guilt instead of innocence and giving thanks to the Almighty that she wasn't the pathetic woman keeping vigil behind the accused.

The sound of dozens of bodies simultaneously sitting down filled the high-ceilinged room.

"At this time, I'm granting the prosecution's motion and ordering prospective witnesses to vacate the courtroom," said Judge Richards.

Attorney Lowery had warned Luella that the judge might exclude witnesses, but when she heard the order, her back stiffened. Leaving, she would be spared the lurid images and vile descriptions that the prosecution would inevitably present, but she had taken a marriage vow to stand by her husband's side through good times and bad. By leaving now, she was abandoning him at the lowest point in his life. She had no choice; August needed her to testify. Exclusion was the price for taking the witness stand on his behalf.

"I'll keep an eye on things," Franklin whispered.

Luella grabbed the back of the bench in front of her, braced herself, and rose slowly, praying her wobbling legs wouldn't buckle. August half turned to face her, nodded almost imperceptibly. She knew he meant to reassure her, although his tentativeness had the opposite effect.

"I love you," she mouthed.

A uniformed officer escorted her down the aisle and said something about taking the elevator to the second floor. As she walked toward the exit, Luella felt every eye on her. *One foot in front of the other, one step at a time.*

When she reached the door, she tried to resist looking over her shoulder, but at the last second, she turned to get a final glimpse of August. He sat ramrod-straight, his back to her. His posture made her recall the countless times he'd said, "Half the key to winning is skill; the other half is attitude. Make your opponent *believe* you're a winner."

Luella prayed he was right. She didn't dare think what would happen if he was wrong.

For months Luella worried about sitting in the courtroom, observing the spectacle, viewing August's humiliation, listening to the lies and venom spewing from the mouths of the prosecutor and witnesses. Sitting in the waiting room, unable to lend August the moral support he so badly needed, proved to be worse.

She paced, checked her phone every few minutes for non-existent emails and texts. She paged through the outdated *Redbook, Sports Illustrated,* and *Field and Stream* magazines stacked on the coffee table at least twice. Every time someone walked by the open doorway, she hoped that it was Franklin coming to tell her the judge had changed her ruling, or better yet, that she'd dismissed the charges for lack of evidence.

August's attorney, unwilling to predict the length of the trial, said only that the prosecution would present its case first and the defense would follow. Since Luella would be testifying for the defense, she would be waiting out most of the trial in this room, a room that looked like an afterthought furnished from a neighborhood garage sale, designed for utility, not comfort.

In one corner, a cooking program played muted on a small flat-screen television placed atop a faux-oak media stand. In another corner, a half-empty coffee pot and an assortment of mismatched cups sat on a square side table. A brown carpet, its nap long since worn thin, covered the floor. Two lightly-padded chairs upholstered in a slubbed mauve fabric—reminiscent of a 1980's dentist office—faced a blue, plaid sofa. An oversized black and white photograph of the courthouse, as it looked before the jail addition, hung too high on the longest wall.

Sitting alone fretting in the unhospitable room was difficult, yet staying home to wander around the house, useless and removed, was unthinkable. Worst of all was her feeling of powerlessness, the realization that the one thing she could do for August was to stand by his side, support him, show the world she had faith in him, and she was prevented from doing that. It may have been a tepid gesture, but sitting behind August in the courtroom would have, at least, been *doing* something.

Idleness provided too much opportunity to obsess on unwanted thoughts. What if the jurors didn't see through the lies? What if August was unjustly convicted? Only once had she allowed herself to ask the question: could August have abused those boys? The answer came back as emphatically as a slammed door. *No!* He would not, could not have molested them. She knew him, trusted him. He had always lived up to her faith in him. August was a good man, a credit to the coaching profession, a pillar of the community. He was a wonderful father, grandfather, and husband. The answer to the question had to be *No!* It was not possible that her entire life had been built on a lie. She would not allow herself to ask that question again.

The shift in their relationship was subtle, their mutual fear corrosive, eating away at the ties that bound them. They'd put up a brave front for each other and for Rosie, but underneath it, Luella knew they both wallowed in the dread of a guilty verdict. They hadn't spoken of it, as though naming their fear would give it power. They had to remain outwardly optimistic—August because it was his nature, Luella because he needed her to be.

Beneath her optimism, lay the abyss—life without August. Unimaginable. She'd built her existence around him, made his dreams hers. Coaching, speaking engagements, Laurent's Basketball Camp, the Hoops and Hearts Foundation, she'd constructed her world around all of it. She'd been introduced as Augie Laurent's wife countless times; yet she couldn't remember a single time when he'd been introduced as Luella Laurent's husband. Who would she be without him? After more than three decades together, she did not know who she was alone.

She would stand firmly by August's side as she always had. She would testify and proclaim his innocence publicly. Forcefully. When this ordeal was over, she and August would mend fences with their only child. They would be a loving family again. They would heal. And their partnership would be restored.

But what about Beth?

August's arrest had been a public humiliation for Beth, who had idolized her father to the point of building a coaching career that paralleled his. Still, Luella wanted to shake Beth until her teeth fell out. How could she believe that her father was capable of sexually violating any child? Heaven help August if the twelve jurors rushed so quickly to judgment.

Luella's head hurt. She was tired of thinking. Tomorrow she would bring a book to busy her mind and knitting to busy her hands.

Through the hour-long lunch break, eaten with Lowery and August in a vacant conference room, Luella picked at her turkey sub. Conversation was sparse, mainly limited to the attorney telling them to keep the faith after August complained, "I'm getting fucking killed in there."

Once alone back in the witness waiting room, Luella stared at the muted television, stood occasionally to stretch her stiff muscles, and scrolled through her phone, checking the weather, news, and social media feeds.

In the late afternoon Luella thought sadly that, if she were still teaching, the school day would just be ending. That meant Beth should be out of class. On impulse she called her number.

Surprisingly, Beth answered. "Mom, I don't really have time to talk. I'm just heading into practice."

"The trial started today."

"I know. I texted you. Remember?"

"Right. That was before the judge ordered witnesses out of court. I've been sitting in the waiting room most of the day."

"Are you alone?"

As shabby as it was, the room was, at least, private. It hadn't before occurred to Luella that other witnesses might share it. The notion of facing her husband's accusers in this small space made her queasy.

"Mom?"

"Yes. I'm alone."

"I'm sorry. I wish I could help."

"I appreciate your concern." Luella regretted her clipped tone. She longed for communication between them to be easy again, to talk about unimportant matters, to laugh spontaneously over ridiculous things. Mostly, she longed for Beth to support her father so that every conversation wasn't laden with unspoken judgment.

Franklin stepped into the room. His sober expression was not reassuring.

Luella's brow furrowed. "I've got to go. Franklin is here."

"Mom, I really am sorry."

"Uh huh."

"I'll call tomorrow."

Before Beth hung up, Luella's attention shifted to her brother and any news he might be bringing from the courtroom.

"They've adjourned until tomorrow," said Franklin.

"How are things going?"

"Not well," he admitted, shaking his head. "The prosecutor's opening statement was compelling. The testimony from the police didn't help."

Luella grimaced. The faces of Sergeant Fossmeyer and Officer Smolinski, the police who had informed her of the charges, were as vivid as if they faced her now. She would never forget how frightened she'd been when they accused August of unspeakable things and hinted at her complicity. She was angry, damn angry. She thought how excruciating it must have been for August to sit silently through their scurrilous testimony.

Franklin looked at her, his expression pained. "Remember, it's early. The prosecution phase of a trial is always discouraging." He said this in a way that made Luella think he was not just trying to reassure her but trying to convince himself.

She stood, the muscles in her back and legs protesting. She scooped up her purse and gathered her coat from the hook by the door. She glanced at her phone—4:49.

"I'll pick up Rosie and bring her by after dinner. You might want some time alone with Augie on the drive home." Franklin held her coat open as she slid her arms into the sleeves.

"Luella?"

"What? I'm sorry. It's hard to concentrate."

"Understandable," he said.

Outside the waiting room the halls of the courthouse seemed ee-rily deserted, the office doors rimming the central staircase, all closed. Franklin's and Luella's footsteps landed heavy on the terrazzo floor. Despite its clean appearance, the place smelled fusty. It was as if, since 1921, the year the structure was erected, there had been a steady build-up of decay, which simply could not be scrubbed away.

Together they rode the elevator up to the third-floor courtroom where August waited outside the locked door. He stood passively, star-ing into the distance. Luella walked up beside him and touched his arm. When he turned to look at her, she saw the toll the day's proceed-ings had taken. His posture was less erect and tiredness had crept in around his eyes.

"We're expected back here tomorrow at 8:30," he said, wearily.

"Let's go home."

"I've got cramps in my legs from sitting all day. Let's take the stairs." said August.

The wide wooden staircase that zigzagged through the center of the building creaked as their feet landed on each tread. The build-ing, which had seemed nearly abandoned only moments ago, filled with echoing voices and footsteps as employees filed out of their offices at the end of the workday. No one spoke to them or acknowledged them, yet Luella felt their eyes on her, imagined she heard their critical thoughts. She resisted breaking into a run.

One foot in front of the other. One step at a time.

"I'm parked on 3ʳᵈ Street," Franklin said when they reached the final landing. He hugged Luella and kissed her cheek.

Luella turned and scrambled to catch up to August, who was al-ready out the door.

Daylight melted into dusk as Luella turned out of the courthouse parking lot, August in the passenger seat, the air between them deathly silent. He usually insisted on driving, but today prudence overrode habit. His prescription anxiety medication taken at a higher dose than hers made driving riskier for him. Getting pulled over by the police for an infraction meant his bail could be revoked. Besides, August seemed to have lost the will to take charge.

Compared to rush hour traffic in Chicago, the streets were practically deserted. Luella turned on her directional, then checked the rearview and sideview mirrors before changing lanes. She glanced at the speedometer, slowed to precisely twenty-five. It felt as though the car was standing still, but she held at that speed. The last thing she needed was a ticket.

The elastic band of her tights pinched her waist, and the cold leather seat chilled her legs. She pressed the toggle to activate the heated seat and turned the thermostat to seventy degrees. August seemed indifferent to the cold as he stared out the side window.

They rode through downtown where most of the storefronts stood dark, past two Lutheran churches, a Catholic church and a daycare center, plus a string of car dealerships, gas stations, and convenience stores. Luella waited for August to speak, stealing glances at him as she drove. She sensed he wanted time to decompress, the way he insisted on alone time after basketball practices and games, but when they reached the edge of town, she could no longer tolerate looking at the back of his head.

"What happened in court?"

August turned toward her. "Haven't I been through enough today?"

"I wouldn't know. I spent the day in the waiting room," she groused. She meant to be kinder, more understanding. She reminded herself being excluded from the courtroom wasn't August's fault. The day had been stressful for her, but it had to have been traumatic for him. Her peevishness made her feel small and selfish. "I'm sorry," she said. "I'm just tired. I know it's been a terrible day for you."

"It's so fucking unfair!" August blurted. "I sat there listening to Fett tell the jury what a demon I am. According to him, I'm evil incarnate, the worst human being since Hitler. And the goddamned police. I didn't recognize who they were talking about. Don't they have actual criminals to arrest? The jury looked at me as though they've already decided I'm guilty."

Luella reached for his hand.

"It's so goddamned hard to sit there and take it without being able to fight back."

"Our turn will come." Luella struggled to sound reassuring when, in truth, she was scared. "Remember what your attorney said. He told you not to lose hope at the beginning because he'll put on a strong defense. Franklin said the same thing. He told me the prosecution phase is always discouraging."

"I'm not sure he actually believes that."

Luella wasn't sure which "he" August meant, but she chose to let it drop.

August let go of her hand and grew quiet again. Since the arrest, his personality seemed to shrink by the day. On the extrovert scale, he'd always been a resounding ten, the most outgoing person she knew. When they'd first met, he'd seemed bigger than life, a strapping, confident athlete out to conquer the world. He commanded a room, made others want to spin in his orbit. To her great surprise, from the moment they'd met that first summer at the lake, he'd pursued her, the quiet, bookish girl. "With you, Lulu, I'm a better man," he'd said. She became his silent partner, his helpmate. The role suited her.

Perhaps her contentment as a wife, mother, and teacher was old-fashioned by modern standards. Some women might believe she should want to step out of Augie Laurent's large shadow, to have her own lofty goals, her own unbridled ambition. Her daughter was the ambitious one. Beth had her father's competitiveness, drive, and need for recognition. At age thirty, she was the head girls' basketball coach at one of the largest high schools in the state, a champion with an eye toward a college coaching job. Luella was proud of her, but she worried that the trial would derail her and ruin her chances of ever finding love again.

Still, Luella learned that a partner was no hedge against loneliness. Assumed friends had fled as though her bad fortune was contagious. Beth kept her distance. August had withdrawn into himself, retreating like a frightened animal burrowing into its hole, lashing out unpredictably. Her attempts to draw him out had been mostly met with failure. There were times when she simply didn't have the energy to coax him into conversation. She missed the gregarious man she'd married. Only Rosie, whom he'd watched over and protected all his life, occasionally elicited a smile.

Rosie! They'd forgotten to pick her up. They'd already driven past Voorhees Road, the turnoff for the sheltered workshop. Luella pictured Rosie anxiously waiting by the front door. Luella pulled in to the empty parking lot of Holt and Son Body Shop.

"What are you doing?" August asked.

"I missed the turn for Horizons." Luella swung the car around. She looked at the digital clock. Sunset would be in less than a half hour. At least they hadn't gone too far past their turnoff.

As they reentered the city limits, street lamps turned on. The leaves stubbornly clinging to the oak trees and the flag flying above the corner convenience store fluttered lazily. The wind, so blustery only that the morning, had faded to an anemic breeze.

Luella turned on to Voorhees Road, drove through a modest residential neighborhood and past an elementary school constructed in a bygone era. In ordinary times, she would be leaving school at this hour, rolling a carry-on-sized suitcase filled with materials to prepare for the next day. That life seemed far away, although only five months had passed since she'd been in the classroom.

Luella pulled in front of Horizons Sheltered Workshop, put the car in park, and left the engine running.

"I'll be right back," she said.

No one stood in the expansive foyer of the large pole building, which had been converted into offices, classrooms, a kitchen, and several work stations. There was a light on in one of the offices off the entryway. Luella poked her head in the door.

"Excuse me. I apologize for being late. I'm here to pick up Rosie Laurent," she said.

The middle-aged social worker looked up at Luella over her purple cheaters and said pleasantly, "Rosie was already picked up."

Then Luella vaguely remembered that Franklin mentioned he would pick up Rosie. She felt foolish. It was one thing to forget an arrangement made days in advance; it was another matter to forget something planned less than an hour ago.

"Thank you," Luella said, sheepishly. "I forgot that my brother was getting Rosie today."

"Not a problem," the woman said and turned back to whatever she'd been doing.

But it *was* a problem. Not being able to keep a thought in her head for five minutes was a problem.

Luella hurried to the car and slumped into the driver's seat.

"Where's Rosie?" asked August.

"I forgot that Franklin told me he was going to pick her up." Luella rubbed her temples. "I can't think. I'm surprised I remember my name."

"Let's just get the hell out of here."

Chapter Eight

~The Vow~

With the third day of the trial over, at seven o'clock in the evening Luella pulled up in front of The Hair Affair salon. She parked on the east end of Main Street next to a yellow Volkswagen beetle with a custom pink rose decal on the driver's side fender, belonging to Trudy, the salon owner.

When Luella entered the salon Trudy stood behind the reception counter. A woman with a pixie cut handed her a tip. As the woman turned to leave, she looked at Luella, the groove between her brow deepening into a scowl.

"You're not going to let *her* in here," she huffed in a stage whisper.

"I invited her."

The woman harrumphed, grabbed her coat from the corner rack, and stomped past Luella on the way out.

"Pay no attention to her," said Trudy as she locked the door behind her and turned the "closed" sign toward the street.

Trudy's look du jour was a shoulder-length beach-wave hairstyle, tipped pink. A colorful floral tattoo vined around her long, slender calf. The salon, its walls decorated with posters of trendily coiffured twenty-somethings and usually echoing with small-talk and natter, had never felt so preternaturally quiet.

"I hope I didn't cost you a client," said Luella, embarrassed.

"Believe me, she's a customer I can afford to lose."

"Thank you for this." Luella hung up her coat and glanced at the array of women's magazines fanned out on the coffee table.

"Honey, when I saw you on the news and heard that you're testifying at the end of the week, I said to myself, 'That woman needs a haircut and color.'" Trudy gestured for Luella to sit at the last of the four stylist's stations. "I knew you'd want to look your best, but if I was in your shoes, I wouldn't want to face a bunch of nosey old gossips when I got my hair done. I figured that's why you haven't been in, so I called."

Trudy turned the chair toward the mirror and stood behind Luella, studying her. She ran her slim fingers from Luella's nape to her crown. "I see you used store-bought color." Her glossed lips pursed disapprovingly. "That stuff will ruin your hair."

"Guilty," Luella admitted. She'd lacked the courage to come to the salon. She'd called and cancelled two weeks ago, making an excuse about a conflicting dental appointment. Although she'd felt guilty for lying, Trudy was right, the thought of tolerating the surreptitious glances and overt rudeness of the salon's patrons was more than she could handle.

Everywhere Luella went judgment pressed in on all sides. She shuddered at the memory of the ugly encounter with Patty Meier at McBride's Grocery Store. The day she'd selected that box of inferior hair dye, it was all she could do to stand in the aisle at Freedman's Pharmacy. Because she was in such a rush, she'd overcompensated, avoiding anything close to "mouse-brown" and chosen poorly, an ash-brown that made her complexion look old and sallow.

"Let's soften this color. I'm thinking of keeping the base fairly dark with softer highlights to frame your face. I know you don't like high contrast, so I'll keep that in mind. What do you think?"

"I'm at your mercy."

"You just relax while I go mix the color," Trudy said and headed for the back room. In less than a minute, however, she returned with a cup of coffee and a *People* magazine. "Something to distract you while you're waiting."

Luella took a sip of coffee and randomly opened the magazine to an article about some young starlet she's never heard of, making her feel old. She read half way down the page and realized she hadn't retained a single word, her thoughts, instead, had returned to the courtroom and to Adlai Fett, who, according to August, had done significant damage when he questioned Roddy Miles on the stand.

Roddy would be twenty-three or twenty-four by now. He was eleven the first summer he attended basketball camp. Luella hadn't seen him for almost ten years, but she remembered him clearly: a shy, fatherless boy with big talent. "The kid's quick as a cat," she remembered August saying that first season. "Needs to be more aggressive and needs more confidence, but we can work with that." Roddy had returned for several summers.

When it came time for high school, August made calls to the coach at St. Michael's Academy and secured a scholarship for Roddy, which at the end of an all-state career, he'd parlayed into a full ride to Loyola University. Luella pictured the stung look on her husband's face when Lowery informed August that Roddy would be testifying against him. "Roddy Miles? You're sure?" August had asked, incredulous. When Luella inquired how the testimony had gone, August teared up and insisted that he couldn't talk about it. After all August had done for him, Luella was grateful she hadn't encountered Roddy Miles—the boy turned Judas—in the courthouse. She couldn't imagine how she would have stomached looking at him without showing murderous resentment.

"Here we go." Trudy carried a tray with three shallow mixing pans. "We'll have you looking like a million in no time flat."

Luella closed her eyes against creeping weariness. Trudy expertly sectioned strands of hair, applying the various dyes and then wrapping them in foil. Luella tried to stay in the moment, listening to Trudy talk about ordinary things—the weather, Givens Knoll High School, people they knew in common—but the ordinary had gone out of life. Her world had become a courtroom drama.

"That'll do the trick," Trudy said, standing back and admiring her work.

Luella opened her eyes and caught her absurd reflection in the mirror. "With all this foil on my head I look like a human antenna. I think I could pull in WJXQ," she chuckled.

It had been a long time since she'd made any attempt at humor. August, who typically used levity to deal with all things serious, often to Luella's consternation, had always been the jester, the hail fellow well met; but these days he could barely lift himself out of bed in the morning.

"I can't remember the last time I laughed."

Trudy touched her shoulder. She set the timer for twenty minutes. Instead of disappearing into the back room as she customarily did, she sat at the next station and swiveled toward Luella.

"You want to hear something beyond funny?" Trudy said. "Howard tells me his mother is visiting us for three months. Three months! The woman drives me nuts after five minutes. She gave up her apartment and is making the rounds from kid to kid, three months at a crack. She's worn out her welcome at Lola's. Now, it's our turn. I'm about to live with Cruella De Vil."

"That sounds dreadful."

"I thought of divorcing Howard, but I'd have to marry him first."

Luella smiled. For as many summers as she could remember Trudy had been sharing entertaining stories about her partner. "You've got a point."

"Besides, Howard's a saint. He's put up with Marty for years."

"How is your nephew?"

"On the wagon today, but there's always tomorrow."

"One day at a time, they say."

"You were his favorite teacher, you know," Trudy said.

Luella had tutored Marty, a lost soul, through summer school math so he could graduate. He'd been a challenge, so quick-witted, so full of promise. If only he could conquer demon alcohol.

"He was a favorite of mine, too," she said.

"Luella, do you mind if I ask you a question?"

Luella's back stiffened. Her guard, let down slightly, stood instantly erect.

"Are you okay?"

It was not the question she'd expected. There had been plenty of questions, spoken and implied: questions about August, questions about the alleged victims, questions about her complicity. But, no one had asked her if she was okay.

"I honestly don't know. This whole thing has been a nightmare. Some days I think I'm coping. Other days I'm not sure I can make it until dinnertime."

"I'm sorry things are so hard."

Luella swallowed, choking back tears. The timer buzzed.

"Let's get you rinsed."

Trudy led Luella to the sink. Leaning back in the chair, Luella settled her neck on the basin's padded curved rim and closed her eyes. Warm, soothing water cascaded through her hair. Trudy gently massaged her scalp with coconut shampoo, the aroma teasing like a tropical breeze. The comfort of it made Luella's knees weak. It had been so, so long since she'd felt such tenderness. Without warning, tears.

"I'm sorry," she whispered.

"Honey, you've got nothing to be sorry about, nothing at all."

The only sound in the living room was the metronomic tick of the grandfather clock. Luella, computer resting in her lap, Bird curled at her feet, relaxed in front of the unlit fireplace. She smoothed a hand over her hair, appreciating its silky texture and coconut scent. Navigating to an e-card site, she sent a thank you note to Trudy to express gratitude for her kindness earlier that evening.

Before going to bed, she decided to check the camp's website. Below their motto—Laurent's Basketball Camp: Developing Skills/Building

Character—a closeup photograph of a player completing a layup, extending full-length to the hoop, the ball rolling off his fingertips, stretched across the screen. Beneath the photo was written a concise description:

"Set in the beautiful Northwoods of Wisconsin, Laurent's Basketball Camp, a 55-acre property with 600 feet of frontage on pristine Whisper Lake, provides three regulation courts, twelve residential cabins, a dining hall and indoor recreation facilities. Originally built in 1928 as a family resort, the property was converted into a youth sports camp in 1995 after its purchase by Jolliet University men's head basketball coach Augie Laurent. The camp offers week long intensive instruction by top coaches for youth between the ages 10-17."

Under the description in bold red letters, it said "Closed for the Summer."

Luella couldn't bear to look further.

She switched to her Facebook page to see how many "friends" remained. Originally, they'd numbered three hundred one. Now there were seventy-nine. A quick mental calculation meant that two hundred twenty-two people had rejected her. Slightly over twenty six percent of her "friends" were still there. Surprising how much the technological rebuff—the cyber equivalent of shunning—hurt. She suspected that those who remained stayed, not out of loyalty, but for voyeuristic reasons, hoping to get a peek beneath the lurid media headlines. They would get little satisfaction. She never posted anything, never left a comment, never pressed "like." Instead, she merely peeked through the crack of a door left ajar.

Scanning her wall, Luella noted the typical array of postings: photos of someone's redheaded grandson, a link to a gun control article, a suggestion to "like" the Green Bay Packers webpage. She scrolled past a quiz to find out what make of automobile best suited her and a video of a six-year-old singing prodigy.

Rubbing her eyes and yawning, she was about to log off when the name "Laurent" caught her eye. She'd avoided reading articles about

August's arrest or articles containing trial propaganda; but this one was different. In bold type, the headline screamed, "**Should Luella Laurent Be Prosecuted?**" The tagline followed: "The wife of accused pedophile, Augie Laurent—victim or accomplice?"

Luella's breath caught. Her eyes fluttered like hummingbird wings. She couldn't believe it! Below the headline sat her unsmiling image, an unflattering close-up taken as she walked into court with August on the first day of the trial. A voice in her head warned, *No good can come of this*. She hesitated and then clicked on the *ftpnews.com* link.

A lime green header with the *Fit to Print News* orange lightning bolt logo burst onto the computer screen. In the column along the right side of the page, beneath capital letters proclaiming CHILD SEX SCANDAL and an ad for Pioneer Insurance, a photograph of August, his drawn face peering through a car window, stared back at her.

Luella skipped to the article's byline belonging to Nanette Hartman. Although she'd never heard of Ms. Hartman, she imagined the woman looking like a hooked-beak bird of prey. She began reading:

Luella Laurent, wife of famed basketball coach and accused pedophile, Augie Laurent, has stood by her husband despite the damning court testimony of six alleged victims. Speculation is that she will testify on his behalf as early as Friday. Shocking details provided in the victims' accounts have raised questions about Ms. Laurent's credibility and possible involvement in the abuse.

Directing the computer arrow to the "x" in the upper right corner of the screen, her finger hovered above the left click key ready to close the page.

Although Ms. Laurent has avoided the limelight, Coach Laurent has often publicly acknowledged her as his helpmate and silent partner.

"She's been instrumental in the establishment of the Hoops and Hearts Foundation," Laurent said in a 2014 interview after receiving the "Philanthropist of the Year Award" from the Stevenson Foundation. "She's been my rock for 30 years. I couldn't do any of this without her."

Luella gritted her teeth. Since when was altruism and loyalty worthy of suspicion?

After the scandal broke, Ms. Laurent issued the following statement of support:

"I am devastated by the false accusations against my husband. He has dedicated his life to the education and welfare of children, as have I. He would never hurt a child. I am certain no child who attended Laurent's Basketball Camp or who was a participant in the Hoops and Hearts Foundation sponsored programs was ever mistreated."

Frustration slithered through her veins. Abandoning her husband might make her more worthy in the public eye but not in her own estimation. She'd taken a marriage vow to love August for better or worse, in sickness and in health, 'til death do us part. It was a vow she intended to keep.

Luella scrolled to the last sentences of the article.

What did Ms. Laurent know and when did she know it? Is she an unwitting victim or a willing accomplice?

Luella's hands shook. An invitation for readers to comment beckoned beneath the article. *Hit escape now,* a voice in her head cautioned. There was nothing to be gained from this self-torture. Slowly, she scrolled down the page. *For heaven's sake, don't do this!* But she couldn't stop.

- *Augie Laurent is a monster and his pathetic wife is the monster's handmaiden. She is as guilty as he is for turning away from children who desperately needed her help. Arrest her and throw away the key.*
- *If a woman married as long as Luella doesn't know what her husband is up to, she's either a fool or a liar.*
- *Luella Laurent is a weak, sick, disgusting pig.*

Luella reached in the pocket of her robe for a tissue and dabbed her welling eyes.

How did any stranger presume, with such certainty, to comprehend another woman's life? She *had* known what her husband was "up to." He'd been "up to" coaching other people's children, creating one of the most respected basketball programs in the country, and raising money so that underprivileged kids could participate in summer camp. He was "up to" being generous to a fault. He was "up to" being a faithful husband, a caring father, and a doting grandfather.

- *I'd divorce Augie so fast it would make your head spin. Sure, it would be hard to give up the money, glory and fame, but any decent woman would give him his marching orders.*

What money? August had lost his job, and they'd dug deep into their savings to pay for a top-notch lawyer. If the unthinkable happened and her husband was found guilty, she could lose everything. If he was found innocent, it would take years for them to recover financially. And how did abandoning your partner translate into decency? As to glory and fame, Luella had tolerated the limelight, not sought it. Any semblance of glory vanished with the arrest. Fame had degenerated into notoriety.

- *Didn't Luella say to herself, what is Augie doing hanging out with all these 12-year-olds? Didn't she ever wash a sheet and wonder where the blood or semen came from?*

Blood? Semen? The only blood and semen she'd ever washed out was from the sheets of her marriage bed.

The words cut Luella wide open. The cruelty took her breath away. She doubled over, hugged her knees, and coughed hard, trying to clear her lungs of the venom. What had she done to generate such animosity? She'd always handled her students with tenderness. She'd brushed away children's tears, picked them up when they'd fallen, loved them even when they acted unlovable.

"Lulu!" August shouted from the kitchen. "Do we have any more peanut butter? This jar's empty."

Luella straightened up, rubbed her eyes, took a deep breath. August must not see her like this. She didn't have the wherewithal to explain how devastating the virtual threat felt when he faced an actual threat. She wouldn't compete with his pain. How foolish she'd been to read these words when, with the press of a button, she'd held the power to ignore them. What these strangers thought of her didn't count. Her vows counted. Tonight, her ally in this terrible ordeal rummaged through the cupboards in the kitchen.

She moved the computer arrow over the "x" in the upper right-hand corner and depressed the left click key. The screen darkened.

"There's a new jar in the pantry," Luella called, struggling to keep her voice steady.

"Where?" he hollered.

"Give me a minute. I'll be right there."

Chapter Nine

~Promise and Protect~

On the fourth day of the trial in the evening, August seemed more somber than ever. When Luella asked for details, he shared nothing, as though living through the experience once was all he could manage. August's fragility kept her from pressing. Franklin was circumspect, too, as though his sole mission was to protect her. All he'd said was that the defense had an uphill climb.

Luella stretched out on the couch in the living room with a Tony Hillerman mystery and a glass of Merlot. Bird lay on the floor vigorously gnawing a large bone. Rosie was already in bed. August sat on the edge of the overstuffed chair, leaning forward, legs wide apart, elbows on knees, swirling the ice in his Manhattan, seemingly hypnotized by the motion. "We have to prepare for the worst," he said, as though talking to himself.

Surprised, Luella glanced up.

"We have to talk about what we'll do if the worst happens," he repeated.

"But the defense starts tomorrow," Luella protested. "I haven't testified yet."

"I'm being realistic." August continued swirling the ice and staring into his glass.

"You're being defeatist." Luella closed her book, sat up straight. "You've got a very good lawyer. Franklin says he's the best."

August swigged his cocktail. "Sure, Lowery will fight like hell, but I've been in enough contests to know that having the best coach doesn't guarantee a win." She'd seen him like this after lost games—flushed cheeks, pinched lips, rounded shoulders.

"You can't give up."

"I'm just saying we have to be prepared for a wrongful conviction. *You* have to be prepared."

She hadn't allowed herself to dwell on that possibility. The thought of August being found guilty and going to prison alarmed her.

"This will all fall to you," he said, gesturing in a wide swoop around the room. "The camp, the foundation, Rosie."

"You'll be acquitted. You have to be. I want my—our—lives back."

"And you think I don't?" His voice was loud and hard-edged. He glanced at the stairs in the direction of Rosie's bedroom, as if suddenly aware that he might awaken her. "Luella," he said, lowering his voice. "Don't you think I'm scared shitless at the prospect of prison? If I owned a gun, I'd put a bullet in my brain. Don't you think I want to turn back the clock to before this shit storm began? Christ, I want to wake up from this nightmare." He raked his fingers through his hair. "This is my life we're talking about. I'm fighting like hell to hold on to my sanity. But ignoring reality won't make it go away."

Luella felt like she was diving underwater and someone cut her oxygen line. She'd longed for August to talk with her about the trial, but now his pessimism made her want to escape the conversation. She considered leaving the room but was certain he would follow. She sipped her wine, stalling to regain her equilibrium. Maybe he would take the hint and drop the subject. Please, she thought, let me read and drink my wine in peace. Let me hold on to hope.

"Franklin can help you with the foundation. He can handle the legal matters." August stood and paced. "Hoops and Hearts doesn't have to have my name attached to it. He'll be able to find another coach to front the organization. It's a great image booster. There'll be plenty of guys who'll want in. Kent McElroy might be a possibility."

Luella didn't react, fingered her Hoops and Hearts necklace, continued to sip her wine, letting the hint of licorice linger on her tongue. Resting her head on the back of the couch, she thought of the extravagant bottle of Le Macchiole Messorio Merlot August had purchased for their thirtieth anniversary, how he had draped a white dishtowel over his arm, bowed, and poured a small sample for her approval, as if he were a five-star restaurant sommelier. She wanted that August back, the grandiose, impractical man who dreamed big and left the worrying to her. This August, this nervous, agitated man whose world had shrunk to the courtroom and this house, made her despondent.

"Keeping the camp operating is going to be trickier. Until the dust settles, enrollment will be a problem. You'll have to be patient until there's an up-tick in participation." August stopped, drained the last drop from his glass, and set it on a side table. "Rely on Franklin to help you with the legal issues. Portman, at the bank, can deal with the financial matters. In the short term, Beth can run the camp. She knows enough to keep things going until you find someone with a national reputation, someone who will lend his name to the camp."

"But she refuses even to visit."

"She'll come around."

Luella wasn't so sure. She worried that Beth might never set foot in the camp again, much less run it. Their phone conversations, which she still had not revealed to August, left no doubt that Beth's anger festered. Luella desperately wanted to keep her daughter in her life, so she changed the subject anytime the arrest or the trial came up, but Beth's rancor, always simmering beneath the surface, contaminated even the most superficial topics. Reconciliation with her father, if it ever came, depended on the outcome of the trial.

August lowered himself onto the couch next to Luella, took the wine glass from her, set it on the coffee table, and took her hands in his. He had the look of a nervous suitor about to propose. "I'm most concerned about what happens to Rosie. When my mother went into the nursing home, we both agreed to have her come live with us. I know having her here hasn't always been easy on you."

Given the difficulty of that first transition, Luella couldn't imagine how Rosie would cope with the loss of the big brother she adored.

"As her legal guardian...if I'm in...if I'm not here..." August squeezed Luella's hands. "Lulu, are you listening?"

Desperately, Luella wanted him to stop talking. She didn't want to think about the what-ifs, to project a future without him, to hear what was coming next.

"I want you to promise me you'll assume guardianship."

Luella pulled away as if his hands were electrified. She wondered if he understood the enormity of what he was asking.

"I need you to promise me you'll take care of Rosie."

Luella closed her eyes, felt his warm hands on her shoulders. The trial was not over. She would testify on August's behalf. Her husband was innocent. Surely twelve reasonable people would see that.

"Luella, I need this from you."

Reassurance cost nothing.

"I promise."

Lying awake, staring at the ceiling, thinking of her conversation with August earlier in the evening, and worrying about her upcoming testimony, Luella heard what sounded like a door slamming outside. Bird growled. Not trusting her senses, Luella considered it might be the imaginings of a restless mind; but she heard the sound again, another door slamming somewhere in the darkness. Bird sprang up from the floor, dashed out of the bedroom.

August, breathing heavily, stirred beside her but did not wake. She hadn't dared ask how many sleeping pills he took each night, certain they exceeded the prescribed limit. If the pills proved addictive, they'd cross that bridge after the trial was over.

Luella slipped out of bed, then padded to the window in her flannel nightgown. She squinted into the shadowy, moonlit night.

Through the bare tree branches she spotted taillights receding down the long driveway and then disappearing as the vehicle turned onto Virgin Timber Road. It was unusual to see a vehicle leaving the remote property at any time of day, much less in the middle of the night.

In the center of the circular drive, dark objects swaying in the branches of a large oak caught Luella's attention. Her heartbeat quickened. Gooseflesh crawled up her arms. From this distance, she couldn't make out the forms. Part of her didn't want to know. Part of her wanted to crawl into bed, pull the covers over her head and pretend she hadn't seen or heard anything. She considered waking August but thought better of it. He needed his rest for what undoubtedly would be another harrowing day in court. Whatever was out there, she decided to face alone.

Luella put on her robe and slippers and tiptoed downstairs. The house felt drafty. The wind must be blowing from the north, she thought. As she walked through the living room, she inhaled the acrid aroma of stale ashes. A few dry logs rested on the andirons, but she couldn't remember the last time they'd built a fire.

Bird whined, paced at the door. Luella pulled her wool jacket from the hall tree, put it on over her robe, and then kicked off her slippers and wedged her bare feet into her hiking boots, hurriedly bending to tie them. From the top shelf, she retrieved an over-sized flashlight.

Outside, the wind rasped through the pines. Despite being bundled, Luella shivered, uncertain if it was the cold or fear making her tremble. She wished she'd put on a stocking cap.

Cautiously, she tromped along the driveway, gravel crunching underfoot, shadows dancing about as she shined the flashlight in a sweeping motion. She heard a cracking noise and pivoted toward the sound of branches breaking on the forest floor. In the flashlight's beam, three large does stared at her through round, alert eyes. For a moment, they stood frozen in the glare of the light before darting into the darkness. Bird gave chase, then soon circled back.

When Luella reached the base of the oak, she inhaled deeply, summoning courage. She pointed the flashlight into the tree. From a long, low-lying branch dangled two scarecrow-like figures, stuffed with straw, one dressed as a man, the other as a woman. Each had a cardboard sign draped around its neck: "Coach Pervert" and "Mrs. Pervert." Luella's lips trembled. Her hands shook, causing the light to flutter erratically through the branches.

Who would do such a cruel thing? Who despised them enough to do something so hateful? Was it strangers? Someone they knew? August must not see this. He'd been constantly on edge. She had to remove these effigies and destroy them. As she scuffed along the driveway to the utility shed, she coughed and wiped her wet cheeks and dripping nose with the back of her hand. Bird scampered beside her.

Tucking the flashlight under her arm, she shined the beam on the padlock. Her mind went blank. The combination. *Think*. Then she remembered that it was August's birthday. After two failed attempts, the lock opened. Luella undid the hasp and opened the double doors.

The shed was packed full. A long, aluminum extension ladder, too heavy and unwieldy for her purpose, hung on the sidewall. Shakily, she shined the light around the shed's perimeter looking for the eight-foot stepladder. Cobwebs threaded the corners. There, behind the riding mower, the ladder leaned against a stack of Adirondack chairs. She skirted piles of clay flowerpots, sidled around the mower, and retrieved the ladder. As she backtracked, her jacket pocket caught on the mower and ripped.

Luella carried the ladder around the drive to the oak tree, leveling it as best she could on the uneven ground. She returned to the shed and grabbed the pruning shears mounted on the wall. She climbed the ladder slowly and held on to the tree branch to steady herself. Cautiously she let go, making sure she was stable, then snipped the clothesline rope. It took several cuts before the effigy of August thudded to the ground. Luella's legs wobbled. Her arms ached. Her hands and feet numbed. *You can do this. You have to do this.* She rebalanced herself and reached for the other effigy. The details struck her—a brown, spray-painted mop-head, which she understood was supposed to mimic her dyed hair, and a bra stuffed with rags. She snipped the rope three times before the figure dropped.

Quivering, Luella descended the ladder and stared down at the crude forms. Under the flashlight's beam, "Mrs. Pervert" shone in pink, day-glow letters on the cardboard sign. She grabbed the sign and ripped it into fist-sized pieces, letting the wind scatter them into the darkness. She dragged one figure at a time back to the shed. For now, she would hide them behind the stack of Adirondack chairs and re-member to burn them later. She put the ladder and pruning shears away and locked the shed doors.

"Bird, come," she commanded. The dog ran to her. "Time to sleep. Tomorrow is a big day." Bird wagged his tail. Wearily, hands still trem-bling, she trudged to the house and up the porch steps. "Remember," she said, as she opened the door, "this is our secret."

Chapter Ten

~Testimony~

From the vantage point of the witness stand Luella scanned the packed courtroom, trying to remain impassive as Attorney Lowery had instructed. She recognized several of the reporters, buzzards all. Interspersed among the strangers were familiar faces: parents of the alleged victims; Father Jeffery, the priest who'd officiated at Beth's wedding; Franklin; and, surprisingly, Trudy, her hairdresser.

Having gotten little sleep after a night of dealing with the effigies hanging in the yard, she felt tired and edgy. The bright overhead lights made her eyes water. Her mouth was sawdust dry. The three bites of the egg salad sandwich she'd eaten at lunch lay in her stomach like a sack of marbles.

She thought of Lowery's advice. "Remember to keep your comments brief. Answer only what's asked, no more. Stay calm. Juries interpret nervousness and fidgeting as guilt." She crossed then uncrossed her legs until firmly planting both feet on the floor. She pulled her knees together.

On Luella's right, Judge Richards loomed shadow-like in her peripheral vision. The court reporter sat stiff-backed at a small table beneath the judge's bench, her hands poised to record every spoken word. Adlai Fett, seated at the prosecutor's table about twenty feet away, scribbled intently on a legal pad. Lowery, seated at the defense table, inclined his head toward August and whispered something that caused him to nod.

Desperately she wanted to convince the jury that August Laurent was a good man incapable of committing any of the vile acts he was accused of. Her responsibility as a character witness weighed heavier than any she'd ever shouldered, the stakes made greater by love, loyalty, and years of shared history. Beneath Luella's loose-fitting coral blouse and cream-colored cardigan—clothing Lowery had suggested to make her appear soft and non-threatening—she perspired heavily. She touched her heart necklace, then to keep from shaking, crossed her arms.

After she was sworn in, Lowery rose slowly from his chair and approached the witness stand. She made fleeting eye contact with August. "Help me," his eyes pleaded. "Be my voice. Tell them all the things I want to say but cannot. Make them believe you. Convince them I am innocent." She smiled at him faintly, intending to convey reassurance she did not feel. He half-smiled at her intending, she imagined, to convey confidence he did not have. Remembering Lowery's instructions—we want the jury to like you, to feel your sincerity—she reminded herself not to scowl, to affect a pleasantness cut from whole cloth. Luella smoothed her skirt over her thighs and sat up straighter in the witness chair.

"Please state your name for the record," Lowery said.

"Luella Margaret Laurent."

"And, where do you reside?"

"Currently?" she asked

"Yes."

"6247 Virgin Timber Road, Givens Knoll, Wisconsin."

Lowery asked a series of factual questions: how long she'd lived at her current residence, her relationship to the defendant, how long they'd been married. He reviewed the trajectory of August's career, established his record of success and her part in it. His voice was firm but gentle, as though trying to impart strength and encouragement. Luella began to relax. She could do this. She must do this.

"Do you have children?"

Luella shifted in her chair.

"Yes, our daughter Beth."

"Did you and your husband want to have a larger family?"

"There was nothing we wanted more."

"Could you tell the court why you didn't have more children?"

Luella believed she'd come to terms with her infertility, had long since convinced herself that one wonderful daughter was enough, but the question posed so publicly sliced open the wound. Her eyes moistened.

"We tried," she said, "but—there were medical problems."

"And how did that affect your husband?" Lowery asked.

"Affect him?"

"That is, how did he cope with the disappointment?"

Luella glanced at August. He stared at his folded hands resting on the table.

"We—he refocused his energies. He became a devoted father. In the beginning years we took in foster kids. He became the best teacher and coach he could be. He started the summer basketball camp. We—August…"

"So, Coach Laurent devoted his life to children. Is that correct?" Lowery cut Luella off, as if to remind her to parcel out her information carefully.

"Yes."

"He also started the Hoops and Hearts Foundation. Is that correct?" Lowery turned toward the jury, cueing her to do the same.

"Yes."

"Please explain how that came about."

"We'd been running the basketball camp for about six summers," she said. "One night there'd been a big storm, almost a tornado, and we spent the day clearing tree branches off the courts. We were exhausted and sitting around the table having coffee. August said, 'We can do more.' I thought he meant we should go back out and clear more branches so I wasn't too thrilled." Luella chuckled and instantly felt foolish.

Lowery looked her in the eye. "Could you please clarify what he meant by doing more?"

"August meant we could do something that would really make a difference in the lives of kids who need the most help."

"So, the foundation was created to help at-risk kids and talented kids whose families didn't have the economic means to send them to camp. Is that correct?"

"Yes, that's right. That's why he started the Hoops and Hearts Foundation, to raise money for those kids. He also got the idea to devote one week of camp each summer to kids who have severely handicapped siblings."

Lowery again half turned toward the jury. "The prosecution claims he used the foundation as a front to select his alleged victims. Can you explain his real motivation to help those particular kids?"

Luella shifted in her chair. "August said some kids get lost in the shuffle, either because they have challenging home lives, live in poverty, or because their handicapped brothers and sisters require so much of the families' time and money. It was out of empathy for them, not some sinister plot."

Pausing, Lowery glanced down at his legal pad and flipped the page. "Does Coach Laurent have any personal experience that would make him aware of the problem?"

Luella's mouth felt as though it had filled with sand. She reached down for the water bottle at her feet, uncapped it, took a large drink, then recapped it and set it back down. "Yes. My brother Franklin had a son, Carter, with DMD. August really loved Carter. He spent a lot of time with him. He even had Carter sit at the end of the bench during basketball games. August was deeply affected by Carter's death."

"Please explain DMD to the jury."

"Duchenne Muscular Dystrophy. It's a terrible degenerative disease that's progressive. It weakens the voluntary muscles. Carter couldn't walk. He ended up in a wheelchair. It weakened his lungs. He died at age eighteen from pneumonia." Luella looked at Franklin who sat stone-still. She knew her testimony must have stirred up unpleasant memories and reminded him that unresolved grief had cost him his first marriage. She regretted exposing his pain so publicly, but the stakes were too high to spare her brother.

"August also has a handicapped sister. Is that correct?"

Luella turned her attention back to the attorney whose facial expression invited her to go on. "Yes. His younger sister, Rosie, is cognitively challenged."

"August became her guardian and caretaker after his mother was institutionalized. Is that correct?"

"Yes."

"How would you characterize your husband's relationship with his sister?"

"August adores Rosie and Rosie adores him." Luella smiled. "He's always been her protector. He's infinitely patient with her."

"So, Mrs. Laurent, you would say the Hoops and Hearts cause is deeply personal?"

"Yes."

She ached to say so much more, to explain August's passion and altruism, but the attorney moved on.

"Mrs. Laurent, you run the summer camp with your husband. Is that correct?"

"Yes. August is responsible for all aspects of the instructional program and I manage the daily operations."

"In your role, do you become familiar with the players?"

"Some I barely get to know and some I get to know quite well. Especially the players that return for multiple years. Certain kids leave a more lasting impression than others."

Lowery quickly checked his notes. He asked Luella about each of the alleged victims. Two of the boys she remembered only vaguely. Three of them she described variously using words like "needy", "troubled", "slight", "immature", and "clingy".

"Mrs. Laurent, the prosecution claims that the alleged victims have been traumatized by their experience at camp. Have any of these boys ever remained in touch with Coach Laurent after they stopped attending camp?"

"Yes."

"In fact, didn't Roddy Miles visit your home?"

"Yes." Luella leaned forward. "August acted like a father to Roddy." Her voice grew louder. "He taught him, coached him, took him under his wing, gave him all the opportunities he's taken full advantage of—scholarships, fame, a sweet life, a…"

Lowery's expression, as he faced her, was a warning. He turned to the jury and said pleasantly, "Under the circumstances, Mrs. Laurent, your emotion is understandable." He turned back toward Luella. "When did you see Mr. Miles after he attended camp?"

Luella reached for her water again, uncapped the bottle, swallowed. "When he was a senior at Loyola, Roddy stopped at our house in Lake Bluff to introduce us to his girlfriend. He sat in our living room for a couple of hours. He was really friendly. I served them cokes and snacks. It was like he wanted August's approval. He even invited us to his wedding."

"Does that sound like the behavior of an abuse victim?" Lowery asked, turning toward the jury.

Adlai Fett was on his feet. "Objection. Your Honor, Mrs. Laurent is not an expert on the characteristics of abused children."

"Sustained."

Lowery's eyebrow arched. "In the twenty-five years you have been running the camp, have you ever seen your husband inappropriately touch a camper?"

"No."

"Has any child ever complained to you that he was being physically or sexually abused?"

"No. Never."

"Thank you, Mrs. Laurent." He smiled at Luella, then looked up at the judge. "Nothing further Your Honor." He strolled to the defense table and placed a reassuring hand on August's shoulder before sitting down.

Luella exhaled. On the record, she had described August's kindness, done her best to reveal the man who had been lost among the lies.

"Mr. Fett, your witness," Judge Richards announced.

Adlai Fett pushed back from the prosecutor's table and rose in slow motion, tugging at the cuffs of his ill-fitting suit jacket as he unfurled to his full five feet ten inches. One deliberate step at a time he approached the witness stand, ran his hand over the top of his shiny head, stroked his goatee, and cleared his throat.

He waited.

And waited.

Any confidence Luella gained under the defense's questioning, dissolved. The room grew hotter, the air thinner.

"Mr. Fett, do you have questions for this witness?" asked the judge.

"Yes, Your Honor."

Fett made laser-like eye contact with Luella. "Mrs. Laurent, just one question. I ask you, why would six boys of different ages who have never met each other, all... decide... to... lie?"

Luella bit her lip. Her eyelids fluttered. Her lungs deflated.

"I...I...I don't know."

Sitting at the small drop-leaf table tucked beneath the kitchen window, Luella picked at the lukewarm chicken casserole on her plate, feeling drained after an arduous afternoon of testifying. She took a sip of wine and glanced up at August, who seemed far away. He scraped his fork around the perimeter of the plate with one hand and drummed on the table with the other.

He'd been stoic on the ride home from the courthouse. She'd expected appreciation, disappointment, anger; anything would have been better than stony silence. Naively, she'd thought testifying would bring relief, that defending her husband, explaining what a good father and exemplary citizen he was, would prove cathartic. Instead, she feared she'd done more harm than good. What could she have said, but hadn't? What had she said, but shouldn't have?

She heard Adlai Fett's deceptively soft voice slithering into her thoughts like a snake through a tight crevice. *Why would six boys of different ages who never met each other all decide to lie?* There had to be an explanation, but logically, this didn't make sense. Any math teacher knew that to find an answer to a problem all the given information had to be accurate; one imprecise fact and it was impossible to arrive at a correct solution. Where was the flaw in this case? On one side of the equation were six alleged victims claiming they'd been abused; on the other side was the man with whom she'd built her life, an honorable man she believed in and loved. The error had to rest with the boys. It had to.

Luella longed to talk about something mundane, anything to keep her mind off of her performance on the witness stand, but the ordinary had gone out of life. Nothing was as it used to be—no ringing telephones, no boisterous campers, no buzzing boat motors, just Rosie's off-key rendition of "Tomorrow" drifting in from the living room, Bird howling along, as she sat in front of the television, eating dinner and watching *Annie*.

Although it was barely past seven o'clock, the late October night was already deep black. Luella stared into the darkness, seeing nothing beyond her reflection in the window. She studied her weary face, its newly carved lines visible in the glass, her reflection a clear reminder that the trial was exacting a heavy toll.

Critically, she eyed the lace valance purchased nearly two decades ago and wondered when it had turned yellow. In all the summers they'd lived at the lake, the lack of a shade on that window had never bothered her. She'd always enjoyed the notion of deer wandering through the woods in the darkness and bedding down in the cool, still nights, but since the incident with the effigies she felt exposed. Before then it hadn't occurred to her that prying eyes might be lurking in the forest, watching. She made a mental note to order blinds.

"The interview was a big mistake," August said.

Luella tensed. Was he saying it would have been better if she hadn't testified?

"I thought if I talked to Pete McCormick—he'd always been an upright guy—and explained, I could make him see that every accusation was a half-truth, a misunderstanding, and people would realize what a farce this whole thing is." August seemed to be talking more to himself than to her.

When she realized that he wasn't referring to her testimony but to the radio interview he'd done recently, she felt relieved.

McCormick, who hosted a sports program on talk radio station WYMX, called and asked August for an interview, convincing him that it was a chance to tell his side of the story, to clear his name. "It's time to play offense," August had said to her. From the outset, Luella thought the interview was ill advised and told him as much. But throughout his career, August finessed the media with the skill of a Ferrari salesman. His charm and loquaciousness made him a reporters' favorite. Besides, he trusted McCormick, who'd often had August on his program. His favorable treatment had made August forget that radio personalities, especially the likes of Pete McCormick, were not predisposed to be allies. August's usually smooth delivery came off disjointed and disingenuous.

"It's water under the bridge," Luella said, trying to contain her frustration.

"McCormick put words in my mouth. I thought he was supposed to at least pretend to be unbiased."

Luella sighed, set her wine glass on the table.

"The questions were loaded," August complained. "It's like asking,

'Have you stopped masturbating every day?' No matter if you answer yes or no, you're screwed." He pressed his temples, as if squeezing hard enough would make the pain seep from his eyes.

A minute into the interview Luella knew it was a mistake.

"Augie, you spend a lot of time with young boys," McCormick prompted. "You must be very attracted to children."

"I really enjoy being around kids," August admitted. "I love their energy and potential. I like working with them, mentoring them."

"Then would you say you're strongly attracted to kids?"

Luella had fantasized shoving the microphone into Pete McCormick's mouth until he choked.

The air went momentarily silent.

"Augie?"

"Look, Pete, the truth is any successful coach has to love kids, believe that he can make a difference in order to dedicate his life to them," August said. "You know my record, Pete. Of course, I enjoy being around kids."

Luella cringed. That wasn't the point. The point was that August was on trial for molesting children. He should have left no doubt that he was not a sexual predator, that he hadn't done the disgusting acts of which he'd been accused. Instead, during the entire interview, he semantically danced around the issue, leaving room for inference when he should have forcefully slammed the door. He should have said, "I never, never touched those boys in a sexual manner. Never. Period." In vain, Luella waited for him to address the issue head-on, to strongly assert his innocence. Instead, he'd used a feather when he should have used a hammer to quash the accusations.

A day later the *Milwaukee Journal Sentinel* reported on the interview in its Sunday edition. The headline, "Laurent Confirms Attraction to Young Boys," appeared in large, boldface type above a photograph of August as he turned unsuspectingly toward the camera. Other newspapers picked up the story at a dizzying rate. Luella discouraged him from reading the article, which was also printed in the *Givens Knoll Weekly*. After he'd read it for the third time, she'd thrown the paper in the recycle bin. He'd fished it out, read it a fourth time, obsessed some more.

In the court of public opinion, it was too late to undo the damage. In the court of law, August could still prevail. That's where they had to focus now. They could not afford to wallow. Losing faith would be as good as tying a stone around their necks and jumping off the boat in the middle of the lake.

"August, listen to me. What's done is done. You have to let this go."

August's eyes glistened.

"Please, for both our sakes."

"You're right, Lulu. As usual, you're right."

Although she'd asked for his compliance, what she actually wanted was for August to resist, as he would have before the arrest and, if he gave in, to do so after engaging in a spirited argument. His docility made her so weary she wanted to collapse on the kitchen floor.

They fell silent again, picking at their food. The furnace kicked in, the rafters groaned, and a blast of hot air escaped from the grate at Luella's feet, slightly lifting the edge of the tablecloth.

Rosie baby-stepped into the kitchen precariously balancing her dinner tray with Bird waggling behind. Luella pushed back from the table and hurried to retrieve it.

"You did a good job eating your vegetables," Luella said.

A broad smile lit Rosie's face.

"Would you like to watch another movie?

"*Shrek!*" Rosie shouted. "I like the donkey. He's really funny."

"I'll find it for you." Luella turned to August. "Be right back."

Luella searched the television app and found the movie. "There you go," she said, tucking the afghan around Rosie, who had settled into her favorite spot on the sofa. Bird stretched out beside her and rested his head on his paws "I'll come and watch with you in a little while."

"Okay," Rosie said, her attention already fixed on the screen.

When she returned to the kitchen Luella asked August if he would like more food, although there was still plenty left on his plate.

"Please just sit down," he said.

Luella warily dropped into her chair.

August cradled her hand in his. "I know you did your best on the stand today. I couldn't survive this nightmare without you." He stroked her fingers.

She fought an emotion she could not name.

He squeezed her hand. "Remember the second summer we opened camp? There was still snow on the courts in May, and we were worried they wouldn't be clear by the time the campers arrived."

She nodded, relieved at the sudden change of topic.

"I was naïve enough to think we could shovel them off," August recalled. "I stood out there with my puny shovel in foot-deep snow. Then my mathematical wife says, 'This eighty-four by fifty-foot court has a surface of 4,200 square feet. And this isn't our only court. Do I really need to calculate how long it will take to shovel the cubic feet of snow off of all of them, or are you ready to be more practical?' I would have ended up in the hospital in traction if you hadn't gotten the idea to call the volunteer fire department to hose them off."

Luella smiled. "And the Greisbachs down the road called the newspaper because they thought the camp was on fire!"

August laughed.

Here was the August of their life before, the man who wore a permanent smile, made everyone around him happy, loved a practical joke. How she missed this man!

He brought her hand to his lips and kissed her palm. His eyes were moist and his expression suddenly serious.

"Lulu, you're the one solid thing in my life. All the rest means nothing." He let go of her hand, spread his fingers and wiggled them slowly, as though sifting grains of sand. "The championships, the awards, the foundation, none of it matters."

"You're mistaken," said Luella. "The young men you coached—you made a difference. The Hoops and Hearts Foundation, the kids you brought to camp—you know how many you helped."

"You were in court today. It all counts for nothing. I'm fucked." August sounded resigned, hopeless.

Luella leaned forward. "August, look at me." Slowly his eyes met hers. "We can't let this beat us. We have to stay strong. Life will be good again. You'll see."

On the last Saturday in October, the day after Luella testified, the late afternoon temperature hovered in the mid-forties. August napped in the living room. Rosie was at Franklin's house, helping his wife, Denise, bake Halloween cookies.

Luella looked out over Whisper Lake. Dressed in a knit stocking cap, wool jacket, and fleece gloves, she sat on the hewn log bench. Bird sat beside her. "Go on," she said. The dog quickly disappeared into the woods.

The lake was quiet, the tourists and summer residents having long since returned home. Blue gray water reflected the partially cloudy sky. The deciduous trees, interspersed among the white pine and spruce, had lost most of their leaves. A flock of Canada geese honked overhead. As Luella squinted skyward, the goose at the point of the V dropped back, relinquishing the lead, causing her to marvel at the flock's cooperation, precision, and instinct.

How she loved this place! It was hard to remember a time when the lake wasn't central to her fondest memories—flaunting her first bikini on Aunt Mavis's and Uncle Walter's dock, meeting August her sophomore year in college, purchasing the camp, teaching Beth to swim. She needed to focus on the good times, to remember all the wonderful life that had been lived here now that it had become as much prison as refuge.

It felt good to focus on the trees, water, and birds rather than on the courtroom, jurors, and testimony. The pure air tingled in her lungs. Sometimes, lately, she felt as though she were scaling a mountain, where the air was too thin, the weight of everything pressing heavily on her chest, making each breath a labor. Sometimes, she thought, it would be easier to give up the struggle, to simply surrender and stop breathing.

She wrapped her arms around her body for warmth and closed her eyes. As concerns about August—his lack of appetite, his fears, his growing depression—crept into her thoughts, she stopped herself. He'd occupied too much of both her waking and sleeping hours. Sometimes her head felt full to bursting. She needed this moment to herself.

Imagining her yoga instructor's voice, a voice she hadn't heard in months—soothing, enticing, hypnotic—she tried to clear her mind. All toxic thoughts—black, tarlike, viscous—drained from her. White, healing light seeped into the unfilled spaces. She sat perfectly still, listening to the sound of the pine boughs overhead swaying gently in the breeze. A cheerful chorus of chickadees, nuthatches, and pine siskins filled the air. The resonant *kak kak kak kak* pecking of a pileated woodpecker intermittently reverberated nearby. She tilted her head back and absorbed the last rays of the sun rapidly descending over the tree line.

From behind came a vague rustling of leaves. Her body tensed. All white light instantly extinguished. Her first thought was that August was coming to disturb her solitude.

"What do you want?" She opened her eyes, turned, and saw that it wasn't August, but Franklin making his way down the path. He was dressed in formal shoes, wool overcoat, and leather gloves. "You certainly don't look ready for a hike."

"I brought Rosie home. I've been searching all over for you."

"I just came down here for a bit of breathing room."

Luella slid to one end of the bench. Franklin sat beside her. He pulled up his coat collar, rubbed his gloved hands together.

The breeze died down; the air hung perfectly still. High overhead a jet contrail silently bisected the sky.

"It's so beautiful here," Luella said.

"You'll get no argument from me." He turned toward her. "Have you considered what you'll do about the camp?"

"What do you mean?" she said, turning to face him.

"With the camp closed this past summer and no revenue coming in to pay upkeep and taxes on the property," Franklin said, "the situation is unsustainable."

"Surely we can hang on until this…this situation passes."

"You have to be realistic. The campers aren't coming back." His voice was firm but not unkind.

"But when August is acquitted, things could turn around. He could get his coaching job back, or find a new one."

"Oh, Lu."

She stood and faced her brother.

Franklin rose, then looked down at his shoes, as if buying time to consider what to say next. He took a deep breath before making eye contact. "We're all sick over this. But I've been sitting in that courtroom every day listening to the testimony, and it doesn't look good. Things are not going well."

"He's innocent!"

"The testimony is…"

"But the defense isn't finished presenting its case yet," said Luella. "The other witnesses for August haven't testified yet."

"The evidence against him is compelling. The testimony has been damning. What those young men have described is…brutal."

"You can't give up on August! You've known him as long as I have. You know who he is."

"I thought I did."

Luella shivered. The air suddenly felt cold, the surroundings inhospitable. She wiped her runny nose with the back of her glove. "Not you, too. I can't bear to have you give up. You just can't.".

"Lu." Franklin's expression was both tender and pained. "I'm sorry the news is not more hopeful." He stepped in close. She stepped back. He moved toward her again and locked his arms around her.

She resisted the urge to push him away. "No. It's not true."

"I'm here for you. You know that. I always have been and I always will be."

The fight drained from her body. She buried her face in his chest. It was as though her boat had capsized, and her brother was the only one substantial enough to cling to.

Franklin spoke softly. "I know this is hard, Lu. I know you love him, but do you honestly believe he's not guilty?"

Chapter Eleven
~Six Plus One~

B eth had been surprisingly insistent when she called to say that she was driving up north and suggested they meet Sunday afternoon in a town forty miles from Givens Knoll. Luella wondered at the urgency and at her own nervousness. She tried to persuade Beth to come to the lake. Beth had refused.

"Not as long as *he's* in the house." She emphasized the "he" as though the word tasted rancid. Finally, Luella relented and agreed to meet in the small town she'd driven through many times on the way to someplace else.

What would she say to her daughter now? Beth, so quick to judge, so slow to forgive.

As she drove through mile after mile of dense forest, the remoteness of the countryside reinforced Luella's isolation. An occasional house set back from the highway appeared, often with an antique, rusted truck embedded in the yard, poking up from the tall grass as though purposefully planted. Raindrops peppering her windshield shrouded the landscape in a veil of gray. She turned on the wipers and tapped her fingers on the steering wheel, matching their rhythm as they swept back and forth as if keeping time to "Pomp and Circumstance." She passed a white, clapboard-sided church tucked among the trees and noticed how full the parking lot was, wondering where all the Lutherans had been hiding in this sparsely populated place.

The rain beat down harder.

She turned on the radio, scanned past a preaching evangelist, two country music and several rock stations, finally landing on the public station and a discussion of medical marijuana. After listening for a few minutes, she pressed the off button. She passed a modest farmhouse with a sagging barn, an old concrete silo, and a small herd of cattle standing in a puddled pasture. A semi sped by, throwing sheets of spray across her windshield, making visibility impossible. She gripped the wheel tightly, slowed to forty-five, feeling not quite in control.

At last, pulling into a parking place in front of the *Java and Scone*, Luella looked for Beth's SUV but didn't see it. Dashing through the rain from her car to the coffee shop, she stepped in ankle-deep water streaming along the gutter. Water seeped into her leather shoes and wicked up her socks.

The *Java and Scone* was a typical small-town coffeehouse—seven tables, a worn sofa tucked in the far corner, a single counter with a cash register, plus an oversized glass display case set perpendicular to the counter, the back wall laid out like a compact apartment kitchen, complete with sink, refrigerator, dishwasher, and stove. It looked as though the furnishings had been salvaged from someone's outdated home remodeling project, giving it the feel of part Grandma's kitchen, part Bohemian living room. The aroma of freshly brewed coffee wafted through the air. The work of local artists hung haphazardly, creating the impression of an art gallery tipped on its axis. In the background, Eva Cassidy sang "Somewhere Over the Rainbow," a version that always touched Luella's soul. Six of the tables were occupied; one by a bearded, middle-aged man whose attention never left his laptop screen; another by a twenty-something woman with her nose buried in a novel; the rest by groups of patrons of various ages, chatting.

Luella approached the counter and scanned the menu posted on the chalkboard hanging behind the counter.

"May I help you?" asked the barista, a fiftyish woman with a Midwestern smile that invited friendship.

"I'll have a medium coffee, black." Luella looked at the woman's face, searching for signs of recognition and disapproval, but there was no evidence in the woman's expression of anything but welcome.

"We're featuring an Ethiopian blend today."

"That's fine."

"I haven't seen you in here before," the woman said, setting the full cup on the counter, her tone encouraging further conversation.

"Just passing through." Luella searched her purse for her wallet. She pulled out her debit card and then decided to pay with cash, not wanting to reveal her name, caution having become a habit. The woman handed her two single bills and some change, which Luella stuffed into the tip jar.

Holding her coffee cup gingerly, she skirted the baby stroller blocking the path to the lone empty table in the corner. She sat down and gazed through the large storefront windows, nervously watching for Beth.

As a child, Beth was a daddy's girl. Competitive. Athletic. She physically favored her father, too—tall, Roman nose, thick hair, blue eyes. Maybe if she could hug her daughter, touch her, look into her eyes, she could help her soften towards him.

Beth, hunched against the cold, jacket dripping, appeared in the doorway. When she looked up, Luella smiled and waved. Beth made her way to the table, removed her jacket and placed it over the back of an unoccupied chair.

Luella rose and embraced her.

"Thank you for meeting me," said Beth, accepting the hug. "Be right back." She stepped away and then threaded her way to the counter.

"Nasty weather," Luella said after Beth returned with an espresso and sat down.

When she got no response, Luella looked down at her hands and fidgeted with her wedding band, thinking that a mother shouldn't feel this uncomfortable talking with her daughter.

Finally, Beth broke the silence. "He's created a mess."

Despite knowing her daughter's no-nonsense nature, Luella wasn't prepared for the bluntness. When she'd mentally rehearsed their meeting, they'd led up to this matter gradually. It was clear that Beth, never one for small talk, was having none of it.

"How can you stand living with him after what he's done?"

Luella looked around the room, trying to see if heads had turned in their direction. No one seemed to pay attention. Still, she lowered her voice almost to a whisper and leaned across the small, round table. "How can you condemn your father so freely after all he's sacrificed for you?"

"How can I condemn him? He's a pedophile! He's done unspeakable harm to those boys and to us!"

Luella jolted backwards, Beth's words landing as hard as a physical blow. "What happened to innocent until proven guilty? What happened to loyalty?"

"Mom, the evidence is overwhelming, and you know it. Thirty-four counts against him. One boy, maybe it's a lie. Two boys who know each other, maybe it's a setup, revenge for some slight. But six boys who don't know each other, who have no known connection, come forward and tell similar stories of being violated over a long period of time? Six, Mom, six!"

It was as though Beth had prepared Attorney Fett's single cross-examination question. Luella was determined to turn this conversation in a more sympathetic direction before Beth's heart permanently hardened.

"If you could see him, Beth, he's really suffering, barely hanging on."

"Do you hear yourself? He, he, he! What about the rest of us? What about those boys? What about all he's put you through? What about *me*?"

Luella reached for Beth's hand, grazing the tops of her fingers. "Beth," she said. "I know it's difficult."

"Difficult? It's unbearable." Beth pulled her hand away. "Do you have any idea what it's been like for me at school, how the other faculty members look at me now, how my students see me, how my players will never view me the same way? I'm Beth Laurent, daughter of Augie Laurent, the pedophile coach." A tear escaped down her cheek, which she quickly brushed away. "Of course, no one has the guts to confront me directly. It's all whispers behind my back. It's all silences and stares."

There was so much Luella could tell her daughter about pain, so much she could share about bottomless grief. "I know," she said, gently, her eyes moistening.

Beth took a sip of her espresso, then focused on her cup.

"I'm so sorry, honey. It's unfair, horribly unfair." Luella sought to make eye contact, but Beth continued to look down. "We're all under terrible stress. It's more important than ever that we stick together."

Beth didn't respond, waiting instead, as though letting her mother's words seep into her like rain soaking into the soil. Finally, she took a deep breath. "I didn't mean to make this all about me. I know this has been terrible for you, too, Mom."

Luella touched her daughter's arm.

"I've been subpoenaed by the defense."

"I didn't know that," said Luella.

"His lawyer wants me to be a character witness, to gush about what a wonderful father Dad is. And it's true. I always felt grateful to have him as my dad. That is, until I found out he's been hiding a very dark side of himself. It makes me doubt that I've ever really known him."

"Oh, honey."

Beth tucked her hair behind her ears and cleared her throat. "This is so hard, Mom." She shifted in her chair. "Do you remember when I was about ten-years-old, I had a friend, Mikey?"

"Mikey?" Luella searched her memory. "Mikey St. James?"

Beth nodded. Her eyes met Luella's. "Remember how he used to come over to our house a lot, and then suddenly he didn't come over anymore?"

"Didn't you have a fight?"

Beth shook her head. "It wasn't really a fight." She gnawed her lower lip, as if working up the courage to continue. "Back then he told me he wouldn't come over because my dad was weird. My best friend said he didn't like the dad I worshiped. When I asked why, he refused to tell me. At the time, I was hurt and angry. I told Mikey he was the weird one, that I didn't want to be friends anymore. That memory has been gnawing at me. Well, I did some research. He wasn't too difficult to locate. Lives in Denver. Doctor Michael St. James, an orthopedic surgeon. I called him."

Luella sat statue still.

"I reminded him what he said about my dad being weird. I asked him what he meant. At first, he said, 'Let the past be the past.' I thought he might hang up on me. But I persisted. I told him it was really important to me. I begged him to tell me the truth."

Luella looked away, focused on the oil painting of the loon on the far wall.

Beth leaned in and lowered her voice. "Dr. St. James told me that Dad fondled him. That's why he never came back."

"That can't be..."

"Dad unzipped his own pants, too. He forced Mikey to stroke Dad's hard penis. He told Mikey it was their secret. If he ever told anyone he'd be in big trouble. Mikey was scared. So, he never told."

Luella's throat closed.

"Mom, how can I testify? I believe Mikey."

Head reeling, Luella staggered toward her car. She stepped off the curb and braced herself against the side of her automobile as she felt her way to the driver's door, barely aware that the rain had turned to icy drizzle. She fumbled in her purse. Her shaking hand found a wallet, makeup case, and hairbrush before locating the fob at the bottom of the bag. She hit the unlock button, opened the driver's door, and slipped behind the steering wheel, then pressed down on the brake and the engine's start button.

A rap on the window startled her.

There stood Beth, raincoat propped over her head like a protective awning. Luella saw Beth's lips move without hearing her words.

A louder rap.

Luella reluctantly opened the window half-way.

"Not now, Beth. I can't—"

"I'm begging you. For both our sakes, wake up!"

"Not now."

"Mom, I don't want to lose you, too," Beth cried.

Luella couldn't remember a time when she hadn't put her daughter's needs first.

"Not now," she said, and closed the window.

Beth continued to plead, but her words drifted into the air, unheard.

Pulse racing, temples throbbing, Luella put the car in gear and pulled away from the curb. A horn blared. She didn't look back.

Standing in the rain, confused and anxious, Beth watched Luella's car disappear down Main Street. The only other time Beth could remember her mother acting so angry and impulsive was back in July, at camp on the dock, when she'd slapped her across the face. Now Beth had that same sickening worry that she'd lost her mother forever.

Tentatively, she stepped along the icy sidewalk to her car, opened the door, and sidled into the driver's seat, her jacket drenched and feet soaked. Shivering, she started the car, turned the temperature dial to seventy-six degrees, and cranked up the fan to full blast, remembering how Gabe used to argue that it didn't pay to turn the fan on until the engine warmed up. "But you're not here," she said aloud, her voice cracking.

She heard Gabe's voice, gentle and reassuring. *Calm down, Bethy. It's going to be okay.* She imagined his arms enfolding her, an image that comforted but also created a longing as strong as the gravitational pull of the Earth. *What did you expect? Gratitude? An instant change of heart?* As Beth thought about it, her expectation that Luella see the truth seemed ridiculously naïve. *Put yourself in her shoes. How would you have reacted if she told you that I molested kids? Be honest, Bethy, it wouldn't have been pretty.*

Gabe had always been willing to see both sides of any issue. At times his even-handedness had been maddening, especially when Beth simply wanted an ally. There's always another point of view, he'd say. She'd argue that she didn't care about being objective; she simply wanted him on her side.

Sleet pelted the windshield. She pressed the weather icon on her phone and found the temperature had dropped to thirty-one degrees. Highway conditions would become dangerous.

Beth turned the dial on the dashboard to Luella's cell phone number and pushed enter. The phone rang. No answer. "I'm unavailable to take your call. Please leave a message." A flash of frustration, then worry.

"Mom, I'm sorry. I know the news was upsetting, but you have to believe me. I didn't mean to hurt you. Please, please call me back."

Beth waited for a few minutes, then sent a text asking Luella to call. Still, no response.

Slowly, she pulled out of her parking spot and headed north to Franklin's house where she'd arranged to stay overnight. As the roads became slipperier, she regretted the choice to meet so far from Givens Knoll. Her gaze darted from one side of the highway to the other in search of a Lincoln Navigator turned upside down or smashed against a utility pole. She pictured her mother's car, the front end smashed, the top flattened, an ambulance siren blasting. If there was an accident, she'd never forgive herself. "Please keep her safe," Beth prayed aloud.

She decelerated, then pressed the phone icon on the dashboard, selecting Gina's number.

"Hi."

"I just left the coffee shop," said Beth.

"You sound a little shaky."

"The roads are icy." It was as though Beth's emotions lay just below the surface of her skin, and the slightest nudge would lay them bare. If she said more, the floodgates would open.

"Don't worry about Wyatt," said Gina. "Anthony's here. They're in the living room playing some dragon fighting game, having the time of their lives."

Beth was tempted to turn the car south; court subpoena be damned. She yearned to hug Wyatt, nuzzle his mop of curly hair, hold onto that one solid part of her life.

"I'll try my best to be back in time to take Wyatt trick-or-treating, but I have no idea when I'll be called to testify," said Beth. "I hate to ask, but can you…"

"Absolutely. I've got his costume here. I'll make sure he gets enough candy to be on a month-long sugar high."

"Thanks, Gina. I couldn't manage without you."

"No worries. Just be safe."

Gina hung up. The deserted highway seemed like the loneliest place on the planet.

Beth's thoughts turned to the witness stand. Although she hadn't spoken to her father since July, she knew what he expected. She was to swear that he was an exemplary father and an honorable man. Thomas Lowery had made that clear when he'd spoken to her on the phone. "Your father is in the battle of his life. His freedom is at stake," he'd said. "He needs you, Beth. Your job is to make him sympathetic to the jury. You're also a camp coach who can swear that you've never seen him abuse anyone." That much was true.

But since talking with Thomas Lowery, she'd had a conversation with Dr. Michael St. James.

The afternoon sky, as gray as worn pavement, hinted at impending nightfall. The road shone like patent leather, a glaze of ice forming on the asphalt. An approaching truck flashed its lights. Luella turned on her headlights and windshield wipers and drove.

Dad fondled him... He forced Mikey to stroke Dad's hard penis.

Beth had tossed a grenade into Luella's life, exploding her fragile certitude.

The weight on her chest felt as though she'd been pinned in a rock-slide. She feared she was having a heart attack. At the first opportunity, she turned into the lot of a closed Chevrolet dealership and parked next to a row of pickup trucks. Pressing her hands over her heart, she applied pressure as she breathed deeply and exhaled slowly, trying to gain control, debating whether to call 911.

She placed a hand over her mouth and fumbled with the door handle. As the car door opened, she bent and threw up onto the wet asphalt. The rancid smell of vomit wafted up from the pavement. A gust of cold, damp air slapped her hair across her face. She closed the car door, pulled a wad of tissues from the box in the console, wiped her lips, and stuffed the tissues into the litter bucket. As her symptoms slowly lessened, she decided she wasn't having a heart attack, although dying of a broken heart seemed possible.

Her cell phone chimed in her purse. Reluctantly, Luella reached for the phone. She set it on the console and ignored Beth's call.

Luella searched for an explanation for Beth's claim. Perhaps Beth needed to manufacture the story of Michael St. James' confession to justify her rage. But Beth was a truth teller. Luella remembered the time that Beth, along with two high school friends, had been suspended for harassing a special needs student. After the punishment had been meted out, Beth admitted to her parents that she was not involved; in fact, she'd volunteered to partner with the girl in the physical education class when no one else would. August wanted to intervene with the principal. Beth insisted that he stay out of the matter, disarming him with her righteousness. "You know what Gandhi said. 'Silence becomes cowardice when occasion demands speaking out the whole truth and acting accordingly.' Dad, I let it happen. I was silent. I should have stood up for her." Beth had the ability to be the source of jaw-clenching frustration and, at the same time, button-popping pride. Even as a little girl, she'd never been one to fib to escape consequences. Sometimes, to her detriment, she seemed incapable of telling even a white lie. Beth might be furious enough with her father to want to hurt him, but she would not lie to do it.

Possibly she'd been deceived by Michael St. James. What did Beth know about the man? Perhaps he'd read about August's arrest in the newspaper and manufactured the story. Being a sweet little boy did not automatically translate into becoming an honest man. But Beth made it clear that she'd had to plead with him to reveal his secret. Michael was a surgeon. It seemed unlikely that his ego was so fragile that he'd invent such a damning story.

There was another possibility. Maybe Michael unwittingly turned an innocent childhood event into a fictional memory that meshed with the other alleged victims. Luella had pored over websites, trying to make sense of the allegations against August, and learned a lot about False Memory Syndrome. It wasn't unheard of for a person to believe himself to be a victim of abuse, which turned out to be objectively untrue. In the 1970's and 1980's, there had been a raft of lawsuits over cases in which recovered memories of sexual abuse and satanic rituals turned out to be false. She desperately wanted Mikey's confession to be a case of False Memory Syndrome.

That was unlikely, too.

Thirty-four counts. Six boys.

Michael St. James made victim number seven.

She thought of the phone call from All-American player, Brett Thibodeau. It was small consolation that she wasn't the only one with blind faith in August. For months, she'd replayed that telephone conversation in her head, hanging on to Brett's words like a rock climber clinging to a hairline crevice. Now, she'd lost even that meager handhold.

A single ping sounded on her cell phone. A text from Beth. *Mom, PLEASE call me. Worried.* She also noticed that she'd missed a call from August. At the sight of his name, she blanched. How was she ever going to face him? How could she go home?

Although the rain had stopped, the windshield wipers continued rasping against the dry glass. There was little traffic on the highway. The few vehicles that did pass by moved slowly. Driving home would be difficult in the worsening road conditions. It occurred to her that careening down an ice-covered road and slamming into a tree at seventy-five miles per hour might not be a bad way to die.

If only she could think straight.

She couldn't sit in the dealership lot all night. Should she find a motel and stay there until—until what? Until clarity magically dawned? Should she drive to Franklin's house and ask to stay overnight? There would be questions asked that she was unprepared to answer. She imagined Denise's disapproving scowl and couldn't bear it. Besides, Beth might be headed there. And what excuse would she give August for not coming home?

If only her head would stop pounding. If only she could catch her breath.

Had it only been two days since she'd testified on August's behalf? A spark of fear traveled the length of Luella's spine. What was her culpability in publicly swearing to the innocence of a guilty man? Was it a matter of humiliating herself, or was she in legal jeopardy? She'd sworn to tell the truth. When she'd taken the witness stand and passionately defended August's virtue, she'd believed in his innocence, still wanted to believe. She wondered, did a lie have to be intentional to be perjury?

How could she take the word of a man who'd reluctantly shared a story with her daughter over the man with whom she shared a life?

Luella reached for her heart necklace, felt reassured by the cool metal on her fingertips. With all her being she wanted to stay loyal to August.

Loyalty wasn't a one-way street. August remained steadfast when her infertility dashed hope of having a large family. He'd remained loyal when cancer took her breast.

The memory of that time was so vivid, Luella could still smell the medicinal odor of the hospital room and feel the chill of the bathroom floor tiles on her feet. She remembered how the trauma of facing her disfigured chest for the first time stopped her cold. She'd looked in the mirror hanging over the sink and seen her heavily lined face in the unflattering light. As she slipped the hospital gown from her shoulders, it fell around her ankles. There she was, exposed in her forty-six-year-old body, one breast whole, the other replaced by a slight mound bisected by a raw, elliptically shaped incision, its suture lines reminding her of a sketch of a tree branch. She might have thought it delicate if not so gruesome. She lifted her arm, tracing its path to her armpit with her index finger without touching the wound. Luella remembered thinking this was her old, new body, both familiar and strange. For a while, she simply stared. A sob gathered in her throat and stuck.

She recalled bending to pick up her gown from the floor and pulling it over her chest. When she straightened, August stood behind her, startling her. She turned toward him.

"I...I...didn't know you were here," she said, her voice timid.

"It's time to go home," he said.

August studied her. She looked at the floor, embarrassed by how unattractive and fragile she felt. He stepped toward her. She stepped back.

"Lulu," he said. "It's all right."

Almost imperceptibly, her head shook back and forth as if to signal that it wasn't all right; it would never be all right. He stepped closer, backing her to the sink. Tears slipped down her cheeks. August gently spread her arms until the gown fell to the floor.

"Don't look at me," she whispered, turning away.

"You're my wife."

Humiliation oozed from her pores. "Please, August. I'm not ready."

"Lulu, it doesn't matter. You'll always be beautiful to me."

She stood silent and still, her arms hanging at her sides, and let him look at the place where her breast used to be.

Now she tenderly ran her hand over the left side of her chest and felt the padding of the mastectomy bra. It occurred to her that if August was sexually drawn to young boys, maybe he preferred a flat chest, maybe the trauma she'd endured, losing that part of herself, was, to him, no loss at all.

Although she had no idea how much time had passed, it seemed as though she'd been sitting in the dealership lot for hours. August would be watching for her. Facing him seemed impossible. One look at her and he would know something was up. How could she hide the seismic shift that had occurred since she'd left home that morning?

And what about the trial? With her testimony completed, she was no longer barred from the courtroom. From now on, August's attorney expected her to sit behind the defense table to demonstrate belief in his innocence. Her absence would be a red flag to the jury, as well as to the reporters, who would sniff out trouble like a pack of bloodhounds. Unless absolutely positive of his guilt, certain beyond any doubt, could she bring herself to let August face that alone? How could she turn off decades of caring because of some second-hand story?

Luella needed firsthand corroboration. She'd call Michael St. James, listen to his story, and decide for herself if his allegation was true. Until she was certain, she would keep quiet, because once she decided August was guilty and confronted him, there would be no turning back.

A county maintenance truck passed by, its rotors flinging a mix of sand and salt on the glistening highway.

Leaning in, Luella examined her face in the sun visor's vanity mirror, scowling at the red puffy eyes that stared back at her. Her blotchy face and neck looked like an archipelago map. She pulled concealer from her purse and applied it to the undereye circles. The pounding in her head lessened. Her breathing slowed. Hopefully, during the drive home, the physical ravages of her crying jag would disappear.

The ravages of her emotional upheaval were another matter. She needed to summon every ounce of strength she possessed, pray she would be able to collect herself enough to face August and pretend, since this morning, nothing had changed.

Chapter Twelve
~Self-preservation~

The over-powering odor of frying bacon greeted Luella when she entered the house. She peeked into the kitchen. The sink was filled with dirty dishes, the countertop littered with broken egg shells. The rangehood fan whirred at full speed. August stood at the stove, his back to her, seemingly unaware of her presence.

On the drive home she'd convinced herself that she could act as though everything was the same between them, but now that August stood there in the flesh, her confidence faded. She considered continuing through the living room and up the stairs, undetected. That would lead to suspicion, to explanations she was unprepared to give. No, better to face him.

She took a single step into the kitchen and waited, her nerves jangling.

August worked at the stove, his gray T-shirt and workout shorts more suited to a gym than a kitchen, his wide stance more suited to a coach than a cook. Tall, broad-shouldered, and muscular, August, who wore his masculinity like other men wore a uniform, looked imposing. The physicality she'd always found alluring now seemed threatening.

Perspiration gathered under her arms. She straightened her shoulders, struggled to breathe.

August reached for the tongs on the counter, his back muscles flexing beneath his shirt, his arms thicker than she remembered, his hands larger. Those arms had held her, and those hands had touched her intimately thousands of times.

August turned, opened the cupboard door, and retrieved two plates. "You're here," he said, glancing over his shoulder. "I was starting to wonder if you'd ever make it home."

There was an edge to his voice that made her want to snap back; how dare you be short with me. Liar! Tell me the truth! But if she opened that floodgate, how could she get through tomorrow? How could she sit behind him in court if the truth was more awful than she could bear?

"The roads were terrible," she replied.

"I'm making bacon and eggs. Rosie's hungry. We couldn't wait." August slid two eggs on to each plate. He turned off the fan. The room grew unnervingly quiet.

Luella hoped he couldn't hear her labored breath or her thumping heart. She stood paralyzed, as though the air around her held an overabundance of gravity, making her limbs heavy, her feet immobile.

"I can put on some extra bacon," he offered, sounding more conciliatory.

"I made a drive-through stop," Luella lied, relieved that August was too preoccupied to make eye contact.

The toaster clicked.

"Could you grab those?" August nodded toward the toaster.

Luella commanded her feet to move. The smell of burnt toast made her queasy. She lifted each of the slices out of the toaster and dropped them on to a plate. Standing over the sink, she scraped the charred surface with a knife, then placed the plate on the counter, never looking at August.

As Luella peered out the kitchen window into the darkness, a ghostlike image of her face, reflected in the glass, stared back at her. The solid person she'd always believed herself to be had morphed into a phantom. August's reflection appeared in the glass behind her. She gasped, or thought she might have. She was sure of nothing. He pressed against her, his body heat searing her skin. His arms encircled her. She stiffened, then willed her muscles to relax.

He bent his head to her ear and confessed, "I'm not angry with you for being late, Lulu. I'm wound tighter than a drum. Honestly,

I'm worried. I don't trust the jury to do the right thing." He turned her toward him, looked into her eyes, and ran his fingers through her hair. "You're the only one I trust. You're my rock. I can't get through tomorrow without you." It was almost as though he read her thoughts, using his body and his voice to push against her doubt. He kissed the top of her head, his lips lingering, his neediness palpable. She knew he craved reassurance, not only that she would be there for him in court tomorrow but that he would be spared the consequences of his actions. It was an extorted gift. She would sit dutifully behind him in the courtroom, display her loyalty in front of the jury, but that was all.

"It's been a long day. I'm going upstairs," she announced, stepping out of his embrace.

"But it's early."

"I'm tired."

"You haven't told me how things went with Beth. Were you able to help her see how unreasonable she's being?"

Luella shook her head.

"No mother's magic?" he said, the edge creeping back into his voice.

"She's angry and hurt."

"*She's* angry? *She's* hurt?" The arteries in his neck pulsed. "Because the arrest embarrassed *her*? Because it's made life difficult for *her*?"

Luella's maternal instincts flared. Beth was a mother, too, who'd chosen her child over her father, protection over loyalty. It shamed Luella to realize that she'd done the opposite. And it appeared as though Beth had been right. It was tempting to fire back at August, to reveal what Beth told her about Michael St. James. She wanted to hurt him the way he'd hurt her and Beth, to make him feel the pain he'd caused. A voice in her head advised caution. Now was not the time for confrontation. There was too much uncertainty, and she was too drained to think clearly.

"I'm going to take a bath and turn in," she said, eager to retreat to the solitude upstairs.

"I don't want to be alone tonight," said August, half pleading, half commanding.

"Rosie is here."

"You know what I mean."

"August, I'm tired. The ride home was exhausting."

Luella didn't wait for a response. She walked into the living room where Rosie sat on the sofa next to Bird, working on a beginner's needlepoint, her mouth pinched and brow wrinkled in concentration.

"I made a mistake," Rosie fretted. "I need help."

Shaking, bone-weary, and in no mood to fuss with a juvenile craft project, Luella was tempted to stride past, ignoring Rosie's plea. Hadn't she endured enough of her family's neediness for one day? Anger and resentment roiled in the eye of a tornado gathering force. If she gave in to that force, no telling where the funnel would touch down. She had to keep control.

"I'm making this for Wyatt cuz he's my great-nephew." Rosie looked up at her expectantly.

Luella studied the needlepoint canvas imprinted with a color-coded teddy bear. It was as though she were seeing a pictorial rendering of innocence, of those who had been swept up in this drama—the boys August had violated, Rosie, Wyatt, Beth. None of them deserved this. None of them asked to have their lives turned upside down. Her rage intersected a deep, deep sorrow. Her heart bled for all of them.

"See, I goofed up the purple bow," complained Rosie, lifting the canvas for Luella to inspect. "And it's my favorite color."

No matter how weary she felt, ignoring Rosie's benign request would only make Luella feel worse. Kneeling down beside her, Luella pulled a row of misaligned stitches from the canvas. "See, it goes this direction."

Rosie nodded, then plunged the purple yarn into the correct square. "Thank you," she said, focused.

"You're welcome, sweetie."

"Dinner's ready," called August.

Rosie set down her needle point and, struggling to keep her feet in her scuffs, shuffled toward the kitchen with Bird following.

Bracing herself on the arm of the sofa, Luella rose from the floor and trudged with heavy limbs up each stair tread to the master bathroom. The scent of August's cologne lingered in the air. Or maybe it was on her skin or in her imagination. He'd worn that same scent since the day they'd met, a fragrance she'd found sexy and alluring. Now it fed her nausea. She took a bottle of antacid medicine from the cabinet, avoiding her haggard image in the mirror, and popped two chalky discs into her mouth.

She drew a hot bath, stripped off her sweater, jeans, and under garments and threw them in the hamper. Slinging one leg and then the other over the side of the claw-foot tub required Herculean effort. She lowered herself into the steaming water, welcoming the initial pain as though it were a purification.

The bedside alarm clock read 8:32 p.m. Luella pulled on her flannel nightgown and climbed into bed, retrieving her journal and a pen from the nightstand, hoping to complete an entry and turn off the lamp before August came upstairs.

She wrote as though she were stepping into the confessional and absolution lay at the end of the page.

Nell, I am lost. I fear I am living with a stranger. I thought I knew him—I'm so angry I can't bring myself to write his name. I don't know what to believe. How is it possible that he forced himself on children? How is it possible that I never knew?

Luella paused, stared at the page, barely recognized her imprecise handwriting, hoping that if she concentrated hard enough the answers might magically appear. Her thoughts fired erratically, sparking in one direction, then another, disorienting her. She'd always loved journaling for its order, word following word, sentence following sentence. Her mathematical mind needed to make two plus two again equal four. Begin with a single word, she told herself. One step at a time. Start and rational thought would follow.

Should I confront him? Tell him I know about Mikey St. James? Get him to admit what he did?

But what if Beth is mistaken?

Luella thought of Beth standing at the car window, pleading, saw her image in the rearview mirror growing smaller and smaller until the distance between them seemed unbridgeable. Was the mother-daughter bond she'd always believed to be absolute, repairable? Would they ever be able to pick up the pieces and return to a place where they trusted one another absolutely?

Beth is slipping farther and farther away. I hoped that meeting her at the coffee shop would be a step toward healing. Instead, it blew us farther apart. I don't want to believe Beth. I'm angry at her for telling me this. I want to believe she's off base. I want to believe Mikey is delusional.

My heart screams LIAR! My head screams TRUTH!

The words on the page blurred as Luella's eyes filled with tears. She set her pen on the journal, pulled a tissue from the box on the nightstand, and dabbed her eyes. She detested this constant weepiness, this fragility that had turned her into the kind of woman she had always found weak. How was it possible that she still had tears to shed? Would the time ever come when they would simply dry up? To stop her hands from shaking, she balled them tightly and pressed them to her chest. Control. She had to get control.

She pictured walking into the courtroom in the morning, pretending she still believed that August possessed the virtues she'd sworn to on the witness stand. As the jurors studied his facial expression and his body language, looking for nuanced clues as to his guilt or innocence, they'd also scrutinize her. Attorney Lowery had warned that optics mattered. Since August was not going to take the witness stand—his lawyer believed that cross-examination by the prosecution was too risky—she'd been cast as the outward manifestation of his morality, a good woman who represented a good man. She felt sullied and used.

She thought of the countless times she'd seen televised press conferences where wives stood stoically behind their famous husbands caught up in sex scandals. The faces of Camille Cosby, Hillary Clinton, and Dotty Sandusky flashed through her mind, a few wives among legions of women who had stood by flawed men. She'd wondered how they could allow themselves to be used as props, knowing full well their husbands had betrayed them. She'd always speculated about their motivation, felt sorry for them. Had any of them considered refusing to stand by their man? Had they considered running away?

She imagined fleeing, leaving August to face the remainder of the trial alone. In her mind it was a flight without a destination, a disappearing act, a magician's trick. She would simply be gone—not to Chicago, New York, or Portland, not to a cabin in the woods or to a deserted island. She would not flee by car, train, or plane. She would be spirited away to another dimension. Think it and be gone. There was no such thing as magic. As a practical matter, she could not figure out where she would go. To Franklin's? To Beth's? Those family entanglements involved their own kind of weight.

Luella retrieved her pen. In a shaky hand, she continued.

I want to confront him. Make him confess. But if he admits to having sex with those boys, I won't have the courage to walk into that courtroom, to face him or the jury or the press. If I disappear, that will be a clear signal that I gave false testimony. It will be evidence beyond a shadow of a doubt that he is guilty.

The defense will rest soon and the jury will begin deliberating. I would never be able to forgive myself if I ran out when he needed me most and I later found out that he was telling the truth.

Luella heard footsteps in the hallway. She quickly closed her journal, turned off the bedside lamp, and slid into a loose fetal position. She wanted to be asleep, or at least pretend to be asleep, before August came to bed. The footsteps drew closer. Her heart beat hard and fast. She waited, feigned sleep. The footsteps continued on past her bedroom door and down the hallway. Rosie.

Relieved, Luella sat up, switched on the lamp, and opened her journal to hastily pen some final thoughts.

When I'm under a public microscope is not the time for confrontation. The vultures are all too eager to circle my carcass and pick at my humiliation. Now I understand why women stand by deceitful men.

Self-preservation.

Luella placed her journal in the nightstand drawer and turned off the lamp. She curled on her side, facing the window, lying awake for nearly an hour before August entered the bedroom, the floorboards creaking beneath his weight. Dresser drawers scraped open and closed. The en suite bathroom door shut with a thud.

While August performed his nightly bedtime ritual, Luella tried to force sleep. She counted backwards from one-hundred by sevens, imagined floating on a billowy cloud. Nothing.

Frustrated, she opened her eyes, squinted into the darkness. The world outside the window loomed moonless and still. A strip of pale-yellow light under the bathroom door and the digital clock provided the only illumination in the room.

As someone who used to abhor anything that dulled her senses, it disturbed her that, since the arrest, she'd become dependent on drugs. But desperation overrode caution. She'd worry about getting off the pills later. She propped herself on her elbow, carefully opened the nightstand drawer, and rummaged for the bottle of sleeping pills, past a stash of pens, her journal, a pile of keepsake greeting cards, bobby pins, and several tubes of lip balm before locating the pills. She sat up, glanced at the bathroom door. Trembling, she twisted the safety cap until it popped off and dropped to the floor, then shook two pills into her hand and downed them with the glass of water kept on the night-stand. She decided to take a third pill. A bitter residue lingered on her tongue. After setting the open bottle on the nightstand, she slipped under the covers.

The toilet flushed. Water poured from the tap. August's electric shaver buzzed. The shower turned on. He would be coming out soon. Luella pulled the covers up to her chin and prayed for oblivion. Like a descending theater curtain, the medication slowly edged downward through her body, beginning at her head and slipping over her shoulders, arms, back, and legs. She became drowsier and drowsier. The noises in the bathroom grew muffled and distant, as though traveling through a long tunnel. Her head sank into the pillow. The down comforter enveloped her like a hug. The mattress shifted beneath her, the sensation, at first, pleasant, as though she were rocking in a boat in the middle of the lake.

"Lulu," August whispered, his voice drifting in dreamlike from the ceiling. His warm body pressed against her back. "Lulu." He touched her shoulder. His voice moved closer. His breath tickled her neck. A cool hand slid under her nightgown and stroked her hip.

"Tired," she muttered.

"This could be our last night together."

Luella's muddled mind fought a tug-of-war between slumber and wakefulness. She longed to remain cocooned, untroubled.

Last night together.

His hand migrated from her hip to her one undamaged breast, his fingers teasing her nipple. Pleasure rippled through her body.

"If the jury fucks up..."

Luella's emotions swirled in circles. Pity—Scorn—Hope—Despair—Love—Hate. Criminal or victim? So complicated, so unclear.

A hand slipped between her legs.

"I need this."

No.

He turned her and pulled her toward him.

"I love you," he said in a honeyed voice, as though he read her doubt, felt it on her goose-bumped skin and in her taut muscles.

Her mind separated from her body. She tried to pull it back, but the sleeping pills had taken over. August kissed her. From somewhere deep within a voice in her head shouted *No!* but her lips didn't move. Her thick tongue filled her mouth. He parted her legs. *No!* The voice echoed. Her arms remained lifeless by her side. As her body pressed further and further into the mattress, surrender. August's hands navigated her body like a blind man who'd memorized his way home.

Chapter Thirteen
~Unholy Sacrifice~

Luella sat in the courtroom one row behind the defense table, the effects of the previous night's sleeping pills—foggy brain, heavy eyelids, weighty limbs—lingering. Was it merely three days since she'd testified? Was it only yesterday she had met Beth, who turned the world on its head? Was it only five months ago that life was perfect?

"All rise," the clerk ordered as Judge Richards entered.

Luella rose, teetered, and grabbed Franklin's arm.

The judge assumed her place on the bench. Everyone sat.

Luella studied August—his resigned expression, deep crow's feet, sagging shoulders. She watched this husband-stranger whom she'd loved most of her life. She thought of the previous night, how she swallowed her anger, avoided him, worried she might implode. The sex act was a drug-fogged memory, more sensation than reality. Yet that morning in the shower she'd nearly scrubbed herself raw washing off his scent.

The media portrayed August as a fiend. Luella admitted how often she'd condemned people she had never met but read or heard about who committed terrible acts—drug traffickers, murderers, thieves. She had not thought of them as individuals with nuanced lives, had not considered their circumstances or the people they loved, the people who loved them, or weighed the good they might have done. Like everyone else, she had failed to recognize their humanity. August's violation of those boys *was* unequivocally depraved, if true. It wasn't the entire story. His positive qualities didn't erase the terrible things he'd done to his victims. Her heart ached for them. However, August could not be reduced to the worst things he had ever done.

It seemed like both a lifetime and a minute had passed since the prosecution began presenting its case and Judge Richards ordered the witnesses from the courtroom. During the days spent in the waiting room Luella was gripped by guilt at leaving August alone. She couldn't recall a single time in their marriage when she failed to stand beside him. Even during chemotherapy after her mastectomy, she attended the NCAA regional final game because August asked her to be there. Today, sitting behind him, a signal to the jury that she still believed in his innocence, she felt deeply ashamed for perpetrating a lie. Yet there she was, the dutiful wife. She resisted the urge to bury her face in her hands like a child to become invisible.

Brett Thibodeau, the All-American guard who had played for Jolliet University twelve years ago and who called the house after August's arrest, took the stand. Luella remembered how she wept from gratitude after Brett's call, how she thought then what courage he had shown, supporting his former coach when so many others abandoned him. Now she was horrified that this honorable young man was about to sacrifice his reputation by testifying on behalf of a child mol—she couldn't bring herself to even think the word—a liar, the same way she had sacrificed her own integrity. When she decided not to confront August and remain silent, she had forgotten to consider the collateral damage suffered by others who would testify. How could she have been so myopic?

STOP! A voice in her head screamed, yet she sat impotent.

"Please tell the jury why you've agreed to testify," said Lowery.

Luella forced herself to look at Brett. Although she saw remnants of the boy, he now had the mien of a successful executive—hair expensively styled, custom-tailored suit fitted to his athletic build, handsome features matured into manhood.

"I owe everything to Coach Laurent," he said, that hint of Kentucky in his voice, his large, earnest brown eyes making contact with the jurors. "Not only did he take a chance on me, offering me a full scholarship when other coaches passed, he was there for me when Dad died my junior year of college. Coach became a second father to me at the lowest point in my life." As he recounted the story he'd shared over the phone, explaining how August had intervened so that his brother Patrick could stay at a private high school despite the family's economic hardship, she thought of the dichotomy of good and evil that August personified.

"How long have you known Coach Laurent?" asked Lowery.

"Fifteen years."

"To your knowledge has he ever sexually abused anyone?"

"Objection." Prosecutor Adlai Fett was on his feet. "It's impossible for the witness to speak as to whether Mr. Laurent has abused other boys."

"Sustained," said Judge Richards.

"Mr. Thibodeaux, Did Coach Laurent ever make advances toward you or do anything sexually inappropriate to you?" asked Lowery.

"No!"

"You explained that your younger brother was sensitive and beholden to Coach Laurent after your dad died. Did Coach Laurent ever take sexual advantage of him?"

"Absolutely not. He helped my brother stay at Saint Ignatius and asked nothing in return."

"Thank you." Lowery walked back to the defense table.

Without looking up from the legal pad he appeared to be studying, Adlai Fett said, "No questions for this witness, Your Honor."

Puzzled, Luella turned to Franklin.

"Nothing there," he whispered.

As Brett left the witness stand and made his way down the center aisle, he appeared confused by the prosecutor's dismissal. Luella resisted the urge to grab his arm and beg forgiveness. When he made eye contact with her, smiling faintly, she could not bring herself to smile back. She hoped her expression conveyed the deep sorrow and shame she felt for allowing him to make an unholy sacrifice he did not yet understand.

Kent McElroy, one of August's oldest friends and coaching colleagues who had worked at Laurent's Basketball Camp since its opening and who was present at August's arrest, took the stand next. He appeared somber and uncomfortable as he lowered his six-foot-eight-inch frame onto the chair in the under-sized witness stand. Luella recalled an image of Kent at camp years ago—Beth was probably six or seven—when he had ridden Beth's bike to the mailbox on the main road to retrieve an expected letter from his fiancée, Annalise. August needled him about being pussy-whipped and told him he looked like a circus bear on that child's bike. Luella half-fell in love with Kent that day for being such an unabashed romantic, willing to look foolish in front of his macho peers, something that, in her experience, didn't happen often among the coaching fraternity.

Kent scanned the back of the courtroom as if searching for someone. Luella turned to follow his gaze and saw Annalise sitting in the last row of the gallery. She had known his wife for almost as long as she'd known Kent and considered her a friend, but it occurred to Luella that she hadn't heard from Annalise since the week of the arrest.

The undersides of Luella's eyelids felt gritty. Hollowness replaced the heaviness of her limbs. Behind her, someone barked with an incessant cough, making it impossible to concentrate as Lowery asked routine questions designed to establish the long-standing association between Kent and August, including Kent's work on behalf of the foundation and at the camp. Luella fumbled in her purse, located the loose stash of ibuprofen in the zippered pocket, grabbed two tablets, popped them in her mouth, and gulped them down with her bottled water.

Franklin looked at her quizzically.

Luella touched her temple. "Headache," she mouthed and turned her attention to Lowery's examination.

"In the twenty-plus summers you worked at Laurent's Basketball Camp did you ever observe any inappropriate sexual contact between Coach Laurent and any of the boys attending the camp?"

"Never."

"Did any of the boys ever indicate to you that Coach Laurent mistreated them?"

Kent chuckled nervously. "If they complained, it was to grouse about how hard Coach worked them." Lowery remained all business. Kent took his cue. "But no, absolutely not," he insisted. "None of the kids ever said he sexually abused them. The kids respected him. They revered him."

Franklin shifted in his seat. "Mistake," he muttered.

"That's all, Your Honor," said Lowery.

Adlai Fett rose from the prosecutor's table in his deliberate fashion and sauntered toward the witness stand. Luella at first avoided looking in his direction, the humiliation suffered at his hands still raw. But like a spectator at a five-alarm fire, she couldn't resist for long. She watched as he tugged at his suit jacket cuffs, ran a hand over his bald head, stroked his goatee, and cleared his throat, just as he'd done before cross-examining her, his obsessive behavior reminiscent of Brett Thibodeaux's ritual before shooting free throws—the sign of the cross, four bounces of the ball, then the shot.

"So, Mr. McElroy, do you think it's possible that these kids who revered a famous coach, an adult whom they admired and looked up to, someone who held the key to their athletic futures, might be very reluctant to report the abuse to you, someone who was clearly his colleague and friend?"

Kent glanced over at the defense table. Luella, who had been on the receiving end of one of Adlai Fett's catch-22 questions, winced.

"Mr. McElroy, I'll repeat the question. Is it possible these hero-worshiping kids would be very reluctant to report abuse by someone they revered to someone who was clearly his ally?"

"I—I guess it's possible."

"I understand there were nightly bed-checks conducted at the camp. Is that correct?"

"That's correct."

"Did you conduct those bed checks?"

"Occasionally."

"How often?"

"I don't know."

"Half the time? A quarter of the time? Less?"

"Less."

"Would you say rarely?"

"Yes."

The questions came at the speed of an automatic weapon's assault.

"In fact, wasn't it common practice for Mr. Laurent to conduct nightly bed-checks by himself?"

Kent hesitated, his expression that of a man who hadn't seen the hazard staring him in the face, but now saw danger everywhere. "There was a perfectly good reason for that. It was a favor to the rest of us, so the staff could prepare for the next day's activities."

"I'll take that as a yes." Fett turned toward the jury. "So, Mr. Laurent could have had sexual contact with any number of campers and you would have had no idea what went on in those cabins."

"He wouldn't do that. He's not that kind of—"

"No further questions," Fett interrupted and returned to the defense table.

As Kent stepped from the witness stand and made his way to the back of the courtroom, he avoided making eye contact. Luella recognized his expression. It was the look she'd seen on every coach's face after a loss, the look of a competitor who knows he's been bested.

"Call your next witness, counselor," ordered Judge Richards.

"The defense calls Beth Laurent."

The subpoena had come as a surprise to Beth. Her last encounter with August ended in anger, accusation, and rejection. Why risk calling her as a witness for the defense? Deep down she knew the answer. Her father understood her well. She loved him and would never intentionally hurt him.

From the back of the courtroom, she made her way down the center aisle, the stone in the pit of her stomach growing heavier with each step. She glanced at Franklin, then at Luella, whose expression was a plea. Beth wanted to reassure her mother; despite how poorly their meeting ended yesterday, she was a loyal daughter.

Beth hated drama. Now, it seemed her life was nothing but. How had everything become such a mess? How had hers become one of those dysfunctional families she used to scorn? Once she lived a charmed life. However, she learned that good fortune was fickle, landing on you one day, disappearing without warning the next.

Television crime shows had not prepared her for the emotional power of the courtroom. Everything about it was intimidating; the judge presiding from the elevated bench; the jurors focused, unsmiling and intent; the room, formal, locked in another era. She tried to calm herself, breathe deeply, but the musty air seemed to grow thicker, as though guilt had an odor and a weight. She lowered herself into the witness chair, her heart beating so fast she feared it would rupture. She imagined everyone staring, their judgment tunneling under her skin like some invisible parasite. Silently, she repeated the mantra playing in her head since early morning—*just tell the truth, just tell the truth.*

She avoided looking at her father. He'd always had the power to level her with a scowl. Even as a child, when teaching her to dribble a basketball, step into a lay-up, or shoot a free throw, he could make her work harder and longer by simply flashing a look that communicated more than any lengthy sermon. If she made eye contact with him now, she would crumble.

After she was sworn in, Lowery stepped from behind the defense table and approached slowly. He smiled and spoke to her like a long-lost friend, although Beth's only contact with him had been a couple of phone conversations. When he asked her to come to his office to prepare, she had refused, hoping he would conclude her testimony would be worthless.

"May I call you Beth?" he asked, his honeyed voice and forced familiarity making her spine stiffen.

She nodded.

Judge Richards interrupted. "Ms. Laurent, please respond verbally so the court reporter can record your answer,"

"Sorry. Um—yes."

"Beth, as you were growing up, how would you characterize your relationship with your father?" asked Lowery.

"We were very close."

"Please explain what you mean by close."

"Because of his job, my dad was gone a lot, but he always made time for me. He was very involved in my life." Beth thought of the many times he had taken her to watch practice and how afterwards they would play shoot-around and h-o-r-s-e in the empty gym. Even as a little girl, her father had talked strategy and reviewed game films with her. He had made her believe she was the center of his universe.

"So, you would say he was a good father?"

"Exceptional. Dad spent hours teaching me. He came to my games whenever he could. Sure, he was demanding. He had high expectations. All good coaches do. But he was also patient and encouraging."

Lowery sauntered toward the jury box, then half-turned toward Beth. "You're a successful coach. At this early stage of your career, you've already won a state championship. Is that correct?"

"Yes."

"Is it fair to say your father was instrumental to your success?"

"Yes. My dad was my role model. He taught me everything I know about basketball. I wanted to be exactly like him."

Lowery paused, letting Beth's words wash over the jury, allowing them to conclude that such an admirable father could not possibly molest children.

"Was your dad a strict disciplinarian?"

"Like I said, my dad set high standards," said Beth. "He expected me to try my best, to use my talents, but he wasn't unreasonable."

"Did he spank you?"

Beth found the question peculiar. She waited several seconds before answering, "No. Never. He didn't believe in physical punishment."

"So, he never hit you. Did he ever touch you in an inappropriate, sexual manner?"

"No! Absolutely not."

Lowery stepped toward her, a satisfied expression lighting his face. "You spent a lot of time over many years with your dad at the camp. When you were a child, you hung around so much the other coaches used to call you 'Little Shadow.' Then, when you became a successful coach, you were hired as his assistant. Is that correct?"

"Yes."

"In all those years, from the time you were a child shadowing him to your employment as a coach, did you ever see your dad inappropriately touch any of the campers?"

Beth had asked herself that question a thousand times. What had she seen? She thought of the way her father would take players by their shoulders and elbows or wrap his hands around their waists and move them into the correct position on the court when they failed to understand his instructions. There never seemed to be anything unusual about that. Many coaches physically handled players. She did it herself. He gave kids encouraging pats on the back and celebratory high fives. At camp, when the day's instruction was over and recreation time began, there would be chicken-fight games in the lake. The combatants tried to knock their opponents off each other's shoulders into the water. She had seen boys sitting atop her father's shoulders countless times, him looking as exuberant as the kids. It had never occurred to her that he might have thrilled to these seemingly innocent contacts, enjoying the touch of young wet bodies and the sensation of young crotches rubbing against his neck. The thought sickened her. Maybe those touches were as innocent as they appeared, but her conversation with Michael St. James made her question everything she thought she knew about her father.

Just tell the truth.

"No. I never saw him inappropriately touch a camper."

Lowery leaned in. "Did your dad ever do anything that caused you to believe he harmed any of the campers in any way?"

Beth paused, glanced at her mother, whose eyes warned her to be careful. She reminded herself that Mikey had been her little playmate, not a camper. *Answer the question as asked. Just tell the truth.* "Dad might verbally dress down a player who didn't listen, but he also seemed to be able to read personalities, to intuitively know when someone needed to be handled more—sensitively. So no, I never saw him intentionally cause harm."

"Thank you, Beth."

Beth was filled with a mix of relief and regret; relief that she'd done no apparent harm; regret that she might be helping to acquit a pedophile. She had the urge to ask, did I do okay, Dad? Did I live up to your expectations? Even now she hoped that she had not disappointed him.

Adlai Fett's chair scraped the floor as he pushed back from the prosecutor's table. Beth watched him approach. If circumstances had been different, she might have felt sorry for the man. She guessed him to be somewhere in his mid-fifties, the stereotypic country lawyer, a guy who had gone to a no-name law school, returned home, and never left. She knew better than to trust him or to let down her guard. Looks could be deceiving. She heard her father's warning; never underestimate an opponent.

Fett's expression was almost apologetic, reminiscent of a farmer who had grown fond of an animal he had raised but was about to slaughter. He stroked his goatee as if considering his first move. "I'll ask you the same question I posed to your mother. Why would six boys of different ages, who never met each other, all decide to lie?"

Beth froze.

Fett stared at her. "Ms. Laurent?"

Her throat squeezed to the diameter of a pinhole. *Just tell the truth.* Her tongue lay useless in her mouth.

He took several steps forward, his expression intense. "Let me re-phrase that. Do you believe those six boys lied?"

Lowery sprang to his feet. "Objection, Your Honor. Counsel knows full well that a witness cannot comment on the veracity of another witness."

"Objection sustained."

Fett's stare drilled into Beth. He took another step closer. She gripped the sides of the witness chair, bore down, her knucks turning white. She closed her eyes and shook her head from side-to-side. Her chest heaved. *Do you believe those six boys lied?* She clamped her quivering lips together.

"Ms. Laurent?" Beth heard Judge Richard's voice. "Do you need a moment?"

Beth opened her eyes, sole a glance at her father.

"That's okay, Your Honor," said Fett, turning away. "I have no further questions for this witness."

Chapter Fourteen
~Collateral Damage~

After testifying Beth fled from the courtroom. During the four-hour drive to Gina's apartment, it was impossible to erase the thought that she had failed the biggest test of her life. She'd frozen when the prosecutor asked if she believed the six boys had lied. Although she hadn't been required to respond, the answer was written on her face.

She couldn't imagine any circumstance under which her father would forgive her for today's betrayal, and she doubted her mother would be able to forgive her, either.

It was dusk by the time she turned off the highway and onto the main artery through the town where Gina lived. As she traveled along the road lined with strip malls and commercial buildings, blue and red emergency lights flashed up ahead. Beth checked her speedometer, then moved to the inside lane to give the police vehicle wide berth. At the four-way stop, she turned left onto MacArthur Avenue. The streetlights glowed faintly in the waning light. Trick-or-treaters flooded the sidewalks and crisscrossed the street in packs. Beth slowed down to navigate through the children costumed as witches, ghosts, and cartoon characters.

Wyatt had insisted on dressing up as a football coach "like my dad-dy." It wasn't a traditional Halloween costume or much of a disguise, but Beth didn't have the heart to dissuade him. As they'd gathered his costume, she had pulled Gabe's coach's cap and whistle from the hook in her bedroom closet and handed them to Wyatt. Often, she told herself that it was time to discard Gabe's things, but she'd been unable to, as if removing them would permanently eliminate him from their lives. "These were Daddy's," she'd said. Wyatt had run his fingers over the cap and whistle as if they were sacred relics.

When she arrived at Gina's—a graceful Victorian divided into upper and lower apartments—Beth parked on the street. A glowing porch light signaled that trick-or-treaters were welcome. She rang the doorbell. Gina answered holding a large plastic cauldron filled with candy and wearing a witch's hat, gray wig, and long black robe. A gnarly wart stuck to the tip of her nose and heavy, black makeup rimmed her eyes.

"You look like you could use some chocolate." Gina stepped aside to let Beth enter.

"It's going to take more than sugar to erase today," said Beth, rubbing her chilled hands together.

"You must have had a helluva day." Gina hugged Beth, then held her at arm's length. "There's an open bottle of red on the counter. I'll join you when I'm done playing witch."

Beth took several steps toward the kitchen. The apartment seemed unnaturally quiet. "Where's Wyatt?" she asked, a seed of panic burrowing into her chest.

"It was getting late and Wyatt was so excited he didn't want to wait any longer, so Anthony took him out trick-or-treating," said Gina.

"I thought *you* were going to take Wyatt trick-or-treating."

Gina shrugged. "I drew the short straw. Anthony wasn't too keen on answering the door a hundred times."

As if on cue, the doorbell rang. A group of costumed children stood on the porch.

"Oh, what a scary ghost! And a beautiful princess! And a fierce Power Ranger! And, oh my goodness, you're a pumpkin!" Gina's actress skills were on full display as she urged the children to plunge their hands into the cauldron and grab a mittful of candy bars.

Beth paced. She loved Anthony, recognized how wonderful he was with Wyatt, but…but what?

He was a man.

The thought that it mattered horrified her. Anthony had never done anything to warrant suspicion. But then neither had her father. She hated

August for blowing trust to smithereens. She knew she was being irrational. It didn't matter. She wondered if she would ever completely trust any man again. If Gabe were alive, would she even be suspicious of him?

How did a boy grow up to be a man who preyed on children? Was deviance genetic? How could she ensure that her son wouldn't grow up to be a predator? He had lost his father. Who would be a trusted, worthy role model? Who would keep him safe?

Her thoughts somersaulted downhill, gathering speed with each tumble. Her mind grappled for a handbrake. If she could just see Wyatt, hold him.

"I need some air," said Beth.

"But you haven't told me about your testimony."

"Later."

Gina looked skeptical. "It's cold out there, and you're still wearing a dress."

"I'll be fine."

"Here." Gina reached into the entry closet. "At least wear my long coat. And take this flashlight. It's getting dark."

Beth walked briskly through the neighborhood searching for Wyatt and Anthony. She had no idea which direction they'd gone, but figured Anthony wouldn't venture too far with a five-year-old. As she passed by parents herding groups of children, some holding on to toddlers' hands, it occurred to her that she might be the one who looked suspicious without a costume or a child in tow. And that was the problem in a nutshell. Danger rarely wore a devil's costume.

After walking several blocks without spotting Wyatt and Anthony, she turned down a side street, walked another block, and headed back in the direction of Gina's apartment. Her cheeks felt cold and damp. Her nose dripped. Goose bumps crawled up her legs. She stumbled on a crack in the sidewalk. "Shit!" She fished the mini-flashlight from her coat pocket. As her hand shook, the beam of light jumped erratically along the sidewalk.

By the time Beth reached Gina's porch, she was gasping for breath. She rang the doorbell. The door flew open.

"Mommy!" Wyatt wrapped his arms around her waist. With Gabe's over-sized cap on his head and whistle around his neck, he looked like a mini-version of his father. "I got lots and lots of candy! Kit-Kats are my favorite. Uncle Anthony says I can only eat two though 'cuz he doesn't want me to get a tummy ache."

Beth scooped Wyatt into her arms, hugged him fiercely. Gina and Anthony stared at her. She reluctantly set Wyatt down.

"Come on, snuggle bug," said Gina, reaching for Wyatt's hand. "Mommy's had a long day. Let's get you out of your costume and into your pj's."

"Are we having another sleepover?"

"Yup. Executive decision," said Gina.

After Gina whisked Wyatt down the hall, Anthony said, "What's happening, Beth?"

"I can't breathe. I can't think. The walls are closing in."

"Sounds like a panic attack." Anthony held her shoulders and turned her toward him. "Beth, look at me. Listen to me. You're going to be okay. I'm here with you."

She met his chestnut eyes, desperate to grasp the lifeline he offered.

"Take off your coat. Come and sit down."

She unbuttoned her borrowed coat and handed it to him, then lowered herself onto the entryway bench.

"I'm going to count out loud. I want you to breathe deeply in and out as I count. Okay?"

Beth nodded.

"One—two—three—four…" In. Out. In. Out. "One—two—three—four…" Anthony's steady voice soothed like warm milk and honey. Gradually her breathing steadied. Her heartbeat slowed. The panic subsided. Beth buried her face in her hands. "I'm sorry. I'm so, so sorry."

"You have nothing to be sorry about."

"On the witness stand I—I froze."

Anthony sat beside her on the bench and held her hand.

"I lost my family today," Beth whimpered.

"You have a wonderful little boy. And you have Gina and me. And let me remind you, we're your family."

"But when I found out that you were alone with Wyatt, I had these insane, evil thoughts," Beth confessed. "I can't even trust the people who mean the world to me."

"It's okay," he said. "It's all going to be okay."

She turned to look at him. "I wish with all my heart I could believe that."

Luella's botched testimony, Beth's revelation about Mikey, her tense relationship with August, plus the day spent sitting in court watching Beth struggle on the witness stand, added together wiped her out.

So that she could privately contact Michael St. James, Luella told August that she was going to the grocery store because they were out of several essentials, which was only partially true. Before entering the store, she dialed the number of Mountain Pass Orthopedic Clinic for the third time, the first two calls having been made from a courthouse bathroom stall. Again, she left a message with the receptionist. "This is Luella Laurent. No. I'm not a patient of his, but this is urgent. Please ask him to return my call."

"I'm sorry. The doctor is very busy. Yes. I'll relay your message," the receptionist replied curtly each time.

She wouldn't blame Dr. St. James if he didn't return her call. How could a relative stranger be expected to get involved in this mess? If he ignored her, she could tell herself that whatever happened all those years ago between August and Mikey was a misunderstanding, a misinterpreted touch that didn't rise to the level of abuse. She could tell herself that Beth was wrong.

Luella moved through the store quickly, checking each aisle to make sure she was alone, picking items off the shelf without noting labels or prices. At the check-out counter the teenage clerk filled two bags without comment.

At 7:05 p.m., as she drove in sparse traffic along the rural highway, chatter on public radio about the decline of the honey bee droned on. Preoccupied with thoughts of Beth's testimony, she paid little attention to the chatter. Beth had looked like a cornered animal on the stand, wide-eyed, nervous, ensnared in the same trap the prosecution had set for her.

The phone rang. She glanced at the caller I.D. on the dashboard screen. *Mtn. Pass Ortho. Clinic. 303-555-8765.*

Luella's hand hovered over the decline button. The phone continued ringing. She thought of Beth standing at the curb outside the Java and Scone, pleading, "I'm begging you. For both our sakes, wake up!"

She turned off the radio, pressed accept.

"Hello."

"Mrs. Laurent?"

"Yes."

"This is Doctor St. James." His deep voice caught her off guard. She still thought of him as ten-year-old Mikey, Beth's timid playmate.

"Thank you for returning my call."

"I've already spoken with your daughter." Again, that bass voice, formal, intimidating. Where was that sweet, young boy of memory, the one with the wide, sincere eyes, the plump cheeks, the shy giggle?

"I'm sorry to bother you, I know you must be very busy," said Luella.

Silence.

She was tempted to hang up, but she had come too far. She hoped that Michael would say, "Nothing happened. Coach Laurent was always good to me, always appropriate. Whatever Beth told you was a product of her overactive imagination." The roiling sensation in her stomach told her otherwise.

To validate the multiple counts against August, Luella needed to hear that his predatory behavior extended beyond the accusations of opportunistic basketball players. If Michael uttered three simple words, "he fondled me," any illusion that this was a conspiracy would crumble.

"I know you talked with Beth, but it's important that I hear what happened directly from you." Luella struggled to keep the tremor from her voice.

Again, silence.

"I know this is difficult."

"It was a long time ago."

"Please."

Luella turned the car onto an abandoned gravel driveway. Her headlights illuminated a thick stand of evergreens. A low hanging pine bow scraped the hood. The left front tire settled into a rut, canting the car at an awkward angle. She put the car in park, leaned back against the headrest, and gripped the steering wheel.

"I was a shy kid. I didn't have many friends. Beth was kind to me, played with me at school and often invited me to your house."

"I remember how much you loved Magic."

"Magic?"

"Our Labrador retriever."

"Right. Magic Johnson." His voice softened. "My brother was allergic to dogs. My mother didn't allow us to have pets."

"Michael, what happened between you and my husband?"

"Mrs. Laurent, I don't think…"

"I need to know."

She heard him inhale.

"My father left shortly after I was born. I envied Beth because she had such a cool dad. I looked up to him. I used to pretend he was my dad, too. He'd toss a basketball around and give me piggyback rides. He made me feel important. At first, I welcomed the contact, a hug, a shoulder rub. Then one day I used your basement bathroom."

Luella swallowed hard.

"Beth must have been outside. He came in and sat down on the edge of the tub. I remember thinking that he shouldn't be in there with me, but it was his house. I thought that maybe dads shared the bathroom with their sons. I didn't know."

"What happened?"

"You want the ugly details?"

"I want the truth."

There was a long pause. For a moment, Luella wondered if the called dropped.

"He asked to feel my bicep. He flattered me, told me how big and strong I was getting. I was so proud." Michael laughed bitterly. "Then he ran his hands down my back. My fly was still unzipped. He touched my crotch. I froze. I didn't tell him to take his hand away. I didn't tell him to stop."

"Oh, Michael!"

"He pulled my pants around my knees and slid his hand down my underwear and—and he fondled me. He unzipped his fly and forced my hand around his hard penis. He wrapped his hand over mine and made me rub faster and faster."

Luella's eyes welled.

"The bastard ejaculated into my fucking hand."

A tear trickled down Luella's cheek.

"It feels good," he said. "It's natural, son. Guys do this all the time." She heard the pain in this grown man's voice. Guilt gripped her.

"Did you tell your mother?"

"He said it was something special just between us. It was our secret. He said my mother wouldn't understand, that women never understood this kind of thing. It was something private that men and boys did. If I wanted to be a man instead of a weak little tattletale, I'd keep this to myself."

"Did you tell anyone?"

"Who would have believed me? *You*? From what I've read in the papers, Mrs. Laurent, you still believe your husband is innocent. What are there, *six* accusers? Back then would you have believed *one* ten-year-old boy?"

Luella's cheeks burned. Shame overwhelmed her. She imagined Mikey, trusting, unguarded, cornered, his pants crumpled around his knees, August hulking over him, cajoling, his strong hand sliding down the front of Mikey's underwear.

"I'm sorry. I'm sorry. I'm sorry," she repeated again and again, until she realized that she was speaking into a disconnected line.

Chapter Fifteen

~One More Night~

The house was shrouded in dread. Dread lurked in the corners, papered the walls. To Luella, the place seemed darker, colder, smaller, all sense of sanctuary abandoned.

An hour after Rosie went to bed, Luella, pretending to read a book, her nerves as taut as piano wire, sat silently in the living room across from August. The call from Michael St. James earlier in the evening destroyed her belief in August's innocence, but she did not confront him. Things would get ugly and become unbearable if she revealed that she knew the truth. She was drained. She could not cope with a scene tonight. Better to wait, she told herself. After Beth's testimony the defense had rested. The lawyers would present their summations tomorrow and then deliberation would begin. If the jury quickly reached a verdict, this would be their last night together. She had to hang on for one more night.

One. More. Night.

Out of the corner of her eye, she anxiously watched August. He held the framed photograph of Beth at seven years old—cradling a basketball, grinning, her front teeth missing. He stared at it for several minutes. His right foot tapped double time. His carotid artery protruded from his neck, pulsing furiously. The tell. She had seen it countless times, mostly in the heat of competition.

She waited. Bird's nose nudged her hand. Absently, she stroked his soft ears. Michael's bitter voice echoed in her head. *The bastard ejaculated into my fucking hand.* An image of August, his lust evident, forcing Mikey to pleasure him, insinuated itself into her thoughts. In five years, Wyatt would be the age Mikey was when August assaulted him.

She shuddered. She had to get control or her simmering rage would boil over. If she was to survive until the end of the trial, she needed to push the image out of her mind.

What a dupe. From the beginning she'd been an auxiliary to this man whose career and star power had defined her. His goals became her goals. They lived where they lived and ran a summer camp because of him. Their friends—now former friends—came from his coaching circle. Even her job at St. Eligius required that she be allowed to accompany August when he needed her. His success was her success. His guilt. Her guilt. For one more night she had to pretend to be Coach Augie Laurent's loyal wife. She needed to get through this, to buy time to decide what to do next.

She had never thought of August as a complex man, rather as someone whose surface mirrored his internal life, an extrovert who preferred thoughts and emotions to be on full display. He had co-authored a book about his life, their life, about his coaching philosophy, fatherhood, the Hoops and Hearts Foundation. He was a man who sought exposure, who thrived in sunlight, while she preferred shade.

The arrest changed everything. Secrets changed everything. There was a darkness to August, a perversion, which had been invisible to her. Had it been there all along and she'd simply refused to see it?

On their ride home from the courthouse, August hadn't said a word about Beth's testimony. As Rosie sat in the backseat chattering about pumpkin carving and a Halloween party, he'd stared out the window as if memorizing every crack and pothole in the road. His silence, although unnerving, didn't surprise Luella. August always protected his sister from unpleasantness. Perhaps it was his tenderness with Rosie that made her believe he was incapable of such callousness toward those boys.

Luella resisted the urge to leave the room. She stared at the unread page, contemplating her next move. Comforting him used to come naturally. Now it was as though she had a kind of sensory amnesia. Before the Dr. St. James revelation, Luella would have soothed him, reassured him, promised to stand by him regardless of the outcome. Now, the man she had loved, the one who deserved her loyalty and compassion, no longer existed. The man sitting across from her deserved to be punished.

"I've lost her," said August, his voice melancholy. He set Beth's photograph face down on the side table. His foot stopped tapping. The artery in his neck no longer throbbed.

Warily, Luella closed her book. His behavior baffled her. She'd expected anger, an explosion. The signs were all there. The tell. His eyes glistened in the lamplight. He'd always despised weakness. Revealing vulnerability must have cost him dearly. They sat in silence for a while, the lone sounds in the room a surging furnace and a branch brushing against the porch roof.

"Remember when Beth was little and people asked her what she wanted to be when she grew up, and she'd say 'I want to be Daddy,'" said August. "Those were the best of times. We've had a good life."

Had, thought Luella. *You destroyed it.*

"I love you, Lulu. Nothing will ever change that."

This was her cue. She remembered. She was supposed to say "I love you" back. She was supposed to go to him, put her arms around his neck, stroke his hair, the way she always had whenever he needed to be soothed. The words didn't come. She didn't move.

"I can't go to prison." August buried his face in his hands.

She saw his pain but could not help him. She could not bear to touch him. "It's been a long day," said Luella, trying to keep the anger from her voice. "I'll let Bird out."

"Wait. Remember you promised me you'll take care of Rosie," said August. "I want you to promise me again."

The gravity of her promise hung around Luella's neck like a yoke. Rosie would grow older but would always need care. Losing her brother would be an enormous blow.

"I need to know she'll be okay."

"I told you, I promise."

The clock on the fireplace mantel chimed eleven bells. Luella headed toward the back porch. "Bird, come," she called. The dog's ears perked up. Slowly, he uncurled, stood, and languidly stretched one hind leg, then the other, before trotting across the living room to follow Luella, his claws clicking on the hardwood floor.

When she returned with Bird, August was sitting in the chair next to the fireplace. "I'm not quite ready to turn in yet. You go ahead. I'll be up a little later," he said, calmly.

Luella stroked the soft fur of Bird's head, relishing the comfort of it. The dog circled twice before settling into his bed.

By the time she got into bed, exhaustion took over. Grateful to be alone, she snuggled under the blankets, tucked an extra pillow along her side, and fell into a fitful sleep.

At first, when Luella heard whimpering, she thought she was dreaming. The whimpering persisted. Gradually, her eyes opened. Bird sat on the floor next to the bed, whining. She checked the alarm clock on the bedside table—2:23. The other side of the bed was empty. She was tempted to turn over, but Bird continued to whine.

Something wasn't right. A knot twisted in her stomach. A needle of fear stabbed at her chest. Sliding her legs over the side of the bed, Luella stood, taking a minute to get her bearings. "What's the matter, boy?" she said, pulling her robe from the hook on the back of the door and heading downstairs.

Dread.

In no mood to relive the earlier drama of the night, she hoped to find August asleep on the couch, rather than sitting awake, brooding. The dim light of a single table lamp glowed in the living room. August slumped in the chair next to the fireplace, chin touching his chest, body listing to the left, and arms dangling at his sides.

Luella stepped lightly. "August, August, wake up."

No response.

She touched his shoulder. Shook him.

Then she saw the open pill bottle on the floor.

"Oh God! What have you done?"

She grabbed his hand, pressed her fingertips along the inside of his wrist, and checked for a pulse. A slow, weak beat fluttered against her fingers. She ran to the phone and dialed 911.

"Hurry! Please hurry!"

"The ambulance is on its way, Ma'am. Stay calm. I'm here." The dispatcher's voice was steady, reassuring.

"What should I do?" asked Luella.

"Talk to him. Try to make him stay with you. Administer CPR if his breathing stops or becomes so shallow that you're not sure he's breathing."

Luella knelt next to August. She grasped both of his shoulders. "August. Do you hear me?"

His eyes fluttered, half opened, then closed again. His lips moved. Luella leaned her ear close to his mouth. He mumbled incoherently. Luella trembled. She remembered her mother on her deathbed, slipping farther and farther away into another dimension, mumbling gibberish, her eyes pleading for Luella to understand. "Mom, I don't know what you're trying to tell me." It was as though her mother had been dreaming aloud. Or speaking with ghosts. At that moment, Luella had realized her mother was leaving forever. The memory terrified her.

Please, God, don't let him die!

The clock indicated that thirteen minutes had passed. Givens Knoll was too small to have its own hospital, the nearest ambulance coming from the next town ten miles away. Before now, she'd never considered the impracticality of living on the lake, down a long, winding country road far from medical facilities. The isolated camp had provided comfort, a haven removed from the cares of challenging careers and city life. Lately, it had become a fortress, protecting her from curiosity seekers and the press. Now it became dangerous.

Desperate, Luella cradled August's wrist and again felt for his pulse. Closing her eyes, concentrating, she detected a faint, slow tap. Her own pulse raced uncontrollably, making it impossible to trust her senses. She reached under his T-shirt and placed an open palm on his chest, praying to feel it rise and fall.

"August, stay with me. I mean it. Don't you dare die!"

A siren wailed in the distance. Bird's ears perked up. He stood protectively near August.

"They're coming. You hold on. Breathe, damn it!"

The siren's scream grew louder as it traveled along Virgin Timber Road, finally turning down their long driveway. At the house, the siren stopped. Flashing red and blue lights flickered in the through the windows, making the living room look like a macabre discotheque. A firm knock on the door. Luella ran to open it. Bird followed. Two paramedics, wearing unisex Ojibwe County Ambulance Service jackets and dark blue slacks, stepped into the foyer wheeling a gurney.

"He's in the living room. He overdosed," Luella said, breathless, pointing.

As she led the way with Bird following, the forty-something paramedic, her brunette hair pulled into a single braid that trailed down her back, asked, "Do you know what he took?"

Luella stooped to retrieve the empty prescription bottle from the floor and handed it to the paramedic. "I'm not sure how many of these he took," said Luella. She pointed to the empty bottle of vodka on the side table. "He drank that, too. I don't know how much."

"Lunesta," the woman said to her partner, who appeared to be somewhere in his thirties, although his bearded face and slightly receding hairline made it difficult to judge.

"Do you know what time he took the pills?" the woman asked.

"He was okay when I went to bed around 11:30. I found him about twenty minutes ago."

"What's his name?"

"August."

Luella held Bird by the collar and stepped aside, giving the paramedics room to work. She suppressed the urge to apologize. For her husband's weakness? The inconvenience of August trying to end his life in the middle of the night? For her failure to anticipate the unimaginable?

They spoke to August, using his name, explaining what they were doing even though he was unresponsive. They lifted him on to the gurney and placed an oxygen mask over his nose.

Yesterday in court, watching Beth testify, Luella thought she had hit rock bottom. It had been like watching her daughter drown as she stood by, unable to swim and with no life preserver in sight. She'd never felt more helpless, until tonight. Was there such a thing as bottom? Perhaps the belief that you had to hit bottom before beginning recovery was a convenient cliché perpetrated by those who had never been there. Maybe she would just keep falling and falling, losing more of herself with each tumble until she disappeared.

"Ma'am. Ma'am."

Luella looked quizzically at the woman.

"Is he taking any other medications?"

"Um…something for high blood pressure; I don't remember the name of the medication," said Luella, her voice tremulous.

"Does he have any other medical problems?"

"No."

"Is he allergic to any medications?"

"I—I don't think so."

Out of the corner of her eye Luella saw Rosie, wearing a pink nightgown, crouched on the bottom stairstep, huddled against the wall. "I had a bad dream," she whimpered, her lower lip quivering. "I heard a loud siren. It scared me."

"Oh, sweetie," said Luella, "you heard the ambulance." She and Bird sat beside Rosie. Luella touched her arm, felt her tremble. Or was she the one shaking? "August is sick. These people are going to take him to the hospital."

Rosie's eyes glistened. "Does he have the flu?"

"I don't know," Luella lied. "The doctors will find out at the hospital."

The paramedics hooked an IV bag to a pole fastened to the gurney, searched for an exposed vein in August's extended arm, and inserted the needle.

Rosie gripped Luella's leg. "Are they hurting him?"

"Not on purpose. They're trying to help."

The woman cut August's T-shirt from hem to neck and attached a cardiac monitor, then covered him with a blanket. The paramedics guided the gurney toward the door.

"I'll be at the hospital as soon as I can," Luella said as she followed them.

Rosie ran to the window, Bird bounding beside her, and watched as the paramedics loaded August into the ambulance.

Luella grabbed her cell phone from the coffee table and called Franklin's number. The phone rang and rang until it reverted to voice mail. She checked the time—2:57. She tried his number again. No answer. Tried again.

"Hello?" mumbled Franklin.

"I'm sorry to call you."

"Lu? What's wrong?"

Glancing over her shoulder to make sure Rosie wasn't listening, Luella lowered her voice to a near whisper. "I need your help. The paramedics just took August away. He tried to kill himself."

"Oh my God! I'm on my way."

It was as though an invisible barricade kept Luella from entering August's hospital room. She stood in the doorway studying him as he slept, a vortex of emotions threatening to pull her down into permanent misery.

The room was a science fiction-like tableau. The fixture on the wall behind August's bed cast a flickering light, exaggerating the wrinkles on his face as if they were outlined in black crayon. A ventilator, heart rate monitor, and I.V. stand flanked the bed. A strip of tape at the side of his lip held an intubation tube in place. His arms and bruised hands lay atop the white blankets pulled tautly over his body, and his wrists were tethered to the railings. No longer the robust and confident man he'd been before the arrest, he looked worn and exposed, as though he'd aged a decade overnight. The room smelled of disinfectant and despair.

"Have you been in to see him yet?" asked Franklin.

Startled, Luella turned.

"I'm sorry it took me so long to get here. I stayed with Denise to make sure Rosie settled down and went back to bed."

"I'm grateful that Denise was willing to come to the house."

"She loves you, Lu. Until now she just hasn't been able to make herself—well, you know, with August there."

"I know." Luella swallowed a sob. "I couldn't get through this without both of you."

Franklin pulled her into a hug. She leaned into the comfort of his embrace. "Will this nightmare ever end?"

"Lu, let's take this one step at a time."

"I'm trying."

"How's he doing?"

"He's stable. The doctor just gave me permission to see him," she said, brushing the tears from her cheeks. "I haven't worked up the nerve to go into his room yet."

"If you're afraid, I can go in with you."

How could she make him understand that it wasn't fear that kept her from walking into the room? Her hesitation was more complex than that. Love and devotion waged a fierce battle against anger and disgust. She weighed their decades together against the terrible crimes August had committed. She couldn't find the words to explain that, although she'd been unaware of the abuse of those boys when it happened, standing by August now made her feel culpable. No matter what she chose to do, she became a betrayer. Soothing August made her an accomplice to the horrible things he'd done. Turning against him made her a traitor to her marriage vows. If only she could walk away, turn off love as simply as twisting a water spigot. If only she could say, "You've created this mess. You're on your own." If only anger and disgust could finally win out.

Placing a hand on the small of her back, Franklin guided Luella into the room. They stood side-by-side next to the bed listening to the rhythmic compression of the ventilator and the high-pitched beep of the monitors. The name of the attending physician, Dr. Neel Mehta, was printed on a whiteboard opposite the bed, along with the names of his nurse and C.N.A. Luella took this as an optimistic sign that August might soon be awake enough to read the board. At the moment, he was unconscious, the only movement the regular rise and fall of his chest. His skin appeared sallow; the corners of his mouth crusted with dried spittle. His thick, silver hair—always a source of vanity—lay matted on one side of his head and disheveled on the other.

"The doctor said another hour and he would have been dead." Luella's blood pressure spiked at the image of August slumped in his chair, terrified that she'd found him too late. She shuddered at the memory of the wailing siren, the EMTs working over August while she silently prayed and Rosie whimpered as they led him away on the gurney. "I almost didn't find him on time. Bird woke me. He owes his life to our dog!"

She stared at the restraint around August's wrists. His helplessness rankled. What if *she* decided to quit? What if *she* abandoned him, Beth, Wyatt, Rosie? What if *she* didn't give a damn about anybody but herself? *Coward!* The thought screamed in her mind. *You leave me here while you choose to slip away. Coward!*

"He's a human wrecking ball, shattering our lives. For what? The sick thrill of fondling pre-pubescent boys?" Bitterness spouted from her like lava from a long dormant volcano. "My God, Franklin, what was he thinking? Damn him. How could he do this?"

Franklin turned her toward him, looked her in the eye. "Death must have seemed less frightening than prison."

His words poured over Luella like a bucket of ice-water. She turned, walked out of the room, and headed down the hall toward the waiting room, her mind reeling with the thought that August's choices had been narrowed to prison or death. Apparently, at least in Franklin's and August's minds, acquittal no longer seemed possible. She passed a bank of windowless patient rooms, all with similar institutional lighting and monitors, and a nurses' station.

Was it day or night?

At the far end of the corridor, she entered a small waiting room. Luella lowered herself into a chair tucked in the far corner. It seemed as though all she did lately was wait. Compared to the courthouse waiting room, which appeared to be decorated with a hodgepodge of castoffs in dated mud browns, this one was decorated with mid-century modern chairs and a loveseat in muted taupe and olive greens. Original watercolor landscapes hung on two of the walls, and a flat screen television hung on another.

Franklin entered and sat across from her.

Pulling out her cell phone, Luella checked the time—7:12 a.m. "I have to call Beth," she muttered.

"I can call her."

"No. It should be me."

"Then I'll get a hold of Thomas Lowery to let him know what's happened and to have him find out how the court will proceed."

"Proceed? Without August?" Luella hadn't considered what came next. It seemed as though the world should stop, that everything should remain in a freeze-frame until August recovered. It had been less than five hours since she'd found him unconscious, draped over the arm of the chair. How could life possibly go on as though nothing had happened?

"It will be up to the judge. Given that the defense has rested, my guess is she won't postpone things. It may sound heartless, Lu, but she'll be concerned about staying on schedule. Plus, there's the matter of holding the jury longer."

"I understand," said Luella. But she didn't understand. She didn't understand any of this.

Franklin pulled his cell phone from his jacket pocket and left the room.

Luella again checked the time—7:16 a.m. Beth would be at home getting ready for the day. Luella pressed Beth's number, hoping that she would not be too busy or too angry to answer the call. The phone rang multiple times until the call was diverted to voice mail. Luella pressed the number again. It rang and rang. No answer. She pressed it a third time. "Please, Beth. Please pick up."

Chapter Sixteen

~The Spinning Earth~

B eth lay staring at the ceiling in Gina's guest room, the plush mattress, down comforter, and plump pillows unable to coax her into a restful sleep. She hadn't intended to stay overnight, but after her panic attack Anthony and Gina convinced her that she was in no condition to drive or to go to work the next day.

"You already applied for a two-day leave, so take it," said Anthony.

"Plus, you look like hell," Gina added. "I traded shifts so I don't have to be at the hospital until mid-afternoon, so you can sleep in and I'll get up with Wyatt. It won't hurt him to miss a day of kindergarten."

Trying to sleep in as Gina suggested, Beth inserted her ear buds and searched for a meditation podcast on her phone. The soothing female voice urged her to envision warm water flowing through her limbs, then lulled her into a steady breathing rhythm. She tried to relax, to let the voice transport her to a place where the trial didn't exist. However, within minutes her thoughts returned to the courtroom.

She'd left with hardly a glance in her mother's direction, not intending to be cruel and dismissive, but unable to bear seeing the disappointment on Luella's face. Her mother's unconditional love had always been taken for granted, undervalued when weighed side-by-side with her father's earned respect. What little value she had placed on her mother's role as supporter, cheerleader, and healer. Throughout Beth's basketball playing career her father served as her teacher, pushing her to excel, but it had been her mother who helped pick up the pieces after a loss.

Soft light peeked through the closed slats of the wooden blinds. Beth removed her ear buds, sat up, turned on the reading lamp, and looked at herself in the dresser mirror on the wall at the foot end of the bed. She looked pale and drawn, the kiss of summer sun on her face long since faded.

Her phone rang. She ignored the call. It rang again. Then again. She checked caller I.D. Mom. Was she calling to express her disapproval of Beth's performance on the witness stand? Her mother couldn't possibly be more disappointed than Beth was in herself. She didn't need to hear a defense of her father, how devastated he was, or how the family needed to stick together through this difficult time. Beth had heard it all. Talking now would just make her feel angrier and guiltier. No, she didn't need that.

Her phone pinged. Voice mail. *Beth, it's Mom. Please call me! It's important! It's an emergency!*

It was unlike her mother to be hyperbolic. A jolt of anxiety coursed through Beth. She swung her legs over the edge of the bed and stood, flexing the tightness in her shoulders.

She hesitated, then pressed Luella's cell phone number.
"Hello?"
In that single word, Beth heard the pain in her mother's voice.
"Hello, Mom,"
"I'm sorry to call so early. Your dad is in the hospital."
"What? He was just in court yesterday."
"There's no easy way to tell you. He overdosed last night. He tried to kill himself."

Beth slumped down on the edge of the bed.

Her father had always seemed invincible, the embodiment of strength. Quit had never been part of his vocabulary. Until now.

It's my fault.

In that brief glance at the end of her testimony, she'd seen the impact of her silence when Fett asked if she believed the boys had lied written on her father's face.

It's my fault.

Beth rested her head in her hands.

Who are you trying to kid? It was Gabe's voice. *You think you have that kind of power over your father? You think you can make him kill himself? Seriously?* To purposely end a life was beyond comprehension. Gabe would have given anything to live, to remain with her and Wyatt. A man born with a happy gene—positive, optimistic, excited about their future together—life was precious to him. Life should be protected, cherished, held on to. It was a slap in the face to throw it away.

Anger versus guilt. It was impossible to sort them out.

Pull it together, sweetheart. Get your head in the game. It was Gabe again. Her head hadn't been in the game for two and a half years. *Wyatt needs you, babe.* She had to pull herself together. Their son deserved a mother who didn't quit, who didn't wallow in self-pity, who fought through every challenge.

Beth lifted her head, squared her shoulders. Walking over to the window, the floor cool against her bare feet, she opened the blinds and squinted into the light. A fat squirrel scrambled, stopped, changed direction, then dashed up the centuries-old oak in the front yard. The neighbor from the house across the street raced down her front steps and then jogged along the sidewalk. A green Subaru rolled slowly down the street. Inexplicably, the sun had risen and the earth continued to spin.

The aroma of freshly brewed coffee seeped under the bedroom door.

Although Beth had classes to teach and a basketball team to coach, she couldn't imagine returning to work, not with her father in the hospital and her mother left alone to face the situation. Before the school year began, she had spoken with Dr. Fitzgerald, the superintendent of schools, about the dilemma with her father. Then she believed it was best to keep working even though he'd offered to grant her a leave of absence. She had been so angry she wanted nothing to do with the trial. With her mother's phone call, everything changed. Her mother needed her. And Beth was too distracted to teach or coach. She had to make a choice. Anything was better than inaction.

Beth slipped her plush robe on over her nightgown, cinched the tie around her waist, and wandered through the living room and into the kitchen, surprised to see Anthony sitting at the table drinking a cup of coffee.

"Hey sunshine," he said. "Gina took Wyatt along to the grocery store so you could get some sleep. You feeling any better?"

Beth shook her head. Her jaw quivered. "M—my m—mom called this morning. My dad is in the hospital. He tried to kill himself last night."

"Jesus!"

"He overdosed on sleeping pills. Mom said he almost didn't make it." Beth brushed a tear from the corner of her eye. "He's in bad shape."

"I'm so sorry." Anthony set his cup on the table, looked at her intently.

"I have a favor to ask." Beth fidgeted with the soft ends of her belt.

"Anything."

"I need you to watch Wyatt. I'm going to go see my superintendent and ask for a leave of absence. I should have done it from the beginning. My assistant, Jordan, is capable of assuming my coaching duties. I'm not sure who Dr. Fitzgerald will find to teach my math classes, but he'll figure it out."

"Are you sure about this?"

Beth shook her head. "I'm not sure about anything. But I'm not in the frame of mind to teach or coach. I feel guilty for abandoning my students and players, but it's unfair to them if I continue, given how messed up I am. You saw me come apart last night. Things have only gotten worse since then."

"Sounds like a wise decision," said Anthony.

"Besides, I need to mend fences with my mom. I thought she and my dad were in this together, but he proved last night that he is willing to abandon her. I need to be there."

"Do you want us to keep Wyatt when you go north?"

"Thanks, but I want him with me. I'll call my Aunt Denise. I'm certain she'll watch Wyatt during the day until the trial is over. She loves him to pieces, plus she's offered to help a million times in a million different ways."

Anthony stood up and hugged Beth. His cleanly shaven face smelled of spice. "I'm really sorry, Beth. If there's anything you need, just say the word."

For a moment, she stood, immobile, not wanting to move out of the comfort of his embrace. Taking that first step meant walking toward uncertainty. "I better get dressed," she said, backing away. "I'll pick Wyatt up after I meet with Dr. Fitzgerald. I'll drive to Givens Knoll this afternoon."

"You sure you're up for that?" asked Anthony. "You've had a pretty rough couple of days."

"I need to be there," Beth insisted. "So, one way or the other, I have to be up for it."

It was mid-afternoon before Luella returned home from the hospital. Bird greeted her at the door, tail wagging. "Good boy," she cooed, bending and stroking his head. "You're a very good boy."

She hung her jacket in the foyer, glanced at her reflection in the mirror above the hooks. After the ambulance left the previous night, she had done her best to calm Rosie, then called Franklin and Denise and asked them to come to the house. As soon as they arrived, Luella had run upstairs to put on a pair of jeans and a sweater before rushing to the hospital, giving no thought to her appearance. All she could think of was August's survival.

Now gravity tugged at her limbs, a headache pulsed in her temples. Exhausted, she scuffled into the kitchen.

Denise stood at the sink washing dishes. "Oh, Luella, I'm so sorry." She dried her hands on the dishtowel slung over her shoulder. "Franklin just called from the hospital. He said Augie still isn't communicating, but the doctor said he'll live."

Luella nodded wearily, too tired to offer more.

"Selfish," Denise grumbled, teeth clenched.

Luella stepped back, leaned against the counter, refused to take the bait. "Thank you for coming to take care of Rosie. She was pretty shaken. How is she now?"

"Asleep. After lunch I encouraged her to take a nap."

Luella took a glass from the cupboard, filled it with tap water, savored the cold liquid as soothed her parched throat.

There was a knock at the door. Luella flinched. The last thing she needed was to deal with the police or a persistent reporter. What she wouldn't give for some peace. Couldn't the outside world just leave her alone? She resisted the urge to ignore the knock, drag herself upstairs, and bury herself under a mound of covers. She peered out the kitchen window. Trudy's yellow Volkswagen was in the driveway, a pop of color incongruous in the stark November landscape. What on earth was her hairstylist doing here?

"Do you want me to handle this?" asked Denise.

"No—no, I'll find out what she wants."

Luella opened the door.

"Hi. I don't mean to impose," said Trudy. "I was worried when I heard about your husband's—overd—ambulance ride to the hospital."

"How did you know?" asked Luella, cautiously.

"Howard is a volunteer firefighter. He has a police scanner. I thought someone should check to see if *you're* okay."

"Do you want to come in?" Luella opened the door wider and gestured for Trudy to come inside.

"Thanks." Trudy took two steps into the foyer. "I can't stay. I have someone coming in at 3:30 for a cut and color. I just wanted to see if you're all right and if there is anything I can do to help."

"Honestly, I don't know how I feel. Numb, I guess. Tired."

"And probably worried sick and pissed as hell."

With each of their encounters Luella became more convinced that Trudy was as much therapist as hairdresser.

"Anyhow, I brought you a bottle of Malbec and a box of chocolates. Lame, I know. I just couldn't think of what else to do."

"Thank you." Luella accepted the wine and the chocolates from Trudy, deeply touched by her kindness.

"If there is anything you need…I know people always say that, but I mean it. If there is anything I can do to help, just say the word."

"Right now, I need sleep."

"I'll check back in a day or two," said Trudy.

"I don't want to put you out."

"Something tells me you could use a friend."

Chapter Seventeen
~The Summation~

Judge Richards presided on the bench. Twelve strangers sat in the jury box. Adlai Fett bent over his notes. Thomas Lowery rifled through his briefcase. Spectators and reporters crowded the gallery. Everything appeared the same as it had since the beginning of the trial, except August no longer sat at the defense table. Without him the scene looked like a complex jigsaw puzzle missing an essential piece. Instead, the jury had an unobstructed view of Luella, his reluctant surrogate.

She'd wrestled with the decision whether to come to court today. There was no law requiring her to sit through the rest of the trial. Absenting herself, she decided, sent the wrong message. The verdict needed to be based on the facts of the case rather than on appearances. Maybe that was naive. Or maybe her sense of loyalty was so deeply ingrained there seemed to be no other choice.

Franklin sat next to her as he had every day of the trial. She wondered how she would ever repay him for all he'd done for her throughout this ordeal.

After spending a second night at the hospital Luella barely had enough time to take a sponge bath, wash her face, apply make-up, and change into her black slacks, pink blouse, and gray blazer. She'd used dry shampoo and a curling iron to make her hair presentable. A generous application of concealer camouflaged the dark circles under her eyes.

Glancing down at her blouse, she noticed a stain on the silk placket. Something so trivial shouldn't matter, she told herself, yet it seemed emblematic of losing control of the most basic things in her life. She pulled her blazer closed and fastened the top two buttons of her blouse.

Luella watched the court reporter's fingers, her nails polished flame red, and marveled as they skittered over the keys of the stenographic machine, recording the judge's every word. Too tired to concentrate, Luella caught only bits and pieces of Judge Richards' explanation to the jury, something about "the closing phase of the trial," moving forward despite the defendant's "illness," and not reading too much into his "temporary absence."

When it came time for Adlai Fett's summation, he rose from the prosecutor's table and sauntered toward the jury box as if he had all the time in the world.

Franklin squeezed her hand reassuringly.

Luella watched as each juror made eye contact with the prosecutor. He waited, as if thinking hard about the message he was about to deliver, as if just at that moment he was deciding what needed to be said. She suspected his closing statement had been memorized days ago. The entire performance was theater.

"You've been told by the defense that August Laurent is a pillar of the community, a man to be admired for his charitable work and all the good he's done for children," Fett began. "I won't deny that he's done *some* good for *some* kids. He's a successful coach. No one has disputed that. He's poised. He's slick. He's charismatic. All of that is true."

Luella brushed her fingers over her Hoops and Hearts necklace hidden beneath her blouse and thought of how proud she'd been when August launched the foundation. It had provided opportunity for many kids, but because of August's criminal behavior, its reputation was forever destroyed and the good that had come from the charity no longer counted.

"Don't be fooled by appearances the way those young boys were fooled." Fett paused for dramatic effect. "The truth? His motives were anything but pure. He used his charity and his basketball camp as a front to troll for vulnerable boys. He gained their trust. He took advantage of his exalted position. He groomed them. He used those children for his sick and perverted pleasure."

The picture in Luella's mind darkened. She imagined August making nightly rounds alone, flashlight illuminating the path as he made his way toward the campers' cabins, entering, smiling, oozing charm, selecting his victim, some boy too passive to resist his advances.

"Imagine sending *your* son to Laurent's Basketball Camp." Fett's attention moved from juror to juror. "You send him there with the expectation that you are entrusting his wellbeing to a skilled coach, a role model, a moral, good man. Instead, your son is groomed. Lured. Sexually assaulted. Repeatedly violated. His innocence robbed. He's scarred for life."

Several jurors looked down. One of the women wiped away tears. Shame snaked through Luella like the tentacles of a poisonous vine.

"You've heard a preponderance of evidence that proves, beyond a reasonable doubt, August Laurent is a sick, clever, remorseless predator, a predator who must be convicted and punished for the permanent damage he's done to these six young men."

Luella's fists lay clenched in her lap. It took every ounce of will she possessed not to flee from the courtroom.

Fett paused, stood in front of the jury far longer than necessary, as if waiting for the weight of his words to land. "Thank you, ladies and gentlemen. I trust that you will do what is right. Only you can deliver justice for his victims. You must return a verdict of guilty on all counts."

When Fett finished and took his place behind the prosecutor's table, the courtroom became so quiet that Luella heard the overhead light buzzing. At least she thought it was the light. Maybe the static was in her head.

Thomas Lowery slowly rose from the defense table, stood for a moment, and fastened the buttons of his suit coat.

Luella studied the jurors. They sat stone still. Lowery faced a gigantic hurdle.

"Coach Augie Laurent has been painted as a monster. That couldn't be further from the truth." Lowery raised his voice for emphasis. He paced from one end of the jury box to the other, then stopped in the middle.

"You heard the testimony from the people who know Augie intimately. His wife." Lowery turned and gestured toward Luella. "His daughter. His players. Fellow coaches. They all paint the exact same picture, and a far different one than the prosecutor would have you believe. They all know that Augie Laurent is an honorable, caring husband, father, and coach. He is a good man. An honorable man. A self-sacrificing man.

"None of them, I repeat, none…of…them…has ever had even an inkling of any sexual misconduct. Not an inkling. Don't you think that the people who know him best, who spent every day with him over a lifetime, would have had some notion that things were not right if what the prosecutor says is true?"

It occurred to Luella that August had never outright denied the sexual abuse accusations. He never said, "I swear to you on my mother's life, Luella, I did not sexually abuse those boys." It's what she desperately wanted to hear, but never had. Every confrontation resulted in obfuscation as he danced around the issue. *You know me. I'm your husband. How can you have so little faith in me? You see two and two and think it equals five. I need you to stand by me, Lulu. I can't do this without you.*

Lowery took a step closer to the jury box. "Brett Thibodaux, told you how much he owed to Coach Laurent. He not only mentored Brett, who became an all-American, but he also became a father to him when Brett's own father died. Coach Laurent went above and beyond by helping Brett's younger brother stay in private school, even paying his tuition. Let that sink in."

Lowery waited as he scanned the jury. "His younger brother was the same kind of fatherless boy the prosecution would have you believe Coach Laurent liked to prey upon. Instead of taking advantage of him,

Augie paid for his schooling. That is not the action of a child molester. That is the action of a patron. This story of care and kindness is not an isolated case. It has been repeated throughout Coach Laurent's career.

"One of the alleged victims testified that he brought his girlfriend to Coach Laurent's home to introduce her long after he was in college and had stopped attending camp. What abuse victim does that? What abuse victim volunteers to visit and invite to his wedding the coach who allegedly assaulted him? It defies logic."

Lowery paused like a symphony conductor between movements. "That doesn't sound like an abuse victim to me. It sounds like a misguided young man who greatly admired his coach but who has been duped into believing there is some monetary gain if he joins the victim brotherhood. Given his family's poor economic circumstances, it would almost be forgivable if an innocent man's freedom weren't at stake."

Luella wondered what impact the picture Lowery painted was having on the jury. If she were in their shoes and only had the word of others to go on, what would she believe?

"You heard the testimony of Kent McElroy, a coaching colleague with an impeccable reputation who has worked side-by-side with Coach Laurent since the opening of the camp. In twenty years…twenty years," Lowery said, slowing his pace, "Coach McElroy has never seen one instance of inappropriate touching. Not one. No child has ever reported any abuse to him. *Never.*"

Luella flashed back to the grand opening of the camp. The energy. The optimism. Kent McElroy had been there. The future lay before them like the road to a magic kingdom. Never did she imagine that the road would lead to such tragedy.

"It's only human to sympathize with these misguided young men, who come from poverty and fatherless homes and who have had many bad breaks in their lives," Lowery conceded. "Anyone with a heart can't help feeling sorry for them. Augie felt sorry for them, too. But he did more than that. He tried to help them. You must ask yourself if a man who has a big heart, who has done so much good for so many, a man whose closest friends and family never saw a hint of inappropriate behavior is actually capable of doing such grievous harm. It simply doesn't make sense.

"There is an overabundance of reasonable doubt in this case. Therefore, as fair-minded men and women, you must return a verdict of not guilty on all counts."

When Lowery ended his summation and assumed his place at the defense table, Judge Richards addressed the jury. She reviewed the thirty-four counts against August, advised the jury of the task before them, and sent them from the courtroom to deliberate.

That was it.

After the judge left the bench, the attorneys packed up their briefcases, and the reporters and spectators filed out of the courtroom.

There was nothing left to do but wait.

Franklin stood and offered his hand to Luella. "It's time to go, Lu." She grasped his hand and rose with effort. As she turned to leave, she saw a lone figure sitting in the back of the courtroom.

Beth.

Chapter Eighteen
~Drip, Drip, Drip~

After tucking Rosie in for the night, Luella retrieved her journal and a pen from the bedroom nightstand and went downstairs to open Trudy's 1.5-liter bottle of Malbec. She poured a liberal glassful, then took a box of photographs from the sideboard and set it on the coffee table. Bird curled beside her as she eased herself onto the floor and rested her back against the sofa.

The day's wrenching testimony, the reporters' barrage, the loneliness, plus growing financial pressure, pressed down hard, leaving Luella anxious, weary, agitated.

She gulped the wine in four large swallows, poured a second glass.

A photo atop the pile caught Luella's attention; her standing next to August in front of the Laurent's Basketball Camp entrance sign after they'd first installed it, both smiling broadly. "Here's to our dashed hopes and dreams," she said, raising her glass in a toast, taking a generous draw. "*Our* hopes. *Our* dreams." He'd convinced her that theirs was a shared life, a shared vision. Did that translate into shared guilt? No! August had created this mess. He'd abandoned her, left her to face this crisis alone.

She ripped the picture in two and tossed it on the floor.

Next was a staged photo of Luella and August at their twenty-fifth wedding anniversary celebration, him kneeling on one knee as if proposing. In a dramatic champaign toast he'd risen and declared his undying love in front of all the partygoers. "To Lulu, the woman who has stood by my side for two-and-a-half decades. I promise the next quarter century will be even better than the first."

Luella sneered. "To your broken promises." She raised her glass and emptied it. "Selfish bastard," she blurted, ripping the picture in two and tossing it on the floor.

She poured a third glass.

Another picture was taken the first summer they'd met. They sat in Uncle Walter's 1940 wooden Chris-Craft Barrelback, August at the wheel. She remembered the thrill of him putting his arm possessively around her as Aunt Mavis snapped the photo with her instamatic camera. Luella studied it, attempting to discern some clue in his expression or body language that hinted at depravity. What she saw was a cocky, fun-loving, athletic college boy with an electric smile sitting next to a bookish, introverted, smitten young woman, looking up adoringly at him. August's self-assurance, ebullience, and sex appeal had been irresistibly attractive. What had he seen in her? He claimed it was her goodness that made him want to be a better man. If that was true, she was an abysmal failure. More likely, he'd selected her for her eager devotion, the way you choose a puppy, she thought.

She imagined climbing out of the boat, prescient, running away to avoid a disastrous future. If she'd resisted August's pursuit, what would she be now? A mathematics professor? Single? The wife of an ordinary man? Anything would be better than this. Anything.

She tore the photo. "To gullible girls everywhere," she scoffed, raising her glass, then taking several swallows.

Another photograph of August instructing a rapt group of players lay on the stack, his charisma undeniable. The kids couldn't have been more vulnerable if he'd led them around with a magic flute. Out of the hundreds of kids who had come to camp, how had August decided which ones to target? His radar for susceptibility was precisely tuned. He'd done a superb job of choosing her. She ripped the photo and crumpled the half with August's image tightly in her fist, then pitched it.

She finished the third glass.

One by one she examined the years of photos taken at the lake:

August coaching on the outdoor courts; Beth as his assistant, first as a gangly teenager, then as a commanding adult; Gabe on his first trip to the camp; Rosie proudly helping in the kitchen, Wyatt playing with the older boys. Anything in which August appeared was destroyed, her ire ratcheting up with each tear. Soon, scraps littered the floor.

Luella picked up the bottle of wine, held it to the light, and squinted, trying to determine how much she'd consumed. Who cared? Oblivion was the goal.

She poured a fourth glass, drank half.

Setting it down, she scrawled a few sentences in her journal, then stopped. Nell Wooden. Luella Laurent. What on earth did they have in common? Basketball. That was it. It certainly wasn't integrity, or the devotion of an exceptional husband. John never humiliated Nell. Never left her to face a frightening future alone. Never made her hate him.

Luella ripped out several pages. What was the point? What was the goddamned point?

She tipped her head back and welcomed the wine sliding down her throat. How many glasses was this? Three? Four? More? How many did it take to make the pain stop? Cradling the bowl with the stem between her fingers, Luella poured another.

When she glanced up, head heavy, thoughts fuzzy, the framed photograph on the mantle of August with the bishop made her laugh bitterly. "You hypocrite." She gripped the floor lamp pole, teetered, wobbled, and stood. "Pillar of the community my ass," she slurred. Lurching toward the fireplace, she caught the corner of the mantle, grabbed the frame, threw it on the floor, and kicked it across the room.

The pillow with an embroidered Hoops and Hearts logo lay on the chair where just two nights ago she'd found an unresponsive August. She thought of Sergeant Fossmeyer insisting that the foundation was more a recruitment tool than a charity. "You were right," she said through numbing lips. Luella touched her heart necklace, fumbled with the clasp, tugged at it. "Damn!" She gave up and yanked the pillow's seam with all her strength. When it didn't give, she staggered to the sideboard and retrieved a scissors from the drawer, plunged it into the fabric, ripped the pillow down the middle, pulled out the spun polyester, and flung it.

Bird chased after the stuffing, grabbed a mouthful, furiously shaking his head, as if inviting Luella to play. Reaching, she lost her balance, fell on all fours. The point of the scissors scratched the hardwood floor. "Shit," she mumbled, crawling back to the coffee table. Bird lost interest in the game and lay next to her. "That's a good boy," she drawled, patting his head.

With both hands, Luella lifted the wine bottle and took a final gulp. Maybe it was possible to drink enough to never wake up. "Coward! You think you're the only one who can give up?"

Exhausted, she rested her head on the coffee table. Her arm knocked over the wine glass. "Drip, drip, drip," she mumbled, and fell into a deep sleep.

It was midnight when Beth brought her SUV to a stop next to her mother's house. Something felt off. The yard light wasn't on and the windows were dark. What would she find when she walked in the door? One suicide attempt per family was enough. Surely, Luella, the steadiest most reliable person she knew, wouldn't do anything so drastic.

Please, God, please let her be all right.

Stepping from the car, Beth braced against the night chill. A sprinkling of snowflakes fell from the early November sky, landing cold and wet on her hair and exposed skin. She grasped the railing and cautiously felt for each slippery stair step. The door was unlocked. She went inside. Silence. Bird didn't greet her with his usual tail-wagging exuberance. Her stomach tightened.

"Mom," she called. No answer. "Mom!"

Beth ventured into the living room. Her mother sat on the floor, knees tucked beneath her, head on the coffee table, snoring. Bird lay next to her, thumped his tail in recognition. In a sweeping glance around the room, Beth noted with alarm that the place looked as though it had been vandalized. As she came farther into the room and her eyes adjusted to the single dim light, she was shocked by her mother's disheveled appearance: hair uncombed, cheek streaked with mascara, sleeve stained with wine. Beth stepped on something hard, teetered, regained her balance. The framed photo of her father posing next to the bishop, accepting the Philanthropist of the Year Award, lay shattered, its glass spider-webbed, as though deliberately smashed.

Kneeling beside Luella, Beth squeezed her shoulder. "Mom. Mom!"

Luella's eyes fluttered open. She looked at Beth glassy-eyed.

"I called and called. What happened?"

"I gave that bastard my whole life, my whole goddamned life!" Bitterness escaped in a sour-breathed slur.

Beth couldn't ever remember seeing her mother inebriated or hearing her use such salty language. Witnessing Luella's vulnerability made Beth feel as though the granite fortress that protected her all her life had fallen to rubble.

"That son-of-a-bitch," Luella seethed. "He ruined my life."

After leading Luella upstairs, careful not to wake Rosie, Beth helped her undress, and fall into bed. She tiptoed downstairs with Bird close on her heels.

"What happened here, boy?" Bird looked up with doleful eyes, head tilted, brow raised, as if to communicate that he was just as baffled. "Looks like I'm not the only one going crazy."

Beth righted the floor lamp, flipped on lights, and made her way to the kitchen. She found a garbage bag under the sink and used her phone to search for instructions on removing red wine from a carpet.

In a large bowl, she mixed a tablespoon of white vinegar, a tablespoon of dish soap, and two cups of warm water. She lifted a roll of paper towels from the dispenser and found a stack of clean, white rags in the laundry room storage closet. In the living room, she set the wine glass upright and mopped up the spill from the tabletop. On her hands and knees, she dipped a rag in the cleaning mixture and laid it over the stain, letting the liquid soak into the carpet, used a dry rag to dab the stain at the edges and worked her way to the middle, alternately applying the mixture and blotting the liquid, until the stain disappeared. She threw the pile of wet paper towels and rags into the garbage bag.

Next, Beth gathered the strewn pillow stuffing and threw it away. She smoothed the casing, tracing the letters that spelled Hoops and Hearts, with the tips of her fingers. She remembered when Mrs. Jackson, a grandparent of one of the sponsored campers, had given her mother the hand-sewn pillow and how touched Luella had been.

She sat on the floor with legs tucked under the coffee table. Bird settled with his large head nestled against her thigh. Absently, Beth stroked his back. She carefully lifted the book with the torn pages and examined it. It was her mother's journal. She flipped to the most recent entry.

What arrogance to think August walked in the footsteps of John Wooden! How delusional I've been for believing that I was his Nell. What a complete fool!

Acrimony dripped from the page. It was as though Beth peered into her mother's soul and saw a reflection of her own humiliation. Tempting as it was to continue reading, prying was too invasive. She replaced the torn pages and set the journal aside.

She had intended to gather the scattered photos and return them to the overturned box, unexamined, but began picking them up one by one, lingering over each image, traveling back to a time when life held happiness and promise.

She found a picture of herself at five years old, hoisted above her father's head, her long hair suspended mid-air as if in motion, a basketball arcing toward the hoop. The photo had been taken the first year the camp opened. She remembered her elation when the ball, almost too big for her small hands, swished through the regulation-height hoop, and her father's enthusiastic high-five after he'd set her on the court. She'd never felt more loved.

Beth picked up the halves of another photo and pieced them together. Her father, his hair not yet completely silver and his crow's-feet barely visible, wore headphones and sat next to Pete McCormick, the nationally syndicated sportscaster, doing a radio interview. Beth stared at it. This must be the interview, recounted until it had become family lore, in which her father insisted that her mother was "the real power behind the throne."

As Beth examined other torn photos, she noticed that in each one August appeared as heroic or a paragon of virtue. The only pictures that remained intact featured Beth.

The grandfather clock chimed two thirty, time to gather the photos, both torn and whole, and place them in the box.

She was exhausted. Rather than drive back to Franklin's, she decided to stay, leave a quick text to tell her uncle not to worry; she would retrieve Wyatt in the morning. "Come on, Bird," Beth said, getting up from the floor. The dog yawned, rose, lazily stretched his legs and arched his back. "What do you say? Outside once more before bed?"

Bird pranced to the back door.

Beth carried the bowl of carpet cleaning solution and bag of garbage into the kitchen. She emptied the carpet cleaner into the sink and put the bowl in the dishwasher. When she opened the door, Bird dashed outside. She turned on the porch light and put on her jacket. Cold air seeped through her clothes. The wind bit her cheeks. Pulling her jacket collar up, she crossed fifty feet to the garage and placed the bag into the garbage can, securely fastening the lid against marauding raccoons and bears.

"Bird!" she called. The dog charged out of the darkness and scampered up the stairs.

Once inside, Beth switched off lights and made her way back to the living room. As she was about to turn off the living room lamp, a photograph she hadn't noticed under the coffee table caught her eye. She picked it up. It was an old photo of her father in his coaching attire, smiling, with his arm around a boy, maybe eleven or twelve. The boy looked intently into the camera, sober, his body stiff and listing away from her father. It was Derrick Boyer, one of the alleged victims. She recalled seeing the photo before. Then she had assumed the boy's discomfort was the reaction of a starstruck kid posing with the famous coach. Now the image screamed "Help!"

Luella woke confused, uncertain whether her anger lingered from a forgotten nightmare or from something real. A dull ache pulsed behind her eyes. Her head felt boulder heavy, her mouth desert dry. Gradually, as the fog of sleep lifted, she remembered finding August passed out in the living room, keeping vigil at the hospital, then sitting in court as though she were the one on trial. She vaguely remembered opening a bottle of wine, intending to dull her pain. But instead of the anesthetizing effect she'd hoped for, the alcohol had turned her sorrow into rage.

She braced herself on an elbow and squinted at the digital alarm clock—6:09 a.m., more than an hour before sunrise. Bird jumped up on the bed, something August never allowed, and rolled on his side. As Luella reached to shoo him away, she hesitated, petted him. "It's all right, boy." She stroked Bird's belly. "He's not here."

Too wired to go back to sleep, she thought of the daunting day ahead. She had to drive Rosie to Horizons, go to the hospital to check with August's doctor and then, as much as she dreaded it, return to court. The jury would be deliberating this morning, and there was no predicting when they would come back with a verdict.

Easing out of bed, she rubbed her aching back, massaged her throbbing temples. Shambling to the bathroom, she relieved herself, washed her hands, splashed cold water on her face, brushed her teeth, and ran a comb through her hair. She put on a sweatshirt, a pair of jeans, and wool socks. Later she would make herself more presentable, but first she needed some air.

Bird sprang off the bed, loped down the stairs and into the living room ahead of her. Luella flipped the wall switch, turning on the lamps. The box with torn photos, neatly stacked, sat on the coffee table. The empty casing of the Hoops and Hearts pillow lay folded on the arm of the sofa. The framed photograph of August, its glass smashed, was placed on a side table. She had only a fuzzy notion of how the pillow had been damaged and the glass broken. She was certain that she hadn't left everything so neat. She had a foggy memory of Beth being in the house last night. Or had she dreamed that? When they'd left the courtroom yesterday, Beth had told her that she wanted "to take things slow," so she chose to stay at Franklin's house with Wyatt.

Thumbing through her journal on the coffee table, she saw that several loose pages had been carefully tucked into the book. She glanced over at the side table. August's face stared up at her behind the shattered glass.

"I'm done," she said. "I'm so done."

Inebriation, though temporary, had been a relief, like a layover on a long-distance flight. Given the pounding in her head, she knew that drunkenness was not a permanent solution.

From the hall closet she retrieved her down jacket, stocking cap, and mittens. She bundled up, pulled on boots, grabbed a flashlight off the top shelf of the closet. When she stepped outside and saw Beth's SUV parked in the driveway, she smiled.

She headed to the lake. Bird dashed past her down the path. A dusting of snow covered the ground. Luella treaded cautiously, keeping her eyes down as she followed the beam of the flashlight. Standing at the shoreline, she breathed in air so bracing, it cooled her lungs as if it were mentholated. A faint glow kissed the tree line on the eastern shore. A pinprick of light from a house on the opposite side of the lake twinkled in the semidarkness. She shined the beam of light over the water. The surface, as silver as a freshly minted quarter, would freeze so solidly in December that fisherman would drive their pick-up trucks out onto the ice. She had no idea what the water temperature was now, but it had to be cold enough to cause hypothermia in a matter of minutes.

Suicide. She thought of August and understood the temptation. The solution to her ruined life beckoned right in front of her, the deep, frigid water, a Siren, calling, seducing. How easy it would be to wade into the lake, heavy clothing dragging her underwater, lungs filling, heart stopping. Had similar thoughts gone through August's mind the night he ingested the sleeping pills? Had he imagined his mind numbing, his heart stopping? Had he stared at the bottle of pills and seen, not death, but peace?

Taking pills was an imprecise way of committing suicide. Too much chance of being found before death mercifully arrived. Drowning would be a more fool-proof method. At first, her arms and legs might involuntarily claw toward the surface, her lungs desperate for a gulp of sweet air. But her water-logged boots would anchor her to the bottom so that there would be no turning back. Soon panic would give way to surrender as her lungs filled and she drifted into oblivion.

She teased the toe of her boot in the water. The sound of pine needles crackling underfoot stopped her.

"Mom?"

Luella turned. Beth, a stocking cap pulled low over her forehead, dressed in a parka and carrying a cup of coffee, made her way down the path. Luella saw that her daughter was no longer a child, someone to be protected, but a woman to be admired. Despite all the heartache— the loss of Gabe, being left alone to raise Wyatt, the betrayal by her father—Beth endured.

Luella knew that she could never voluntarily leave Beth or Wyatt, never burden them with the legacy of suicide. No. She could not do that to them. She, too, had to endure.

Bird scampered up to Beth in greeting and then darted off, nose sniffing the ground.

"I thought I might find you here." Beth's tone was tender. "I didn't expect to see you up so early after—after last night."

Luella walked over to the bench, patted it. "Come sit with me," she said.

Beth handed Luella the steaming mug of coffee, then settled in next to her mother.

"Honestly, I don't remember much," Luella admitted.

"The living room was pretty trashed."

Luella sipped her coffee. "Mm. Strong."

"I thought you might need it."

Luella stared out at the lake. Beth waited quietly. The sun peeked over the tops of the pines. Light danced on the rippling water. Overhead, crows called *caw-caw, caw-caw.*

"Before I met your father I had big dreams," Luella said. "I planned to earn a doctorate in mathematics. I wanted to be a college professor. Did you know that I was accepted into the graduate program at the University of Chicago?"

"You never told me that."

"Now I can't even keep a job teaching eighth graders."

"Mom, I always thought you were happy."

"I was. The sacrifice seemed worth it when I thought my life meant something. I gave up everything for your dad. Now I feel like a fool, and I can't stop resenting him. I can't stop regretting my choices."

"Do you regret having me?"

"Oh, honey. No! I'm so sorry. I didn't mean that." Luella looked into Beth's moist eyes. "I could never regret having you. You and Wyatt are the joys of my life. You keep me from—giving up."

"I'm sorry that I haven't been there for you, Mom."

"I'm the one who should be sorry," said Luella. "I didn't want to believe your father was capable of—of molesting those boys."

"What made you change your mind?"

"I talked to Michael St. James."

Chapter Nineteen
~The Verdict~

The jury entered the courtroom single file. Luella sat behind the defense table next to Franklin, studying the jurors' stoic faces, searching for any hint that might reveal their verdict. They had become so familiar—the middle-aged woman with dyed red hair and exposed gray roots; the elderly man, stooped at the waist; the millennial who compulsively gnawed her cheek—that Luella had to remind herself these were twelve strangers who would decide August's fate, and by extension, hers.

Twelve. A sublime number, Luella thought, with a perfect number of divisors. Ubiquitous. Twelve months of the year. Twelve numbers on a clock face. Twelve apostles.

August had told her he saw the jury as a rival team to be out-coached, out-maneuvered. Now he lay in the hospital, survivor of an attempted suicide. It was clear he had underestimated his opponent. When the trial began, she believed these twelve jurors would be convinced of his innocence. As the trial progressed, she adjusted her expectation, hoping that a percentage of them would be persuaded August was an honorable man incapable of molesting children. Now, she realized, just one holdout would make him a free man.

At first, she had hoped for August's acquittal. Now what did she dare hope for? Six boys, plus Michael, (and perhaps others), had been deeply scarred, some damaged for life. Justice demanded a guilty verdict, yet she could not bring herself to pray for August's imprisonment. Nor could she pray for his exoneration. She would save her prayers for his victims, if she could bring herself to pray at all.

Before coming to court, Luella had stopped at the hospital. August, now conscious, had been transferred to the psychiatric ward and placed on suicide watch. After consulting with his doctor, who assured her that her husband would survive, she cautiously stepped into his room, stood ten feet from the bed and observed him as he slept, grateful he was not awake. His wrists were still tethered to the rails, and his pallor was the color of paste.

Judge Richards's voice brought Luella back to the moment. "Has the jury reached a verdict?"

"Yes, Your Honor." The foreperson, a sixty-something, somber woman, rose as though her knees ached from the effort.

The clerk delivered the paper with the verdict to the judge. She scanned the page and handed it back to the clerk, who then returned it to the foreperson.

"Will the defendant's counsel please rise?" It was a command, not a request.

Thomas Lowery unbuttoned his suitcoat and stood, expressionless.

"On count number one, sexual assault in the first degree, how do you find?" asked the judge.

Luella held her breath, clutched the edge of the bench. Next to her, Franklin shifted, then leaned forward.

The foreperson stood rigid. "We find the defendant—guilty."

Lowery's shoulders slumped slightly.

Luella gasped. Franklin touched her shoulder.

Guilty. The word, announced emphatically, made the unimaginable real.

Excited chatter erupted in the gallery. Luella bristled. She didn't begrudge the victims their justice, but she resented their glee. Unable to bear the satisfaction on the spectators' faces, she stared at the floor and fought back tears. Many times she had been in the stands when August's team suffered a defeat, and she'd had to endure the winning side's victory celebration. This did not compare.

Judge Richards lowered her gavel. "Quiet! Ladies and gentlemen, quiet, please! These proceedings are not complete." She paused, and waited for the murmuring to die down before asking, "On count number two, child enticement, how do you find?"

"We find the defendant guilty."

One by one the judge enumerated each of the thirty-four counts. Each time the verdict came back guilty. The word screamed in Luella's head. GUILTY! GUILTY! GUILTY!

Then without fanfare the trial was over. The jury was dismissed and the judge exited the courtroom.

The murmuring of the spectators grew into excited conversations, celebratory pats on the back, hugs, and handshakes. Adlai Fett, attempting to pack his briefcase and leave, was waylaid by well-wishers and reporters.

Luella thought of August lying in his hospital bed. She imagined his reaction when informed that he had been found guilty on all counts. He would be taken to jail to await sentencing once he became well enough to be released from the hospital. After sentencing, he would be sent to prison. He would never set foot at the camp again, coach another team, watch his grandson grow to adulthood. Everything that mattered to him, that defined him, would be stripped away.

As Luella sat stunned, absorbing the resounding verdicts August had foreseen, she realized that, to him, death had been welcome. She pictured him slumped in his chair the night he overdosed, life seeping from his body. She had reacted, called 911, pleaded with him, willed him to hang on. Now she understood why he wanted to die.

The word "guilty" hit Beth with the force of a stun gun. She sat in the last row of the gallery, trembling. Naively, she thought she was prepared for today's verdict, but the impact proved more devastating than imagined. Despite her belief in his guilt, she secretly hoped that her father was innocent. Now that illusion was shattered. She was also unprepared for the intensity of the celebrations around her. The middle-aged woman in the row ahead fiercely hugged the young man sitting next to her, repeating again and again, "You won! You won!" Two spectators gave each other high-fives. Across the aisle she heard a bitter voice growl, "That bastard deserves to get life for what he did."

A tsunami of emotion washed over her. This was her father whose downfall they cheered: the father who read her bedtime stories when she was a child, taught her how to master a hook shot, walked her down the aisle at her wedding, teared up the first time he held Wyatt, and comforted her as she sobbed at Gabe's funeral. To the revelers, he was pedophile August Laurent, nothing more.

Burying her face in her hands, she let the tears flow.

Gradually the celebratory chatter died down, and the spectators filed out of the courtroom. Beth swiped away her tears, took a deep breath. She made her way up the aisle toward her mother and Franklin, who were standing with Thomas Lowery. Franklin, his expression somber, nodded as he listened intently to the attorney. Luella, eyes red and puffy, looked as if she were the most distraught mourner at a funeral.

"I can't believe it," murmured her mother. "This doesn't seem real."

"I'm sorry," said Lowery.

"Under the circumstances you did your best." Franklin shook his hand. "It was impossible to offset the evidence against him."

Lowery brushed off the lapels of his suit jacket and straightened his tie. "Time to face the media. I'll try to run interference while the three of you go directly to your vehicles. If they stick a microphone in your face, don't say anything. There's nothing to be gained by speaking with the press."

"What about August?" asked Luella. "Who is going to tell him?"

"It's my job to break the news," said Lowery. "I'll head to the hospital now." He picked up his briefcase and, as he left the courtroom, glanced over his shoulder. "I'm sorry. I'm truly sorry."

"Beth, I'll drive your mother home." Franklin wrapped a scarf around his neck and slipped on his overcoat. "I assume you're staying at our house tonight."

"Actually, I'd like to stay at the camp if it's all right with you, Mom," said Beth cautiously.

"I'd like that."

"What about Wyatt?" asked Franklin. "Do you want him to stay with Denise and me tonight?"

"If you and Denise wouldn't mind. I could use a night to recover, and I don't think it would help Wyatt to see his mother and grandmother looking like basket cases." Beth, biting her lower lip, turned to her mother as if to apologize for the insult. "Plus, I have to figure out how to explain all this to him. He idolizes his grandpa."

"I'm sure Denise will agree to keeping Wyatt overnight." Franklin pulled his phone from his pocket and called his wife. Denise had strong feelings about August's transgressions, so Beth assumed she wasn't circumspect about expressing her approval when Franklin told her the verdict. "Yes...I'll tell her...M-hmm...I'll be home soon...Yah, me too."

Franklin slid the phone into his pocket and turned to Beth. "Denise said to tell you that Wyatt can stay as long as you need him to. He's an angel, and she can't think of anything she'd rather do than spend time with him. She also suggested I pick up Rosie and have her spend the night so you and your mother can have some uninterrupted time together."

"Thank you." Beth hugged her uncle and kissed him lightly on the cheek. "I can drive Mom home now and get Wyatt in the morning."

The three of them were the last to leave the courtroom. A number of people still milled about in the corridor. Prosecutor Fett, spouting phrases such as "justice served" and "a step toward healing for these young men," spoke with reporters. Several reporters spotted Beth, Luella, and Franklin and rushed toward them. All three kept their heads down and pushed through the group until they reached the outside, finally making it to their cars.

As Beth pulled away from the courthouse, Luella sitting silent in the passenger seat, she remembered a quote from *The Merchant of Venice*; "The sins of the father are to be laid upon the children." The verdict wasn't the end, thought Beth. Far from it. She and her family would be paying a price for her father's sins for a long, long time.

Before the guilty verdict was announced earlier in the day, Beth mistakenly believed that anger with her father would protect her from the heartbreak that now overwhelmed her. Back at the camp, weepy, agitated, and fragile, it took every ounce of energy she possessed to hold it together.

Luella, sitting on the living room sofa, had barely spoken since leaving the courthouse.

The silence made Beth anxious.

She opened the media cabinet door where August stored his vinyl records, surprised to find Norah Jones' recent *Day Breaks* album among his collection of 1970's and 80's favorites. She pulled the album from its sleeve, raised the dust cover, and set the disc on the turntable, carefully lowering the tone arm so the needle wouldn't scratch the record, the way her father had taught her when she was a little girl. "Like this, Bethy," he'd said, his large hand guiding her small child's hand.

Piano music, then Norah Jones' breathy voice began singing "Burn. " The melancholy tone reflected Beth's mood.

The guilty verdict made the split with her father real and permanent. She should just feel relieved that Wyatt was safe. After all, that was the main reason she'd rejected her father so abruptly. To protect her son. She couldn't take the chance that her father would groom him early, eventually abuse him. The possibility was too awful to contemplate. Yet she couldn't help feeling searing loss. Never again would they listen to music together. Never again would he say, "Listen to that riff, Bethy. Pure magic."

She sat down on the opposite end of the sofa from Luella, picked up the plate of take-out cashew shrimp, and balanced it on her lap. Bird, lounging between them, sniffed her food before nestling his large Newfie head against her leg.

Beth glanced at her mother, spoke cautiously. "Things got pretty intense today. It made me sick to watch people celebrating."

"That's an understatement." Luella ignored her food. "I don't know whether to feel relieved or devastated."

"I know what you mean. On one hand, I believe the verdict was just, and I'm glad that the trial is over. On the other hand, I feel gutted." Beth set down her plate and shoved it to the corner of the coffee table.

"Today's drama was too much. I'm exhausted." Luella stood and carried her plate into the kitchen. Bird jumped from the sofa and followed her, leaving Beth alone.

Alone.

She couldn't help thinking of her father, imagined him still on suicide watch, lying helpless and alone in his hospital bed. By now Lowery would have broken the news that he'd been found guilty on all counts. She was still furious with him, yet she couldn't fathom the despondency that must come from knowing that you would spend years locked away, that life as you knew it was over.

Luella returned from the kitchen emptyhanded, Bird, hovering alongside. She wandered over to the French doors and stared out toward the lake into the darkness. Several minutes passed before she spoke. "Turns out, it takes a lot of energy to get drunk and act like a lunatic, then sit in court the next day and have your husband found guilty of molesting kids."

"Yeah, who knew?"

Luella turned and smiled at Beth, who was relieved that her quip was received as intended.

"Mom, it was a relief to see you lose it last night. I mean, for months now I've thought maybe I was the only one going nuts. Now I see you're as cuckoo as I am." Beth twirled her index finger beside her temple.

"Maybe we'd actually be certifiably crazy if this whole awful situation wasn't making us a little crazy." Luella crossed the room to the oversized chair next to the fireplace, grabbed the afghan draped over its back. "Maybe we're normal." She wrapped the afghan around her shoulders and settled into the chair. Bird nestled at her feet.

"I wouldn't go that far," Beth teased.

Another small smile from Luella, as though the slightest expression took effort. Beth understood that vulnerability. For her, any revealed emotion threatened to make her burst into tears.

Beth closed her eyes, listened to the music softly filling the room.

"I've been thinking," said Luella after a long interlude.

Beth opened her eyes, turned toward Luella.

"Whoever said, 'God never gives you more than you can handle' must have been delusional. Some people would rather die than face whatever God is dishing out. I mean, look at your dad."

"Mom, please. Let's not go there." Beth's muscles tensed. Things between them had been going so well; she was sick to death of hearing her mother defend her father.

Bird, as though sensing the change in mood, looked up at Luella, then at Beth.

"Wait, hear me out." Luella rose wearily, walked over and picked up the cracked, framed photograph, still lying upside down on the side table, of August standing next to the bishop. She lowered herself next to Beth. Bird followed, wedged himself between the sofa and the coffee table, and plopped down at their feet. Luella held out the photo. "Look at this. Really look at it." She handed it to Beth. "Did you ever in your wildest dreams think he was capable of trying to commit suicide? Your dad with his hair styled. His suit fitted. His teeth whitened. I thought he was far too vain for that. I found him slumped over, drooling, looking like hell. He would be horrified if he'd seen himself. August is always so concerned with his image."

"Apparently not concerned enough."

"Good point."

"The thing that bothers me most about his suicide attempt is the timing," said Beth, handing the photo back to Luella, her tone hardening. "He doesn't down a bottle of pills when he's arrested or when his victims testify. He waits until you and I take the stand, as though the verdict becomes our fault."

"Yeah. Too bad he didn't kill himself *before* he molested those boys."

"Mom!" Beth gasped.

Luella covered her mouth, giggled. She slammed the photo on the coffee table, facedown.

Bird jumped up, crawled up on the sofa and curled next to Luella.

"It's not funny," said Beth. "This isn't a laughing matter."

They held eye contact. Beth tried not to, but burst out laughing.

Both women laughed harder.

"Way to rock the gallows humor, Mom." Beth said, then snorted. "I didn't know you had it in you."

Bird's tail beat happily against the cushions. It took several starts and stops for Beth and Luella to regain their composure.

Luella placed her hand over Beth's, lightly stroked it, then put it back in her lap. "Seriously, you know I'm sorry for everything that's happened between us."

"I'm sorry for everything, too. Mom, can we just offer a blanket apology to each other and call it good? Right now, I don't have the strength to rehash the past."

They grew quiet. Norah Jones' sultry voice, singing "Carry On," filled the silence.

Beth waited, screwed up her courage, hoping her mother, who had been fired, would understand her decision to voluntarily give up teaching. "I have something to tell you. I took a leave of absence from my job."

"Oh, honey."

"I just couldn't stay. My head wasn't there. My heart wasn't in it. It wasn't fair to my students or my team. The superintendent agreed."

"For how long?"

"The rest of the year."

"Will you be okay for…"

"Moneywise, I'm all right. I have the life insurance settlement from Gabe. It'll hold me until I figure out if I want to go back or find another job."

"Two unemployed teachers."

"I have a favor to ask." Beth sat straighter, faced Luella, hesitated. "I—I'm not ready to go home. Gina offered to let Wyatt and me stay at her place, but it's pretty small." She tucked loose strands of hair behind her ear. Her heartbeat sped up. She bit her lip. "I thought—I mean was wondering if I could stay with you for a while. I could help you with Rosie."

Luella's eyes shimmered.

"Honey, you don't need an excuse. I'd love to have you and Wyatt stay with me. I won't be rattling around in this place alone. If you're here it won't feel so empty."

Beth wrapped her arms around Luella in a tight hug. "Thank you, Mom. I love you." A warmth like sunshine breaking through clouds filled Beth with hope.

Luella held on, kissed Beth on the cheek. "It's going to be okay, kiddo. We're going to be okay."

"Mom, where do we go from here?"

"I have no idea."

The next evening, as she snuggled with Wyatt for their nightly reading ritual, Beth nestled into the pillow propped against the headboard of his bed. He'd selected one of his favorite stories about the elephant and pig who tried to play catch with a snake. When they came to the page where the ball hit the armless snake in the head, Wyatt shouted, "BONK! BONK! BONK!" His infectious, little-boy glee reassured her that she'd made the right decision to move back to the camp.

She hadn't been so sure when they'd arrived that morning. The leafless trees, the overcast November sky, the eerie quiet—a jarring contrast to the lushness, warmth, and hum of summer at the lake—made her question the wisdom of uprooting Wyatt. The grass was bleached brown. Every cabin stood empty. The temperature dipped to thirty degrees. An unsettling bleakness enveloped the place.

She couldn't help reliving the argument with her father on the summer night she'd fled; he'd accused her of disloyalty, kicked her duffel bags down the stairs, yelled at her to never return. And yet, the camp was filled with years of special memories. For Wyatt's sake, if not for her own, she would push the most recent heartbreak to the back of her mind and focus on the positive.

In the afternoon, as she'd stepped from the car, her mother had greeted her with open arms and an expression Beth interpreted as gratitude. Wyatt ran to her, hugged her, and exclaimed, "Grandma, I'm here! I bet you're happy I'm coming to live with you." Bird bounded toward him and nearly knocked him off his feet. "Hi, Bird! I'm back!" Wyatt wrapped his arms around the dog's neck and giggled as Bird covered his face in slurping kisses.

"BONK, BONK, BONK!" Wyatt yelled again as the ball ricocheted off the snake.

Beth read the last few pages, then closed the book.

"Can we read another story?" begged Wyatt. "Just one more."

"Not tonight, honey. We've already read two stories." Beth kissed the top of his head. "I'm tired. It's been a long day for both of us. Tomorrow night we can read three."

"Promise?"

"Promise."

Wyatt yawned, rubbed his eyes. "Mommy? When do I go to my new school?"

"Monday. Two days from now. I know starting new things can be a little scary. But your teacher, Ms. Simmons, is really nice, and you'll make lots of new friends."

"Are you coming with me?" Wyatt looked up at her expectantly.

"Of course. I'll drive you to your new school and help you meet your teacher. In fact, let's go there tomorrow and check out the playground. Would you like that?"

Wide-eyed, Wyatt nodded.

Beth scooted to the edge of the bed, swung her feet to the floor.

The bedroom door opened slightly. Bird wedged through the opening, dashed into the room, jumped onto the foot of the bed. Wyatt smiled and made room for the dog, who lay down and pressed against him.

Rosie peeked around the door.

"Come in." Beth smiled and patted the spot next to her on the bed.

Rosie, wearing her pink ankle-length nightgown and over-sized fuzzy slippers, shuffled in and sat down next to Beth. "Luella said you're going to live here."

"That's right."

"I'm happy."

"Me, too."

"Me, three," added Wyatt.

Rosie laid her head on Beth's shoulder. Her lower lip quivered. "I was sad when you were gone."

"Oh, Rosie Posie, don't be sad." Beth smoothed Rosie's hair; then stopped mid-stroke. She'd used August's pet name for his sister. There was no avoiding it; her father was present even though he would never return to this house.

"Sweetie, look at me." Beth gently held Rosie's shoulders. "No matter where I am, I think about you and love you. And now we're here."

Wyatt inched forward. "I'm going to a new school with lots of new friends. And we can play when I come home."

"And when I come home from Horizons." Rosie beamed, stretching her arms above her head and yawning.

"It looks as though you're ready for bed, too," said Beth.

Rosie stood, shuffled to the door, and looked over her shoulder. "I'll see you tomorrow." She waited, her face the picture of anticipation. Beth knew that in their nightly ritual August always responded, "Not if I see you first, Rosie Posie." It was a small thing, but Beth couldn't bring herself to say it. "Sweet dreams," she replied instead, and blew a kiss. Rosie looked confused. Slowly, she broke into a grin. "Sweet dreams," she repeated and toddled down the hall.

"Mommy," said Wyatt as he nestled under the covers. "Is Grandpa going to live here, too?"

A pang of grief traveled from Beth's stomach into her chest and to the ends of her limbs. How could she again explain to her five-year-old that the grandfather, with whom he'd had nothing but happy experiences, the grandfather he loved and idolized, was a convicted pedophile and a possible danger to him? August wouldn't be out of prison until Wyatt was well into adulthood, if ever. She resented her father for putting her in this position, for making her break her son's heart.

"Honey, remember I told you that Grandpa did some bad things so he had to go to prison."

"Can he visit us?"

"No. He has to stay in prison.

"But what if he just came for a little while."

"Not even that."

Wyatt looked stricken.

"Can we call him?"

"No, honey, we can't. We're not allowed to call." That much was true. But it was equally true that Beth had been unwilling to speak to her father when he had called. Maybe someday she would be able to, but not yet. "It's still okay to love him and think about all the fun things you did together." She leaned in, settled his teddy bear in the crook of his arm, pulled the covers up to his chin, and kissed his cheek. She scratched Bird behind an ear. "It's time for sleep, buddy. If you have more questions, we can talk tomorrow."

Wyatt yawned; his eyelids heavy.

Beth edged toward the door.

"Mommy," he said, "I'm going to make a special card for Grandpa and put lots of dinosaur stickers on it. Grandpa and I love dinosaurs. Our favorit-ist is the Velociraptor 'cuz of the Raptor basketball team. And I'm going to tell him I can dribble my basketball he gave me thirty-six times. He won't believe it."

If it wasn't clear before, it was perfectly clear now; August's presence in their lives would not be easily erased. Wyatt's memories of a grandfather who let him ride on his shoulders to shoot baskets, taught him to reel in a fish, engaged in plastic dinosaur battles, was permanently imprinted. Beth was unsure whether she would mail Wyatt's card to the prison or if she would post it, like a child's letter to Santa, to a fictious address. At his age, Wyatt would be none the wiser. Still, didn't he have a right to a connection with his grandfather? Someday, would Wyatt resent her if she kept him from that relationship?

"You're right. Grandpa would like that." Beth turned off the light. "I love you, buddy"

"I love you, too, Mommy."

Chapter Twenty
~A Faulty Star~

On a Tuesday afternoon in mid-November, Luella waited at the Ojibwe County Jail to see August. She hadn't seen him since the guilty verdict and since his release from the hospital. The entry smelled faintly of body odor. Every surface seemed hard and unforgiving. The thought of being confined in this place made her shudder.

As required, Luella arrived early for the pre-scheduled visit. She mentally checked off the long list of visitation rules posted on-line. Pockets empty. Cell phone and purse locked in the car with the windows rolled up. Hair free of clips and bobby pins. No jewelry other than her wedding ring. Modest clothing and a bra without an underwire so that she could successfully pass through the metal detector. Hopefully, she hadn't forgotten anything.

A stocky officer, his uniform snug around his middle, verified that her photo I.D. matched the information on his computer. She successfully passed through the metal detector before being led into the visitation room where she was escorted to a table to wait for August. Her nerves were on edge as she anticipated the tightrope she was about to walk, between the urge to confront August about his guilt and the awareness that he was fragile after his suicide attempt. She sat in the plastic chair with her fingers laced, hands in her lap, both feet planted on the floor.

Several tables in the room were occupied by other inmates and their visitors. The air vibrated with a low hum of conversation. On the table nearest her a very pregnant young woman also sat waiting. Remembering another rule—no conversing with other inmates or their visitors—Luella kept her eyes on the tabletop in front of her.

After a few minutes, August walked in looking somber. She stiffly accepted the brief kiss and hug the rules allowed at the beginning of the visit. He lowered himself into the chair on the opposite side of the small table.

His complexion was wrinkled and pallid, aging him dramatically. His facial stubble and cheap haircut made him appear like the inmate he was and not the fastidiously groomed man who used to have his hair styled at one of the most expensive salons in Chicago.

He'd always been vain about his full head of wavy hair. Even as a beginning coach, when money was tight, August had splurged on first-rate haircuts. "You've got to dress for the job you want, not for the one you have," he'd remark whenever she'd remind him that they were on a tight budget. "If you want to be a success, you have to look like a success, and that includes haircuts." It pained her to see him now appearing like a man who no longer strove for success, but for survival.

"Hi," said Luella, fumbling for a way to begin. "You okay?"

"What do you think?" His tone teetered between anger and despair.

He had no idea the emotional toll this visit exacted from her, or if he had an inkling, his loneliness and boredom trumped her discomfort. Stalling, she described the ceramic pot Rosie painted at the sheltered workshop, reported that Wyatt now called the refrigerator bin the "veg-able cripser," and explained the plot of the latest novel she'd read—anything to avoid the one topic she still needed to broach—his guilt. She fought to strike a balance between her anger and the forced cheerfulness she knew rankled him. August said little. Given the sameness of his days, she supposed that there was nothing new to say.

"You received *Shoe Dog,* the Phil Knight book I sent to you?" Luella had ordered books to be delivered to August since, to prevent contraband from being smuggled into the jail, it was against the rules to hand-deliver packages. "The story of how the Nike Company was created sounded pretty interesting. The reviews were positive. Are you enjoying it?"

"It's slow in places, but he's an impressive guy." August squirmed in his chair, drummed his fingers on the table.

She waited for him to say more. When he didn't, she asked, "Are you ready for more books?"

"Sure. There's nothing else to do in here. Watching paint dry would be more exciting."

He'd always been a restless, high-energy person who flourished when over-extending himself. She imagined confinement was especially hard on him. Plus, Franklin had told her that while the other inmates might play cards or games in the common room, it was likely that August would be shunned by the general population, since pedophiles were considered the lowest of the low.

"I need you to deposit some more cash in my account," he said quietly. "The toothpaste and soap they give us isn't fit for a dog, and the air in here is so dry you could start a fire by rubbing your hands together. I need to buy some ChapStick." For the third time, he ran his tongue over his lips, a newly acquired habit Luella found distracting.

Before August's incarceration she knew nothing about life in jail. Since then, she'd learned that while inmates' basic needs were met—three meals per day that provided 2,000 calories, plus generic grooming supplies—those who had relatives with the financial means had accounts from which they drew funds for items from the canteen, such as snacks and upgraded grooming products. Phone calls made from the jail were routed through a private company and excessively expensive. Inmates used their accounts to pay for those calls. However, if too much money was deposited and spent each month, the authorities would suspect an inmate was engaged in illegal activity like drug purchases or extortion payments to other inmates. Because August had tried to end his life by ingesting too many pills, he was watched especially carefully.

"How much?" she asked.

"Two hundred dollars should be enough for now."

"I'll make a deposit before I leave."

As the allotted time for the visitation ticked away, an awkward silence fell between them. Luella nervously twisted her wedding ring, working up the nerve to confront August. She heard Michael St. James' deep voice. *He fondled me.* "I have something I want to—"

"Dammit, Luella, you should have let me go."

"You don't mean that."

"Don't tell me what I mean," he growled. "Look around you. This is what you've consigned me to, life in a hellhole."

"I—I didn't..."

"Didn't what?" The blue eyes that used to melt her heart, now stared at her, steely and cold. "Didn't think? Didn't want to face reality?"

"Didn't want you to die."

"It wasn't an impulse. It was a choice."

"I'm sorry."

"I can't do this," he said, running his fingers through his short-cropped hair, his voice edgy. "I've got to find a way out." August glanced over his shoulder as if checking to see if the officer standing watch was listening. "I talked with my lawyer about an appeal," he confided, lowering his voice.

Luella bristled. All moisture drained from her mouth.

Apparently, August didn't notice that the earth had shifted because he continued speaking as though he thought she'd be thrilled. "Lowery couldn't make any promises, but he said he's been scouring the trial transcript checking for possible grounds for an appeal. He's looking for any errors on the part of Judge Richards or the prosecutor. I know he doesn't think much of Adlai Fett, that self-righteous prick."

She thought of the thousands of dollars they'd already spent on the high-priced attorney. Both she and August had been fired from their jobs. They no longer had an income. The university had discontinued his benefits, including their health insurance. They were threatening to void his pension. She'd spoken to Franklin about the depletion of their resources and about the liability of the highly-taxed camp property that no longer generated revenue. There was their large house in Lake Bluff, which sat empty, to worry about. Franklin had also warned her that August's victims would likely file civil lawsuits, which could put *her* at risk financially. In fact, she could lose everything.

Guilty! She heard the words of the jury foreperson. She stared at August. Saw his mouth moving. Heard nothing. August may be depressed about being locked up, but he had the luxury of not having to maintain their properties or agonize over their finances. Resentment festered in her like an infected wound. If he was innocent, no amount spent to free him would have been too much.

But he's guilty!

"I know it's a long-shot, Lulu, but I have to keep fighting or die trying."

"B-but you…"

"Time's up," the officer interrupted, his voice as forceful as a slammed door. "Visitation is over."

Luella left the visitation room sickened. August clearly thought she still believed in his innocence. He still counted on her loyalty, played on her trust, relied on her gullibility.

During the hour Luella spent at the county jail, light snowfall had turned into a full-blown storm. She pulled the hood of her coat over her head, pushed through the double entrance doors of the building, and trudged through the parking lot to her SUV, which was already covered in two inches of snow. Snowflakes pelted her face with icy needles and clung to her eyelashes. With her mittened hand, she swiped the handle of the rear driver's side door, then opened it to retrieve the telescoping snow brush.

As she worked her way around the vehicle, wiping snow from the roof and windows, her mind reeled, alarmed by the news that August was seeking an appeal. Not long ago she would have been adamant that he fight for his freedom, been ecstatic that he hadn't given up. But there had been a sea change. She fought the urge to march back into the jail to confront August, an irrational impulse since access to him was strictly controlled. Until her next visit, she'd be left to stew over her inability to tell him the truth.

She opened the car door and tossed the snowbrush onto the floor and then sidled into the driver's seat, kicked snow from her wet shoes, closed the door, and started the engine. She adjusted the thermostat to 72 degrees, pressed the switches for the heated seat and the lumbar adjustment. When she pushed off her hood, snow tumbled through the air. Her limbs and face felt chilled, the car seat stiff, her heart numb.

Although not yet four o'clock, the thick cloud cover and relentless snow made it seem like dusk. Luella turned the wipers on high.

A hunched female figure, bundled in a tight-fitting jacket, stocking cap, and Sorel boots, tramped past the front of her car, making her way to a rusted Chevy sedan parked about thirty feet away. The woman attempted to clear the snow from the windshield using her bare hands. Luella pulled her vehicle alongside, got out and offered to help. It was the young pregnant woman who had waited at the table next to her. Barely out of girlhood, she had apparently hitched her wagon to a faulty star.

What crime had her loved one committed? Drug possession? Repeated DWIs? Assault? Robbery? Luella saw the woman's future clearly. It was a future marred by disappointment and desperation. She fantasized taking the woman by the shoulders, looking her in the eye, shaking her, and saying, "Run, don't walk! It's not too late! You have a choice. Don't waste decades on someone who will cause you years of heartache."

"Thanks," said the young woman as she clumsily dropped into the driver's seat.

"You're welcome."

Before closing her car door, the woman gestured toward Luella's Lincoln Navigator. "Fancy wheels," she said with raised eyebrows and no hint of a smile. Then she started the engine, which turned over after three attempts, and drove away.

Back inside her vehicle, where the air and leather seat steadily warmed, Luella couldn't stop thinking about the young woman, who obviously saw her as a person of means. Perhaps the woman envied her, or perhaps she hadn't given her a second thought. But Luella couldn't shake the image of the woman, immature, pregnant, with a husband or boyfriend in jail. What chance did either she or her unborn child have?

Who are you to judge, thought Luella. At age twenty, she had thrown her lot in with a pedophile. She'd felt so certain, so sure of him. No one could have persuaded her to walk away from the man she loved. Was he already flawed or had he changed? The notion that she had wasted decades with a sexual predator made her feel more worthless than a tarnished penny.

The longer she remained in the parking lot, the more treacherous conditions became. Putting the car in drive, she cautiously steered through the unplowed lot onto the street, where she followed the tire tracks of previous traffic. Her headlights illuminated the plump snowflakes falling faster now, impairing her vision. Going was slow. She thought of the pregnant young woman driving the rusted sedan, probably with balding tires.

As she tried to concentrate on driving, August's words distracted her. *I have to keep fighting or die trying.* It had always been about him. He'd thought only of *I. I have urges. I want sex. I will fuck children. I...I...I.* Bitterness bored into her like a drill through stone.

Keep fighting. He was right about that. She had to keep fighting for herself.

What if Thomas Lowery uncovered some mistake in the proceedings, figured out a way for August to get a new trial? How could she pretend that his immoral behavior didn't matter? How could she keep up this charade? His hope for a new trial was a pipedream, she told herself. He hadn't even been sentenced yet.

Luella followed a slow line of commuter traffic queued behind a huge plow that sent snow tumbling unto the shoulder. A drive that should have taken forty-five minutes from jail to home had already stretched to over an hour. By the time she neared the south end of Given's Knoll, she was almost alone on the highway. Once off the main road the snow became deeper and the blacktop nearly undetectable from the shoulder.

She pressed the phone button on the steering wheel and called Franklin.

"Hi. I—I'm sorry to bother you," she stammered. "I just came from the jail."

"What is it, Lu? Are you out in this storm?"

"I'm fine. I'm almost home." She gripped the steering wheel tighter. "August is hoping to appeal his conviction. I feel terrible because I know he deserves to be punished, but without him, everything feels… heavy. The camp. The house. Taxes. Insurance. The possibility of civil lawsuits. It's like there's a weight around my neck and I'm drowning."

"You know I'm here for you. I can help you sort things out, sell the house, the camp."

"I keep hoping this nightmare will end."

"I know you don't want to hear this," Franklin pressed, "but the hard truth is you need to divorce him."

Divorce. There it was; the word Luella had not dared to say out loud. "I don't want to hurt him when he's at the lowest point in his life."

"Damn it, Lu," Franklin snapped, "for once in your life think of yourself instead of him. You need to protect your assets or you will end up with nothing. And I mean nothing."

His intensity startled her.

"You've always been a giver, not a taker, thinking of others first," he said more gently. "I admire your generosity, seriously, I do. Heaven knows I've been on the receiving end of your caretaking more times than I care to count. You've always had a soft heart. Even as a kid, you put everyone before yourself. You never met a stray cat or dog you didn't bring home."

Cautiously, Luella turned the corner of Virgin Timber Road and then down the unplowed driveway. Through the cascading snow she saw that the porchlight was on. Warm lights glowed in the downstairs windows of her big house, the cedar-clad house that had once been the resort lodge. Beth, Wyatt, and Rosie would welcome her home.

"You've been a wonderful wife, Lu. No one disputes that. But this is not the time to be selfless. You have a future to think about."

"I was so angry with Beth for turning her back on her father, and now I'm about to do the same thing."

"Does that mean you agree to divorce him?"

Luella let the word settle in.

"Yes."

Chapter Twenty-one
~Thanksgiving~

Luella was surprised when Denise called with an invitation to Thanksgiving dinner.

"Nothing fancy. Just family—Franklin, Beth, Wyatt, Rosie, you and me," said Denise.

When, Luella wondered, was the last time she had received a social invitation? It was as though she'd contracted a virulent disease that sent everyone scattering. The exception was her hairdresser, Trudy, who apparently hadn't gotten the message that marrying a pedophile was contagious.

Luella hesitated a beat longer than was polite.

"Luella?"

"I'm here."

"Please say yes. Beth has already agreed."

So, Beth had accepted the invitation without consulting her. She had moved back to camp more than two week ago. There had been plenty of opportunity to discuss holiday plans.

"What time?" asked Luella.

"Around five-ish."

"What can I bring?"

"Just yourself. I've got the meal covered."

Luella waited. For what exactly? For Denise to apologize? For the sisterly ease they once enjoyed to magically reappear? Although distant, Denise, in her own way, had been supportive. She hadn't stopped Franklin from coming to court every day of the trial. She'd welcomed Beth and Wyatt into her home, had helped with Rosie more times than Luella could count, and had been a godsend the night of August's suicide attempt.

All arrangements had been made through Franklin. "Denise says she'd be happy to have Rosie stay overnight." "Denise says she'd love it if Rosie would come to the Fourth of July parade with us." "Denise says she'll pick up Rosie from Horizons."

While Luella was grateful for her help, she resented the distance Denise put between them. They used to be as close as actual sisters, or so Luella had thought. When Franklin's first marriage fell apart after his son, Carter, died, and he brought his secretary, Denise, fifteen years his junior, into the family, other relatives gossiped and outright rejected her. Not Luella. Yet Denise slammed the door so immediately that Luella didn't have the chance to explain or defend herself.

Defend herself? *She* hadn't molested those boys. *She* hadn't groomed them, lured them, violated them. Then Beth's words came back to her. "I didn't *choose* to be Coach Augie Laurent's daughter." That was her offense. Choosing August. How could she defend herself against that?

"Thank you for the invitation," said Luella, hoping that a family dinner would be a step toward normalcy.

What harm could it do?

Franklin's three-story log home with its huge, angular windows was worthy of *House Beautiful*. He was so unassuming that Luella sometimes forgot how hugely successful he had become as founder of the law firm Martin Campbell & Ross LLP.

Four years ago, after Aunt Mavis died, he and Denise razed the seventy-five-year-old cottage and erected their dream home on the property that Luella had inherited with her brother. At August's urging Luella sold her half of the land to Franklin, rationalizing that she already owned the camp on this same chain-of-lakes, and it was wise to keep the valuable land in the family. She greatly preferred the small cottage that, since childhood, had been a place of refuge with its charm and irreplaceable memories. It was a thought she kept to herself.

She missed her Aunt Mavis and Uncle Walter, the way they'd doted on her, loved her unconditionally. She missed the simple things:
sleeping in the trundle bed on the screened-in porch, sunning on the
wooden raft, swinging in the hammock tied between the huge white
pines—the two-hundred-year-old trees that had been cut down to
build this over-sized house.

As an awkward teenager she'd often talked with Aunt Mavis into
the wee hours about "girl things" that she'd been too embarrassed to
discuss with her secretive mother. When Luella was a college sophomore, Aunt Mavis was the first person to whom she'd admitted that she
might be falling in love with the tall, handsome basketball player who
"wasn't really her type."

Now Luella stood in the glow of the porch lantern that accentuated the custom-made walnut front door. She adjusted her coat collar,
finger-combed her hair, and rang the doorbell.

As she waited, she wondered what her life might have been if
she'd never met August that summer, or if she hadn't transferred to
the University of Wisconsin to be near him. What if she had pursued
a graduate degree at the University of Chicago instead of marrying
him and moving from one town to another so he could build his career? Fate. Happenstance. Choices. Life was built around them, yet one
could never see far enough down the road to know where it all led. The
path she'd been on had seemed so right, so comfortable, until one day
it wasn't.

She rang the doorbell again. When Franklin opened the door,
Wyatt scooted past him and threw his arms around her waist, hugging
her fiercely, even though he was now living with her and had only left
that afternoon with Beth and Rosie to help Denise prepare dinner.

"Grandma!"

"Oh, it's my favorite boy!" She picked him up. "You've gotten so
big I can hardly lift you."

"Aunt Denise says I'm growing like a weed."

A stab of jealousy. Luella had lost so many months with her grandson while Denise had enjoyed frequent contact. She reminded herself that was Beth's doing and not her sister-in-law's.

"You sure are." She set Wyatt down and ruffled his hair.

"Hey, sis." Franklin leaned in and kissed her cheek.

"Hey, yourself," she replied, leaning in. She'd always gotten along with Franklin, but an unforeseen benefit of the trial—the only positive outcome she could see—was becoming closer to her brother. Getting through the trial without him sitting by her side day after day would have been impossible.

Luella removed her coat and handed it to Franklin.

"Uncle Franklin buyed me, a Nintendo DS." Wyatt announced.

"Wow! That's quite a gift." She raised an eyebrow at Franklin, who ignored her incredulous expression. "You're a lucky boy."

"He's been showing me the intricacies of Animal Crossing and leaving me in the dust. Someday this kid is going to own a cyber company or invent something we haven't even imagined."

How enviable to have a future filled with such promise. Luella's own uncertain future loomed like a swollen storm cloud, blotting out the sun, constantly threatening to unleash more pounding rain. She was too proud of Wyatt to actually envy him. It was more that she imagined restarting her life, taking roads she'd previously rejected, making choices that would have led her down a path far away from August Laurent. The future, gloomy as it seemed, was worth struggling through, if for no other reason than to watch Wyatt grow into adulthood.

"Beth and Rosie are in the kitchen helping Denise. They've been waiting for you," said Franklin, gesturing toward the lake side of the house. "Come on, buddy." Franklin took Wyatt's hand. "We'll hang out with your grandma after dinner. Now let's go finish that game."

Luella crossed from the foyer into the music room with the baby grand piano at its center. From there she entered the great room, which was open to the kitchen, a stylistic mix of French country and Northwoods rustic, complete with a six-burner La Cornue range and a commercial-grade Sub Zero refrigerator. Although she'd been in the house dozens of times and acknowledged that Denise's culinary skills warranted such extravagance, Luella never failed to note that Aunt Mavis's entire cottage could have comfortably fit inside the kitchen and dining space of the new house.

"Luella's here!" exclaimed Rosie.

"Hi, Mom." Beth maneuvered around the ten-foot island to give Luella a hug. "We've got a crisis on our hands. We're trying to choose an appropriate wine to pair with beef Wellington." Beth conspiratorially winked at her mother.

Luella grinned. "Beef Wellington?"

"Denise thought a change of pace from turkey might be nice."

"I'm thinking either a Burgundy or a Bordeaux," said Denise, puzzling over the pricey bottle in each hand. "What do *you* think, Luella?" She spoke matter-of-factly, as though no distance had grown between them.

"Oh, definitely the Bordeaux," said Luella, who knew little to nothing about wine pairings. She winked back at Beth.

"Bordeaux it is."

"I wish Augie was here," blurted Rosie.

It was as though one of the parties in a ceasefire had unwittingly fired a shot across the demilitarized zone.

"Rosie, honey," Denise said evenly. "Franklin and Wyatt are downstairs in the rec room. Please tell them dinner will be served in about a half-hour."

As soon as Rosie left the room, Luella rounded on Denise. "So, we're going to act as though August doesn't exist. We're going to erase years of history with a snap of the finger. Is that the plan?"

"I didn't say that," Denise shot back.

"Oh, we're just not allowed to mention his name."

"You can talk about him all you want, Luella. You can defend him to the hilt. Just—not—in—my—house."

"Mom. Denise." Beth stepped between them. "Please stop! It's not bad enough Dad hurt those boys. Can't you see that we're letting him destroy this family?"

"Like it or not, Beth, he's still my husband and he's still your father. And, Denise, like it or not, he's still your brother-in-law. Refusing to face this isn't going to magically make things better. Believe me, I've tried," said Luella, splaying her hand across her chest. "I've pretended for far too long. I *want* to talk about what happened. I *need* to talk about what happened. It's eating me up inside. And if I can't talk about it with the people I love most in the world, then I don't know where to turn."

"I'm sorry. I'm just being honest. I'm beyond disgusted," confessed Denise. "I thought I could do this, but I'm not ready to dredge up all that—muck."

"You're not just angry with him," said Luella. "You're angry with me."

Chapter Twenty-two
~Joyeux Noël~

An undecorated ten-foot spruce stood in the corner of the cathe-dral-ceilinged living room. Beth sat cross-legged on the floor opening the boxes of mini-Christmas tree lights she'd purchased that afternoon at the local hardware store, while Luella sat on the couch, huddled around the coffee table with Wyatt and Rosie, making chain garland from red and green construction paper. Bird sprawled on the floor near them, watching intently.

It would be their first Christmas at the camp. For as long as Beth could remember, they had spent holidays attending college basket-ball tournaments, the family's activities revolving around her father's coaching schedule. The holidays at Whisper Lake should have been magical. The setting resembled a scene from a vintage Christmas card. A foot of pristine snow covered the ground; majestic pines, their branches bending with the weight of the snow, stood watch over the house; a sliver of pale blue sky peeked through the trees. It would also be the first Christmas without her father, whose presence loomed large even in his absence. The sentencing hearing, mere weeks away, infected the mood in the house. Her mother's detachment, more no-ticeable the past few days, made the atmosphere seem all the more gloomy

That morning, out of earshot of Wyatt and Rosie, Beth confronted her mother. "I know the holidays are hard for you. They're hard for me, too. But I'm not going to let anything rob Wyatt of his childhood. He's already had too much loss in his short life. Nothing can bring his father back, and I can't undo the damage his grandfather has caused, but I'll be damned if I let anything ruin Christmas for him."

Instead of the pushback Beth had anticipated, her mother said simply, "I'm trying."

"Try harder." Beth snapped.

Luella said nothing.

"I appreciate that you agreed to invite Gina and Anthony," Beth added, attempting to lighten the mood. "Since their parents decided to take a holiday cruise, it worked out well."

"I hope they don't regret coming," Luella replied.

It was unlike her mother to be so overtly negative. Beth chalked it up to the strain they'd been under. Since she'd moved back to the camp they had arrived at an understanding of sorts, both acknowledging her father's guilt, both struggling with the deep sadness his actions had caused, and both wrestling with anger. As far as Beth was concerned, he'd brought the consequences upon himself and sullied the rest of the family in the process. Her mother, on the other hand, couldn't seem to shake the burden of obligation. Unable to see eye-to-eye, they'd settled on silence. At some point, Beth believed, they would have to hash this out, but, at least for now, the holidays created an unspoken cease-fire, a truce that could end without warning.

"Is it time for Aunt Gina and Uncle Anthony to come yet?" asked Wyatt, looping a green strip of construction paper through a red one. "Uncle Anthony said he has a special surprise for me."

Beth glanced over at the grandfather clock. It was just past two o'clock. "They'll be here soon, honey."

Gabe would have been impressed with how his younger brother had stepped up as the father figure. It would have been understandable if Anthony, a handsome, eligible bachelor, an entrepreneur with a successful internet business and an active social calendar, had simply walked away. Instead, he'd committed to being in Wyatt's life. A surge of gratitude coursed through Beth. She was also grateful that Anthony and Gina had accepted the invitation to spend the holidays at the lake, hoping they would bring some measure of cheer and provide a distraction from the constant focus on her father.

Beth plugged the ends of the light cords together and into the outlet to make sure that all the bulbs worked. Satisfied that none were defective, she laid them out carefully side-by-side, climbed the ladder, and wound the first strand among the top branches of the tree.

"Rosie, could you help me?" asked Beth.

Smiling, Rosie put down her green paper strip and glue stick and got up from the couch.

"Please hand me the next one." Beth pointed to the floor.

"Jingle bells, jingle bells, jingle all the way. Hey!" Rosie belted out off key.

Beth's spirits lifted. She hummed along, started to believe it was possible to have a pleasant, if not a joyful, Christmas. From her perch, she could look out the window at the frozen lake, now a smooth plain of blinding white. In any other year, it would have been impossible not to find peace in this place.

"I'm not sure why you bought such a tall tree," Luella complained. "We don't have any ornaments, and I'm not sure we can make enough chain to decorate the whole thing."

Beth swallowed her annoyance. "It's okay, Mom. The lights will make it festive."

"Grandma, I have an idea," Wyatt offered. "At school we drawed our faces on paper plates and hanged them up. We could draw faces on paper plates and hang them on our tree."

"That's a great idea!" said Beth.

"I love drawing!" Rosie gave Wyatt a high five.

"Out of the mouths of babes," said Luella. "I'll go see how many paper plates are left over from summer."

"Come on, Wyatt. Let's go get my craft supplies." Rosie took Wyatt's hand and climbed up the stairs with Bird chasing.

Beth stepped from the ladder and wound the remaining lights

around the lower branches of the tree, the needles scratching her hands as she worked near the trunk. The aroma of spruce and the prickly needles against her skin evoked a memory of the first Christmas after she'd married Gabe. They'd argued over the best way to string the lights, whether to wrap the strands in a continuous spiral or to go vertically up and down the tree. Beth insisted on doing it her way, aggressively removing the lights Gabe had already strung. As she tugged at the entwined cords, the tree toppled over, scattering dried needles across the floor. Gabe had looked at her incredulously, and they'd burst out laughing. They'd ended up making love next to the fallen tree. For weeks she'd pulled out needles stuck in her cable knit sweater.

Rosie returned carrying a large plastic bin filled with art supplies. Wyatt trailed with a smaller container. Bird pranced behind him. Rosie opened both bins and spread the markers, yarn, ribbon, glitter, pipe cleaners, fabric swatches, buttons, glue sticks, and scissors on the dining table.

"This is perfect," said Beth.

Rosie glowed.

Luella came from the kitchen holding a stack of white paper plates. "This ought to do."

The four of them sat at the table constructing face ornaments. Soon the table was littered with glitter and scraps of construction paper. Beth smiled at Rosie's and Wyatt's Picassoesque creations, faces with features that didn't quite line up.

The doorbell rang.

Bird scampered to the door. Wyatt and Beth trailed after him.

"Uncle Anthony! Aunt Gina!"

"Come in. Come in," said Beth.

Their arms were laden with wrapped presents.

"You have no idea how glad I am to see you," Beth whispered into Gina's ear.

Rosie and Luella joined the group in the foyer.

"We're happy that you could join us for the holidays," said Luella. "Wyatt has been especially anxious for you to get here. Did you have any trouble finding the camp?"

"We vaguely remembered how to get here, although it looked different in the summer when we came for Beth's wedding. Our G.P.S. worked surprisingly well in the woods, plus your directions were flawless," said Anthony. "Hey, buddy, can you help me carry these presents?" Anthony handed Wyatt a couple of the smallest packages.

Once the gifts were deposited under the tree and suitcases were brought in and taken up to two upstairs guest bedrooms, everyone sat around the table making small talk and more paper plate ornaments.

"I was going for Lady Gaga" said Anthony, holding up his plate, "but I think this looks more like Hilary Clinton."

Gina giggled and gave his arm a friendly shove.

"Don't get me wrong. I voted for her, but I think a Christmas ornament in her honor is a bridge too far."

Beth laughed and was gratified to hear her mother laugh, too.

"Well, I'm making your face." Gina showed her plate with its black pipe cleaner hair and toothy grin, to everyone. "And I think I've created an exact likeness."

Wyatt giggled. "It doesn't look like Uncle Anthony at all."

The tension drained from Beth's neck, as though an iron shroud had been lifted from her shoulders.

"Hey, buddy, you've been working on that same ornament a long time," Anthony observed. "Whose face are you making?"

"Grandpa Augie," said Wyatt, solemnly, as he glued a black button on the plate underneath an arched eyebrow. "He's in jail. Mommy says he's never coming back."

"Grandma! Santa came! He ate the cookies, and the reindeer ate the carrots!"

Luella's eyes slowly opened, the haze of sleep clearing as Wyatt, breathless, wearing his dinosaur pajamas, his curly hair tousled, climbed on her bed. Bird nestled at the foot end, tail thumping.

"He left lots of presents!"

Slowly, Luella sat up, propped her pillow against the headboard, and leaned back. She pulled Wyatt toward her, hugged him, kissed his forehead, her spirits rising. His skin, warm and child-soft, smelling faintly of sweet perspiration, soothed her. Beth was right; her grandson deserved a joy-filled Christmas.

"Presents? Are you sure?"

Wyatt nodded vigorously. "I peeked downstairs. There's a giant pile of presents under the tree." To demonstrate, he thrust his arms up as high as he could reach.

Luella chuckled.

"Grandma, when can we open the presents?"

Glancing at the clock, she saw that it was just shy of six thirty. "Is anyone else up?"

"No," he admitted. "But I can wake them up!"

"Go for it." She gave Wyatt another squeeze. "Wake up Gina, Anthony, Rosie, and your mom. Tell them it's time to open presents, and tell them Grandma says there is no turning over and going back to sleep."

"Okay!" Wyatt slid off the bed. Bird stood, stretched his front legs to their full length, arched his back, then leapt to the floor and followed Wyatt.

Once downstairs, Luella made a pot of coffee, set small plates on the counter along with cream, sugar, mugs, glasses, and a pitcher of orange juice. She also arranged a plate of Danish pastries Beth had purchased at the bakery.

She poured a cup of coffee for herself, inhaling the aroma as she ambled into the living room. The warmth from the cup seeped into her fingers and palms. Snow blanketed the ground and the frozen lake. A decorated tree stood in the corner of the living room, yet things felt off, as though she'd awoken to Christmas in a foreign country. It wouldn't have surprised her if, instead of Merry Christmas, she was greeted with Joyeux Noël, or if she discovered the presents had been delivered by Sinterklaas.

Thinking of August sitting in his stark cell, acutely aware of his family celebrating Christmas without him and knowing that for years to come holidays would pass with the same oppressive monotony, tore at Luella's heart. Perhaps after all the years of frenzied sports activity she should have been grateful for this peace, for the low-key holiday. But it seemed unbearably sad. She told herself to quit wallowing, reminded herself to adjust her attitude for Wyatt's sake.

Bird bounded down the stairs, followed by Wyatt. "I waked everybody. I had to sit on Uncle Anthony cuz he snores and he didn't hear me."

"Good idea," said Luella, smiling.

Rosie, still in her nightgown and wearing scuffs, came down the stairs first. "Can I turn on the lights?" she asked, pointing to the tree. "It's prettier with the lights on."

"Of course."

Rosie flipped the wall switch. The tree lights glowed in the room's half-light, making the room instantly more festive. The paper chain garland and paper plate face ornaments, Luella had to admit, lent the tree a childlike charm.

Beth came downstairs next wearing Gabe's navy fleece robe with his initials monogrammed on the breast pocket. Before the loss of her own husband, Luella might have suggested it was time to stop wearing it, believing that hanging on was prolonging Beth's pain. She might have said something insensitive, such as "it's time to move on," as if the future without Gabe held more appeal than the past.

Next, Anthony arrived in plaid pajama pants and a long-sleeve University of Wisconsin T-shirt. He was a handsomer version of Gabe;

the resemblance to his older brother, however, was unmistakable. She wondered how their likeness affected Beth.

Gina was the last to enter the living room. Her hair, put up loosely on the top of her head, revealed full, high cheek bones. She had the same penetrating eyes and dark hair as her brothers, revealing Italian ancestry that Beth referred to as the "Mancuso look." She wore a pink satin robe tied around her slim waist. Her flawless skin glowed.

"Before we get started, coffee, juice, and rolls are in the kitchen. But hurry. We have one anxious little boy," said Luella.

Beth, Anthony, and Gina each came back carrying a mug and a plate. Rosie held a glass of juice and ate a Danish, its telltale crumbs trailing down the front of her gown. Gina and Beth arranged themselves on either end of the sofa with Rosie seated in the middle.

"Ooh, I see Santa was here, a very generous Santa at that," said Gina. "I'm pretty sure if Santa checked his list once or twice, he wouldn't be leaving all these presents for me." She grinned at Beth. "I wonder who has been extra good to get so many presents."

"Me!" exclaimed Wyatt.

"Well then let's see what Santa brought you," said Anthony, who lowered himself to the floor next to the presents. He handed Wyatt a package wrapped in blue, snowman-print paper.

Carefully, Wyatt pulled one taped flap, then the other.

"It's okay to rip away, buddy, or we'll be here all day," Anthony assured him.

Wyatt turned to his mother. Beth nodded permission. Tearing the first strip of paper from one end of the package to the other, Wyatt again turned to Beth, as though he couldn't quite believe it was okay to be so destructive. She smiled. From infancy, Luella observed, Wyatt had always been cautious, unlike other little boys who dove into the fray without a second thought, who climbed to the highest rung of the jungle gym before an adult could corral them, who sped down the driveway on their bikes without a second glance for on-coming traffic.

Not old soul Wyatt. It pained Luella to think that the losses he'd suffered in his young life had exacerbated that inborn caution to the point where tearing paper had become an act of bravery.

"It's a dinosaur robot! Just what I wanted!"

After Wyatt unwrapped a Lego set, a pair of walkie talkies, a six-pack of dinosaur cars, a star nightlight projector, and a saucer snow sled, all from Santa, Anthony said, "Wait here, buddy, Aunt Gina and I have something for you." He left the room and returned carrying a huge gift covered with a patchwork quilt. "It was too big to wrap, so we're going to have an unveiling."

Wyatt's eyes widened.

Anthony set the gift on the floor. "With any unveiling, you need magic words. Ready?"

Wyatt nodded solemnly.

"Gaboo boo—raboy boy—taleek leek—kaboom boom," Anthony chanted while waving his arms wildly over the gift.

Wyatt giggled.

"All right, already," Gina snickered.

"Shazzim, shazzam!" Anthony pulled the blanket off, revealing a cerulean blue bicycle.

Wyatt's eyes grew into wide circles. "It's a bike. It doesn't have training wheels!" Wyatt threw his arms around Anthony's waist and then ran to Gina, wrapping his arms around her neck.

"You guys are too much," said Beth. "It's a big gift for a little boy."

"Don't worry. I'll teach him to ride," Anthony reassured her as he lifted Wyatt onto the seat. "We just need to adjust the pedals and the handlebars."

Wyatt dismounted. "It's the bestest bike in the whole world."

"What do you say," said Anthony, "after lunch we bundle up, shovel a path on the driveway, and take this for a little winter spin."

"Santa brought a present for you, too, Rosie," said Beth, handing her a box wrapped in silver with white embossed pine trees.

With great care Rosie undid the taped ends of the wrapping and slid it from the box. "I'm saving this pretty paper for my crafts," she declared. Inside the box she found abundant needlepoint supplies.

After the adults finished exchanging gifts Luella said, "Look. There are two more presents here. One says 'to Rosie from Augie.' The other one says 'to Wyatt from Grandpa.'"

Luella handed a palm-sized box, topped with a red bow, to Rosie. Flipping open the hinged lid, Rosie discovered a pair of silver butterfly earrings. Like sunrise, a smile slowly spread across her face. "Augie always gives me really good presents."

Beth, Anthony, and Gina sat silent.

From under the tree and against the back wall, Luella retrieved a cube-like box covered in Mickey Mouse wrapping paper.

"From Grandpa?" Wyatt looked both puzzled and delighted.

"He didn't want you to think he had forgotten you."

Wyatt dropped to his knees and tore the paper. Luella helped him open the box. Inside was a junior-sized basketball. He lifted it out of the box and rested his cheek against the dimpled surface.

"Mom," said Beth, her voice tense. "Could you please help me in the kitchen?"

Luella stared at Beth, confused.

"The kitchen," said Beth, nodding in that direction, her mouth dipping into a frown.

Reluctantly, Luella followed.

Once in the kitchen out of earshot of the others, Luella said, "What?"

"Mom, you've got to stop this."

"Stop what?"

"This." Beth gestured toward the living room. "This charade. You have to stop trying to make Dad better than he is."

Not in the frame of mind to explain why she'd visited the jail that afternoon, especially given Beth's stern admonition on Christmas day, Luella excused herself after Wyatt and Rosie turned in for the night, leaving Beth to enjoy time with Anthony and Gina.

She sat propped up in bed and opened her journal. The most recent entry was dated more than a month ago. Several torn pages were tucked into the spine, reminding her of the night she'd fallen apart, and Beth had to pick up the pieces. She wondered how much of her journal Beth had read.

From the back pocket she pulled out a clipping from Nell Wooden's obituary, published in *The Los Angeles Times* in 1984, now creased and yellowed from age. She carefully unfolded it, and read:

The Woodens' daughter, Nancy, recently said: "I've known a lot of married people, and I've always said what they (her parents) had was rare. It's like they were one person, and totally devoted to each other and the family."

Luella had held up the Woodens' marriage as an ideal to be admired and emulated, and used to believe she'd achieved it. How ridiculous to think that for she and August oneness was desirable or even possible.

She flipped to a blank page and wrote *December 29* at the top.

My visit to the jail this afternoon made me heartsick. There was no evidence of the holidays anywhere.

Luella had been nervous as she trudged up the long sidewalk to the jail and checked in with the stoic officer at the reception window. Being in that building made her feel as though she, too, were a criminal. Glancing around the entry at the young woman with a teardrop tattoo, the middle-aged man with wire-rimmed glasses, and the pregnant teenager who looked too young to vote, Luella wondered if they felt the same shame, whether they also wanted to explain to the desk officer that they had nothing to do with the crime perpetrated by the inmate they'd come to visit.

Facing August was more difficult than I imagined. My last visit after his suicide attempt should have prepared me for seeing him in that place looking so diminished. It did not.

On the way there I practiced confronting him. How could you ruin those boys? How could you hurt our daughter? How could you destroy everything we worked for? Do we mean so little to you? I wanted to demand answers. But when I saw him walk in wearing that orange jumpsuit with Ojibwe County Jail stenciled on it, as though he now belonged to the county and not to me, I lost my nerve.

He felt like a stranger.

There had been times when August would be away from home for a week or two, working a basketball camp or recruiting, he immersed in his work, she fixed in her routine, and there would be a distance between them when he returned, the first hug and kiss always tentative. They had to work back into their rhythm as a couple. But this was different. August was not coming back.

He talked about lack of sleep due to the constant noise and the inadequacy of the food. At least he was able to purchase better supplies since I put money in his account.

I tried to talk about what was going on at home, to tell him about the presents I'd purchased for Rosie and Wyatt on his behalf, as much to distract myself as to inform him, but he kept changing the subject back to life in jail. I think it's too painful for him to hear about all he is missing.

The longer they spoke the more the walls had closed in, her suffocating on the accusatory words lodged in her throat, him shrinking his world to the size of a cell.

Just before it was time to leave, he did inquire after Rosie and Beth and Wyatt. He asked if I could bring them for a visit. I made no promises. With enough preparation I might manage a visit with Rosie. It would upset her to see August in jail and to realize that he cannot come home. Despite what he wants, I don't think I'm prepared to deal with that. Beth has no intention of seeing her dad, and I can't imagine that she will let Wyatt visit his grandfather. Ever.

There was a soft knock on the door. The door opened a crack. "Mom? Are you awake?"

"I'm up."

As the door opened wider, the light from the hallway fanned across the floor, glinted off the dresser mirror. Beth's tall, lean figure glided into the room. Luella set her journal on the nightstand and moved to the middle of the bed. Beth curled up next to her, the way she used to as a child when August was away.

"I know you went to see Dad."

"I'm not going to justify that to you."

"How is he?" Beth spoke so softly that at first Luella thought she might not have heard her correctly.

"Subdued. Lonely. He seems smaller somehow."

Beth rested her head on Luella's shoulder. Luella stroked her daughter's hair, inhaled its flowery scent.

"Mom, I don't know how to stop being so angry. All I know is that I'm tired of hating him."

Chapter Twenty-three
~The Mancusos~

Bird bounded through the deep snow, ears flapping, tongue lolling, then tunneled toward Beth, headfirst like a canine plow. A snowball exploded in the middle of Beth's back, shooting ice crystals into her hair and down her neck. She shivered and laughed.

"You got her Uncle Anthony!" cried Wyatt, his conspiratorial glee delighting Beth.

"Okay you two, this means war!" Beth bent down, scooped a mound of snow into her thick mittens, packing and shaping it into a softball-sized sphere.

Anthony hoisted Wyatt, using him as a human shield, Wyatt giggling as Anthony trundled backwards, bouncing through the foot-deep snow, flinging another snowball sidearm that winged Beth's coat sleeve.

"If you think a child is going to save you, you have another thing coming," yelled Gina.

Anthony twirled to face her, sending Wyatt's legs sailing into the air and making him giggle all the harder.

Gina, looking very much the city girl, wearing a white quilted jacket belted at the waist, her hair stylishly held back by a bright red headband and her feet in fashionable leather boots, threw a snowball that landed several feet short.

"No chance you'll be drafted into the Majors anytime soon," Anthony taunted.

Beth, dressed in a wool jacket and Sorel boots, closed within twenty feet and lobbed the snowball, which burst on top of Anthony's stocking-capped head.

"Three points!" exclaimed Beth, "Swoosh! Nothing but net."

"Come on, buddy. We're sitting ducks." Carrying Wyatt, Anthony trudged through the snow, Bird romping alongside, and hid behind the trunk of a century-old pine. He set Wyatt on the ground, scooped up a fistful of snow, and packed a small snowball. "Boys against the girls. Our dignity is at stake. You ready?" Wyatt, wide-eyed, nodded. "Let's see how far you can throw this one." Anthony placed the snowball in Wyatt's outstretched hand. "First we have to see if the coast is clear," Anthony said loudly and slowly for Beth's and Gina's benefit.

Two heads peeked from behind the tree. Their mutual resemblance to Gabe took Beth's breath away. She'd recognized this resemblance in the past—the way they tilted their heads, set their jaws, smiled impishly—yet seeing their faces, one poised above the other, made Gabe seem alive, not a memory but an in-the-flesh presence. How she wished he could be here with her, with his son and brother and sister to savor this beautiful day. She braced herself, resisted the melancholy that threatened to reinsert itself, determined not to succumb to the sadness. Not today. Not during this rare, joyful respite.

The faces disappeared behind the tree.

"I wonder where they could be," Gina shouted, her hand poised above her eyes, her head turning dramatically from side-to-side like a lookout. "Have you seen them anywhere?"

"They seem to have disappeared into thin air." Bird circled the tree, barking, as if trying to alert them to the obvious hiding place. Beth didn't know whether her eyes were watering from the cold or from laughter.

Wyatt and Anthony burst from behind the tree and launched their missiles, Wyatt's landing on Beth's thigh, Anthony's hitting its mark on Gina's shoulder. Anthony bent down, scooping more snow, packing snowballs, swiftly, expertly hurling them in a barrage. Wyatt imitated him with half the efficiency but twice the determination. Gina waded through the snow away from the onslaught. Beth stood her ground, packing snowballs and whipping them as fast as she could manage. In her peripheral vision she saw Gina throwing snowballs that landed far short of their intended target. Bird leaped into the air, jaw snapping in a vain attempt to catch each snowball. Anthony and Wyatt advanced until they were within ten feet of Beth.

"We surrender!" she yelled.

"What?" Gina hollered back, giggling, slogging through the deep snow toward the others. "I thought we had them on the ropes."

"I don't know about everyone else, but I'm ready for some hot chocolate," said Beth, her hat, jacket, and jeans covered in white.

"I love hot chocolate," said Wyatt. "With marshmallows."

"Sounds good to me. How about you, sis?" said Anthony, giving Gina's shoulder an affectionate squeeze.

"I never turn down chocolate, solid or liquid," she said.

"Boys rule," declared Wyatt.

Heading to the house, Anthony gave Wyatt a high five. "To the victors!"

"That was the funnest time ever," said Wyatt. "I wish you and Aunt Gina could stay forever."

In the foyer, everyone removed their jackets and hats and hung them on the hooks to dry, then lined up their wet boots on the rubber mat. Wyatt's cheeks glowed and his eyes sparkled. Beth kissed the top of his head before he disappeared into the house with Anthony and Gina.

As her hands and feet warmed, the pleasant burn reminded Beth of her childhood, when she spent hours building snow forts with her friends. Afterward she would come indoors and savor the sensation of her body thawing. The snowball fight harkened back to that innocent, less complicated time, when she found pleasure from simply coming in from the cold.

In the kitchen Luella prepared a tray of cookies and Rosie stirred cocoa and milk in a large saucepan.

"Looks like you were having a good time out there." As Beth lifted a cookie from the tray, Luella playfully slapped her hand. "Now you've ruined the symmetry."

"A little OCD are we?" Beth swiped a second cookie.

Luella smiled. "Out! I'll bring these in when the hot chocolate is ready."

Beth joined the others, all red-cheeked and in stocking feet, gathered in the living room around the fireplace. The room, as cozy as a down comforter, smelled of tangy woodsmoke. Bird lay on the floor near the hearth gnawing the ice balls between his pads.

"It's really beautiful here. Isolated, but beautiful," said Gina, gathering her damp hair into a ponytail and twisting the band in place.

Winter had a special beauty—pristine snow sparkling in the sunlight, laden boughs curtsying to the earth, wispy clouds floating in the ice blue sky. Magical. The isolation didn't bother Beth, but the memories troubled her. Before she'd decided to return, she wondered whether living at the camp would be tolerable; it held so many reminders of her father. She'd discovered that because the family had never spent the winter months at the camp, she could focus less on basketball, campers, and her father, and more on the refuge-like quality of the place.

Still, before Anthony and Gina had arrived, there existed a pervasive sadness that Beth attributed to her mother's insistence on keeping her father's presence alive in the house. Like a ghost whose maleficence is revealed through whistling tea kettles, slammed cupboard doors, and flickering lights, he was invisible but omnipresent. His clothes still hung in the closets. His watch sat on his dresser. His prescriptions, toothbrush, and shaving cream were still in the medicine cabinet. It was as though her mother couldn't make up her mind, one minute smashing and tearing up old photos and ripping the stuffing out of a pillow, the next continuing to wear the Hoops and Hearts necklace, encouraging Wyatt to make a paper plate ornament of her father's face, and neglecting to tell Rosie the truth.

It was hypocritical, Beth knew, to be too hard on her mother. One minute she despised her father, the next, she missed him, or at least missed the father she'd idolized. She missed talking basketball strategy, sharing team stories, seeking advice. She missed the way he doted on Wyatt, the pride he'd displayed in being a grandfather, as though she'd given him the most precious gift possible. She longed to have her father back; then the anger would fester. There were times when she simply wanted to wish away the past several years, before Gabe died, before her father assaulted those boys. But perhaps it wouldn't be enough to erase a few years. Who knew how long her father had been preying on children. She might have to wish away her entire life.

"The hot chocolate is ready," Luella called from the kitchen.

The fire sputtered and crackled, sending sparks up the chimney. Kenny G played in the background, his soprano saxophone humming richly somewhere between woodwind and brass. Luella entered the room carrying a tray of hot-chocolate-filled mugs. Rosie followed with a plateful of frosted cookies.

Tomorrow morning, New Year's Day, Gina and Anthony would be leaving. Beth dreaded their departure. Having them visit through the holidays had been a godsend. They'd brought laughter into a house otherwise devoid of it. Wyatt had told Anthony exactly what she had been thinking but dared not say, "I wish you and Aunt Gina could stay forever." Anthony and Gina, Gabe's brother and sister, were the siblings she'd never had. Gabe's family had become her family. She had grown to love them as much as any blood relatives. Being together, seeing the uplifting impact they had on her son, her mother, and Rosie reinforced their essential place in her life.

When she'd married Gabe Mancuso, she'd insisted on keeping her surname. She'd been proud of the Laurent name and all that it stood for: success, morality, and integrity. Then she knew who she was. She was Beth Laurent, daughter of August and Luella, a new teacher, an up-and-coming coach. She was a feminist who believed that giving up her name meant giving up a part of herself. Gabe had respected that, never pushed. Now the Laurent name stood for failure, sin, and deceit. She was ashamed. Her father had destroyed the stellar reputation she had enjoyed. It didn't matter that she was not the one who had molested those boys, been arrested, found guilty. As long as she kept the Laurent name, she would be forever linked to Augie Laurent, the pedophile coach. Guilt by association. No matter what she did, as long as she was Beth Laurent, she could not completely escape the stink that would cling to her.

Like a snakeskin, she would shed that old self. She would start over, an adult tabula rasa.

"Luella, these are the best gingerbread cookies I've ever eaten," Gina gushed. "Seriously."

"Grandma this is the bestest hot chocolate *I* ever had. Seriously," Wyatt mimicked.

In that moment Beth made the decision she'd avoided for months. She would not sign her teaching and coaching contract for the following year. She would get a new job in a new city. If she had a chance to transform herself into a new person, she had to be in a place where she could build an impeccable reputation herself. Beth Laurent would be no more. She would be Elizabeth Grace Mancuso, woman, mother, teacher, coach.

The next hurdle was to tell her mother.

As the grandfather clock struck ten the blare of party horns resounded in the living room. "Happy New Year!" everyone shouted.

"It was a stroke of genius to celebrate New Year's Eve on Puerto Rico time rather than central time," Luella gushed.

"As much as I'd like to take credit for the idea," said Gina, "I can't. When I was in college, I worked at a tavern that catered to an older crowd. We'd set up a theme party and call it New Year's in San Juan. It's where I developed a taste for *arroz con dulce* and rum punch. We'd pop the champagne at ten, have the place cleaned up by eleven-thirty, and be out partying and dancing at Club D'Angelo by midnight."

"I never in a million years would have thought of that," Luella admitted.

"This calls for a toast." Anthony raised his champagne flute filled with sparkling cider. Glasses were hoisted all around.

"*Alla tua salute!* To your health!" he said. "May this new year be a thousand times better than all the years that came before."

It couldn't get much worse, thought Beth. The past couple of years had been the most miserable of her life. Hopefully, Anthony's toast was a harbinger of better days ahead.

"*Alla tua salute!*" everyone repeated.

The New Year holiday had never been especially meaningful to Beth; it had simply been a day devoted to watching college football games. Making New Year's resolutions struck her as an exercise in futility. A competitor and planner, she had never needed one special day devoted to setting goals. Tonight, however, the notion of a fresh start held great appeal. "Happy New Year!" Silently she dissected each word.

Happy. Since Gabe died, she'd been a million miles from happy. Grief had settled in like a permanent boarder. There had been glimmers of joy that would ignite, only to quickly fade. The previous summer she'd come to camp determined to regain her footing, and then her father had been arrested, knocking her sideways. Sometimes she wondered if she'd forgotten how to be happy, whether the ability was like a muscle that needed exercising lest it atrophy.

New. She had the chance to shed the old, to look forward rather than backward. It was impossible to erase the past; besides there were memories she cherished, memories she wanted to fiercely hold on to. Obsessing on the pain strewn in her past was like revving a car engine when stuck in a snow bank, causing the tires to sink into a deepening rut. She was tired of sinking, tired of being stuck. New beckoned her to stop staring in the rearview mirror and to focus on what lay ahead.

Year. Three hundred and sixty-five days stretched out before her like an untraveled road. The moment Gabe quit breathing it was as though time had stopped, but implausibly life around her continued. She'd wanted to shout, "Don't you know that everything has changed!" A Technicolor world had turned black and white. If it hadn't been for Wyatt, who gave her a reason to get out of bed each day, she would have pulled the covers over her head and never gotten up. He was the reason she had to heal.

"We need a selfie," insisted Gina, bringing Beth back to the moment.

Beth, Anthony, Gina, Rosie, and Luella crowded together in front of the fireplace with Wyatt sandwiched in the middle.

"Bird should be in the picture, too," said Wyatt.

"You're right, buddy. He's part of the family." Beth patted her leg and commanded, "Bird, come." The dog obediently loped to her and sat next to Wyatt.

Handing the phone to Anthony, Gina said, "Here, brother, put those freakishly long arms to good use."

Anthony gave her a playful nudge before extending his arm to its full length. "Smile!" he said.

Click.

"Take one more just in case," said Gina.

Click.

"Good. Let's see how fabulous we all look." She took the phone from Anthony, enlarged the first photo on the screen for everyone to see, and then scrolled to the second photo.

"Not bad. We look pretty dapper in these party hats, especially you, Wyatt." Anthony grinned at Beth. He picked up Wyatt, whose oversized top hat rested on his ears and sat cockeyed on his head, and hoisted him under his arm.

Wyatt giggled as Anthony jiggled and twirled. A wave of affection flooded over Beth. She had to admit that with their wide grins, glinting eyes, and shiny foil hats they looked festive and, yes, happy. Even her mother looked younger in the photo than she had in months.

"Are you sure you can't stay to watch the Rose Bowl on Monday?" Luella asked. "I've invited Franklin and Denise over to watch the game. It would be more fun with the two of you here."

"It's a tempting offer." Anthony set Wyatt down gently. "But we need to leave tomorrow. Both of us have to get back to work."

The look of disappointment on her mother's face mirrored Beth's dread at their departure. She had feared that Christmas and New Year's Eve would be funereal, the reality of her father's absence hitting home with a vengeance, so she'd invited Anthony and Gina to the lake to provide an antidote to the blues. They hadn't disappointed, but they were not a permanent cure.

It had been such a relief to laugh and play, to think about something other than her father or that she had no clue where to go or what to do next. Her mother must have been wrestling with the same demons, since she'd caught her staring into space more than once. Beth silently repeated Anthony's toast. *May this New Year be a thousand times better than all the years that came before.* If life was going to improve, she had to take control.

"Luella, this is a beautiful place, plus you've been such a gracious host it's hard to leave," said Gina. "I'm sorry we have to go, but if you'll have us, we'll be back."

"I'd like that. You're always welcome."

Beth was heartened to see that her mother would miss them, too. Perhaps that would help smooth the waters when she broached the subject of changing her last name to Mancuso. Perhaps her mother would see that it was not only about disavowing her father but about the love she had for Gabe's family.

The grandfather clock chimed on the half hour.

"Okay, kiddo. It's way past your bedtime," said Beth. "Say good night to everyone."

"Aunt Gina, will you read stories to me tonight?" Wyatt asked, yawning and rubbing his eyes.

Beth shot Gina a sympathetic look.

"Absolutely. I'm always ready to read to my favorite nephew. Rosie, do you want to help me tuck Wyatt in?"

"Sure! I love stories."

Wyatt made a loop around the room hugging everyone. Rosie followed, hugging everyone, too.

"I'll be up as soon as you've brushed your teeth and read *one* book," said Beth, kissing Wyatt's cheek.

"Two?" Wyatt pressed.

"Not tonight," said Beth. "Remember, we had a deal. You got to stay up for the New Year's celebration in exchange for only reading one book tonight."

Wyatt yawned again, his eyes turning into slits.

"All this merriment has worn me out, too," Luella admitted. "I'm going to call it a night."

She followed Gina, Wyatt, Rosie, and Bird upstairs, leaving Beth and Anthony alone in the living room.

Beth paged through the vinyl albums in the record cabinet. "Lionel Richie, Marvin Gaye, or Gladys Knight?" she asked, looking over her shoulder.

"How about Marvin?"

"Marvin and *Midnight Love* it is," said Beth. She pulled the album from its sleeve, How many times had she heard her father play "Midnight Lady," the first song on the album? "Listen to that perfect percussion mix. That's Marvin clapping and playing the keyboard riffs. The guy had more talent than any one man deserves," he'd say each time before the guitar joined in and the horns began playing. A pang of grief slithered through her.

Anthony leaned forward in her father's oversized chair, his forearms resting on his knees. "Do you think Luella realizes that USC is playing Penn State in the Rose Bowl tomorrow?"

"Am I missing something?"

"Penn State," said Anthony. "You remember—Jerry Sandusky? The huge child abuse sex scandal. Minimum prison sentence of 60 years. The university was assessed a sixty million dollar fine and a four-year post-season ban. They're eligible to play bowl games again."

"Oh, no!" Beth groaned. "I hope Mom doesn't freak out."

Gina bounded down the stairs. "Wyatt fell asleep half way through *The Lorax*. He's all tucked in snug as a bug in a rug. Rosie's in for the night, too."

Beth smiled weakly.

Gina looked from Beth to Anthony. "What?"

"Beth didn't realize USC is playing Penn State tomorrow, and she's pretty sure Luella doesn't know either."

"Oh, no," said Gina. "That's not good, not good at all."

Chapter Twenty-four
~Revelation~

In the kitchen Luella prepared a tray of cheese, crackers, and sliced Anjou pears for the family Rose Bowl party. She lifted the lid from the slow-cooker to check the cranberry chili meatballs, inhaling their tangy sweetness. Satisfied that they were fully cooked, she opened the liquor cabinet and retrieved bottles of Pinot Noir, Denise's favorite wine, and Maker's Mark whiskey, Franklin's drink of choice, and arranged them alongside a corkscrew, cocktail napkins, and a tray of glasses.

After the dustup at Thanksgiving, Luella was pleased, although wary, when her sister-in-law agreed to come with Franklin to the house to watch the football game. It was a chance to start the New Year off on the right foot, although she couldn't imagine how the coming year could be worse than the previous one. They would arrive in about a half-hour, and she wanted everything to be ready.

When Anthony and Gina left, she'd been disappointed. Beth's disposition had greatly improved with them in the house. She had been more relaxed, frequently smiling and laughing, something Luella had not seen in a long while. Wyatt lit up around them, too. Luella had to admit that Anthony and Gina, who brought a palpable levity into the house, had a similar effect on her. Without them, she wondered if family tensions would resurface and if she and Beth would revert to the melancholic state they'd floundered in before Christmas. She vowed to do everything in her power to prevent that.

Luella carried the tray of glasses into the living room, where she found Rosie standing, shoulders shaking, face buried in her hands, crying.

"Why are you sad, sweetie?" Luella asked gently, setting the tray on the coffee table and putting her arm around Rosie's shoulder.

"I miss Augie," Rosie whimpered.

"Me, too." As soon as she uttered the words, Luella wondered if they were true.

Rosie looked up at Luella with rheumy eyes and a runny nose. "When is he—c-coming h-home?" she sniffed.

Guilt pricked Luella's conscience. She'd avoided explaining to Rosie that her brother would never come home. Luella hadn't meant to deceive her; it had just been easier to let the truth slide. At first, she herself had held tight to the belief that August was innocent, that after the trial they would resume their lives as a couple and as a family. Even after his suicide attempt, she had harbored the possibility he would return home. After his conviction, she knew she would have to find a way to tell Rosie the truth.

The more time that passed, the more difficult it had become to broach the subject. No matter how often she'd silently rehearsed the conversation, Luella hadn't found the words to explain to her cognitively challenged sister-in-law that the brother she worshipped would spend many years in prison for molesting children. How could she distill a complex situation into something simple enough for Rosie to grasp, especially when she didn't understand it herself? She would never understand the desire to have sex with children or how that urge became more powerful than preserving a reputation, a career, a family. She would never comprehend how August could maintain the charade of respectability, all the while lurking in the perverse shadows. Understand it or not, there was no way now to postpone the inevitable.

"Honey, I have something important to tell you," said Luella, guiding Rosie to the sofa. They sat down side-by-side. Rosie looked at Luella expectantly. Luella handed her a tissue. Rosie blew her nose loudly and then crumpled the tissue in her fist.

"Do you remember why Augie is in jail?"

"Because the police said he did something bad," said Rosie solemnly, parroting the explanation she'd heard earlier.

"Yes, he did something very bad."

"What did he do?"

Luella cleared her throat. "You know what sex is?"

Rosie nodded. "It's when people kiss and touch each other in their private parts and that's how they get babies."

"Yes. And adults are only supposed to have sex with other adults and never with children."

"B-because children aren't s-supposed to have b-babies?"

"That's right." Luella felt as though she were tiptoeing along a tightrope strung between canyon walls. Rosie idolized August. It broke Luella's heart to hurt her, but she could think of no way to explain the situation without offering some version of the truth.

Rosie blew her nose again, bit her lower lip.

"Augie had sex with children. He touched them in their private parts many times. What he did was very wrong, and it was against the law."

Tears pooled in Rosie's eyes. "Are those children going to have babies?"

"No, honey. The children were boys and boys can't have babies. But it was just as wrong to have sex with them. The law says he has to be punished. When adults do something against the law they go to jail. Augie is going to be in jail for a long time."

"How long?"

"I don't know. The judge hasn't decided yet."

"Will he be home for my birthday?"

"No. I'm sorry. He will be in jail for many years. That means he won't be coming home at all."

Rosie's stricken expression made Luella want to take back everything she'd said.

"Do you understand?"

Rosie nodded. Tears rolled down her flushed cheeks. "W-why was he b-bad?"

"I don't know, sweetie. Sometimes good people do bad things. They make terrible mistakes."

Was that true? Despite the numerous articles Luella had pored over, she still wasn't sure what to believe. Was it true that August was a good person who made a terrible mistake, or was he a bad human being who feigned goodness? Clearly, he suffered from a psychiatric disorder. Still, it was difficult to believe that his actions had been beyond his control. She had looked up the criteria for Pedophilic Disorder in the Diagnostic and Statistical Manual of Mental Disorders (DSM-5), published by the American Psychiatric Association: recurrent intense sexual arousal, fantasies, sexual urges or behaviors involving prepubescent children.

Experts didn't seem to know the exact origins of the disorder. Some research pointed to the faulty development of neurological pathways in the brain, others to early trauma, still others to head injuries or experiences of sexual abuse as a child. According to her reading, pedophiles often had to repeat grades in school and had a lower I.Q than the general population. That certainly wasn't true of August, and it wasn't true of other high-profile pedophiles, like that famous Penn State football coach, or the USA Gymnastics doctor, or countless Roman Catholic priests. It seemed as though no one could explain what drove men to behave so egregiously. With all the competing and often contradictory information, Luella didn't know what to make of August's behavior, so how could she explain it to someone with Rosie's intellectual limitations?

"I st-still m-miss him," Rosie snuffled.

"And he misses you." Luella brushed a strand of hair away from Rosie's eyes. "Don't think about the bad. Remember the good times with Augie. You're still his Rosie Posie."

Rosie wiped her wet cheeks with the sleeve of her Jolliet University sweatshirt.

"Remember all the basketball games you watched together and how you helped him hand out water to the players at practice. Think about all the Saturday mornings just the two of you went to breakfast at The Squawking Hen and both of you ordered chocolate chip pancakes."

Rosie managed a faint smile. "And he always bought my favorite daiquiri jelly beans that nobody else likes."

"That's right. You have lots of good memories. The most important thing to remember is that he loves you. Even though he's not here he will always be your big brother and you will always be his little sister. Nothing will change that."

"He'll always be my big brother," Rosie repeated.

Luella envied Rosie. What a luxury to focus on the good in August and ignore the terrible harm he had done.

She sensed a presence in the room and turned. Beth stood a few feet behind her. "How long have you been standing there?"

"Long enough."

Luella carried a tray of hors d' oeuvres into the living room and set it on the coffee table. "Does anyone need me to top off your drink before I settle in to watch the game?" she asked, glancing at the television where two broad-shouldered, suit-clad announcers filled the screen.

"I think we're all good," said Franklin.

Luella sat on the sofa next to Wyatt, who wore the Green Bay Packers football helmet August purchased for him the previous year. Wyatt had torn into the package, eyes wide with delight as he'd opened the box and lifted out the helmet. "Grandpa, it's just what I always wanted my whole life!" She and August had laughed hard at his earnestness. What a difference a year makes, she thought.

"I'm surprised that you're willing to watch Penn State play given their huge sexual abuse scandal," said Denise, grabbing a slice of cheese and pear from the tray and placing them on a cracker.

Franklin shot his wife a withering look.

Penn State. Recognition dawned. A lead weight dropped into Luella's stomach. She knew all about the Penn State scandal, about the firing of iconic coach Joe Paterno over the handling of the Jerry Sandusky pedophile ordeal. When it happened, August obsessively followed the case in the news and had been vocal about his disgust. "Sandusky." August practically spit his name. "What a loser! They ought to lock him up and throw away the key." In hindsight, she wondered if August was trying to provide cover for himself or if his reaction was simply projected self-loathing.

It hadn't occurred to her to find out who was playing this year. For as long as she could remember the family watched the Rose Bowl regardless of which teams played. August was the one who ginned up interest by reciting the teams' records, analyzing their strengths and weaknesses, and describing their star players. By the time the game started, everyone caught his enthusiasm, chose a team to root for, and raucously cheered like a lifelong fan, betting on the outcome and slapping high-fives with each score.

Everyone played a part in the day. The family was like a Jenga game, each member a piece of a delicately balanced tower; now with a big piece missing, the whole thing threatened to topple.

"Do you want to turn off the game?" asked Franklin.

Luella shook her head.

Needing a moment to compose herself, she rose from the sofa and headed into the kitchen. She braced her hands against the cold granite counter, leaned her head on the upper cabinet, and closed her eyes.

"I didn't mean to stir up trouble." said Denise.

When Luella opened her eyes, she was surprised to see Denise standing behind her.

She touched Luella's shoulder. "I thought you knew who was playing."

Luella stiffened and Denise pulled her hand away.

"I owe you an apology. I—I just haven't been able to find the right words." Denise set her glass of wine down on the counter.

Perhaps it was petty, but her sister-in-law's obvious discomfort gave Luella a measure of satisfaction.

"I'm ashamed of the way I've behaved," said Denise. "I haven't been fair to you. When I married Franklin, you accepted me when others wouldn't. I should have been more supportive. It's just that I couldn't believe you didn't know."

"I didn't."

"I've finally come around."

"You expect gratitude?"

"No. No. I've been a real shit." Denise stared down at her hands, fingered her wedding ring. "I just meant—well—it's just that—this is hard."

Luella waited.

"I—I was abused." The words exploded from Denise's mouth as if propelled from a slingshot.

Luella stared at her.

"My uncle. He sexually abused me when I was a child." She gnawed her lower lip. "And my mother let it happen. I waited and waited for her to notice how I recoiled whenever he came near me, but she adored him, doted on him, and I hated her for it." Her eyes brimmed with tears. "When I finally worked up the courage to tell her, she didn't believe me."

Luella felt empathy for Denise's pain, yet she wondered if she was expected to carry the blame for every abuse victim simply because she had married August. "I'm sorry that happened to you," said Luella, softly. "I had no idea. And I swear I had no idea August abused those boys."

"I believe you."

"I'm not looking for your absolution." The words came out more defensively than Luella intended.

"Maybe not my absolution, but your own," Denise suggested, her tone conciliatory. "I'm no psychologist and I'm not trying to offend you, Luella, or to make things worse. Honestly, I'm not. I've done a lot of thinking about this. In fact, I've been able to think of little else. I know how hard it was to forgive myself for letting my uncle abuse me. For a long time, I thought I should have fought back, told my mother over and over until she finally believed me. I hated myself for being a victim. I know how easy it is to blame yourself for something the abuser did."

Luella's shoulders slumped. Her defenses crumbled.

"I'm sorry for not being a better friend," said Denise. "It's just that..."

Beth walked into the kitchen. "Hey, you're missing a barnburner of a game. Deontay Burnett is a wunderkind and Saquon Barkley is a stud."

Beth looked at her mother and then at Denise.

"Okay, what have I missed?"

"We can deal with this later. Right now, we should get back to the game," insisted Luella. She hurried from the kitchen, leaving Denise and Beth lagging behind.

Luella flipped the wall switch, turning on several lamps. Franklin, Rosie, and Wyatt engrossed in the game, seemed to barely notice. Denise nestled next to Franklin on the loveseat, while Beth chose the recliner. Settling on the sofa next to Rosie and Wyatt, Luella leaned over and touched the top of Wyatt's helmet, as if her grandson were the talisman that could restore her equilibrium.

Suddenly Rosie and Wyatt leaped up from the couch and danced around cheering wildly. Bird joined them, prancing and turning in circles.

"Grandma, Saquon Barkley scored another touchdown. He's a stud!"

Luella couldn't help laughing at Wyatt parroting Beth. She glanced at the television. Penn State 49, USC 35. Wyatt turned to give her a high-five. She raised her hand to receive the slap, although she couldn't help secretly wishing that Penn State would lose.

Her thoughts turned to the conversation with Denise, whose judgment hadn't been harsher than her own. Luella had asked herself a hundred times why she didn't see what was happening in her own home. Given the speed with which friends had fallen away, it was clear that most people believed her lack of awareness was a result of willful ignorance. Self-doubt led to self-accusation. She'd once believed, like most others, that predatory behavior must be obvious. There was a time when she would have thought it impossible to live with a man, be intimate with him, and not know that he lusted after young boys, that he led a secret life.

She'd gone over dozens of scenarios in her mind, trying to remember times when she'd seen August with children. Images that came to mind were young boys basking in his praise, puffing out their chests after a pat on the back, angling to be near him. Had her eyes deceived her? Was that a friendly touch or a sexual overture? Was each bed check he'd conducted alone a responsible necessity or a covert opportunity? Was paying special attention to an underprivileged child an act of compassion or nefarious wooing? Even hindsight hadn't provided answers.

She'd read a raft of studies that examined abusive behavior and a number of victims' anecdotal accounts. Her personal experience, along with that of others, led her to conclude that abusers could live under the radar, hide in plain sight, regardless of what the unscathed may believe.

Franklin let out a whoop, startling Luella and bringing her attention back to the game. Ronald Jones had scored a three-yard touchdown for USC. That, plus an extra point, brought them to within seven points of Penn State. Wyatt and Rosie groaned.

"They're coming ba-ack," Franklin crooned.

With a minute and twenty seconds remaining, USC's Deontay Burnett caught a twenty-seven-yard touchdown pass from Sam Darnold. The extra point tied the game at 49-49.

"Unbelievable!" Franklin exclaimed.

Then, in the final play of the game, the USC kicker made a field goal for the 52-49 win.

Franklin gave both Wyatt and Rosie a high-five. "Your team played a heck-of-a game," he said. "And they had the best runner."

"Saquon Barkley," said Wyatt.

"He is a stud," Rosie declared.

Luella was glad that USC pulled off the upset.

Denise sashayed over to Franklin and whispered in his ear. She gave him a coquettish smile and a kiss on the cheek.

"Okay, sure." he said, nodding. "Rosie and Wyatt, how about we go out for pizza to celebrate a great game."

"I love pizza!" exclaimed Rosie.

"Me, too," said Wyatt.

"The women will hold down the fort. You can bring some pizza back for us," said Denise.

After Franklin, Rosie, and Wyatt bundled up and left the house, Luella went to the kitchen and brought back an open bottle of Pinot Noir and three wine glasses.

"Mmm. Excellent choice," gushed Denise, curled up on the love seat, her bare feet tucked beneath her.

"Truthfully, I don't know one wine from another," admitted Luella, lounging cross-legged on the sofa. "I asked the owner of the liquor store for a recommendation."

"Makes me think of Paul Giamatti in *Sideways,* obsessing over the perfect Pinot Noir, scoffing at anyone who drank Merlot," said Denise, holding the long-stemmed glass up to the lamplight, swirling the liquid languorously, examining its blood-red glow. "I have to say I agree with him."

"I love that movie," said Beth. "I'm a huge Sandra Oh fan."

"Pinot Noir is considered an elite wine because it's made from hard-to-grow, thin-skinned grapes," said Denise.

"How fitting," murmured Luella under her breath.

The intimacy in the kitchen earlier had dissolved in favor of small talk. An underlying tension, like the eerie calm before a tornado, pulsed in the room.

"You know they aren't just growing pinot noir grapes in France anymore. California, Oregon, South Africa, Australia, New Zealand, and even Tasmania are producing this variety." It was as though Denise needed to show off her encyclopedic knowledge of wine, a skill she'd worked hard to acquire after she'd married Franklin and had to entertain his wealthy clients. Sometimes her pretentiousness rankled. Today Luella was more sympathetic, knowing that this insecure side of her sister-in-law emerged when she was anxious.

"Well," Beth began, ignoring Denise's wine lecture. "This is later."

"What?" said Luella.

"When I walked into the kitchen earlier you two stopped talking, and when I asked about it, you said we'd deal with it later. It's later."

Luella looked over at Denise who continued to swirl the wine around in her glass. "Denise, it's up to you whether you want to revisit our earlier conversation."

"It's why I asked Franklin to take Rosie and Wyatt out for pizza. I just thought there would be a little more foreplay," said Denise. She took a large swallow of her wine. "Beth, I apologized to your mother for keeping my distance from her. I've been angry. I—I…"

"Haven't we all," Beth interrupted.

"I was sexually abused." Denise's admission hung in the air like a foul odor.

Beth's eyes narrowed. "I'm sorry."

"It started when I was nine-years-old." Denise pressed her lips together and paused as though needing to work up the courage to continue. "I hated my mother for being so blind." Her wine glass shook in her hand. "She should have stopped it."

Seconds ticked by. Beth and Luella sat stone silent.

"I find it hard to believe that someone wouldn't know if a person was an abuser," said Denise, finally. "She let it happen."

"Are you talking about your mother or mine?"

"Mine. Both, I guess."

Luella's muscles went rigid.

Beth looked from her mother and then to Denise. "Are you saying that you are mad at Mom because she didn't know my dad was having sex with boys?"

"Before—not... I *was* mad at her."

"But you were so kind and welcoming to Wyatt and me," said Beth, meeting Denise's gaze. "Weren't you mad at *me* for not knowing?"

"You aren't married to him."

There it is, thought Luella.

"But I was really close to him, too. And I didn't know." Emotion crept into Beth's voice. "Maybe I should have, but I didn't."

"I'm not accusing you, Beth."

"Aunt Denise, I appreciate that. But let me ask you something. Did *you* ever suspect my dad?"

"No."

"Why not?"

Denise turned red. She gnawed the inside of her cheek. "He was successful and charming. He was proud of his family. Everybody admired him. He was the biggest presence in any room. And he was always doing things for charity."

"What if you had thrown *love* into the equation?" Beth continued. "Would it have made it easier or more difficult to suspect him?"

Luella held her breath.

Denise closed her eyes as though surrendering. "More difficult," she whispered.

"Well, there you have it," said Beth.

The day filled with relatives and revelations left Luella depleted. After a long hot bath, she nestled under the comforter, her knees slightly bent, her back resting against a pile of down-filled pillows, and listened to a podcast on her phone. In the moonless January night, the only illumination came from the bedside lamp that shone a halo on the ceiling. She ran her hand over the empty space reserved for Bird, who tonight opted to sleep with Wyatt, thinking that she'd almost adjusted to sleeping alone. Almost.

She thought of August in the county jail sleeping on a thin, single mattress in a concrete cell. He would be there until his sentencing hearing set for the third week in January. From there he'd be transferred to prison somewhere in Wisconsin.

Her attention turned back to the podcast.

After twenty minutes there was a gentle knock on the door. Beth opened it a crack. "Mom, are you asleep," she said softly.

"No, honey. I'm awake."

"Do you mind if I come in?"

Luella paused the podcast and set her phone on the nightstand. "Please, join me," she said, patting the bed. These moments when Beth joined her in the bedroom after Wyatt and Rosie were asleep had become a source of enjoyment.

Beth wore blue pajama pants and a white Nike T-shirt. She hoisted herself up on the end of the tall bed and crawled in next to Luella. She arranged pillows against the headboard, eased under the comforter, and nestled in.

Luella remembered the night Beth was born. August had stood next to the hospital bed, cradling the swaddled baby in his arms, rocking gently from one foot to another. Luella, exhausted from a twenty-hour labor, listened to him softly sing Joe Cocker's "You Are So Beautiful."

"You're not disappointed that I didn't give you a son?" she'd asked

"Lulu, you've given me the world," he'd said. "You've made me a father and the happiest man alive. You've given me a daughter. We're a family."

We're a family. Wellbeing, stronger than she'd ever known, had enveloped her body, creating an overwhelming pride at being the woman who gave him the thing he most wanted.

"I was thinking about Aunt Denise," said Beth. "That was quite a bomb she dropped. I'm feeling guilty for being so hard on her. I was just mad at her for blaming you."

Luella reached over and swiped a strand of Beth's hair from her eyes. "I know, honey. Me, too. To be fair, I don't think Denise has been more judgmental than you or me. I'm angry, but I'm also trying to be honest with myself."

"Yes, honesty." Beth shifted to face Luella. "Which brings me to something else that's on my mind." Beth bent her knees to match the angle of Luella's, creating a tent along the width of the bed. "I've been thinking about Dad's sentencing hearing. I assume you're planning on going to it."

Never quite sure how Beth would react, Luella stepped lightly. "Yes. I dread it. I'm sorry, but no matter how angry I am, I can't bear to have your father face it alone."

"I assumed that." Beth smoothed her hands over the comforter. "I'll go to court, too. It's not just Dad who shouldn't face sentencing alone, *you* shouldn't have to face it alone either."

"Oh, honey, thank you." Luella put her arms around Beth and pulled her into a long hug.

After both women settled back against the pillows, Beth said, "There is something else. I've given this a lot of thought. I'm afraid it might upset you, so I've been reluctant to bring it up."

"Well?"

"I'm willing to support you and to try to be around Dad, at least as much as I can handle. But I've decided to change my last name." Beth sat up straighter, set her jaw. "The Laurent name has become lethal for me. It's a problem professionally. It's a problem personally. If I take Gabe's last name, which I could have done but didn't when we got married, I'll have the same surname as my son. I think it makes sense."

"Changing your name won't take away the pain," said Luella.

"But it will give me a fresh start. It will make it so that every time I introduce myself the person on the other end of the handshake won't recoil or give me that look of revulsion. Mom, I'm not doing this to hurt you. I just can't bear to think of myself as a Laurent anymore."

Luella had been on the receiving end of those handshakes and looks too often to dismiss Beth's logic—the reporters calling out the Laurent name as though it were a curse word; Ardan Connelly, the St. Eligius school board president who fired her, extending his hand and uttering "Mrs. Laurent" as though it was poison on his tongue; the Fourth of July boaters taunting, "Hey Laurent, you sick bastard"—so that any argument she might make to dissuade Beth dropped away as quickly as a stone sinking to the bottom of the lake.

"Elizabeth Grace Mancuso," said Luella. "It has a nice ring to it."

Chapter Twenty-five
~The Transcript~

Luella sat at the office desk with a cup of herbal tea to tackle the stacks of mail that had accumulated, separating bills that hadn't been paid from advertisements for credit cards, solicitations for political contributions, and pleas from charities she'd never heard of.

Bird lay next to the desk, basking in the pale winter rays spilling onto the floor.

Luella tossed the junk mail stack into the recycle bin. A thick 9x12 manila envelope addressed to her and without a return address still lay on the desk. She had no memory of receiving it, but then, these days, she often found herself forgetting and misplacing things. The package could have been sandwiched between the mountain of magazines and catalogs that daily filled the mailbox. Checking the postmark, Luella saw that it had been mailed from the county seat.

She unfastened the metal clasp, peeled back the glued flap, and pulled out a two-inch thick document. A brief, unsigned message scrawled on a half sheet of plain white paper was clipped to the top page.

Mrs. Laurent,

You testified that your pedophile husband was a good and honorable man. You should be ashamed of yourself! Read the testimony of his victims in the trial transcript and see if you still believe he's good and honorable.

Trial transcript? She leafed through the document. The copy was weighty, intimidating. She stared at it as though it were an alien object, held it as though it might scald her hands. Who would have sent the package? Who could have gotten a copy of the transcript? Who hated her that much? Names did not come readily to mind. It could have been any number of people—a lawyer, one of the victims, a member of a victim's family, a jurist, someone from the press. It was impossible to know. There was a time not long ago, Luella thought, when her list of detractors would have been very short. Now the list seemed limitless.

She glanced down at Bird, dozing, his legs twitching as he dreamed. "Let sleeping dogs lie," she thought. What could be gained by reading pages and pages of testimony? Remembering the first day of the trial when Judge Richards ordered the witnesses to be sequestered, she recalled how helpless and guilty she'd felt about abandoning August. While she'd been reluctant to leave the courtroom, there had been comfort in sitting out the trial, shielded from the tawdriness. Since then, her husband had been found guilty. There was nothing more to be done. She should throw the packet in the trash. Why torture herself? The answer was simple. It was the same reason she'd called Michael St. James.

Fanning through the transcript Luella noticed highlighted sections. She also noted that the accusers, who in the media had been identified only as Victims One, Two, Three, Four, Five, and Six, were named. Curious, she began to read a highlighted section from one of prosecutor Adlai Fett's examinations on day two of the trial.

Q. Please state your name for the record.
A. Derrick Jeffries Boyer.
Q. What is your current age?
A. Nineteen.

Luella vaguely remembered Derrick as a slight, quiet, shy, somewhat clingy boy, a camp regular.

Q. You attended the camp through a referral from The Hoops and Hearts Foundation. Is that correct?
A. Yes.
Q. How many years did you attend the camp?
A. Four years.

Derrick testified that while growing up his father was never in his life, that he lived with his mother and younger brother, that he'd been an average student but an exceptional athlete. He answered questions about the activities at camp, how Coach Laurent had noticed him and paid special attention to him, and how the relationship grew over time. As Luella read, it became clear that testifying was difficult for Derrick.

Fett started slowly and gently, building his case, leading to the most embarrassing and traumatic events.

Q. Where did the abuse take place?
A. At Laurent's Basketball Camp.
Q. Where at the camp?
A. Coach took me to a cabin that wasn't used for the campers.
Q. Could you be more specific?
A. It was at the far edge of the grounds. It was mostly used for storage for extra basketballs and hoops and other equipment, but there was an old bed hidden in the back corner that you couldn't see from the doorway. The place was cold and dark. The mattress was old and smelled.

A bed? When Luella had suggested that they restore that cabin for occupancy as they had all the others, August convinced her they didn't need the space for the campers; they needed extra storage. "Why build an expensive shed," he'd argued, "when we already have this perfectly good structure?" His reason seemed logical then. They had an over-sized shed near the house in which they stored lawn care and beach equipment. The basketball side of the operation belonged to August. She'd trusted him to know what they needed. She couldn't remember ever entering that storage cabin.

Q. How did he get you to go into that cabin?

A. Well, the first summer I was at camp, he just had me help get extra basketballs and other stuff. He told me I was like an assistant. He made me feel important, special, you know. He didn't do anything, you know, weird. He'd put his arm around my shoulders, give me a high five. Guy stuff.

Q. But things changed the other years you attended camp?

A. Yes.

Q. How did his behavior change?

A. One night he had me lay face down on the bed. He rubbed my back. Said it was good to loosen my muscles after playing so hard. He massaged my shoulders. At first, I thought he was being nice, you know, acting like a trainer would.

Q. But it didn't stop there, did it?

A. That night he didn't do anything more.

Q. But the times after that?

A. The next time he took me to that cabin he put his hand on my thigh and rubbed it, and his hand kept going higher, you know, toward my privates. I felt weird. Like that wasn't right. But I don't have a dad. I thought maybe dads might do something, you know, personal like that. I should have run out of there, but he was Coach Laurent, this really famous coach. And he treated me like his son, like I was a special player. He told me I had

potential to play college ball. I mean, it's really hard to explain. I was twelve. I didn't know much.

Luella pressed her fingers against her temples. She swallowed hard and swallowed again, took a swig of tea, then continued reading.

Q. Mr. Boyer, I know this is difficult, but I need you to explain to the jury what he did to you after that.

A. Coach told me to meet him there after bed check. He had me lay down on the bed and he laid down next to me. He put his hands down my shorts and rubbed my penis. He showed me how to—to, I don't know how to say this.

Q. I know this is embarrassing, but the jury needs to hear what he did to you.

A. He showed me how to—um—get him off.

Q. Did you ever engage in oral sex?

A. Yes.

Q. Did he perform oral sex on you?

A. Yes.

Q. Did you ever perform oral sex on him?

A. Yes.

Q. How many times?

A. I don't remember exactly.

Q. More than once?

A. Yes.

Q. More than ten times?

A. Yes. I stopped counting.

Q. Did you ever engage in anal sex?

A. [Witness crying.]

It was as though someone shoved a hot poker down Luella's

esophagus, into her stomach, and twisted. Tears trickled down her cheeks.

Dirty. That was it. Dirty. The same hands and mouth that violated this innocent boy had explored every inch of her body. She felt August cupping her breast, thrusting his tongue into her mouth. She'd welcomed him inside her thousands of times. She felt his weight pressing down on her, heard him moaning in her ear. She wanted to peel off her skin.

All these years she'd believed he had been faithful. Never in her wildest dreams had she thought he might be uninterested in cheating with other women because he wanted to have sex with children. *Children!*

She wondered how many times he'd come directly from molesting a boy to their marriage bed, or how many times he had made excuses that he was "too tired" when she had tried to initiate love making. It was too disgusting to fathom. Yet she couldn't stop thinking about it, couldn't help imagining August taking a twelve-year-old boy's penis into his mouth or lying back while a terrified child accommodated him.

Her heart pounded. Bile burned her throat.

She pushed away from the desk, paced from one side of the room to the other and back again. She stared out the window. The red rolled roofs of the closed white-sided cabins visible from the window were blanketed in pristine snow, yet the buildings, which she'd always associated with youthful laughter, appeared dark and sinister. She thought of the hundreds of boys who had bunked there. Why had she never seen or heard anything that made her suspicious of August? Maybe she'd been deaf, dumb, and blind. If she had the courage, she would storm out there and light each of those cabins on fire.

And Derrick. How must that boy, now a young man, have felt? Dirty probably didn't begin to describe it. If she felt betrayed, how great was August's betrayal of all six of his accusers, mere boys who had given him their complete trust? Their anguish must be unbearable. Nothing could ever make up for all that August had stolen from them. Nothing.

Luella staggered across the room and sat back down at her desk. She turned to another highlighted page where she found Fett's examination of Victim Three, Jared Victor Palowski. Jared was another camper referred through the Hoops and Hearts Foundation, another fatherless boy who had come to the camp for several years. It occurred to her that, just like Derrick, as a twelve-year-old, he was slight. Jared's testimony was eerily similar to Derrick's. He described the deliberate wooing, the flattery, and the gradual increase in sexual demands. The one major difference was the coercion August had used to keep him in line.

Q. Jared, what made you go along with Mr. Laurent's advances, why didn't you just tell him no or tell an adult?

A. I was afraid.

Q. Afraid, physically?

A. Yes. He was big and strong. But mostly I was afraid because he told me that he would call social services and tell them my mom wasn't a fit parent because I had gotten into some trouble with the police, and they would put me in foster care. I was afraid that I would lose the only family I had. He said that they would believe him and not me. I believed him.

Luella clamped her jaw so hard she feared she might break her teeth. Leaning back in the chair she closed her eyes and tried to gain control. After several minutes she opened her eyes and finished reading Fett's examination. Then she forced herself to read the aggressive questioning of Jared by August's defense attorney, Thomas Lowery.

Q. Mr. Palowski, Isn't it true that you hoped to make a large sum of money from these accusations against Coach Laurent?

A. No.

Q. Think carefully. Have you ever talked with anyone about making money by accusing Coach Laurent?

A. No.

Q. Isn't it true that you hoped to get a college basketball scholarship with Coach Laurent's help?

A. Sure, I thought he would help me.

Q. And when that didn't happen because you lacked the talent to play Division I basketball you decided to make money by making false accusations against him.

A. I hoped to get a basketball scholarship, but I didn't intend to make money from him.

Q. But you were clearly disappointed when you failed to get the scholarship.

A. Yes, but—

Q. Isn't it true that you plan to buy a new car from the money you make from selling your story to the press?

A. No.

The barrage of questions from August's attorney continued, hammering away at the same issue from different angles, like cascading water battering rock, trying to wear down the witness. Luella remembered how nervous she'd been on the stand, but her cross-examination had been kid-glove gentle by comparison. The lawyers hadn't impugned her motives or implied extortion. Jared Palowski was being assaulted all over again.

She set the transcript down. Stood. Massaged the small of her back. Ran her fingers through her hair. Sat down. Picked the document up again. Found a highlighted section in which Fett examined Victim

One, Marty Nelson Goddard. Many of the questions were the same as the ones asked of Derrick Boyer, just as graphic, just as sickening.

She forced herself to read further.

Q. Mr. Goddard, was Mrs. Laurent ever present when August Laurent performed sex acts on you?

The question stopped Luella cold. She thought back to her experience with Sergeant Fossmeyer at the sheriff's department. "So far you haven't been implicated in any wrongdoing," he'd said. How aggrieved and frightened she'd been. Obviously, the police had their suspicions. It appeared that the prosecutor also believed she might be complicit!

A. No, she was never in the same room, but she came close. One time she walked by the storage cabin that Coach always called our special place. She yelled through the door, It's getting late. What are you doing? He put his hand over my mouth to keep me quiet. I couldn't breathe. He hollered back. Just checking out some equipment for tomorrow. I'll be in the house as soon as I finish bed check. I remember he looked nervous. Then it got quiet. This sickening smile was on his face. He made me put my hand over his hard penis and he whispered in my ear, let's see how good of a player you really are. In my head I begged her to stop and open that door, but she just walked away.

"Oh, God...oh, God...oh, God..." Luella moaned. Her breath escaped in rasping gulps. A sharp pain stabbed behind her eyes. If only she hadn't trusted August when he'd dismissively turned her away, if only she had opened that cabin door, kicked it in. How could she not have suspected him? Why hadn't warning signs flashed neon red?

Mentally she retraced her steps, making her way along the path that wound through the trees between the campers' cabins, flashlight in hand, concentrating on her feet so as not to trip on the random roots that crisscrossed the path. The night air had been cool, the woods still. The high energy of the day had faded with the evening sun. As she passed by the darkened cabins, she heard occasional bursts of youthful laughter, smiled to herself, never bothering to stop to knock on doors or check for lights out. That was August's job, had been since the day they'd opened camp. Sometimes Luella, and in later years Beth, had checked on the girls' cabins, but never the boys'. At the time the division of labor had seemed perfectly reasonable. It seemed impossible that something so terrible could have gone on within earshot without her even suspecting. Love and loyalty had proven to be effective blinders.

The thick transcript shook in Luella's hands, making the skittering words impossible to read. A voice in her head told her to stop torturing herself, warned her that the pain might forever break her, but a competing voice urged her to read on, beckoned her toward the undisguised truth. If she did not confront the truth now, how would she ever be able to face it?

She set the transcript on the desk, flattened the pages with her trembling hand, and found another highlighted section. This time the testimony was from Officer Raymond Jeffers of the Ojibwe County Sheriff's Department. Prosecuting attorney Fett questioned him.

Q. Please describe what you found on Mr. Laurent's computer.

A. Well, there were four computers on the premises. One computer belonged to Mrs. Laurent. We found nothing suspicious on her laptop. An office PC was used for business purposes, such as camp records and foundation issues, and that was clean; one laptop that Mr.

Laurent used for coaching purposes, also clean. When we executed the search warrant, we discovered a laptop hidden in the cabin where most of the abuse took place. That one contained several child pornography sites.

A hidden computer? Luella had no memory of August ever purchasing a fourth computer. As far as she knew, they had the desktop computer in the camp office, and they each had one laptop. Period. According to the officer, though, August had stowed a secret computer in a place he knew she would never venture. His duplicity was another hammer blow.

At the time the officers executed the search warrant she had resented them for invading the camp and their home, detested them, vowed to sue as they turned over mattresses, opened drawers, pawed through their personal belongings. She'd believed then that there was nothing to find, nothing that would possibly point to August's guilt.

Q. What specifically did you find on his hidden computer?
A. There were multiple sites with pictures and videos of pre-pubescent boys engaging in explicit sexual acts with adult males. Some of the sites showed boys posing naked alone or with other boys and other sites showed the children receiving and performing fellatio and anal sex.

Pornographic videos of young boys on August's hidden computer. Luella threw her head back desperate to open her airway. Bird stood, alert, edging protectively toward Luella, who wheezed as she gulped for air and pressed her hands over her roiling stomach.

Slow down. Breathe in. Breathe out. Get control. In. Out.

August had deceived her, acted wrongly accused. He'd hidden more than an extra computer; he'd hidden who he was at his core. If even a miniscule sliver of doubt about his guilt lingered after Michael

St. James' call, it evaporated as quickly as raindrops in one-hundred-degree heat. He was a liar and had made her one as well. She'd sat in the witness stand and declared him to be a moral and honorable man who could never do the awful things he'd been accused of doing. She'd sworn to tell the truth. Instead, she'd told the opposite of the truth.

What a fool! What a pathetic fool!

She bent and vomited into the waste basket.

Chapter Twenty-six
~Untethering~

L uella sat at the desk shattered, her life broken into pieces. She wished August was dead. If only she'd never laid eyes on him. If only it was possible to wish him out of existence. If only she had let him die.

Thinking of the six victims, especially Derrick, Jared, and Marty, whose testimony had been the most vivid and damning, she tried to picture their young faces. She closed her eyes hoping that their features would vividly appear, but only vague images of them came to mind. They'd been among hundreds of aspiring basketball players who had passed through the camp each summer and who, because of their shy, quiet demeanors, had been forgettable. She was ashamed that she didn't remember them more clearly.

As a teacher, Luella encountered plenty of children who fit the profile of August's victims—reticent kids without the confidence or experience to stand up to authority. They were the kids used to keeping secrets: Dad's alcoholism. Mom's depression. Their family's particular form of dysfunction. Names and faces came to mind. Jason. Andrew. Kyle. Garret. All young, immature, vulnerable. The thought of August violating those kids enraged her. She imagined swinging a baseball bat at his head.

And Wyatt. If August had been allowed to continue preying on children, would Wyatt have become a target, too? In July, when Beth stormed out of the house, insisting that she needed to protect her son, Luella had thought her overly dramatic and irrational. Luella was embarrassed to admit that she was the one with faulty judgment.

The glint of the diamonds on her wedding band caught her eye. She stared at her ring.

Thirty-two years ago, August proposed after the last game of his college basketball career. He'd knelt down on one knee on the porch outside her apartment, taken her hand in his, and vowed to spend the rest of his life making her happy. The white gold engagement ring he'd slipped on her finger bore a tiny diamond chip barely visible in the center of a narrow band. "I wish I could afford a diamond worthy of your sparkle," he'd said. "I don't care a whit about the size," she'd insisted. "It's enough to know you love me."

On their wedding day he'd placed a ring on her finger with a large cushion cut diamond set in the center of a wide band. She suspected that on a beginning coach's salary it took him years to pay for it, but she also knew August's attitude about image, so she'd accepted it and worn it as a measure of his devotion. On their fifteenth anniversary, he'd had the diamond on the engagement ring replaced with a two-carat gem. Luella had the engagement and wedding rings fused into a single exquisite piece of jewelry. Now she looked at it as if she'd never seen anything so ugly.

During their wedding ceremony the priest emphasized the significance of the ring, which was supposed to be the symbol of a perfect union and eternal oneness. It represented the completeness of God, he'd said, an ever-present reminder that He sanctified their marriage for all eternity. Now the ring on her hand seemed a mockery. Their marriage couldn't possibly be a less perfect union. The last thing Luella wanted was to be one with August, to be tied to him for eternity. She didn't want to be tethered to him for another second. Suddenly, she felt desperate to remove the ring.

The band grew tighter, and she began to panic as it seemed to cut off the circulation in her finger. Instead of representing fidelity it had become an object of betrayal, a tangible reminder that their life together was a lie. She tried to pull it off, but the heat of her hand had swollen her fingers so that the ring would not ease over her knuckle. She twisted it, pulled harder, tried to force it over the joint until the pain stopped her.

Anxiety buzzed in her chest like a trapped hornet. She had to remove the ring. She sprang from the chair and raced toward the kitchen, Bird trotting closely at her heels.

Turning on the kitchen faucet, Luella held her trembling hand under the stream of tap water, then pumped dish soap from the dispenser onto her ring finger. Back and forth she worked the ring, twisting until it slipped over her knuckle. She stared at the white swath of skin and the indentation left by her wedding band. Like an amputee who still felt phantom pain in a missing limb, Luella felt the weight of her absent ring.

She fished in the utensil drawer and found the meat tenderizing hammer. Placing the ring in the center of the cutting board, she slowly raised the hammer, concentrated, and slammed it down as hard as she could. Crash! The blow had little effect. Luella looked desperately around the kitchen for something heavier to smash the ring. Nothing. She needed a mallet or a sledgehammer.

The camp storage shed next to the wood splitting station was visible from the kitchen window. Luella grabbed the ring and headed toward the door with Bird scurrying beside her. She flung the door open and ran down the steps, unfazed by the biting winter air. At the bottom of the stairs, she grabbed the snow shovel. Bird bounded ahead leaping as Luella trudged through the knee-deep snow, dragging the shovel behind her. She stuffed the ring in her pocket, then sliced the shovel into the snow and filled it again and again until she cleared a section in front of the shed wide enough to open one half of the double door.

Unhooking the latch, she pried the door open and ventured inside. Bird sat in the doorway, panting. She scanned the array of tools mounted on the pegboard wall above the narrow workbench. She spotted the bolt cutter. It felt heavy and lethal in her hands. She pulled the ring from her pocket, stood it on edge on the workbench, opened the jaws of the cutter, aligned the ring inside the blades, then squeezed the long handles of the bolt cutter with all her strength. Snap! One side of the ring gave way. Luella turned the ring, realigned it, and repeated the process, squeezing, squeezing, squeezing, until the other side of the ring broke.

She scooped up the two halves. Once outside, she closed the shed door and plowed through the snow to the side of the shed where August hung his splitting ax, saw, and hatchet. Bird, barking, paced in the cleared driveway. Grabbing the hatchet, Luella trudged over to the tree stump that August used for wood splitting.

With several swipes of her hand, she cleared the snow from the top of the stump. She placed the two halves of the ring on the stump's surface and brought the flat side of the hatchet down with such force the blow reverberated up her arm and rattled her teeth. "Damn you!" she shouted as she hit the halves of the ring, hot tears running down her frozen cheeks. "Damn you!" Her voice echoed through the pines. "Damn you!" She swung the hatchet and hit the ring again and again until, exhausted, she crumpled to the ground.

Sitting curled in the deep snow, spent, Luella shivered, her toes numb. She'd run out of the house without her winter jacket, boots, or gloves. If she sat long enough, she would freeze to death. Tempting. Her teeth chattered. Her fingertips turned white. Bird plunged through the snow and licked Luella's face. "Okay, boy." She braced herself on the splitting log and pulled herself up. In her shaking hands she scooped up the shattered pieces of her wedding ring. With all her strength she flung them into the woods, then headed for shelter.

The first step toward healing, Luella knew, was to face August, look him in the eye, and tell him that she believed he was guilty.

Handling confrontation had always been August's forte. He seemed to relish battle. Whether taking on players, coaches, or referees, he never backed away from a fight. Because in any contentious situation Luella looked to calm the waters, August had once jokingly dubbed her the "smoother in chief." Today he held a clear advantage.

Through a sleepless night she'd mentally rehearsed a script until she knew it by rote. The longer she waited, the more doubt picked away at her resolve, until she wondered if she could summon the courage to utter her practiced words aloud.

Every synapse crackled as she waited for him to be brought into the jail's visitation room. She rubbed her arms against the chill. Eyeing the exit sign above the door, she squirmed in the uncomfortable chair, crossed and uncrossed her legs. It wasn't too late to walk out. After his sentencing hearing August would be transferred to a prison several counties away. She would never have to face him. She could erase him from her life, pretend he'd never existed. She told herself his crimes had shattered any obligation she might once have felt.

Eyeing the clock above the door, she slid to the edge of the chair poised to leave. Just as she stood up August entered wearing the county-issued jumpsuit, looking sober and more pallid than on her previous visit. When he leaned in to kiss her on the lips, she turned so the kiss brushed her cheek. Then she backed away to avoid his hug.

"What the hell, Lulu," he said, looking hurt. He sat and faced her across the small table. The glaring light accentuated the bags under his eyes and the lines on his face. She wished that he didn't look so defenseless.

Luella sat back in her chair, pulse thumping. She glanced around the room in which several other tables were occupied with inmates and their visitors. The lack of privacy made her task all the more daunting.

"Thanks for coming," he said. "You have no idea how good it is to see you."

She said nothing.

"And for putting more money in my account. I got some deodorant and decent soap to wash off the stink of this place."

She sat frozen, her insides churning.

"Oh, and I got the package of books you sent. If it weren't for you, Lulu, I think I'd go mad in here."

Under the overhead glare, Luella felt exposed. August looked at her as though he could see through her and read her thoughts. The confrontation of her imagination had not included sitting across from him while he showered her with appreciation. In her rehearsed version she'd hardened her heart, sat indifferently as he'd complained about mistreatment. She'd replied that she no longer cared about his suffering. He could go to hell.

The battle between hatred and pity raged inside her. Breaking the pattern of years of ingrained behavior, she found, took uncommon strength. It was much easier to hate from a distance.

She saw him glance at her hands.

"Where's your wedding ring?" he asked, his expression a cross between wounded and perturbed.

Luella stared at the pale white flesh where her ring had been. She swallowed hard, straightened her shoulders, and slowly met August's gaze.

"Once I read the court transcript, I couldn't bear to wear it."

His eyes narrowed. "You read the transcript?"

"Yes. And it made me sick."

"Lulu, surely you don't believe those liars. I've told you, they'll say anything to ruin me. I'm your husband. How many times do I have to tell you, you know me?"

"I thought I did, but I don't know you at all."

August flinched. "Think of all the good I've done…we've done. All the kids *our* foundation has helped. How can you just turn your back on that?"

"Me, turn my back!" A ripple of revulsion traveled the length of Luella's body. "You can't be serious."

"I need you on my team."

"What team is that, August? This isn't a game. What you did to those boys is unforgivable. You destroyed their lives!"

"How can you say that?" August's jaw tightened and his jugular vein pulsed. "All I ever tried to do was help those kids."

"No! You had sex with those boys!"

"How can you take their word over mine?"

Luella's heart thundered in her chest. She clenched her fists. "It's not just their word. The police found child pornography on the computer you *hid* in the storage cabin. Disgusting photos of young boys performing sex acts on grown men."

"Those are just *pictures*. They don't mean anything."

"If they didn't mean anything you wouldn't have bought a special computer to hide them from me."

"I knew you'd overreact."

"Stop! Just stop!" Luella slapped her palm on the table.

August recoiled. Heads turned. An officer stepped forward, made eye contact, and frowned, as though sending a stern reminder that acting out violated the visitation rules. Embarrassed, Luella lowered her voice. "Admit what you've done. At least have the decency to tell me the truth."

The twitch at the corner of his mouth was nearly imperceptible, but she saw it. "Men look at pornography, Lulu. It's a fact of life, our dirty little secret. We just don't share it with our prudish wives. It's harmless."

Luella glared at him. She no longer saw the face of a man she loved and devoted her life to, but a man who was sick, broken, and self-deluding. A steel cage locked around her heart.

"Harmless?"

August leaned forward. "I love you," he crooned. "I always have. I always will."

"I'm divorcing you."

August blanched. His eyes glistened. "Don't do this to me. I need you!"

"I needed you, too. I needed you to be the honorable man I thought I married." Luella pushed back in her chair. "I needed a husband who didn't molest children."

"Lulu, please! You'll regret this."

She stood, turned her back on him, and walked out.

Chapter Twenty-seven
~Out of the Shadows~

The January sky was overcast. The temperature dipped to minus twenty-one. Luella, bundled in a down coat, wool muffler, winter boots, stocking cap, and heavy mittens, her breath escaping as a frosty white ribbon, trudged alone up the courthouse steps.

She recalled the first day of the trial in October, when the sun shone and leaves tumbled across the lawn. She'd clung to August as they pushed through the crush of reporters, intimidated by the bombardment of hostile comments, and naïve in her reliance on him for protection. Today, entering court to attend his sentencing hearing, she was anxious and in no mood to deal with a barrage of questions, although she knew it was inevitable. Television station vans were parked in front of the courthouse, but there were no reporters milling about on the frozen lawn. A small mercy, thought Luella.

This was going to be a gut-wrenching day. She'd spent a sleepless night, fretting whether or not to come to court. It would be easier to stay home out of the public eye, easier not to face the humiliation. August did not deserve her support. But despite believing that he was guilty and despite her bitterness, she decided that the only way to live with herself was to see this through.

He had no one else. His father was deceased; his mother was in a nursing home suffering with Alzheimer's; his sister Rosie was childlike in her understanding of events. Former friends and colleagues abandoned him as though pedophilia was as contagious as the Black Death. To them, August had become one thing and one thing only, the coach who molested boys. His positive attributes dropped from memory as abruptly as if a trap door had opened.

If Luella had learned anything by living through this nightmare, it was that human beings were complicated; good and evil could coexist in a person. August was not a unidimensional criminal but a deeply flawed human being who had done evil things, and was now about to face his just punishment.

As she approached the courtroom, several television reporters rushed toward her and thrust microphones in her face. The questions continued even as she wordlessly pushed past them.

"Mrs. Laurent, do you still maintain that you knew nothing about the abuse, even though it took place at *your* camp?"

"How do you feel now that Augie faces years in prison?"

"Will you divorce him?"

Spectators' stares burrowed into her back as she made her way up the courtroom aisle. It surprised her to see Trudy sitting at the end of a row in back of the prosecutor's table. Trudy caught her eye and nodded. Luella slid in next to Franklin on the bench behind August and his attorney. August half turned from his place at the defense table and made eye contact. He looked surprised to see her. She looked away.

Clothes do make the man, she thought. When he'd first appeared in court August had been attired in an expensive, custom-tailored suit, and he'd had a haircut that had been meticulously styled. Instead of glasses he'd worn contact lenses. Now, wearing a jail-issued orange jumpsuit, a cheap haircut, and smudged glasses, it was as though his appearance shouted "convict."

Luella's stomach and shoulders ached the way they had on the first day of the trial three months ago. The courtroom had the same old varnish smell and high-ceilinged, echoey acoustics. The padded bench remained uncomfortable. Prosecutor Fett occupied the same table as did August and his attorney. As before, the room was filled with curious, hostile observers. This time the jury box stood empty.

She stared at the witness stand, the place where she'd publicly vouched for August's upright character, and felt nauseous. Appearing in court today, Luella knew, gave the impression she stood by her testimony, still believed in August's innocence. The enmity of the spectators wouldn't be reserved for August; they would judge her, too. There was no do-over, no opportunity for rebuttal. She would have to live with that mistake for the rest of her life.

"All rise," the bailiff commanded. Judge Richards entered from the left side of the room. Her sober expression revealed little as she looked down from her perch.

As the judge summarized the pre-sentence report Luella's thoughts wandered to images of August locked away in an eight by ten-foot cell, growing old and distant, while she struggled through life, while the family moved on without him. He would miss every significant event in Wyatt's life—athletic achievements, graduation, marriage. Maybe Beth would fall in love and marry again. The once delicious memory of August proudly escorting Beth down the aisle of the Chapel in the Woods turned sour.

Adlai Fett rose to make his statement. Luella studied his mannerisms, slow, deliberate, calculated. Even in profile she recognized his bushy-browed scowl. "Given the number of victims and their young ages, I urge Your Honor to impose the maximum sentence. His predatory behavior went on for years. He groomed his victims. August Laurent was a person of authority, a coach whom the boys and their parents looked up to and trusted, which makes his crimes all the more grievous."

The judge's expression remained inscrutable.

Attorney Thomas Lowery attempted to counter the prosecutor's argument by enumerating August's charitable enterprises, leaving out the fact that several of the victims participated in the basketball camp after being referred through the Hoops and Hearts Foundation. He emphasized that August had never before been arrested for any offense, that he'd led a law-abiding life, that he was a loving family man. "Mr. Laurent is fifty-seven years old. If you impose the maximum sentence, Your Honor, he will likely spend the rest of his life in jail."

The rest of his life. The reality of those words took Luella's breath away.

Next came several victim impact statements.

Derrick Boyer stood at the microphone set up just behind the bar. Luella recalled reading his testimony on the trial transcript. The slight pre-teen of her memory now looked to be over six feet tall. As he read from the paper, his hands shook; but his deep voice, although soft, was clear and steady. "Coach Laurent sexually assaulted me so many times I lost count. I've gone to counseling to try to stop the nightmares and to try to put my life back together. I honestly don't know if I'll ever be able to have a normal relationship, because I see him every time anyone tries to touch me."

As he continued reading, a fist squeezed Luella's heart. Derrick Boyer was not an abstraction, a notion of abuse, or a name on a transcript; he was a flesh and blood young man whose raw wound, laid bare, begged to be avenged.

Next, Jared Palowski, lanky, blonde, and somewhere in his mid-twenties, stood before the microphone. Instead of reading from a prepared statement, he spoke without notes. From the trial transcript, Luella recalled how aggressively Thomas Lowery had questioned Jared, accusing him of trying to make money by fabricating abuse accusations. Jared had not faltered.

"It is impossible to over-estimate the trauma you caused," he said, looking defiantly at August. "You not only stole my innocence, you threatened to have me removed from my family. You kept me beholden to you by using a toxic combination of flattery and intimidation. I went along with all of the disgusting sexual things you had me do. For years, I blamed myself for not being strong enough to resist. I know now that none of this was my fault. I was a kid, a scared, vulnerable kid. You were the adult. You ruined my childhood, but I refuse to let you ruin my life."

Luella admired the courage it took to look his tormenter in the eye and confront him. By comparison she felt meek, weak, and ashamed.

Marty Goddard stood next. He was the young man, now tattooed, bearded, in his late twenties, who had testified that Luella once spoke to August through the cabin door while they were lying together on the bed. "She just walked away," he'd said. His testimony haunted her ever since she'd read the transcript. In her dreams, she fantasized breaking down the door, rescuing Marty before August laid a hand on him. Then she would wake up. The reality that she could never go back and open that door would stun her all over again.

"I still have nightmares," Marty read, his eyes never leaving his prepared statement. "Whenever my bed creaks, I think of his heavy body next to mine, his hands touching my skin. Whenever a sliver of light shines under my bedroom door, I think of the shadows in that old cabin where he assaulted me. Whenever I smell mold, I think of that musty mattress and the disgusting things he made me do. I hope the Lord forgives him for what he did to me and the others, because I haven't been able to find it in my heart to forgive him."

Judge Richards leaned forward, listening intently, her dark eyes moist.

Jane Cleary, the mother of one of the victims, approached the microphone. She smoothed her side-swept bangs away from her face. "Today I am speaking on behalf of my son Jason because he could not be here. He is currently in a treatment facility. Coach Laurent nearly destroyed him." Her voice caught as she spoke. "Jason has attempted suicide twice and turned to drugs. As his mother, I continue to look for help for him and to pray that someday he can lead a normal life. He suffered unspeakable trauma at the hands of that man. I urge the court to lock this predator away for as long as the law allows."

Luella reached into her jacket pocket for a tissue. As the tears escaped, she dabbed her eyes and wiped her cheeks. The enormity of what August's victims had endured became almost too great to bear. Her pity had been misplaced. Her compassion belonged with these young men.

"Mr. Laurent, do you wish to make a statement before I pass sentence?" the judge asked.

"No," he said. "I have nothing to say."

Judge Richards peered down at August, locking him in her hardened stare. Then she looked beyond him to the spectators. "This portion of the sentencing hearing always moves me," she said. "Today I'm especially impressed by the way each of you who spoke conducted yourselves, with uncommon dignity and courage. As you heal from the deep wounds inflicted upon you by Mr. Laurent, remember that you are no longer victims. You are survivors. Hopefully, today was one more important step toward living a full and meaningful life. You have a powerful voice that will give others the courage to speak out, to come out of the shadows and report abuse that might otherwise have been hidden underground. And for that I am grateful."

As Luella listened to the judge address the victims, she desperately wanted to rewind the proceedings to the moment August refused to speak, then to press pause so she could plead with him to beg forgiveness, to demonstrate to the court and to his victims that he was deeply sorry for all the harm he'd inflicted. She fantasized grabbing Thomas Lowery by his collar. "You're his attorney," she imagined shouting. "Tell him that if he doesn't demonstrate remorse the judge will show no mercy. She'll hand down the maximum sentence allowed under the law. Tell him!" But Lowery was no fool. Undoubtedly, he'd already given August his best advice.

August was proud, headstrong, always a leader not easily swayed by what others thought. It was part of the makeup of a head coach who constantly lived with the pressure to win, to make tough on-the-spot decisions, to believe his judgment best. Even if remorseful, he would be loath to publicly humble himself. If only this time he would set aside his pride.

She remembered their conversation at the jail when he informed her that his attorney had discussed an appeal. *I know it's a long shot,*

Lulu, but I have to keep fighting. She was horrified. He was guilty. He should accept whatever just punishment was imposed and live with it. Then it dawned on her, his silence now was no accident; it was purposeful. Admitting guilt now would interfere with any future appeal.

August, with his attorney by his side, stood to face the judge.

"Mr. Laurent, your actions have caused incalculable damage in the lives of these young men," she said. "No number of charitable efforts—and I question whether those public efforts were merely a means of covering up your sexual predation—could ever counterbalance the destruction you have caused. By your lack of publicly expressed remorse, it is clear to me that you do not fully comprehend the depravity of your behavior."

Luella could not imagine standing mute, as August did, while the judge berated her in front of a roomful of spectators. She would have sobbed uncontrollably, collapsed to her knees. It took a combination of strength and narcissism to withstand such public humiliation.

"You were not a stranger," Judge Richards said. "You were a trusted adult, trusted by the community, the parents, and their children. Your crimes are all the more heinous because you used your position to recruit, entice, and violate the children entrusted to your care. You are a calculating predator, a danger to society."

The judge's words sliced through Luella like a razor. Perhaps the victims would never find it in their hearts to forgive her myopia, but she hoped one day to be able to forgive herself.

"Mr. Laurent, it is my duty to impose a sentence that is just and fits the magnitude of the crime," said the judge. "Throughout the trial, I have done my solemn best to remain impartial, to listen to the facts of the case, to remain as open-minded as humanly possible. That phase is over. A jury of your peers has listened to all the evidence and has found you guilty beyond a reasonable doubt. Now I can I admit that I am deeply troubled by your behavior." Judge Richards' voice remained controlled, although her gestures and animated facial expression belied her emotion. "I have three children who have not yet graduated from high school. When I think of entrusting them to you to be guided, taught, and coached the way many of these unsuspecting parents did, I am sickened.

"I do not believe in one-size-fits-all justice. I do, however, believe in the Constitution and the law, which provide sentencing guidelines for the serious felonies you have committed. It is within my discretion as to how to apply those guidelines."

Every muscle in Luella's body tensed.

"While you are in prison, I am making a recommendation for on-going mental health treatment," said the judge. "You clearly have long-standing deviant proclivities that need to be addressed. And in the report before me, I also see that you owe $527.00 in state costs."

The judge turned to prosecutor Fett. "Do I understand correctly that the county has waived the trial costs?"

"Yes, Your Honor," answered Fett.

"Mr. Laurent, you will receive jail time credit of eighty-two days, which will be subtracted from your sentence." Then Judge Richards listed the multiple counts of first-degree sexual assault of a child, plus the first-degree counts of engaging in repeated acts of sexual assault of the same child, of which August had been found guilty. She enumerated the numerous counts of assault by a person who works with children, causing mental harm to a child, exposing his genitals, and child enticement.

She sentenced him to thirty years.

Thirty years! Luella covered her mouth to stifle a gasp.

In addition, for possession of child pornography the judge sentenced him to five years. "To be served consecutively," she said.

Thirty plus five. The sum hit Luella with the force of a battering ram.

August stood mute.

"That is thirty-five years, minus the days for which you are receiving credit. Further, if you live long enough to get out of prison, I order that you remain on lifetime supervision as outlined in section 939.615 of the Wisconsin state statutes."

Luella was unable to see August's face. Beyond a slight slump of the shoulders, it appeared as though he showed no emotion. When his lawyer whispered in his ear August leaned in. Luella saw him in profile. A barely perceptible twitch quivered at the corner of his mouth.

"Is there anything else for the record?" the judge asked, turning to the prosecutor and then to the defense lawyer.

"No, Your Honor," they replied simultaneously.

"All rise," said the clerk.

As Judge Richards exited and August was handcuffed and led from the courtroom, never looking back, many of the spectators applauded.

Luella quietly wept. Franklin touched her shoulder.

Unlike an objective mathematical equation in which A plus B equals C, sentencing was subjective—the crime plus sentencing guidelines equaled whatever the judge determined to be just. Luella wondered at the steel it took to look a man in the eye and tell him that he was a disgraceful human being, that he would most likely die in prison. What nerve it must require to take away a man's freedom, no matter how justified. She could not fathom the responsibility of sitting in judgment.

Awash in grief, Luella leaned against Franklin, who, after the spectators cleared the room, put his arm around her and guided her down the aisle. She remembered leaning on him this same way as they'd left the church after their mother's funeral, sadness overtaking her as it dawned on her, then as now, that life would never be the same.

Beth, her cheeks wet, her expression somber, waited for them in the back.

"Thank you for coming," Luella managed.

"I couldn't make myself sit near him. I'm sorry."

Luella reached for Beth's hand and squeezed it gently.

"Thirty-five years, Mom. He'll be ninety-two years old if he ever gets out of prison. I'll be sixty-five. Wyatt will be forty."

The anguish in Beth's voice pierced Luella's heart.

These past months, when Beth refused to speak with her father, Luella had thought her stubborn, selfish, and callous. She'd been angry at Beth's abandonment, resented her for taking what seemed like the path of least resistance. She'd considered her weak for failing to face August. Like so much else Luella had gotten wrong, she'd been mistaken about Beth. Like an addict, Luella had chosen to wean herself from the poison slowly, making excuses for continuing her dependence. Beth had chosen to suffer the pain of withdrawal immediately. Her daughter had been more honest all along. She had recognized sooner the depth of August's deviancy. Turning away from him had been an act of courage rather than cowardice.

Chapter Twenty-eight
~The Amethyst Month~

The sub-zero cold lingered in early February like an unwelcome guest. Luella, Bird curled by her side, sat on the living room sofa across from Franklin and Beth, staring out at the expanse of snow-covered lake, the absence of color apropos of her wintery mood.

"It's time," Franklin said, laying a document on the coffee table. "You've been holding on to these divorce papers for weeks."

Luella glanced at the papers, then looked back toward the lake.

"We've talked about this. Your properties are a liability you can no longer afford. You need to sell both the Chicago house and the camp," Franklin insisted. "You're aware that the numbers don't add up. The upkeep is rapidly draining your assets. The steep attorney's fees will continue with the civil law suits. There's no guarantee how this will all turn out. The situation is only going to get worse. You can't afford to stay married to August. You've got to get out from under all of this."

It was as though her rational mind was as frozen as the winter ground. Nothing made sense. In trying to solve the equation of her life, thinking that she'd taken all the right steps, followed all the rules, she'd unintentionally divided by zero. She'd gone from having a stable life, an enviable marriage, a fulfilling job, a beautiful house, and a camp that spoke to her spirit, to losing it all.

"Mom, Uncle Franklin is right," said Beth. "To do nothing will spell disaster."

Her brother and daughter had her best interest at heart, but she was still struggling to cope with a confusing mix of fury and longing. There were times when she thought she might be crazy, one minute wishing August dead, the next minute wanting to keep him, or at least the memory of him, in her life. She fantasized various ways he could meet his end: choking, falling, disease, murder. Then her grief would make sense. She could collect his life insurance money and buy time to make measured decisions about what to do with the house and the camp. The cruelty of her thoughts horrified her.

No one would understand missing a man who harmed children. How could she explain that it wasn't that she missed August, the man who preyed on young boys? She missed her loving husband and partner. It was impossible to erase decades of life together with the snap of a finger. She thought of him often, sometimes in a murderous rage, sometimes in a moment of unbearable loneliness.

"Sign these divorce papers now," Franklin urged. "I can see to it that they get to August so you don't have to face him."

A memory of her nine-year-old self teetering on the edge of a three-meter diving board came to mind, her looking down into the twelve-foot-deep pool, paralyzed by fear, the board bouncing as her best friend Janie, the adventurous daredevil, strode out to the end of the board, grabbed Luella's hand, and jumped. She could still feel the sensation of falling through the air, legs akimbo, hair flying, plunging into the water, kicking furiously to the surface. She'd been livid at first, spluttering as her head broke the plane, then a feeling of triumph overtaking her as she realized she'd made the jump that had eluded her for most of the summer. Perhaps this was one of those plunging-off-of-the-high-dive moments.

"Luella?"

She felt the weight of the heart necklace around her neck, invisible under her cable-knit sweater. If Franklin and Beth knew that she still wore it, they would disapprove. Beth had long since stopped wearing her identical necklace. Even to herself, Luella couldn't explain why or justify wearing it; she just knew that it had become her guilty secret, a reminder of all the other forbidden thoughts she kept hidden.

Franklin laid a pen on the coffee table next to the divorce papers. Luella noticed that he'd already filled in the date on the signature line.

Today was August's birthday. She wondered if either Franklin or Beth remembered. She didn't mention it.

She reached for the pen, then hesitated.

As a Catholic, she'd spent a lifetime believing that divorce was not permitted for valid sacramental marriages. Franklin, who had divorced and then married his secretary after a torrid affair, had years ago abandoned the Catholic faith. Still, he seemed to read her mind. "Under the circumstances, do you have any doubt the Church will grant you an annulment? You can worry about what the Church thinks later. Now we have to deal with your legal entanglements."

Church rules? Why should she care? She'd grown up Catholic, attended parochial schools, and been a regular churchgoer even after the Church's disgraceful handling of the priest pedophilia scandal. She continued to work at St. Eligius School until her firing. But the memory of Ardan Connelly, the school board president, hypocritically interrogating her—*are you telling me you had no idea what was going on right under your nose?*— humiliated her. Worse was the acquiescence of Sister Marian Lee, the school principal, whom Luella had considered an ally.

After August's arrest she'd begged God to give back her life. Nothing. More and more she wondered if she were praying into the void. More and more she wondered if her faith was just one more thing, like marriage, family, career, and friendship, she had taken for granted and lost.

Luella scratched Bird behind his ear. He rolled to his side, exposed his underbelly. She stroked the pink skin, as soft as a baby blanket.

Finally, she picked up the pen and scrawled *Luella Margaret Laurent* on the signature line.

Franklin smiled. "Good. It's a start."

The plain white envelope, postmarked February 14, bore the return address of Dodge Correctional Institution in Waupun, Wisconsin.

Luella glanced at Beth, then tucked the envelope under her sweater and carried it up to her bedroom, feeling like a teenager hiding contraband from a parent.

She sat on the edge of the bed, stalling, wishing she had the strength to throw the envelope in the trash, unopened. She slid her finger under the flap and pulled out the letter, handwritten on yellow legal paper.

Dear Lulu,

I'm disappointed you haven't answered my letter, but I don't completely blame you for being angry.

One sentence and her blood boiled. August still believed he was not one hundred percent to blame. How did he parse that percentage? Fifty-fifty? Sixty-forty? How dare he assign her any amount.

I hated the way we left things the last time you visited me in the county jail. When you told me that you're filing for divorce, I was stunned. I don't understand, Lulu. I tried to end my life. I would have been spared this misery and you would have had your freedom. You wouldn't allow it, but now you are willing to kick me to the curb. If you didn't plan to stay with me, why didn't you just let me go?

That self-pitying bastard! August's accusatory tone sent her heart rate skyrocketing. Her hands trembled. She stood. Paced. How dare he lay his misery at her feet. She'd simply reacted when she'd found him slumped in his chair, head lolling, barely breathing. Calling 911 had been a reflex.

Clearly, August expected her to carry the emotional load for both of them as she'd done throughout their marriage. She was so damned tired of the burden. He blamed her for his suffering, expected her to feel guilty, enlisted her to shoulder the weight.

Guilty? No. Enraged!

She glared at the page.

Divorce means you believe I will never get out of here. You have no idea what it is like to be caged, to lose every freedom you took for granted, to answer to people who think they are your superior even though they barely graduated from high school. Humiliation lives with you every minute of every day.

Did he give a moment's thought to her humiliation? His victims' pain?

She'd learned the same personality trait could be positive or negative depending on a person's vantage point. August's self-confidence, what made him a winning coach able to stand toe-to-toe with anyone, a quality that made him seem invincible when they'd first met, had become self-absorption. That made him nothing more than an egoist. Maybe it had been that way from the beginning; she'd simply been too naïve or too much in love to see it.

I told you Lowery is looking to file an appeal. To survive in here, I have to hold on to hope. I need your support. I need you to stand with me.

Too late, she thought.

Don't do this to me, Lulu. You know I love you. Until death do us part.

Yours Always,
August

He couldn't possibly love her, not the way she had fiercely loved him, or he never would have betrayed her in such a vile way. He might love what she provided—family, respectability, loyalty—but not the flesh and blood woman who had given him her heart. Longing for the life she'd clung to these many months suddenly seemed absurd, like longing to be part of a theatrical drama, the actors playing parts and the props creating an illusion. No more.

She ripped the letter in half, tore it again and again, before stuffing the pieces into the envelope. Glancing at the postmark, she grimaced, then tossed the envelope in the trash.

"Oh sweetheart," she sneered. "Happy Valentine's Day."

Chapter Twenty-nine
~Outrunning the Avalanche~

O n the first day of spring the trees remained bare and a foot of snow still covered the ground. The outside thermometer read forty-six degrees, a welcome relief from the sub-freezing temperatures that lingered through December, January, and February.

To Beth, the afternoon sunlight streaming through the kitchen window seemed brighter and more optimistic than it had in months. She cradled a cup of herbal tea in her hands and peered out the window, studying a two-foot icicle, glinting like a crystal stalactite, stubbornly hanging from the roof's soffit. Droplets of water slid down its length, racing to the tip, then having arrived, clung and trembled, as if reluctant to let go.

Winter had been long, with arctic temperatures and record snowfall. When she'd fled north in November, she'd found the seclusion of the camp comforting. At times the house was as silent as an isolation tank, the soundlessness interrupted only by a creaking floorboard or the soft rumble of the furnace. The leisurely days brought solace—driving Wyatt to school, bundling up and taking long walks with Bird, curling up on the couch with a book.

As the weeks ticked by, the remoteness began to wear thin. Winter had overstayed its welcome. She was tired of the cold and snow, tired of being frozen in place. She missed teaching and coaching, missed the energy and optimism of her students, the collegiality of her colleagues. She ached for Gabe, for his humor, his love, his touch. Nights proved especially lonely as she lay in bed, longing to share her innermost thoughts, craving the warmth of his body. And in her most honest moments, she admitted that she missed her dad, their shared love of basketball, his encouragement, his approval. She wondered whether that inner voice seeking his blessing would ever go away.

Beth continued to study the water rilling, fascinated as, drip by drip, the icicle became smaller. She had never spent spring at the camp, never had the luxury of focusing on such minutiae. By now, two hundred and fifty miles south, the ground would be bare, the trees leafing out, and daffodils and irises poking through the soil. This far north, however, where spring often came as a single month sandwiched between the final snow melt and full-blown summer, the arrival of spring could be as subtle as droplets shimmying down a melting icicle.

She saw a vehicle rolling down the driveway. Uncle Franklin's Land Rover. It was unusual for him to come to the camp in the middle of the day. He pulled up next to the house and stepped out of his car looking official, carrying a briefcase and wearing a wool camel overcoat and brown fedora. He sidestepped a patch of melting ice on the wet gravel driveway. Always careful, always deliberate, thought Beth.

A knock.

"Anyone home?" called Franklin.

Bird pranced past the kitchen door, tail wagging double time. Luella hurried behind him. The house was so quiet, Beth forgot her mother was there. The voices in the foyer were muffled, but she heard her name. Curious, she set her cup on the counter and wandered toward the entryway. As she approached, she overheard her mother say, "I think Beth needs to be in on the discussion."

Franklin set his briefcase on the floor, hung his coat and hat on a hook by the door, and rubbed his hands together so vigorously it reminded Beth of a Boy Scout twirling sticks to start a fire.

"What discussion?" asked Beth.

Franklin picked up his briefcase. "I came to talk with your mother about what her next logistical moves need to be, about securing her future."

As an only child, growing up with a mother who never talked down to her and a father who shared coaching strategy with her from the time she was old enough to dribble a basketball, Beth was accustomed to being included in her parents' world. Still, her mother's obvious nervousness made her uneasy.

Bird pranced ahead, leading them into the living room.

"Would you like something to drink?" asked Luella.

"No, I'm good," said Franklin.

Beth and Luella sat on the sofa. Bird curled on the floor at Beth's feet. Franklin chose the chair near the fireplace. He opened his briefcase and withdrew a large manila envelope. He leaned over, stretched out his arm, and handed the envelope to Luella. "The signed divorce papers," he said.

Divorce. It surprised Beth how sad she felt, despite believing that her mother needed to end her marriage. As a teenager, she'd been proud her parents were together, lived in the same house, unlike so many of her friends who were being raised by a single parent or who had step-parents they called by their first names. She'd felt sorry for them. The bond her parents shared had made her secure, protected. She'd told Gabe when he'd proposed that he'd better be sure he wanted to marry her because she would never divorce him. Never. "You're stuck with me forever," she'd declared. How brief forever turned out to be.

Beth glanced at Luella, whose eyes glistened, the sadness in them obvious.

"You should change your name," said Beth. She had already filed her own Petition for Name Change in Ojibwe County Circuit Court. She was now Elizabeth Mancuso, widow of Gabriel Mancuso, mother of Wyatt Mancuso.

"I don't know."

"You can't seriously want to keep the Laurent name?"

"Beth has a valid point," argued Franklin. "Make a clean break. Distance yourself from this scandal."

"The first time I signed the name Elizabeth Mancuso, I felt transformed."

"Luella Martin." Luella timidly tried out her maiden name. "I'll think about it."

"It's really easy to file the petition," urged Beth. "I can help you."

"I said I'll think about it."

Beth glanced at her uncle, but his lawyerly expression remained neutral. "There's also the matter of real estate," he said, deftly shifting gears. "I've contacted Gordon-Mistel Realty in Chicago about selling your Lake Bluff house. I've brought the listing contract for you to sign." He reached into his briefcase and pulled out a legal-sized file folder and a pen. "Duncan Coyle, the agent, checked the comparables, and he's suggesting that you list the property for $1.4 million. It's a fair price. The house is in a preferred location surrounded by more expensive properties, which is ideal. Of course, there is still a substantial mortgage on the property."

Luella accepted the pen and the file folder, opened it slowly.

"I think you have to be prepared for it to sell quickly," said Franklin. "You should drive down and sort through personal possessions as soon as possible."

Beth pictured the four-bedroom house with its intricate millwork, vaulted-ceilinged living room with tall windows, and chef's kitchen with the limestone fireplace. She thought of the lush lawn, tended by a hired landscaper. It was such a contrast to the camp lodge. Whenever she visited her parents' home, she stayed in an upstairs guest bedroom with its charming window seat and *en suite* bathroom anchored by a vintage claw-foot bathtub. The final time Gabe had slept in that room with her they'd made love, and he'd tenderly washed her back as she soaked in that tub. Luella had even decorated one of the bedrooms with a racing car bed for Wyatt. It was a beautiful home that held positive memories, but not having been raised there, Beth didn't have a strong attachment to it.

Stoically, Luella worked the pen between her thumb and index finger.

"Spring is the ideal time to sell," Franklin reminded her.

Luella signed the listing agreement, tucked it in the file folder, and wordlessly handed it back.

"There's also the matter of the camp. You have to sell," said Franklin. "That's going to be tougher. It's worth a lot more. You have acreage and six-hundred feet of prime frontage, but there isn't a hot market for a basketball camp where kids…a camp associated with trouble."

Since age five, Beth had lived there with her parents every summer. The camp had been forever tainted, yet it was hard to think about giving it up. She'd imagined one day taking over the camp when her father retired. Rationally, she knew it was impossible to keep.

"I thought I would grow old here," Luella said, wistfully.

"Rhonda Merring from North Country Realty is coming out to take a look at the property on Tuesday at 9:30." Franklin handed Luella a business card. "The sooner you get the camp listed the better."

Bird jumped up on the sofa and settled between Beth and Luella, resting his head in Luella's lap. She stroked his head tenderly. "How is it possible to love a place with all your heart and yet hate it, too?"

"It's time to move on," said Franklin. "There's simply no other choice."

Easy for him to be so dispassionate, thought Beth, given that he and Denise now owned Great Aunt Mavis's and Great Uncle Albert's property.

"That's just it; move on where?" asked Luella. "The Lake Bluff house will be gone. The camp will be sold. I will be homeless. Not penniless, but homeless. So, tell me, Franklin, where should I go? Please, tell me, what comes next?"

On the gray and gloomy early spring morning Luella was alone in the house. Rosie was at the sheltered workshop. Wyatt was at school. Beth, with Bird as her eager companion, had left hours ago to run errands.

Through the living room windows Luella watched sheets of rain pour down from steel-colored clouds. The incessant drumming on the roof of the high-ceilinged room played counterpoint to the tick of the grandfather clock. The beat pounded inside her chest. In the empty house the marking of time was a haunting sound.

Luella pulled her sweater tight against the damp air and folded her arms across her chest. She considered building a fire in the fireplace, a task August used to perform, arranging the kindling, stacking the wood, leaving just the right amount of airspace between the logs, and crumpling enough newspaper to make the fire catch easily. The wood box was empty. In no mood to don a raincoat and slosh through the yard to the woodpile, she curled up on the sofa and covered herself with the afghan.

She turned on the floor lamp and opened the Barbara Kingsolver novel sitting on the side table to the bookmarked page. After reading several pages she stopped, having no idea what she'd just read. The recent conversation she'd had with Franklin about her finances preoccupied her thoughts. She was worried. About the camp. The Lake Bluff house. Unemployment. Taxes. The future.

Admittedly she had it better than many women with fewer resources. She would not go hungry. Her brother would never let her starve or be without a roof over her head. That, at least, was reassuring. Her savings would only last so long. She wasn't old enough to pull from a retirement account without significant penalty. Who would hire the wife of a notorious pedophile, especially when so many automatically assumed she knew, yet had said nothing? Where would she live? Her future waited, not as an opportunity to begin anew but as a void where the unknown loomed dark and scary.

In her marriage, she'd always been the calm one, the stabilizing force, the balance to August's energetic, mercurial personality. But over the past months, anxiety niggled at her constantly. A whirl of emotions burst to the surface at the most inopportune times. Disgust. Frustration. Rage. Like an extreme skier barreling down a mountainside with an avalanche rumbling behind her, she was barely able to keep control or to stay ahead of problems that threatened to bury her. Who was there to keep her in balance? Beth had worries of her own. Franklin tried, but it seemed unfair to become his responsibility.

With too much time to obsess on all that she'd lost, the quiet, alone times were the worst. Now, like a slow-moving wave, her anxiety gained momentum. The sensation started at her core and tumbled through her limbs. Her heart beat faster. The temptation to numb herself almost overpowered her. This is how people became alcoholics or drug addicts, she thought. Anything to dull the pain. She gnawed the tip of her thumb, concentrated on breathing deeply. Setting her book on the side table, not bothering to insert the bookmark, she stood and wandered around the living room.

"Come on, Luella," she said aloud. "Pull it together."

The rain pummeled the roof. The clock ticked. Louder. Louder.

She picked up her cell phone from the coffee table and scanned the contact list. Who could she reach out to? Who would care? Scrolling through the alphabet served as a reminder of how many friends had deserted her. Rhonda Ahlborn, her closest friend on the St. Eligius faculty. Sophia Giovani, her Lake Bluff next door neighbor. Annalise McElroy, a member of the sorority of coaches' wives. Trudy Nilsen. She paused. She thought of Trudy's kindness, her evening invitations to the hair salon, showing up in court, coming to camp after August's suicide attempt. Impulsively, Luella touched the call icon. Trudy answered on the fourth ring.

"Hello. Luella?"

Trudy's instant recognition caught Luella off guard. In the background she heard voices and the hum of a hairdryer.

"I—I'm sorry. I forgot. You're working."

"What's up?"

"Nothing. It's not important. I'm sorry to have bothered you."

"Actually, you caught me at a good time. I'm waiting on someone's color."

Silence.

"Luella, what is it?"

"I'm embarrassed. It's nothing."

"Nothing?"

"It's just that I'm here alone. The rain. The gray."

"Pretty depressing."

The invitation in Trudy's voice kept Luella talking.

"I'm just feeling sorry for myself. Pretty pathetic." Luella slumped into the sofa.

"August is the pathetic one," Trudy insisted. "Not you. That bastard is the one who put you in this position, made you feel like nothing."

"I'm worried all the time. I have no idea what to do next," Luella confessed, her voice quavering.

"The unknown is scary. I've been there. But, Luella, you're a strong woman, a survivor. What you're going through is damn hard. It's unfair. Shitty. Life sucks right now. Who do you think would handle this awful situation better?" Trudy waited. The hairdryer continued to hum. "You're not weak. You're human. You don't have to do this alone. You don't have to be Superwoman."

Luella leaned into the soft back cushion of the sofa, swept the hair from her forehead, glanced out the window. The torrent had turned to a slow, steady rain, the drumming on the roof, a soft patter.

"My brother says I have to sell the camp and my house. I'll have no home."

"We will figure this out."

We. The word, a lifeline.

"You've been kicked and bloodied, but you're still here."

As Trudy listened Luella's anxiety lessened. Her breathing slowed. The throbbing in her head subsided.

She heard the back door close. Bird bounded into the living room. Beth was home.

"I have to go. The timer just went off." Trudy lowered her voice.

"If I wait too long that stunning auburn color will morph into a shade Mrs. High-and-Mighty wouldn't be too pleased with. Although I admit, it's really tempting."

Luella smiled.

"But seriously, I can call you back later." Trudy's tone was tender, sympathetic.

"That's not necessary. Beth's home. And I'm feeling much better."

"If you're sure."

"I am. And, Trudy, thank you."

Chapter Thirty
~The Purge~

O n Saturday during the third week in April, the last stubborn patch of ice floating in the middle of Whisper Lake melted in the afternoon sun. A raft of mallards paddled ten yards from the shoreline. The deciduous trees still showed no signs of budding.

Beth, wearing a down vest and stocking cap, stood at the water's edge breathing in the crisp, earthy air. She surveyed the beach littered with branches, which over winter had broken off and fallen from the snow-laden trees. As a child, when her parents came north during spring break to begin readying the camp for summer, she had been assigned the task of cleaning the beach. Now, Wyatt and Rosie helped her gather the branches, stacking them in small piles to be hauled into the woods.

Bird grabbed the end of a four-foot branch that Wyatt dragged along the sand. The dog playfully growled, locked his front legs, thrust his rump into the air, and tugged. Wyatt pulled on his end of the stick, growled, then giggled as Bird triumphantly jerked it from his hands and pranced along the beach, head held high like a victorious Olympian. Beth smiled. She was reminded of herself at Wyatt's age, playing with her dog, a lanky golden lab and shepherd mix her father had named Walton, after Bill Walton the UCLA and NBA basketball star.

Beth remembered the first time, when they'd only been dating for a couple of weeks, she'd brought Gabe to camp. She'd watched as he wrestled a log forced ashore by the powerful ice, his muscles flexing through his red plaid shirt, his mop of dark curls blowing in the breeze. When he'd caught her gawking, she'd been flustered and feigned disinterest. "Looks like you're thinking what I'm thinking," Gabe had said, glancing over his shoulder, waggling his eyebrows, and grinning.

"Gina Marie Mancuso reporting for clean-up duty," Gina shouted as she came down the path toward the beach.

"You're here!" Beth ran toward Gina. "I was afraid you'd have to cancel this weekend because of work."

"What, and miss all this fun?" said Gina. "Not on your life. I was able to find another nurse to cover for me. All I had to do was promise to work his hours Memorial Day weekend."

"Ouch."

"Honestly, I don't mind."

"What about Anthony?"

"He's talking with your mom," said Gina, nodding toward the house.

Bird scampered over, tail wagging, and brushed against her legs. She stroked his head and patted his haunch. "Hey, good dog. I'm happy to see you, too."

Wyatt and Rosie ran to greet Gina.

"How are my favorite nephew and aunt-in-law?" She kissed Wyatt on the top of his head and Rosie on her cheek.

"We're taking all the sticks off the beach so our feet don't get poked when we go swimming," said Wyatt.

"But the water is still too cold," Rosie chimed in. "Beth says we have to wait until summer."

"But Bird is allowed to go in the lake 'cuz his fur gives him 'installation'," said Wyatt.

Gina sucked in her cheeks. "Uncle Anthony's up at the house. I think he has a treat for each of you, that is, if you can take a break from your hard work."

"Can we, Mom?"

"Sure, honey."

Wyatt grabbed Rosie's hand and pulled her up the path toward the house. Bird bounded ahead, as if begging them to give chase.

"I take it you haven't told them about selling the camp," said Gina.

"No. I'm still trying to wrap my head around the idea." Beth turned away, wiped her forehead with the back of her sleeve, and stooped to pick up a pile of branches.

Gina, stylishly attired in an olive Sherpa jacket, matching stocking cap, and new boots, grabbed one end of the largest pile and helped Beth haul it into the woods. When they returned to the beach, Gina cupped her hand visor-like above her eyes and craned her neck to watch a bald eagle, its head and tail brilliant white against the cloudless sky. It glided over the lake, circled, and then landed on the bare branch of a giant pine.

"Breathtaking!" exclaimed Gina.

"I never tire of watching the eagles. They've built a nest just around the bay," said Beth.

"I can't get over how peaceful it is here."

"I wish that were enough. I wish I could just be grateful, but I'm still so angry." Beth kicked a small branch toward one of the piles. "After losing Gabe, I thought I'd finally gotten through the anger stage and into some fragile level of acceptance. But the anger I feel for my dad spills over into rage. I try to control it, but I can't seem to get past it."

Gina guided Beth by her elbow to the log bench, urged her to sit. "You're too hard on yourself. Anyone who suffered the losses you have in the past couple of years would be reeling. I know it's hard for you to be patient, but you need to give yourself time to heal." Gina sat beside Beth, turned toward her, looked her in the eye. "True confession? I'm mad, too. I'm angry that my brother died so young, and I'm enraged that your dad has put you through hell."

"I'm mostly angry at him for the unspeakable things he did to those boys, but selfishly I'm furious with him for spoiling this place," said Beth. "So much of my life has been spent here. It's part of my DNA. Yet every time I look at the cabin where he molested those boys, I think I can't run far enough away. Then an eagle flies over and I desperately want to stay."

"Oh Beth."

"I know I sound schizophrenic."

Gina touched Beth's shoulder. "You sound human."

Twenty feet from where Beth and Gina sat, a white-throated sparrow flew from a branch of a nearby spruce and landed on the leaf-covered ground bordering the beach. Beth watched it scratch for food and thought, when she returned to life in the city, how much she would miss these simple moments.

"Have you told your mother about your job offer?"

"No. I haven't decided whether to take it. Coaching at a junior college wasn't exactly in my plans."

"You know the saying, 'Life is what happens to you while you're busy making other plans.'"

"Believe me, I get that. It would be easier to drift if I didn't have Wyatt's future to consider."

"You're a great mom, Beth. And he's a remarkable kid. He's got a family who loves and adores him. He'll be fine."

"I hope you're right."

A pair of ducks swam parallel to the shoreline. Beth wondered if she would be living at camp long enough to see them raise a brood. "I hate muskies!" she'd declared the summer she turned nine, when she'd realized that only two of twelve ducklings had survived. "Oh, honey," her mother had explained. "Muskies and other predators need nutrition. They're part of the food chain. It's nature's way of making sure species survive." Back then Beth had resented her mother's practicality, much preferring her father's quixotic manner. Now she bristled at the thought.

"I'm worried about my mom," Beth confided. "Once she sells the house and the camp, I don't know what she's going to do. I'm not sure about her prospects at age fifty-six."

"Your mom is a smart woman." Gina stood and brushed off the back of her pants. "And tougher than I think you give her credit for."

"She's devoted her life to taking care of my dad and me. She deserves better than ending up alone. I'm thinking of inviting her to live with Wyatt and me."

Gina looked down at Beth. "Is that what you actually want? Is that what your mom wants?"

"I have no idea. But I can't keep living in limbo. I've got to do something. And soon."

Luella had never entered the cabin where August molested the boys. It had been his domain, a space for storing athletic equipment. Since she'd read the trial transcript, it had become a sinful place that turned her stomach every time she looked at it.

There were times when she'd been tempted to enter the whitewashed structure, her curiosity egging her on like a schoolyard bully. *Come on, coward! I dare you.* Several times she'd walked close, but each time she came near it, she lost her nerve and retreated. More often, she was tempted to burn it to the ground, until all that remained of August's lair was a pile of ashes. She'd fantasize building a purifying pyre, a ritualistic sacrifice that would return the camp to the spiritual haven it used to be, a place she could love again.

Today was different. The realtor insisted that she remove any items that would interfere with the sale of the camp. "It's going to be a hard sell, beautiful as it is," Rhonda Merring had said, "given that there isn't a market for basketball camps with this kind of—ahem—notoriety. It's likely whoever purchases it is going to buy it for the lake frontage, condo off the cabins, or tear everything down and build a mansion." The reality stung. But if she hoped to sell the camp and move on with her life, she would have to follow the woman's advice.

Now she stood at the cabin door.

He showed me how to…get him off.

He performed oral sex on me.
How many times?
I stopped counting.

Luella fumbled with a large key ring, hands trembling, searching for two keys, one for the hasp latch lock, the other for the lock in the door knob.

Two locks. One door.

None of the other cabins had double locks. Why had she never found that unusual?

You should have known.

She fingered the smallest key. Shakily, she inserted it into the pad-lock. It fit. She turned the key, pulled the shackle from the body of the lock, released it from the metal loop, and opened the latch. Next, she counted until she reached the key for cabin number twelve. She inserted it in the knob, hesitated. The sound of a pickup truck backing down the narrow road between the cabins distracted her. The truck stopped within fifteen feet of the door.

Anthony jumped out of the driver's side and strode toward her. "Beth sent Gina and me to help. She thought maybe you weren't ready for this."

Gina sat in the passenger seat, texting.

Luella looked down at her trembling hands, took a deep breath. "Thanks," she replied, "but I have to face this." She turned the key. The knob refused to budge.

"Here, let me try," Anthony offered.

Luella stepped aside. Anthony jiggled the key, turned it, twisted the knob, and opened the door.

Cautiously, Luella followed Anthony into the musty cabin, stood just inside the door, resisted the urge to turn and run. Faint afternoon sunlight shone through the top of the dirty west-facing window mostly covered by an old basketball backboard standing upright on a wooden table. A large cobweb hung in the top right corner of the window. The east-facing window was completely obscured by a tall shelving unit filled with plastic storage containers. She squinted into the dimness.

In his testimony, Derrick Boyer described the cabin as "cold and dark." Gooseflesh crawled up her arms. She switched on the overhead light and waited for her eyes to adjust. Several large mesh bins, over-flowing with underinflated basketballs, sat in the middle of the room. Three newer backboards leaned against the walls. Shelves placed per-pendicular to the outside walls divided the eighteen by-twenty-foot room, leaving a narrow makeshift doorway between them.

Derrick also testified that a mattress in the cabin was "old and smelled." Luella glanced around the front half of the room. No mat-tress. Maybe Derrick had lied. Maybe the jury had been duped. Slowly she ventured farther into the room and ducked through the improvised doorway, brushing away cobwebs that clung to her face and hair. There in the far corner, shoved against the wall in the windowless side of the room, was a bare double mattress resting atop a metal frame.

She blanched at the stained blue and gray striped ticking of the tufted mattress. Several buttons were missing. The middle sagged like a sway-back horse. The seediness disgusted her. She didn't want to think about what had happened on that mattress, didn't want to fill her mind with images of frightened young boys lying next to August as he abused them.

Luella scanned the room. In the opposite corner sat an overstuffed chair with the seat cushion askew, an old end table turned on its side, and a black pole lamp with three shades, one bulb. An array of maga-zines was scattered around the base of the chair. An orange extension cord, plugged into the back wall, snaked across the floor. It looked as though, when the police searched the cabin, they'd upended things without regard to restoring them. Somewhere in the room they'd found a laptop computer filled with images of naked young boys. Luella won-dered if August had hidden it or whether, in his arrogance, he'd left it out in plain sight. She pictured him sitting in that grimy chair, his laptop plugged into the extension cord, masturbating.

Her heartbeat thundered in her chest. She again fixed on the mattress. Images in high-definition of August lying next to Marty Goddard came to her. She remembered Marty's testimony. *He got this sickening smile on his face. He made me put my hand over his hard penis and he whispered in my ear, let's see how good of a player you really are.* He'd testified that Luella had come to the door that night, shouted through it, walked away when August assured her that he'd be along soon. She could smell Marty Goddard's fear and desperation in that room, hear his silent plea for help.

"Marty, I'm so, so sorry," she said. "Please forgive me."

"You okay, Luella?" asked Anthony.

Luella jumped.

"I can feel the evil in here." Tears stung her eyes.

Anthony's strong arms enfolded her. "It's going to be okay. You're going to be okay." Luella allowed herself to soak in his kindness, the comfort of his touch.

"I thought I'd be out of tears by now," she said, looking up and wiping her eyes. "I thought I'd be stronger."

Anthony stepped back and looked her in the eye. "Luella, this is not your fault."

"That's right." Gina strolled into the back half of the room. "And you're not alone. We're here to help." She glanced at the bed, scowled. "You don't have to be weak to be creeped out by this."

"We'll empty the cabin." Anthony gently turned Luella toward the door. "You go back to the house."

"Just tell us what you want us to do," said Gina.

"I don't want to keep anything in here. Nothing. Whatever is in good condition can go to the thrift store. Whatever is in poor condition can be taken to the landfill."

"Got it," said Anthony.

"And the mattress—burn it."

After more than a ten-month absence, driving through tree-lined Lake Bluff with its manicured lawns and elegant houses left Luella with a déjà vu sensation. Returning to the home she'd shared with August for nine years, a home where she'd lived a lie, set her nerves on edge.

Beth steered the car pulling the rented trailer onto the brick-paved driveway and parked in front of the garage. Purple irises flourished under the stately shellbark hickory. Luella rolled down the passenger window and welcomed in the aroma of newly mown grass and the spring breeze blowing off of Lake Michigan, two blocks away.

When August was hired as the head coach at Jolliet University, he'd signed a lucrative contract. Together, they'd house hunted in this affluent neighborhood, a step up in status from all the places they'd previously lived. She would have been satisfied to move to a more modest neighborhood in the Chicago area, but August lobbied to buy the English Tudor house on this prestigious street.

The house was beautiful, with its slate shingled roof, gray stack-stone exterior, and multiple dormers. By the time she'd strolled through the 4,000 square foot home, run her hands over the soapstone kitchen countertops, basked in the sunlight streaming through the ten-foot paned windows in the family room, and ambled along the winding path of the English garden in the backyard—a garden she would rarely enjoy since she spent her summers at the camp—she'd convinced herself that she wanted the house as much as he did. The proximity to the lake sealed the deal.

From the backseat, Wyatt giggled, "Grandma, Bird's tail is swishing really fast and tickling my face. I think he remembers you used to live here."

Used to. This is where she *used to* live, *used to* believe her marriage was rock-solid, *used to* be happy.

Luella stepped out of the car and studied the house as though she were a buyer forming a first impression. The landscaping company kept the mophead hydrangeas and perennial flower beds, not yet in bloom, pruned and well-tended. At least that was a plus.

Beth helped Wyatt out of his car seat, and Bird jumped from the back and dashed around the front yard, nose surveying the ground.

Next door Sheila MacFarland, her hair dyed henna and wearing a form-fitting sweater and skinny jeans, sashayed to the roadside mail-box. Luella waved. Sheila acknowledged her with a curt nod, then, stiff and cold as an icicle, kept walking. Sheila, eight years younger than Luella, was on the dramatic side. They'd been friends, not intimates, but close neighbors. In the past, Sheila would have wandered over and chatted, shared neighborhood gossip, invited Luella in for a cup of cof-fee. The snub stung. Luella wondered if Sophia Giovani, her next-door neighbor to the north, whom she'd hand held through a messy divorce, had the same frosty attitude. She consoled herself with the idea that their rejection would make letting go easier.

Luella keyed in the entry code to unlock the front door with its round beveled glass window. The realtor who'd first shown the home bragged that the chestnut door had been reclaimed from a 19th century English manor. At the time, Luella had been impressed; now she won-dered if it was true.

Although the outside temperature inched up to sixty-eight degrees, the interior of the house remained chilly. Luella kept her sweater on as she stood in the large foyer and looked around with a critical eye. She ran her hand over the thick oak banister. A beam of sunlight poured in through the stairway dormer and spilled across the Oriental area rug centered on the tiled floor. The space she once found warm and invit-ing now seemed sterile and abandoned.

"I thought we could start with these," Beth suggested as she charged through the door, carrying an armful of empty boxes and over-sized garbage bags.

"Mom said I'm in charge of Bird," declared Wyatt, holding a tennis ball and following the dog into the house.

"Bird has been cooped up in the car for a long time. I think he would enjoy playing in the backyard," said Beth.

Wyatt cheerfully skipped through the foyer. "Come on, boy. Let's go outside. I'll show you how to fetch."

Luella turned up the thermostat. "I'm not sure where to begin."

"How about starting in the master bedroom. They always advise tackling the hardest things first." Beth handed her mother a stack of garbage bags and three nested boxes. "I'll empty the kitchen."

A framed wedding picture sat atop the dresser in the spacious first-floor master bedroom. It had occupied that same place in every house August and Luella owned. In the photograph, they faced each other, smiling broadly, Luella in her white off-the-shoulder gown, August in his black tux. He was heart-stoppingly handsome. They looked young, joyful, optimistic. She'd been so deeply in love with him she would have given up everything to be with him. And she had.

The large walk-in closet was filled with winter clothes. When Luella left for camp in early June, she'd expected to return. She'd believed that she and August would resume their lives as they had so many times before, he returning to coaching, she to teaching. Now it was as if she were stepping into to a museum chronicling the lives they'd once lived. His side of the closet was filled with Jolliet University athletic apparel, plus custom-tailored suits and shirts, which he wore on game days and at numerous public engagements. Her side held work outfits and dresses worn when accompanying August to his events.

She pulled out her favorite dress, teal, with a deep V back, held it against her body, and examined her image in the full-length mirror mounted on the wall at the far end of the closet. She'd lost weight since the last time she'd worn that dress at the alumni athletic boosters' banquet where August had been the keynote speaker. She'd been so proud and grateful to be his wife. Before walking to the podium, he'd leaned in close and whispered in her ear, "Babe, you still give me a hard-on." She'd tried to suppress her grin and ignore the heat traveling up her neck. At the time, she'd felt sexy and desired. In retrospect, she felt dirty and as manipulated as a believer bilked out of her life savings.

Two black dresses, a red chemise that had always draped awkwardly, and the teal dress, were folded and put in a bag marked "give away." She gathered a boat-necked black dress—good for funerals, she thought—and an olive-green shift that flattered her figure, and folded them into a box marked "save." Slacks, blouses, and sweaters were also sorted. She filled three additional "give away" bags and a single "save" box. Having done without these clothes for the past winter, she could not justify keeping most of them. Besides, too many of them held distasteful memories.

She stared at August's clothes, frowned at the "give away" bag, wondered if this was how widows felt. She'd heard of women who could not bring themselves to let go of their husband's possessions, could not bear to remove fabric that still carried their scent. She stepped closer to August's dress shirts, inhaled. Did she smell his Brut cologne, or did she imagine it? A seed of nausea burrowed into her stomach.

A special rack with twenty ties, arranged by color, hung on the wall by the closet doorway. Luella pulled down the navy paisley tie August had worn when he'd received the Philanthropist of the Year Award. It nearly seared her hand. She threw it on the floor. One by one, she ripped the ties from the rack and dropped them in a pile.

There were undoubtedly men who would be able to wear his clothes, all in excellent condition, even the athletic T-shirts, because August was too fastidious to have it otherwise. But it seemed wrong to pass these clothes along to unsuspecting strangers, men who would not realize they wore these outwardly perfect clothes marked by an invisible stain. Luella imagined a priest performing an exorcism, sprinkling holy water, uttering some Latin incantation, casting out whatever evil infected every fiber.

She tugged each T-shirt from its hanger and flung it on the pile in the middle of the floor. Next the sweat pants. Then the dress shirts

CEONE FENN

and immaculate suits. Adrenaline coursed through her. Perspiration beaded on her forehead. She removed her sweater and laid it on a shelf. From the caddy she grabbed several pairs of August's expensive shoes and tossed them on the pile. Furiously, she jammed his clothes into the garbage bags until the pile disappeared.

She scanned the empty closet. The barrenness seemed to mock her. A wave of sadness threw her off balance. She steadied herself by grabbing onto a shelf. Spent, she lowered herself to the floor. Knees pressed against her chest, she tried to calm her breathing. She wondered if widowhood would be easier, if death of a spouse was preferable to willful betrayal. Then she thought of Beth at Gabe's funeral and how bereft her father had been when her mother died and decided comparing the pain of loss was futile. It all hurt like hell.

"Mom?"

Luella looked up as though she'd forgotten Beth was in the house.

"Please help me carry these out to the garbage cans," said Luella, pointing to the mound of overstuffed bags.

"Are you sure?"

"I've never been more certain of anything in my life."

Chapter Thirty-one

~The Invitation~

On Thursday evening during the first week of May, a line of vehicles—mostly SUVs and pickup trucks, many hauling rigged-out fishing boats—parked in downtown Givens Knoll in front of Millie's Café and Fuddy-duddy's Tap. As she drove past them, Luella slowed and searched for a parking spot in front of The Hair Affair.

Halfway down the block she spotted an empty parking space next to Trudy's Volkswagen beetle. By comparison, Luella thought her large black Lincoln Navigator seemed severe and ostentatious. Buying it had been August's idea. Luella decided she would trade it in for a car more suited to her, maybe a Prius or a Rio.

At 7:30 p.m., day had not completely given way to night. Ordinarily, she welcomed the lengthening days, savored the lingering blue-gray light, but tonight she would have preferred to enter town under cover of darkness.

Except for a pinpoint of interior light visible from the street, the salon appeared to be closed. She knocked on the front door, timidly at first, then with more authority. Trudy opened it and greeted Luella with a smile and a hug.

"I hope you weren't waiting long," said Trudy. "I was just in the back room mixing your color." She locked the door behind her, closed the venetian blinds on the large picture windows, and turned on a bright overhead light.

Luella removed her jacket and hung it on a hook by the entry door.

The salon smelled of floral shampoo, nail polish, and coffee, with a faint chemical undertone, a blend of aromas Luella had come to associate with compassion. It was impossible to express the gratitude she felt for Trudy's kindness. It wasn't as though everyone Luella encountered had been intentionally cruel—although there had been no shortage of snide comments or dirty looks. It was the lack of warmth, a Midwestern, small-town staple she used to take for granted that had disappeared. It was as if there was an invisible do-not-engage zone surrounding her. People abruptly turned away when they saw her coming down the grocery aisle, ignored her at the post office, refused to acknowledge her as she drove by. It created such loneliness that some days she wondered if she would go through the rest of her life friendless. But then Trudy would call and invite her to come to the salon after hours so that she would not have to face prying eyes.

"How are you doing?" Trudy's low, sultry voice was a balm.

To anyone else she would have responded a vague "fine," but Trudy's sincerity told Luella that she actually cared to hear the truth. Luella searched for words to describe the emptiness she felt.

"Stupid question," said Trudy.

"No, no. Not at all." Luella brushed away the comment.

"Given everything that's happened, I imagine you feel like an old worn-out sock."

"Sometimes I feel so hopeless I just pray I won't wake up in the morning." Luella swallowed hard. "Then I look at Wyatt and desperately want to live to see him grow up."

"Oh, honey."

"I keep waiting for someone to make this all better."

Trudy gestured for Luella to sit in the swivel chair in front of the vanity. "I've been kicked in the teeth by a worthless man and survived. No white knight rides up on his horse and rescues you. That's in fairytales."

Trudy swung the purple haircutting cape around the front of Luella and fastened it at the back of her neck. "If I've learned anything in this life, it's that you have to rescue yourself. I'm not saying it happens right away. If you need more time to lick your wounds, okay, but at some point, you have to pick yourself up, stiffen your backbone, and get a new life."

"It's just so damn hard," said Luella.

"When I say you have to rescue yourself, I don't mean you have to do this alone. You have your family and you have me." With a large-toothed comb Trudy expertly divided Luella's hair into sections, brushed on the color, and wrapped the sections in foil.

"I never thanked you for showing up at the sentencing hearing. It meant a lot to me." Luella looked at her reflection in the mirror. Trudy stood behind her, hands working, eyes occasionally glancing up as she talked.

"That's what friends do."

Before August's arrest Luella would have considered Trudy a friendly acquaintance, the woman who styled her hair, regaled her with amusing stories about her live-in boyfriend, Howard, remembered to send a birthday text. They had never been social friends. Luella had never invited her to dinner or to share a glass of wine on the dock. It pained her to admit she had not considered Trudy an intimate, yet when everything fell apart, there she was. Kind. Understanding. Supportive.

"I'm curious," said Luella. "Everyone treats me like a pariah, but not you. Why?"

Trudy stopped brushing on the hair dye. She looked into the mirror, making reflected eye contact. "I've told you my first marriage was a train wreck. What I haven't told you is that my husband, I mean my lousy-crook-of-an-ex-husband, embezzled over one-hundred thousand dollars from the business he worked for. Apparently, he'd been at it for several years."

"Oh, Trudy, I'm so sorry."

"See, that's a woman's first instinct, to apologize. We have nothing to apologize for. Everyone assumed I knew what he was up to. I swear," said Trudy, gesturing with her empty hand for emphasis, "I had no idea. It's as though people can't imagine being married to someone and not knowing every dark, dirty secret they have. Well, I've got news for them. Sometimes the person you love, or think you love, turns out to be into some terrible shit that you have nothing to do with."

Luella heard the anger and pain still lingering beneath Trudy's outward confidence and understood that her own pain would not be going away anytime soon. She also heard strength and resilience.

"You're such a good listener, always asking about me, I never thought to ask about you," said Luella, almost apologizing, then catching herself.

"You're feeling guilty enough without piling on another reason to feel bad," said Trudy, setting the handheld timer for twenty minutes. She sat down in the swivel chair in front of the next vanity. "I divorced my useless husband years ago. Things are good. I've got Howard in my life and he's solid. He comes with some baggage. Namely his mother." Trudy rolled her eyes.

"I can't imagine getting married again."

"Who said anything about getting married?" Trudy held up both hands, palms out. "Besides, you're still raw. The last thing you need is an entanglement right now. Take it from one who knows, you've got a lot of work ahead of you just figuring out who you are without that man."

"Did I tell you I'm going to take back my maiden name?"

"A good first step."

"And I signed the divorce papers."

"Great."

"And I have a pending offer on our…my…house in Lake Bluff."

"You *are* making progress."

Progress. Yes, Luella thought, she *had* made progress. Forward. But forward into what? A condo? An apartment? What about uprooting Rosie? And Bird? He was used to having a place to run and explore. And where? Back to Chicago? No. She was a woman without a home or a city. Rootless. A vagabond. Would she have to sell everything she owned? Did she even want to keep a stick of furniture she and August had purchased together?

When the timer sounded, Trudy gestured for Luella to move to the rinsing sink where she nestled into the padded seat. Luella rested her neck on the curve of the sink's lip, tipped her head back, and closed her eyes. Trudy carefully removed the foils and turned on a soothing stream of warm water. As the water cascaded through her hair, tension drained from Luella's body. Gently, Trudy messaged lavender-fragranced shampoo into Luella's hair, rinsed it, and applied a conditioner. The tender touch made her mentally swoon. After another rinsing, Trudy wrung out the excess moisture and wrapped a towel around Luella's head.

Once back in the cutting chair, Trudy removed the towel and slowly pulled a comb through Luella's hair. She squeezed a dab of styling cream onto her hand, rubbed it between her fingers, and then drew them through Luella's hair from roots to ends. As Trudy began to wield her shears, Luella's mind wandered to their discussion about progress. It surprised her how much Trudy's opinion mattered. She admired her, sought her approval. She had to toughen up if she wanted her friend to see her, not as a victim, but as a survivor.

"Don't take offense," said Trudy, "but I think it would be a really good idea for you to get some counseling. Find a support group of women who have experienced the same thing you have. There's strength in numbers. I know I couldn't have recovered without that kind of help."

Like a clam who'd dared open up to the light only to find a threat looming, Luella's shell quickly closed. She'd resisted sharing her pain for so long, relying instead on writing in her journal to the long-departed Nell Wooden that opening up to a group of strangers who would judge her seemed impossible. She'd been very selective in what she revealed to Beth and Franklin, and had chosen not to confide in Denise, even after the revelation of her abuse.

"I—I don't know," stammered Luella. "I'm a pretty private person."

"And how is that working for you?" asked Trudy, direct as always. "You don't have to do this alone. I know my experience isn't the same as yours, but I do know that there are people who can help, women who do understand what you're going through."

"I have you."

"Yes, you do. But I'm no therapist. I don't mean to tell you what to do. You're a smart woman. It's just a suggestion. Every woman has to find her own path forward."

Maybe Trudy was right. Maybe it would be a relief to unburden herself. Maybe she'd been unnecessarily carrying this heavy load alone.

Trudy stepped back and examined her work. She tilted her head slightly to one side and then the other. She took several extra snips to feather the ends on the left side of Luella's hairdo. Then she attached a diffuser to the hairdryer and blew Luella's hair dry.

When Trudy finished Luella asked, "Where would I find a support group for women who married, you know, a flawed man?"

"Flawed?"

"Oh hell—a pedophile," said Luella.

"That's the spirit. Tell it like it is." Trudy fist pumped and giggled. "You've got a point. I doubt you could find a group like that around here. The place is too small. Not enough perverts."

Luella laughed.

"I think you'll need a city."

Luella thought of Chicago. Returning there seemed like no progress at all.

"You're not thinking of staying in Givens Knoll, are you?"

"No. I have to put the camp up for sale. It kills me to do it, but I no longer feel welcome here. It's as if the place has become an alien planet. I never imagined leaving. Now it's hard to imagine staying."

Trudy brushed the hair from the back of Luella's neck, then lifted off the cape, careful to spill the clippings onto the floor. She gave her a hand mirror, slowly turning the chair so Luella could examine the sides and back of her head.

"I know what you mean. Skipping town will be a relief. I haven't told another soul this yet, other than Howard, of course. I'm selling this building to Jerry Jacobs. He wants to expand his business." Trudy tidied the cutting station, gathered the scissors and comb and placed them in the sink. "The timing is good. I've gotten an offer to work in an upscale salon, Casa de Estética, in downtown Minneapolis. My sister lives there. She's been urging me to move for a long time. Howard's job travels well. Besides, he said he'd follow me anywhere. And, of course, it isn't a problem for his mother. She'd find us if we moved to Mars."

Luella smiled. She wanted to be happy for her friend, yet she couldn't help feeling abandoned.

"Which brings me to something I wanted to ask you," said Trudy. "Promise me you won't dismiss my idea without seriously considering it."

Luella's brow furrowed.

"Promise?"

"Okay. Promise."

"Will you consider Minneapolis?"

"Minneapolis? You mean move there? I—I've never even been there."

"Well, how about a visit to check it out? It beats throwing darts at a map."

"I don't know what to say."

"Just say yes."

When Trudy called, inviting Luella to come along to visit her sister in Minneapolis, Luella hesitated.

"You've been cooped up in your house for months," said Trudy. "You've become as much of a prisoner as your husband. I mean your soon-to-be ex-husband."

Luella wanted to disagree, to say that she walked in the woods every day, that she was free to come and go, but deep down she knew her world had become very small. Since August's arrest, she'd driven to Chicago alone to be fired from her teaching job, then with Beth to ready the Lake Bluff house for sale. Otherwise, she'd been holed up at the camp, only venturing out to go to the courthouse, jail, Rosie's sheltered workshop, or to the grocery store. Each time she left the house she avoided people, always scurrying back like a fearful mouse.

"At any rate, that's not healthy, my friend. You're overdue for a road trip."

"I don't know."

"Look at it this way," Trudy argued. "You have nothing to lose and everything to gain."

Luella relented, knowing that she needed an attitude adjustment. She told Beth only that she wanted some time with her friend, but little about any secretly contemplated future. She vowed to keep an open mind. Trudy was right. What did she have to lose?

She'd heard every platitude in the book about life being determined by a positive attitude. Her favorite poster, the one that appealed to her mathematical mind, hung on her classroom door; *Attitude is everything. Life is 10% what happens to you and 90% how you react to it.* The quote was attributed to an evangelical Christian pastor. She wondered if the reverend had ever suffered a devastating loss—the betrayal of a spouse, the death of a son-in-law, the destruction of his home—or if he had sailed through life preaching positivity while suffering little. Until August's arrest, she'd believed the ten percent/ninety percent ratio. Current circumstances had taught her that life can inflict an event so devastating the ratio becomes inverted, forcing you to belly crawl toward even a flicker of optimism. Then you grabbed on to a scrap of control, made yourself get up in the morning, convinced yourself to live one more day. Slowly, you dragged yourself toward the light.

Now, as the car sped down Interstate 94 toward the Twin Cities, crossing from Wisconsin into Minnesota over the bridge spanning the St. Croix River, Luella savored her conversation with Trudy. The interstate widened to eight lanes and the traffic increased as they approached St. Paul, the capital city skyline dominated by hospitals, churches, and museums.

Trudy deftly changed lanes, kept her eyes on the road. "St. Paul is the more traditional of the Twin Cities, lots of old money, quieter downtown, a good place to raise a family." She glanced in the rearview mirror. "Minneapolis has more of the new money, a vibrant night scene, the U of M, lots to do and see. My sister is a professor at the university. She loves it here."

"The sister whose house we're going to stay at?"

"Shocking. I know it doesn't quite fit, a sister who teaches at the university and one who's a lowly hairstylist." Trudy glanced at Luella, then quickly turned back to the road.

"I didn't mean any offense."

"I dropped out of college a year shy of a degree. It drove my dad the neurosurgeon nuts. I take after my artist mom. As a kid I always loved fashion, make-up, and styling hair. I finally decided to do what I liked, not what others expected me to do."

"I admire your backbone."

"My dad wouldn't speak to me at first. Told me he didn't want to watch me waste my life. But my sister was always in my corner. I want to move closer to her. I've done the small-town thing, had enough of styling senior blue hairs and cutting boring bobs. I'm ready to move back to the city where I can use my creative skills." She again glanced at Luella. "No offense." Trudy grinned, then giggled.

Luella smiled, self-consciously touched her boring bob, then laughed, too.

Friday afternoon traffic slowed to a crawl. A half mile from the intersection of Interstate 94 and 35, Trudy maneuvered into the left exit lane. "Welcome to Minneapolis." She pulled onto I-35 and inched into the flow of traffic. The drivers courteously took turns, allowing vehicles to easily merge as they came off the ramp.

"This is nothing compared to Chicago rush hour." Luella noted the lack of aggressive driving. "I see that the reputation of 'Minnesota nice' is deserved."

After exiting the Interstate, they drove through a residential area of mixed architectural style homes—Victorian, Dutch Colonial, English Tudor, Mid-century modern—with apartment buildings and condos interspersed. Parents jogged along the sidewalks pushing strollers, pet owners walked their dogs, cyclists pedaled through the streets. The neighborhood appeared safe, vibrant. Luella tried to picture herself living there.

Trudy pulled up to the curb in front of a two-story craftsman style home with a brick front porch, large tapered support columns, and a wide street-facing dormer. The exterior was painted gray with white trim. The classic looking home set in the tree lined neighborhood wasn't what Luella had pictured when she thought of Trudy whose taste ran toward the Bohemian.

Trudy's sister, dressed in gray slacks and a rose-colored silk blouse, opened the door. Her blonde hair fell to her shoulders in loose curls. She was an inch or two taller than Trudy, but her distinctive silver blue eyes instantly identified her as Trudy's sibling.

The sisters lovingly embraced.

"This is my friend Luella," said Trudy, stepping aside.

"Hi, I'm Angeline." She extended her hand and smiled warmly. "Tru tells me you're looking for a new life."

After settling into the upstairs guest bedroom, Luella joined Trudy and Angeline in the living room for a glass of wine.

The room had Angeline's understated elegance. The walls on either side of the tiled fireplace were lined with floor-to-ceiling shelves that held a mix of hardcover books and artistically arranged objects. A loden green sectional anchored the space, and matching walnut and leather z-armed chairs flanked the fireplace. While the style was distinctly craftsman, Angeline clearly favored an eclectic mix of décor. A large abstract oil in hues of white, cobalt, and lime green, with a swath of crimson hung over the fireplace.

"What a beautiful painting," said Luella.

"It's one of Tru's."

"You painted this?" Luella turned to Trudy. "I had no idea you were an artist."

"She's always been the creative one of the family." Angeline, who sat next to Trudy on the sofa, affectionately nudged her sister.

Luella settled into one of the leather chairs, sipped her wine. "I understand that you teach at the University of Minnesota."

"I'm a professor of psychology. Father would have preferred I become a doctor, but I've always been more intrigued by human behavior."

A sense of unease washed over Luella. The last thing she needed was another person assessing her, casting judgment. She shifted in her chair, wondered if Trudy had an ulterior motive for inviting her.

"Don't worry, it's not necessary to lie on the couch," said Angeline, smiling. "You're not here as a test subject."

"Is my skittishness that obvious?"

"I can see you're uncomfortable."

"I'm sorry."

"No apology necessary. You'd be amazed at how many people begin a conversation with, 'I suppose you're going to try to analyze me.' I'm not a clinical psychologist. My interests are in cognitive research, mainly neurodevelopmental disorders."

Luella thought of Rosie, who might be interesting to Angeline.

"Besides, according to what Tru tells me about your situation, I don't blame you for being skittish. In your shoes, I'd feel—cautious."

It had been a long time since Luella enjoyed the companionship of women. Friends either overtly shunned her or subtly faded away. Abandonment wounded so deeply she had shut herself off from everyone, preempting rejection. While the camp, with its soaring pines, pristine air, and crystal waters, was a beautiful place, Luella realized that it had become her gilded cage.

She took a deep breath and sat up taller. This was not the moment, when finally connecting to other women, to dwell on her loneliness. This was a time to grasp the hands extended in friendship, to trust that there remained people who did not reject her because she had the misfortune of marrying the wrong man.

The conversation turned toward stories of childhood, politics, and music. Hours passed. They sipped their wine. Shared. Sympathized. Laughed. Angeline seemed genuinely interested in getting to know Luella, not as a curiosity or an object to be studied, but as a person. Trudy was a born listener, and although she didn't have a degree in psychology, Luella had experienced Trudy's empathy and innate understanding of people.

The longer the women talked, the more Luella relaxed. She discovered that both she and Angeline had been reserved, bookish teenagers, who shared a passion for teaching. She and Trudy enjoyed a love of folk music. All three of them had political views that aligned. Maybe it was possible, thought Luella, to shed her identity as the wife of a notorious pedophile and to create a reinvented life.

"I'm lost," Luella confessed. "It's been more than thirty years since I've been on my own. I have no idea who I am." She hadn't intended to be so candid, but the acceptance of these women was like an irresistible open gate into the safety of a private garden.

Trudy rose from the sofa and knelt down next to Luella. "You've been through hell," she said, looking her in the eye. "But take it from one who knows, you're going to survive. You're going to figure this out and come out stronger on the other side."

Angeline put down her glass and leaned forward. "You don't have to do this alone. There's still a tough road ahead. When you're ready, I know of a support group for women who have been betrayed the same way you have. Just say the word."

The heaviness Luella carried deep inside seemed to leach from her bones, radiate through her skin, and lift into the air. This, she thought, must be what hope feels like.

Chapter Thirty-two
~The Letter~

Rapid, high-pitched trills drifted through the open office window on a mild morning breeze. Sitting at the desk, Luella tried unsuccessfully to spot the warbler among the branches of a maple whose greenish-yellow buds were poised to bloom. She thought about last May, a mere twelve months ago, when her life had not yet imploded, when she was still teaching and looking forward to a successful summer at the camp.

Pen in hand, she turned her attention to August's most recent letter, smelling of stale cigarettes. Was it possible August, always health conscious, had taken up smoking? Desperation and boredom could change a person. Or maybe he had a cellmate who chain-smoked. She knew very little about his day-to-day existence and hadn't asked. Knowing his reality might make her pity him, and she couldn't let it weaken her resolve.

Since his incarceration she hadn't responded to any of his correspondence. Today she felt compelled to answer his letter, although she wasn't sure what was driving that need. Closure? What did that even mean? Most likely it was the trip with Trudy to Minneapolis that spurred her to move forward.

She thought of the admonition to "Love the sinner, hate the sin." When she imagined August in that cabin sexually assaulting his victims, hatred burst in her like water through a breached dam. She pictured his exploring hands and mouth, erect penis, heavy breathing, all belonging to the sinner. She imagined his unchecked libido driving him to violate those boys. It would take a magician, she decided, to separate the doer from the deed, the sinner from the sin.

She also thought about the platitude "Hate hurts the hater more than the hated." Who said that? St. Augustine? Gandhi? Obviously, a saint. Although she intuitively felt the truth of it, felt hate's destructive power eating at her, controlling it was a different matter. What force of will it would take to purge the spirit of hate, even if it was for one's own benefit. She was a long way from showing herself that measure of kindness. She was a long way from sainthood.

Luella pulled a page of flowered stationery from the desk drawer and wrote "*Dear August*" at the top. She stared at her handwriting for a moment, then crumpled the page and threw it in the wastebasket. She replaced the stationery with a piece of plain, white typing paper, touched the nib of her pen to the page, hesitated, then began again.

August,

You broke my heart. I haven't written to you because I've been too angry to express anything but hatred. What you did to those innocent boys sickens me. What you did to me and our family makes me despise you. All those years of deception hurt more than I can possibly say.

I keep waiting for you to admit what you did, to take responsibility for your actions. You are a PEDOPHILE. You continue to make excuses, to deny the truth. Without remorse there can be no redemption for you.

Luella paused, leaned back in her chair, read what she'd written. Her words were harsh. They were also honest. For too long she also had denied the full, ugly reality. No more. She ran her index finger over PEDOPHILE like a blind woman deciphering braille, as though touching the ink would force the word to soak through her skin, enter her bloodstream, help her to never forget who August Laurent had always been.

She continued to write.

You have not sought my forgiveness, only my loyalty. You will have neither as long as you refuse to admit the truth. I will not write to you or visit you until I see these words—I did it. I molested those boys. I beg their forgiveness. I beg your forgiveness. I beg God's forgiveness.

Forgiveness. Luella had been obsessed with the idea, seeking guidance from religious leaders, ancient philosophers, famous writers, and new age psychologists. She collected favorite quotes and wrote them in her journal.

The first entry was a metaphor written by Mark Twain. "*Forgiveness is the fragrance the violet sheds on the heel that has crushed it.*" The quote had played in her head for days. Crushed. That was exactly it, being broken and stomped into the ground. Then the perfume of the flower offered her whiffs of hope. Her second entry was by inspirational speaker, Shannon Alder, who said, "*Forgiveness is the one gift you don't give to others. Rather, it is the gift you give yourself, so you can finally be free.*" She thought of Trudy's claim that Luella had made herself as much a prisoner as August. What would it feel like to be truly free of him? Was it only through forgiveness that she would achieve freedom? Her third entry was from C. S Lewis, who said, "*To be a Christian means to forgive the inexcusable because God has forgiven the inexcusable in you.*" Was she Christian enough to ever excuse August?

She'd read about the process of reconciliation in which the victims bravely sat face-to-face with the perpetrators of crimes that had caused them so much pain. She thought of Nelson Mandela who'd spent twenty-seven years in prison and forgave his captors, and of the members of the Emanuel African Methodist Episcopal Church in Charleston, South Carolina, whose loved ones had been gunned down by white supremacist, Dylan Roof. In a remarkable act of individual and collective grace, they forgave him. She wondered at the strength it took to forgive a murderer who had taken someone so precious from you.

She wasn't there. Yet she knew if she was ever to know peace she had to let go of her hatred. She desperately wished she had the level of faith that would lift this burden from her and place it in God's hands. She longed for His grace. Peace was something she would have to work toward, a goal on the horizon. She had only begun to walk the path of acceptance.

> *Do not write to me again until you are ready to take responsibility for your actions. August, I pray that you seek help, that you take advantage of any psychological and religious services available to you. Meanwhile, I will work at healing myself.*
>
> *Luella*

August would have to chart his own course to redemption. She vowed to have no contact with him until he admitted his crime. Privately, unattached to him, she would work at releasing the hate consuming her. For her own sake, she would find a way to forgive him, regardless of his actions, no matter how long it took.

The avian high-pitched trills became louder. Luella put down her pen, closed her eyes and listened. *Sweet sweet sweet I'm so sweet.* The calming birdsong floated around the room. She opened her eyes and gazed out at the maple tree. Less than twenty feet from the window, perched on a bare branch, she spotted a warbler, its tail furiously flicking, its yellow breast like a watercolor sunrise.

Chapter Thirty-three
~Duck Jokes~

Soft morning light filtered through the pines. Maple, aspen, and birch trees bloomed in muted shades of yellow-green and dusty rose. The temperature had already reached sixty-six degrees. The awakening land was primed with possibility. A seed of optimism, once taken for granted and now almost unrecognizable, planted itself deep in Luella.

In a few weeks it would be a year since August's arrest, yet it seemed like decades since she'd felt happy. She hadn't slept through a single night since that day. Restlessness had settled in like a permanent squatter. At times she wondered if life would ever return to normal, whatever normal meant. Still, today Luella couldn't help feeling a touch lighter as she and Wyatt walked along the path toward the lake, Bird dashing ahead and then doubling back, as if to say, "hurry, you're missing some amazing sights and smells."

Given the losses Wyatt had endured in five years of life—the death of his father, the imprisonment of his grandfather, a move away from his home—his buoyancy amazed her. He'd started kindergarten and after a few months had moved north to live at the camp, necessitating more adjustments. But Wyatt proved to be resilient. He adored Ms. Simmons, his teacher, and he'd readily made friends. That first week at his new school he'd come home and announced, "Porter is my best friend. He has a giant dog named Goliath." Wyatt stretched his arms out so far to demonstrate the size of the dog, he'd had to widen his stance to keep his balance. "Goliath is a Saint Bernard. Porter wants me to come to his house and meet him. And I told him I had a big dog named Bird and they could be friends just like us."

More change was coming. Beth would move again. It couldn't be avoided. The camp had to be sold. Beth needed to resume her career. Luella prayed that Wyatt would be okay, that all the upheaval in his life would make him an adaptable adult, not a damaged man unable to trust or make commitments. There were reasons for optimism, which lessened her worries. Wyatt was loved. He had solid role models. And despite the differences she'd had with Beth, Luella knew that Beth was an exceptional mother. Patient. Devoted. Wise.

Luella thought back to the previous summer, remembered with shame slapping Beth across the face when told that Wyatt needed protection from his grandfather. Beth was right to be fiercely protective of her son. Luella was the one with misplaced loyalty. Although Beth had forgiven her, Luella was still struggling to forgive herself.

As she watched her grandson, dressed in jeans and a blue hooded jacket, running along the path, stopping intermittently to pick up a rock or examine a wildflower, she envied his innocence, his trust that the world was safe and amazing. He looked at the world through unsullied eyes, seeing the possible in everything. Every person he met was assumed to be good. Never would she have that blind faith again. Hopefully, she would get back to a place where trust was possible and she recognized the goodness in others.

In the distance an unmistakable tremolo wavered through the air.

Wyatt grabbed her hand. "Grandma, listen."

"Ah, the loons are back," said Luella, savoring the sound.

"Hurry, Grandma! Maybe we'll see them." Wyatt tugged her arm. "They are my favoritest bird."

"Better than hawks or eagles?"

"Well, I like them too, but I still like loons the best."

"Me, too."

"Grandma, did you know they have red eyes, and their babies ride on their backs, and they can dive really deep? Uncle Anthony says they start building nests when they're five years old, just like me."

Wyatt's enthusiasm was contagious. She picked up her pace as they approached the beach. Again, the tremolo echoed across the lake.

"Look! I see them!" Wyatt pointed toward the bay.

About fifty feet off shore, riding low in the water, a pair of loons, regal, with their arrow-like beaks, black and white banding and slender profiles, fished near the point. Luella recalled the thrill she'd felt as a child each summer at Uncle Walter's and Aunt Mavis's when the loons returned, how at night, tucked under a handmade quilt, she'd relished their plaintive cry, telling her that she was back in the place she felt most at home.

Bird sat at attention at the edge of the shoreline, ears perked up, nose sniffing the air.

"Grandma, look! The ducks are coming to see us."

Light glinted off the water's surface. A sord of mallards swam twenty feet off shore, leaving their wake rippling behind them. An image of August waddling along the beach that first year they'd bought the camp, Beth giggling and trying to imitate him, flashed through Luella's mind. "You two look more like Charlie Chaplin than ducks," she'd said, laughing. Then he'd quacked loudly, sending the sound reverberating across the lake. She almost said to Wyatt, "Your grandpa loved to imitate ducks," then thought better of it. She still hadn't decided whether August would be a presence in Wyatt's life or would vanish as though he'd never existed. She resolved to discuss the matter with Beth, soon.

"Grandma, do you know what ducks have with soup?"

"No. What?"

"Quackers."

Luella chuckled. "You're a corker."

"What's a corker?"

"Someone who is really funny."

"Uncle Anthony taught me lots of jokes." Wyatt rested his chin in his hand and scrunched his brow as though thinking hard. Luella had seen this same exaggerated expression on Anthony. She bit her cheeks to stifle a laugh.

Wyatt blurted, "What did the duck say when he dropped the dishes?"

"I don't know."

"No, Grandma, he didn't say that. He said, 'I hope I didn't *quack* any.' Get it? *Quack.*"

Luella laughed.

Bird plunged into the water, as though staring at the ducks was temptation denied one second too long. The mallards paddled furiously toward the middle of the lake, the dog giving chase. "Bird!" Luella hollered. "Come!" The dog swam ahead a few more yards, then turned in a wide semi-circle, creating a small wake, and headed back toward shore. When he reached dry land, he shook and shimmied, sending water flying in every direction. Luella and Wyatt scampered away, chortling.

"Do you want to hear my favoritest joke?" asked Wyatt, gleefully.

"Absolutely."

"Do you know why ducks have tail feathers?" Wyatt pressed his hand over his mouth and snickered.

"No. Why do ducks have tail feathers?"

He pulled his hand away. "To cover up their butt *quacks*," he shouted. His eyes glinted, both hands sprang over his mouth, and he giggled louder.

Luella threw her head back and laughed. Then harder. And harder.

Wyatt's little-boy glee unlocked something in her. That seed of optimism cracked open. She hunched, raised her hands in front of her face and wiggled her fingers. Pulling him to her, she tickled his sides. Wyatt squirmed and squealed, then twisted away from her grasp.

"Grandma, you're a corker, too!" he said, grinning.

Luella knelt, opened her arms wide. "Sweetie, that is the nicest thing you could have said to me."

The rental truck was nearly loaded. Anthony and Franklin, lifting opposite ends of a tall pine bookcase, hoisted it up the ramp and pushed it against the truck wall.

"Is this the last of it?" asked Franklin, breathing heavily.

"I certainly hope so," Anthony replied.

"This was a lot easier when I was a young man." Franklin took a handkerchief from the pocket of his shorts and wiped his forehead. "It didn't look like much when we started, but I feel as though we just loaded a palace-worth of furniture."

"I didn't think I had this much stuff," admitted Beth, who stood in the driveway, peering into the truck through sunglasses, pleased they had finished loading. "I'm grateful for your help." Sweat trickled down the middle of her back. The temperature was eighty-seven degrees, unusually hot for a late morning during the first week of June. The oak flanking the driveway was nearly leafed-out, and all that remained of the daffodils circling its base were spikey leaves.

Gina came down the porch steps carrying a lampshade protected with bubble wrap. "We nearly forgot this." She marched up the ramp, dramatically placed the shade on top of a dresser, and gave Anthony an enthusiastic high five. "Fini, finito, finished!" She dance-stepped down the ramp and grabbed Beth, twirling her around.

Beth threw her head back, grinning.

Anthony strode down the ramp, Franklin following.

"This is one tightly packed truck." Anthony stepped back to admire their work. "You must have been a geometry whiz in school."

"Let's just say I like order," said Franklin. "Everything in its place and a place for everything."

"I can attest to that," Denise chimed in, emerging from the house, carrying a tray loaded with bottled lemonade. "The books on his office shelf are alphabetized by author. You'd think he was running a lending library." She offered Franklin a drink and kissed him on the cheek. "Come to think of it, he does make people sign a ledger if they borrow one of his books."

Everyone grabbed a lemonade.

"To a job well done," said Franklin, raising a toast.

Wyatt, dragging a blue tote bag down the steps, Bird prancing beside him, said, "Wait! Don't forget this."

"Let's see what you've got there, kiddo." Gina peeked inside the tote.

There were rocks of various sizes, several giant pinecones, a jar filled with sand, and a curled piece of birch bark.

"That's quite a collection," said Gina.

"Mom said Grandma has to sell the camp so I won't be here ever again. It makes me real sad cuz it's my favorit-ist place in the whole world." Wyatt, his lower lip jutting out, reached into the tote and pulled out a rock with a quartz vein running down the middle.

"It's beautiful," Gina gushed.

Wyatt held the treasure in his open palm. "Aunt Gina, you can keep it so you can remember here, too."

"Are you sure? This rock is pretty special."

"That's okay. I have lots of other rocks."

"I'll cherish this." She held the stone to her heart.

"We can put this in the car, honey," said Beth, taking the tote from Wyatt and placing it in the front seat of her SUV. "That way you can put your treasures in your room as soon as we get to our new apartment."

From the backdoor Rosie shouted, "Luella says time for lunch."

On the porch, an assortment of sandwiches, a mandarin orange salad, a plate of brownies, and two pitchers of lemon-infused ice water were laid out on a long folding table. The screened windows were open, inviting in the drone of boat motors crisscrossing the lake. The overhead fan whirred as it pushed the muggy air around the room that smelled of sunscreen. Bird noisily lapped up water from his dish tucked in the corner.

Conversation was lively as the sandwiches and salad were passed around. Lost in thought, Beth barely heard a word. She was thinking of her move, alternately excited and nervous. It was time. She had a challenging job awaiting her, yet knowing she would never return to the camp she had called home every summer for most of her life left her deeply saddened. Wyatt had gathered his tote bag of treasures so he could remember the place. She had spent the past several days taking pictures of the house and property.

Beth thought of each person sitting around the table. Uncle Franklin, at the head where her father used to sit, was the rock, the voice of reason, the man who quietly took care of business. Aunt Denise welcomed Beth into her home when she couldn't stay at the camp after the arrest. She'd taken care of Wyatt and Rosie whenever a helping hand was needed, no questions asked. Anthony, a constant reminder of Gabe, stepped in as a role model for her son and came to her rescue always when she most needed him. Gina encouraged her to breathe, to laugh, to live life despite the challenges. She had become a sister. Gentle, generous, loving Rosie was a constant reminder that kindness mattered. Wyatt, a miniature Gabe, was her reason to get up each morning, even during the lowest moments. She loved him so deeply it hurt.

And her mother. What a complicated relationship. They'd endured contentious times, vehemently arguing over her father. At first, it was impossible to comprehend Luella's refusal to acknowledge his guilt. To Beth, her father's transgressions were so egregious that disavowing him seemed obvious. She had a son to protect. Her mother's blind loyalty seemed naïve at best, willfully ignorant at worst. But when Beth thought of Gabe, how deep the love ran, how even in death her loyalty had not waivered, she began to see her mother, not as a parent, but as a woman who had devoted her life to a man she passionately loved. Giving that up could not have been easy.

At first, Beth blamed her mother for failing to see her father's perversion, but when honest with herself she admitted that she also had been fooled. Before the arrest, neither Beth nor Luella had been realistic about August. Both had adored him in their own way. Neither had seen his dark side. Both had to work through guilt for having been blind. Both had been taken in by a manipulator and accomplished actor. They were two women simply struggling to find their way.

Beth now understood that Luella's loyalty extended to her, too. Even during the most antagonistic times, her mother had loved her, welcomed her home, accepted her. They had grown closer. Beth would miss her terribly. She had always thought of her father as the strong one. It turned out that her mother was the one with the backbone.

"We need a group picture," Gina announced when everyone had finished eating.

All eight of them crowded together, faces close, arms around each other, Wyatt on Beth's lap, his arm around Bird's neck. Anthony squatted in the front, extending the phone.

"One, two, three, smile!" He examined the photo, then passed his phone around for everyone's approval.

"We should get on the road," said Anthony. "We've got a long drive and a truck to unload before dark."

Beth began to clear the table.

"I can take care of this," Denise offered. "You have places to go."

"I'll help," said Rosie.

"Anthony, do you mind if I take one more look at the lake?" asked Beth. "I promise I'll be quick."

"I'm sure we can spare fifteen minutes," he said.

"Can I come with you?" Wyatt looked up expectantly.

"Of course."

They hurried down the path toward the lake, Bird running ahead. Beth regretted that she could not memorize the shape of every pine, fern, and protruding tree root. She was losing this place, as spiritual to her as a cathedral. At the beach, she gazed out over the lake, the water glimmering like liquid fire in the sunlight, boats gliding over the surface. Next to the dock a row of ducklings paddled after their mother.

Wyatt laughed. "Grandma loves my duck jokes."

"You are a good joke teller," said Beth.

"Mom, are you sad?"

"Yes, honey. I'm going to miss the camp."

"Me, too."

"But we have lots of exciting things to look forward to." Beth knelt, put her hands on Wyatt's shoulders, met his eyes. "We have a new town, new apartment, new school, and new friends waiting for us. We're in this together, buddy."

Wyatt hugged her tightly. "And Uncle Franklin and Aunt Denise said we can come to the lake and visit them anytime we want to."

"You're right," Beth agreed. "We'll see the lake again."

"Good-bye lake," said Wyatt, waving. "Good-bye ducks. You quack me up."

Beth laughed.

"Last one there is a rotten egg," shouted Wyatt, as he dashed up the path toward the house, Beth chasing, Bird bounding alongside.

"One last bathroom stop, buddy," Beth insisted, as they ran up the porch steps and into the house.

In the driveway, Anthony and Gina were already in the truck, windows rolled down, chatting with Luella, Franklin, Denise, and Rosie. When Beth and Wyatt joined the group, there were hugs all around.

"Don't worry, Grandma," said Wyatt, from his car seat in the back of the SUV. "We're going to FaceTime with you tomorrow."

Beth hugged her mother and held on. "Thank you for everything. I love you."

"I love you, too."

"I'll call when we get there." Beth, eyes glistening, slid into the driver's side of the SUV.

Anthony slowly drove the truck down the long driveway. Beth followed in her vehicle. Both honked a final good-bye. In the rearview mirror, Beth watched everyone waving. Franklin's arm was around her mother, who was wiping away tears.

Chapter Thirty-four
~Another Story~

Luella paced the shoreline at dawn. Mist hovered over Whisper Lake like an ethereal blanket. The air was cool, but the forecast held the promise of a warm summer day.

Bird raced ahead. "Come!" called Luella. He scampered to her side. She pulled a liver treat from her jacket pocket. "Good boy." The dog sniffed her pocket, then lost interest when she didn't produce another treat.

The June landscape painted in vibrant shades of green was a welcome relief from the late-arriving spring. She thought about the first time she and August had driven down Virgin Timber Road to the camp. In mid-April, the understory had not yet leafed out; the forest floor was a tangle of branches and downed trees with patches of snow still covering the shaded ground. Eagerly, he'd shown her the main house with its floor-to-ceiling stone fireplace and breathtaking view of the lake, hoping the disrepair of the courts and cabins would fade in importance. He'd been right; she'd fallen in love with the place. Buying it had been an easy choice.

Selling the camp, on the other hand, had been a difficult decision and no decision at all. As the realtor predicted, the valuable lake frontage would likely be subdivided to build mansions or developed into condominiums. The realization pained Luella, but it couldn't be helped. Even if she'd wanted to stay, she couldn't manage the upkeep or taxes. August's legal bills and the loss of revenue had put her in a financial squeeze. The sale would bring a measure of security.

Marking more than the beginning of a new chapter, selling the camp meant throwing away the entire book and searching for another story, as if everything about her past had been built on swampland, leaving nothing solid on which to rebuild. Things she had assumed to be true about life before August's arrest could not be trusted. Everything—her home, her career, her relationships, her very name— had been tainted. Like oil oozing from a tanker run aground, his deception clung to everything. She could no longer enter the campers' cabins without imagining the violations that had taken place there, or eat at the kitchen table without seeing August sitting across from her feigning innocence, or watch moonlight stream through the bedroom window without feeling his betraying body lying next to hers.

The self-help book she'd been reading advised her to let go of the past, to focus on the now. Acknowledge your anger, the author counseled, but don't let it control you. To Luella, rage was a living force, like the invasive milfoil threatening the ecology of the lake. Let the plant take hold and its tangled stems and thick surface mat would take over, choking out the native vegetation, starving the fish. She must not allow her anger to take such solid root.

The lake's iridescent surface quivered as the wake from a fishing boat rolled hypnotically toward shore and broke gently against the rocks. An avian symphony of chirps, caws, and whistles filled the air. She stood still, inviting a perfume of crystal-clear water, damp earth, and new vegetation into her lungs, savored the soft breeze kissing her face. It was as though a year-long fever had finally broken.

She imagined bottling the serenity of the morning, taking it with her, swallowing a dose whenever she needed it in the challenging days ahead. Three weeks ago, in a burst of determination, she'd thrown her sleeping pills into the garbage. That first week had been torturous. She'd even been tempted to paw through the trash. When restlessness overtook her, she paced and read, resorting to hot baths to lull her back to sleep. The past several nights had gone much better.

Bird bounded past, nearly knocking her over, then plunged into the lake, seeming unfazed by the cool water. Whatever had enticed him remained invisible to Luella. Perhaps it was the pure joy of being wet on a perfect morning. What a luxury to be so carefree. As he emerged from the water the dog loped to Luella, tail wagging, tongue lolling, shimmied from nose to tail, spraying her from head to foot.

"You rascal!" She knelt, stroked his damp head. Bird sniffed the air. "Go on." She gave him an affectionate nudge. The dog lowered his nose, then dashed along the shoreline in pursuit of a chipmunk that scurried into the riprap.

She bent down and scooped up a handful of water. As it trickled through her fingers, Luella heard August's voice—"too cold for skinny dipping, just right for making ice cubes"—the same thing he said every year when they'd first arrive at camp. She wondered if his voice would ever quiet, if she would ever stop sifting experiences through an August-centric filter. Things would be far simpler if she could forget him, but she knew that was impossible. Maybe she could learn to edit him out of her most cherished experiences. Maybe someday anger would fade and she would be granted the grace to forgive him.

A heron stood statue-still, patiently waiting in the reedy shallows one-hundred-fifty feet away. Suddenly, its serpentine neck bent, its head darted below the surface, and it emerged with a fish clamped in its spear-like beak.

Luella looked out toward McGinty's Island, three-quarters of a mile in the distance, its towering spruces silhouetted against the early-morning sky. She'd always thought of it merely as a place that marked the channel between Whisper Lake and Nagadan Lake. Today it stood as a metaphor, independent, self-sufficient, its separateness a sign of strength.

Her cell phone chimed, a text from Beth. *Thinking of you. Be safe. Call when you get there.*

Luella smiled. At least something positive had come from her marriage—Beth, head-strong, determined, dear Beth, whom she would never completely understand, but whom she fiercely loved. Much heartache had passed between them over the past year. They'd walked through the shadows, clawing and scratching their way out of a place, if not trouble-free, real. And, although there was a distance to go, at least they were in a far healthier place.

She tucked her phone into her pocket.

"Luella! Luella!" Rosie yelled, interrupting Luella's thoughts.

"I'm at the beach," Luella shouted.

The heron launched into the air, flapped its massive wings, glided low over the water to a spot on the far side of the bay.

Rosie, wearing capris and a pink flamingo T-shirt, hurried down the path. "Trudy brought cookies! For our new 'partment."

"Yes, today we're going to find a new place to live."

"Trudy told me, 'Don't be sad.'"

"She's right. We'll see her soon, and we'll make new friends, too."

Rosie's eyes widened. "But Rudi can still be my friend."

"Of course," Luella reassured her, keeping her doubts to herself.

"I forgot." Rosie tilted her head. "I'm supposed to say..." She paused and squinted as if trying to remember her memorized line. "Don't worry." She scratched her head. "Um...all the time you can take."

Luella grinned. "Okay. Just help me straighten this loose "For Sale" sign, then we'll go say good-bye to Trudy and have some cookies." Luella grabbed hold of the sign and wiggled it. "Here," she said, pointing to one end. "You push on that side and I'll push on this side." They each leaned with all their weight, driving the sign's pointed metal legs into the ground until it gained a firmer foothold. She checked to make sure it was secure.

"Thanks, sweetie." Luella put her arm around Rosie's shoulders and gave an affectionate squeeze. "Tell Trudy I'll be right up."

"Come on, Bird!" shouted Rosie. "We're going on a trip!"

The dog raced ahead up the path.

Luella mentally reviewed her "to do" list. Appointment to sign a lease for a dog-friendly apartment in St. Paul. Check. Appointment to visit the Apricus Day Workshop with Rosie. Check. Appointment to meet with the ARK group home social worker that Trudy's sister, Angeline, a specialist in neurodevelopmental disorders, highly recommended for Rosie. Check.

Starting over in a new city felt daunting, yet despite her trepidation, Luella was eager to move on. Once she secured an apartment, she would return to sort through her belongings, only keeping items that fit into her current life. She would find a quality placement for Rosie. Trudy's sister Angeline had suggested that Rosie's life would be fuller and more rewarding with friends and activities if she were living with other adults with developmental challenges. Luella would take her time deciding, making certain that Rosie would be in a place where she was happy. She would be part of Rosie's life, continue to be her guardian, and live up to her promise to August, perhaps just not in the way he envisioned. She would find a teaching job. She already had three interviews scheduled, one at a school that sounded very promising. She would join a women's support group and trade in her over-sized car for an eco-friendly model. She vowed to do everything in her power to take care of herself.

Luella took her Hoops and Hearts necklace from her jeans pocket, held it in her palm, stared at it. How could such a small object contain so many vivid memories? It was as though she held the past in her hand. When she'd tucked the necklace in her pocket, she'd intended to fling it into the lake, pictured it sinking, mired on the bottom, buried forever. She hesitated, traced the small open heart with the tip of her finger.

Closing her eyes, she listened to the lacy waves lapping against rock in a rhythm as timeless as a heartbeat, felt the movement, the swaying, the lulling dance of the water coax the tension from her muscles into surrender.

When she opened her eyes, the golden sun had fully cleared

the trees. "Okay, Luella Margaret Martin, it's time," she said aloud. Grasping the necklace by its clasp, she carefully hung the chain over the corner of the "For Sale" sign. Then she kissed her fingers, touched the cool metal of the sign, looked out over the lake, and whispered "Good-bye."

Acknowledgements

Although novel writing is a solitary endeavor involving countless hours spent alone at the computer, it takes a team of people to bring the story to fruition. I am grateful to everyone who provided information and ideas that enhanced the story, weighed in on the quality of the writing, and offered needed encouragement.

My appreciation for their thorough and honest critiques goes to members of our local writing group: Ted Rulseh, Andreé Graveley, Sue Drum, Elaine Hohense, Barbara Kane, and David Foster. I owe a huge debt of gratitude for their encouragement and fiction writing acumen to Writing Sisters: Barbara (Bibi) Belford, Lisa Kusko, Julie Holmes, Blair Hull, Martha Miles, Roi Solberg, and Christine DeSmet. Roi, thank you for going above and beyond, helping me sculpt the pages through your thoughtful editing. Bibi, your edits on the book group questions and back page were right on. And Chris, titling the book was just the final touch I was searching for.

I am beholden to beta readers Kate Rahimzadeh, Robert Hanson, Susie Davis, Sandy Kinney, and retired circuit court judge Robert Kinney. All of you found errors and made suggestions that lent credibility to the story. You provided more help than I had the right to ask for. Any remaining errors belong to me. Also, thank you to hair stylist Samantha Pluister for inspiring Trudy's character and suggesting a way for Luella to dispose of her wedding ring. A bolt cutter, really? And to my friend and neighbor Marian Boschek, my thanks for her willingness to lend her maiden name to any character of my choosing. And thank you to photographer Amy Jakubowski for shooting my author photo.

Several nonfiction authors provided source material regarding pedophilia and the emotional toll it takes on its victims and their loved ones. Court transcripts of high-profile cases were invaluable. I am also grateful to the readers of my first novel, *To Reap the Finest Wheat*, who continually asked when my next one would be published. Your inquiries kept me motivated.

Finally, to my husband, Bob Hanson, a consummate listener, insightful contributor, and loving supporter, you make everything possible.

It Happened at Whisper Lake
Book Group Discussion Questions

1. Why does Luella believe so strongly in August's innocence?

2. Why does Beth quickly conclude that her father is guilty?

3. What emotions does the story evoke in you? Empathy? Pity? Indignation?

4. Swiss psychiatrist Elizabeth Kubler-Ross identified five stages of grief: denial, anger, bargaining, depression, and acceptance. How do these stages apply to Luella's story arc? To Beth's?

5. Luella reflects on the countless times she had seen wives on television standing behind famous husbands caught up in sex scandals and believes she now understands why. What is that reason and do you agree or disagree?

6. What role does August's sister Rosie play in the story?

7. What role does Beth's son Wyatt play in the story?

8. Discuss the changing relationship between Luella and Beth. How do they come to view each other differently than before August's arrest?

9. Has Beth inherited any traits from her parents? If so, describe them.

10. In what way does the fact that Luella and Beth are teachers influence their attitudes?

11. Nell Wooden is a real-life figure who features prominently in Luella's imagination. Discuss the role Nell plays in Luella's life.

12. Beth's husband, Gabe, died at a young age of a heart attack. How does he still figure prominently in her life? Is hanging on to his memory constructive?

13. What is the turning point for Luella in the novel?

14. What do you consider Luella's fatal flaw? What is the upside of that quality?

15. Luella comes to believe that people are complicated, that they are not defined by the worst thing they've ever done. What leads her to that conclusion? Do you agree?

16. What is the significance of Luella's and Beth's matching Hoops and Hearts necklaces?

17. Both Luella and Beth have allies in the story. Who are Luella's allies? Who are Beth's allies? In what way are each of them significant?

18. Does your perspective on Luella change from the beginning to the end of the story? Does your perspective on Beth change?

19. What does Luella learn about the causes of pedophilia and how does she apply that understanding to August?

20. What is the collateral damage to others because of August's choices?

21. Is August's anger over Luella thwarting his suicide attempt justified?

22. What is the importance of setting the story at Laurent's Basketball Camp on Whisper Lake?

CPSIA information can be obtained
at www.ICGtesting.com
Printed in the USA
JSHW071733251122
33809JS00002B/2